ITALY EVER AFTER

LEONIE MACK

B

Boldwood

First published in Great Britain in 2021 by Boldwood Books Ltd.

This paperback edition first published in 2022.

1

Copyright © Leonie Mack, 2021

Cover Design: Alice Moore Design

Cover Photography: Shutterstock and iStock

The moral right of Leonie Mack to be identified as the author of this work has been asserted in accordance with the Copyright, Designs and Patents Act 1988.

A CIP catalogue record for this book is available from the British Library.

Paperback ISBN: 978-1-80415-285-0

Ebook ISBN: 978-1-80048-129-9

Kindle ISBN: 978-1-80048-128-2

Audio CD ISBN: 978-1-80048-121-3

Digital audio download ISBN: 978-1-80048-124-4

Large Print ISBN: 978-1-80048-126-8

Boldwood Books Ltd.

23 Bowerdean Street, London, SW6 3TN

www.boldwoodbooks.com

For my Lucys: Lucy Morris (Flatman) and Lucy Keeling. I wrote Lou for us in 2020...

1

Damn him. Phil was winning this game. His look was tolerant. His eyes were warm, even vaguely fond. Lou was losing. Her jaw was clenched so hard she felt like a petulant child with braces. She smoothed her hand down her tailored skirt. Confronting him in her work clothes was supposed to remind her she could deal with him like an adult. But really, she wanted to run home and change into her sweats, as she usually did after her shift.

'She's eleven, Lou. This is her last summer before secondary school. Can't you let up a little?'

He was the voice of reason, too? Phil never raised his voice because he never needed to. He was the kind of man who spoke and it was done. He was attractive, too – even now at forty-four – which meant he'd never had to stay single for long. She couldn't blame the woman who'd become his girlfriend only a few months after their separation – except that she could blame her and she would. It was the right of a nearly officially ex-wife, right?

'All Edie wants to do is play music. Elite tuition and orchestra rehearsals is her idea of paradise. I'm not forcing her to do anything.'

His lips twitched. 'And a few weeks in the Italian sunshine is your idea of a nice free holiday?'

Strike one. She would have been satisfied to hear him behaving like the juvenile ex-husband, except that he was an expert at pressing her overdeveloped sense of her own inadequacy button.

'It's not a holiday for me. I'm going as a chaperone and I have to pay my own way. The only reason I've volunteered is because Edie is one of the youngest kids going. Most of the parents are looking forward to the three weeks of childcare before the competition'

'You can always send her to us. You know that. You don't have to martyr yourself.'

Lou choked on his sympathy, wishing he would do the same. She took a deep breath. She should have accepted by now that Phil's wiring where she was concerned would never change.

'Can we get back to the point? Edie wants to go and it's a unique opportunity. This youth music festival only happens every four years. She'll get to play in an orchestra under a professional conductor and participate in a competition.'

Phil held up a hand. 'I did read the information you emailed me. But I fail to see why our eleven-year-old has to participate in a very *expensive* competition. You've already forced my hand with the school choice. I'd say you're pretty low on credit with me at the moment.'

Lou recoiled. She needed 'credit' to get Phil to consider her opinion about their daughter? How was an ex-wife supposed to earn credit? Not only was she forced to serenely ignore the practical difficulties of having day-to-day responsibility for their daughter alone, but Phil still required her to manage him to make sure they did their best by Edie. Good God, it was miserable.

Phil looked at her with his unflappably perfect haircut and

warm eyes with their distinguished crinkles that on her would be called crow's feet. It was clear why she'd thrown herself at him twelve years ago when she'd been a young and stupid graduate with too little understanding of the world's faults – and far too little contraception. What was less clear was how she was supposed to deal with him now.

'You know how much she loves playing the violin.'

'I know, she does little else.'

Edie practised especially diligently at Phil's because it meant less time with the obsequious girlfriend.

'I'm still not sure I want to encourage her obsession.'

'Then you'll be happy to know the camp takes that into account. Although they rehearse every day, there's also time dedicated to outdoor activities and confidence-building. I think we can both agree that it would be good for Edie to have some confidence outside her musical talent.'

The faintest glint in his eye was the only clue that he was feeling the pressure. But Phil never backed off. Instead, he calmly went on the offensive. 'So, you plan to make Edie do a high ropes course while you sit in the sun at Sirmione sipping an Aperol Spritz?'

Lou swallowed her defensive response with some difficulty. She had to keep him thinking he was free to make the decision, while also pinning him down until he couldn't refuse. She would manipulate him into compliance if necessary. Why hadn't she thought of this while they were still married?

'You see it won't be a holiday for me. I have to help supervise at the high ropes course – whatever that involves.'

His gaze flickered. 'I'm not sure they'll be safe with you in charge.'

She wasn't sure, either, but she was fairly certain it was beside the point. 'The music teacher from school is organising the trip.

There are kids coming from all over the UK and I won't be the only chaperone.'

'You realise she was supposed to spend a week with us in the summer.'

'That's why I'm asking five months early. What she'd really like is for you to come to the competition in Milan after the camp.' She cut herself off before she added something caustic like: *since you haven't made it to any of her concerts since we split up.* 'If that's not possible, then there is a week of holiday at either end that would work. I'm not trying to keep her from you.'

Phil sighed and she inwardly rolled her eyes. He was about to serve up a big old ball of blame and lob it at her, but he would probably agree afterwards. The sigh had been just deep enough to give that away. 'Look, Lou, are you sure you're not pushing her because of your own issues?'

Lou stilled. The advance warning hadn't helped. She felt that dig as deeply as he'd known she would. 'What issues?'

'Well, you're not musical…'

'I know. I still don't understand where Edie got her talent from, but she has loved music since she picked up a recorder in year one. It doesn't have anything to do with me.'

'I agree that music is a suitable passion to pursue since she's obviously about as sporty as you are. But other kids her age are out playing with their friends. I don't want her to miss out on her childhood because you're worried she'll turn out like you – ordinary and talentless.'

Lou swayed. God knew he was correct, but that didn't give him the right to say it out loud. 'I'm not pushing her.' Was she? She hated how Phil, with all his handsome certainty, could fill her with doubt and cut her down without even intending to.

He knew her better than anyone else, as much as that thought made her sick. He knew she only had her job because he'd twisted arms at the TV station once she was ready to return to work after Edie started nursery. He also knew what the other producers said about her when she wasn't at the studio due to her part-time hours. He knew her professional image hid a person who felt sure she had no right to calmly present the news to a trusting TV audience.

He crossed his arms over his chest and studied her. She tried to muster some outrage at his patronising superiority, but her throat was thick with doubt and hurt. 'All right,' he said suddenly.

'What?'

'I said all right. You win. She can go on this camp. I can't promise Winny and I can come to the competition, but I'll try.'

You win... Yeah, right. But Edie would be pleased. She adored her teacher and had been worried about Phil saying no, when Lou had explained she would have to ask him to pay for it.

'Great,' she said with a forced smile. 'I'll let her teacher know and get in touch when the first payment is due. Can you sign the permission form?'

She fished around in her handbag for the crumpled piece of paper. A year ago, she would never have realised how many forms required the signatures of both parents – or how much heartache collecting a signature could cause.

Phil leaned on his desk and signed with a flourish, returning the form to her with a smile that she used to describe as 'charming'. 'Actually, while you're here, there's one other thing we could tick off the to-do list.'

His voice was mild and kind – as it always was – so she wasn't prepared when he retrieved an official-looking envelope from the drawer of his desk. 'Look what arrived this morning. This will save me posting it to your solicitor. I'm sure the approval of the court will only be a formality. Are you going to apply for the decree, or shall I?'

She fumbled as she accepted the paper with trembling fingers. *I'm in such a hurry to divorce you that I can do the nasty paperwork, if you like. Since you're so ordinary and talentless and I'm deliriously happy with skinny Winny, how about I take the steps to rid myself of you and the daughter I never wanted but whom I will now have shared custody of, thank you very much?*

Lou winced. She was too good at hearing his bitingly smooth voice in her head. 'I'll do it.'

He raised an eyebrow. 'Are you sure? It took you so long to get on to your solicitor about the consent order. I'm happy to take care of the rest.'

Heat rose to her cheeks. He must think she was reluctant to finalise the divorce. She wasn't sure why she had dawdled over the financial agreements. After the awkwardness of calling his relationship with Winny 'adultery' and therefore grounds for divorce, she'd had enough of the horrible proceedings. So what, if he'd felt single from the moment they'd separated and found a girlfriend in a matter of months? She should be happy it had saved them from waiting the full two years to divorce on grounds of separation.

'Fine,' she said, 'I'll let you know when the court has approved the consent order and you can do the application.'

'Good. I'm glad that's settled.'

Of course you are. He bent to kiss her cheek in farewell and she forced herself not to recoil. Did he care so little that he could kiss her casually, after the dissolution of a nearly twelve-year marriage?

She made for the door, careful to turn slowly in her heels. At the door, she remembered she wasn't quite finished. 'Is Edie's spring concert in your calendar?'

'Yes, of course.'

'I've already bought the tickets.'

'We have to buy tickets?'

'Yes, it's in support of the PTA. They want to buy new sports equipment.'

'Are you still on the committee?'

She pressed her lips together. How did he imagine she'd be able to go to PTA meetings now she had to be home to look after Edie every evening? 'No.' She paused for a moment longer. 'The concert's at the theatre in the secondary school.'

'Yes, I haven't forgotten.' He knew he'd missed her last two concerts but he wasn't going to let her point it out.

'I'll see you then.' She walked out before either of them could broach any more of the many topics that remained unmentionable. She'd see him just before Easter – ordinary, talentless and officially divorced.

* * *

Her planning and organisational skills – never particularly strong – lasted right up until the moment she got into her car. She'd driven to work that morning – and paid the exorbitant parking fee – so she'd have time to meet Phil in his office before driving back to collect Edie from school.

She'd made the appointment – since she needed an appointment to see the father of her child, apparently – on a Thursday, because Edie was in choir until four so Lou would have more time to make it back.

The plan had been to put on her newsreader hat, pretend she knew what was going on in the world for the half-hour of lunchtime news that luckily no one watched, head to Phil's building and then leave with a confident strut. Perhaps that was where she'd gone wrong. Lou couldn't strut in heels at the best of times and that afternoon had not been the best of times.

After getting through the meeting, somehow, she'd lost half an hour. She'd sat behind the steering wheel of her little car, her mind trapped between the letter signifying the end of their marriage and the words 'ordinary' and 'talentless'. She suspected she'd also lost a large quantity of salt and water as her face was hot and her eyes still damp when she finally snapped out of it with a curse and slammed the car into gear.

How dare Phil accuse her of pushing Edie because of her own inadequacies? He was the one who was involved with a bloody ballet dancer. What kind of childhood had the sainted Winny had? But Phil obviously thought her sacrifices for her art had been worth it, because she was so much more desirable than his talentless ex. What kind of a message was he sending to his daughter?

Lou wasn't perfect, but at least she had her priorities right – although right now she was running late for her biggest priority.

She pulled up outside the school at ten past four, relieved that none of the other parents were there to see her, dressed up like the serious journalist she pretended to be for twenty hours a week. One of the teachers was leaving, so Lou slipped through the gate behind her, thankful to be spared the extra embarrassment of buzzing through to the staff room to be let in.

She rushed up the ramp to the music room – the part of the school she knew best – and burst through the door.

'I'm so sorry I'm late!'

Edie's dear, cringing smile churned Lou's stomach with the queer mix of relief, pride and anxiety. She was swinging her legs on a stool by the piano, her choir music clasped tightly in her arms. Lou held her arm out for Edie and her daughter dashed over, making Lou's world right again when she fitted against her side – a miracle Lou never tired of appreciating.

Only then could she take a deep breath and face the music...

teacher. She pasted a smile on to her face. He was looking at her. That in itself was strange. Mr Romano kept a particular distant smile for the parents of his pupils and had a quiet way of discouraging further communication.

But that afternoon as he looked at her through his black-framed glasses and as his hand rose to his curly black hair, Lou was awkwardly reminded that Mr Romano held the title of 'hottest teacher' among the more unruly mums she occasionally socialised with.

'Erm... Don't worry about it. Edie was helping me sort out this music for next week.'

She was sure his comment was supposed to put her at ease, but he was still looking at her as though something wasn't right. Was her flashing neon 'loser' sign suddenly visible to everyone and not just Phil?

Gosh, he had such nice eyes – the colour of 80 per cent dark chocolate and rimmed with thick black lashes. But Lou was a Cadbury's Milk sort of girl – Mr Romano with his dishy black glasses, broad shoulders and posh chocolate eyes was too fine even for her inappropriate fantasies.

But why was he still looking at her?

'I'll be on time next time,' she mumbled, forcing her eyes away.

'Truly, it's okay. We all have... lives.'

She glanced back to find him looking at her heels and smiled with a flood of relief. She wasn't usually dressed for work when she collected Edie. The departure from her usual sloppy-track-suit-and-sneakers attire must have surprised him.

She straightened and lifted her foot daintily, showing off the patent-leather pump. 'Nice, huh? Not sure if they make them in your size.'

His gaze snapped back to hers with a flash of something like mortification. The feeling was catching. She inwardly berated herself for the one talent she couldn't deny she had: making bad jokes at the wrong times.

'Sorry, I didn't mean to imply... although there's nothing wrong with it, if you did... You'd probably look good...' She bit her lip to stop digging herself deeper.

He swallowed and she couldn't help noticing the bob of his Adam's apple. 'In drag?' he completed, his voice high with disbelief.

She blinked. Edie was looking between them with alarm. Had she offended him? What kind of crazy divorced mum talked to the hot teacher like this? An ordinary, talentless one.

She was about to make a grovelling apology when a baffled smile formed on his features. His shoulders rose as he let out a half-laugh. Thankfully it appeared that he was too polite to express offence.

'Take it as a compliment,' she muttered and he laughed again.

He stared at her as he rubbed the back of his hand on his forehead, mussing his dark, curly hair that was too long for the neatness of his clothes. A nod to fashion? Was Mr Romano fashionable? He probably was.

He looked as though he was about to say something, but Lou was done for the day with caring what men thought of her and certainly didn't want to explain why she was wearing her work disguise. She swung her handbag around and rummaged in it.

'I've got the permission form for you.' She brushed her hair out of her face as she thrust the piece of paper at him.

Edie turned to her with an excited hop, her hands clasped in front of her. 'Dad said I can go?'

She nodded and glanced back at Mr Romano, who was smiling, but still inspecting her face in that unnerving way that made her feel as if he saw all her faults.

Edie threw her arms around Lou. 'Thanks for asking him, Mum. I knew you'd get him to agree.'

Mr Romano looked quickly away, which only upped Lou's embarrassment. Yes, it was none of his business, but it was also true that she had to beg and grovel for her ex-husband's beneficence.

'Come on, Edie.' She steered her daughter towards the door. 'Sorry again for being late.'

He nodded and lifted his hand in farewell. 'Uh, Mrs Saunders?' Lou froze and turned back with a sharp breath. 'I mean... uh, Ms...'

Lou searched the ceiling for her dignity.

'Oh, God, I'm sorry,' he murmured.

She bit her lip, not sure whether to laugh or cry. 'I think you'd better call me Louise.'

He inclined his head, the baffled half-smile back. He had very distracting lips. What was going on with her today? Mr Romano was probably younger than her – and that was the least of the reasons why he was way out of her league.

'Are you still interested in coming along as a chaperone?'

Lou blushed to the roots of her hair, praying he didn't notice – or at least wouldn't suspect the direction of her thoughts.

'Yes?' she said, her voice too high.

He paused. 'Good,' he said eventually. 'I... uh... I've been asked to organise the schedule because... well, I have, anyway. And I could do with some help with the extra programme?' He rubbed his forehead again and straightened his glasses.

Lou's thoughts raced back to Phil's dig about the high ropes course with a stab of hurt. She smiled brightly. 'Sure. Happy to help.'

'Great, thanks.' He seemed genuinely relieved and she belatedly wondered what his feelings about the sports programme were.

'No problem. Just let me know what I can do.'

'I will. We've got a bit of time. I'm pleased Edie can come.'

Lou grinned. 'Not as pleased as she is.' She gave Edie a squeeze and they turned to go.

'Bye, Mr Romano!'

'See you tomorrow, Edie.'

Lou felt like less of a freak with her daughter by her side and let out a sigh as they clipped their seat belts and she turned on the ignition.

'Mum, what's with your make-up?'

She shot Edie a look. 'I stayed longer at work to talk to your dad.'

Her daughter's look softened to something like pity and Lou frowned. 'No, I mean your mascara.'

Lou froze and flipped down the mirror, gasping when she saw the black smudges beneath her eyes and a drop or two of diluted mascara on her cheek that clearly showed she'd been crying. She groaned.

Her chest prickled as the light bulb finally flashed on. It wasn't a neon 'loser' sign, but it might as well have been.

2

'Cheers! To your freedom!' Zoe held her glass high.

Lou's arm was sluggish as she raised her own flute. She mustered a smile and swigged some prosecco. Too bubbly. Cheap gin and tonic were closer to her mood, but her friends had gone to so much effort to get her out to the pub, and she wasn't going to waste the alcohol. She wasn't so much elegantly sipping the sparkling wine as desperately slurping it.

'There's still one more step in the process,' she pointed out. But she was staring down a new, horrible reality.

'You can still celebrate this step. He's agreed to give you money. Party time!' Tina lifted her glass again and took a long sip.

'The money isn't the hard part,' Lou said. 'At least, not the hard-est part,' she continued with a grimace.

They hadn't argued over finances, but, although Phil was a hot-shot TV producer, he wasn't rich by London standards. And when you took 'not rich' plus 'part-time income' and divided it into two households, it didn't add up to their previous lifestyle. She'd been lucky to find the tiny house to rent in East Dulwich. Edie had told Lou about Phil's new apartment with its open-plan kitchen and views of Westminster, but he'd sneaked in a mort-gage before the legal settlement had been finalised and he didn't have to take Edie to school, so hurrah for him.

Sarah-Jane squeezed her hand. 'You're not feeling sad about the divorce, are you?'

'No!' she denied immediately with an emphatic shake of her head. But she was feeling sad. Not about Phil, good riddance, but about... something. 'Phil accused me of wanting to put off the divorce.'

'Oh, he's just talking crap. Don't listen to him,' Tina said.

Lou wished it were so easy. 'But he's right.' No one replied for a long moment.

'Is it about the girlfriend?' Zoe finally asked.

Lou shook her head. 'They're welcome to each other. And I don't want Phil back.'

'Then why don't you want to divorce him?'

'I do,' she insisted weakly. 'I know. I'm making no sense. It's like, I don't want to have his name any more, but if I change it back, that's twelve years gone and a daughter with a different surname. I don't want to be with Phil. But I don't want to be divorced from Phil either. I don't want to be the ex. I don't want to have to beg him each time to be allowed to make decisions about my life and Edie's! I had to listen to so much crap, just to get him to agree to Edie's music camp.'

She'd shocked her friends into silence again. Tina's muttered, 'Phil's a jerk,' was the only sound around the table.

'He told me I was talentless,' Lou choked. 'He accused me of pushing Edie because of my own deficiencies.'

'It's not true, sweetie,' Sarah-Jane assured her.

Her friend's earnest loyalty made Lou smile ruefully. 'Isn't it? What talent do I have?'

'You're an excellent newsreader,' Zoe said immediately. 'I watch you every day.'

'Thanks,' Lou replied weakly, 'but I got that job because Phil pulled strings at the station and I've only managed to keep it because it's such a pared-down position that no one else wants it. Besides, it's not really me. I don't know anything about the world and I was crazy to think I could be a journalist. Everyone at the station knows it, so I always get the fluffy stories – or plain research.'

'You don't mean that,' Sarah-Jane said.

Lou shrugged and took another long slug of her drink. 'Why not?'

'You're letting Phil get to you,' Tina pointed out.

'That's nothing new,' she said drily.

'You just need some confidence,' Zoe remarked helpfully.

'Is that like a dietary supplement?'

Tina snorted. 'See? You're funny. That's a talent.'

'No one will be booking me in for *Live at the Apollo*,' she said, her lips thin. 'I'm ordinary. Phil said that, too.'

'You're not ordinary. You're our hero!' Tina said with a grin. 'You're the queen of disregard for fashion.'

'Gee, thanks – I think,' Lou replied.

'I'm serious,' continued Tina. 'If it weren't for you, we might all think we had to get dolled up for the school run.'

'I wouldn't give me so much credit.'

Zoe smiled. 'You've got a point. I would never get properly dressed anyway. Between hubby and the four rabble-rousers, there's enough swearing in my house in the morning without adding a fight with the mascara wand. But it's nice I'm not alone.'

Lou swallowed as the mention of mascara took her right back to another part of that day. 'And that's another thing. I never know when to shut up. I told Mr Romano he'd look good in drag.'

'You what?'

Lou wasn't sure she'd ever heard that volume level from Tina. 'It's a long story.'

Zoe was guffawing into her wrist while her flute of prosecco swayed precariously. 'He probably would, you know. That man would look good in anything.'

Tina giggled. 'Yes! A fifties frock with a silk scarf tied around his neck, just so.'

'And no fake boobs – just his real chest showing out the top. Oh my God!'

'Guys! *Guys!*' Lou said, stricken. 'It's going to be hard enough to face him for the rest of the year without these images!'

'You're the one who made things awkward with the hot teacher,' Tina teased.

'He's our kids' teacher,' Lou groaned, looking to Sarah-Jane for support, but her friend was trying not to laugh.

'It doesn't mean we all have to refrain from objectifying him from time to time,' said Zoe. 'What did he say, anyway, when you told him he'd look good in drag?' Tina tittered again.

Lou sighed heavily. 'He just smiled. I'd come straight from seeing Phil. I thought he was puzzled to see me in my work clothes, but what I didn't realise was that my mascara had run and I looked like a pathetic raccoon!'

'I bet he likes sexy racoons,' Tina said with a giggle. 'He's got hidden passions, that one.'

'If he does, then they have nothing to do with me,' Lou said with a frown she hoped was firm and not pitiful.

'Oh, but you want them to, don't you, honey?' Tina said, dropping her voice to a sexy rasp.

Lou flushed, but fought for composure. They were joking, right? They were teasing her about Mr Romano because nothing would ever happen. It was impossible for her to look at him and see anyone other than a teacher – right?

She took a deep breath. 'I'm not in the market for a toy boy,' she said, hoping her dry tone would cover up her confusion.

'Are you still going on the music camp? Did Phil agree to pay for it in the end? Isn't it somewhere lovely, like Italy?' Sarah-Jane asked.

Zoe and Tina bobbed their heads up like a pair of meerkats. 'You're going on the camp?'

Lou nodded as nonchalantly as she could, skimming condensation off her glass.

'Several weeks in Italy?' Zoe asked. 'With Mr Romano?'

Lou studied the ceiling. 'Yes, and yes. But it's not a romantic holiday with a hot Italian man, for goodness' sake. It's a music camp with thirty kids!'

'And a hot Italian man,' Tina added behind her hand. 'It's just what you need, Lou. And he won't even be Edie's teacher after the end of the year.'

'He will still be her teacher for the duration of the camp. And besides, it's not what I "need". What I need is some space from Phil and some peace to sort out... everything.'

'Did you not hear "hot Italian man"?' asked Zoe.

'Shut up, guys. It's not like he's properly Italian anyway, right?'

'Oh, he is,' said Tina, leaning forward. 'Genuine Italian-born, Italian-speaking, passport-holding hot man.'

'Fine, but it doesn't make any difference. How do you even know that?'

She shrugged. 'It's not illegal to ask personal questions.'

The conversation was spiralling and Lou was afraid her dignity was travelling with it. 'A hypothetical romance with someone who is not interested in me is very much not the next step in sorting my life out,' she said with what she hoped was finality.

'You're right.' Thank God for Sarah-Jane. 'But the trip could still be just what you need.'

'I *am* looking forward to getting away.'

'But make sure you take some time for yourself. I've been so much happier since I took up running.'

Lou choked on her sip of prosecco. 'I don't know if I'm quite ready to do that to myself.' She grimaced when it reminded her of the few extra squishy bits she'd developed over the past few years.

But when she imagined the time in Italy, the peace of the warm summer sun, the different art and architecture, she suddenly saw the opportunity. 'But I do have an idea.' She ignored Tina and Zoe's shared look of wariness. 'I've got a few weeks away from home. I'm going to find a talent.'

She'd hoped for applause and vociferous nodding, but her friends just stared at her. Tina reached out a sympathetic hand. 'Lou...'

'I'm serious.' She pulled her hand away. 'There must be something I'm good at! I'm going to try everything until I find it.'

Her friends exchanged glances around the table. 'At least she's sure to have a good time trying,' said Sarah-Jane.

Lou laughed, finally happy with a decision she'd made. 'You'll see. I'll come back and I'll be the best darn basket weaver you've ever seen.'

'I don't know if they weave baskets in Italy.'

Lou grinned. 'I don't know either. But I'm looking forward to finding out.'

* * *

Nick batted his mother's fingers away when they swerved back in the direction of his tie. It was bad enough that his collar had enough starch to send it into battle. He didn't need his tie to suffocate him as it had during every day of secondary school.

He had to move out. After nearly three months living back with his mother, he was losing his dignity with every load of washing. Not to mention he was delaying his mother's planned return to Italy. She'd just retired and, after sixteen years living in the UK, had decided to take up his grandparents' offer to help out with the family farm. He hoped it was also something to do with finally being willing to live in the same country as his dad, who'd never left Milan.

But instead of starting out on the new chapter in her life, she was regressing too, coming to his concerts and fussing with his tie as though he were a teenage prodigy again, instead of a staid music teacher.

'It's not the Royal Albert Hall, Mum,' he grumbled. 'Go and find your seat. I need to round up the kids.'

He peered out on to the stage, set with seats for the violin ensemble and risers for the choir. A technician was testing the lighting and Nick caught it in the eyes with a wince. He sighed and pulled on the knot of his tie again, anticipating the rows of wide, terrified eyes and cacophonous squeak of wrong notes as his poor students squirmed under the pressure.

Some would cope better than others – as he well understood.

The violin ensemble was particularly woeful this year. He was trying to forget the fact that he was going to play as well as conduct. He didn't play on stage any more, but he didn't have much choice that night. If he didn't prop up the second violins, they lost their place, and the students, parents, friends and staff would all be subjected to the out-of-tune howl of instruments being tormented by a bunch of fidgety nine-to-eleven-year-olds.

That might be unavoidable, no matter what he did, but he had to try.

He pushed back his own difficult memories and headed for the green room, where hopefully the parents had delivered all of the children. He would inevitably have to go looking for one or two.

'Nick?'

He stopped up short when he heard his name called from near the stage door. *Oh, God, not now.* He stifled a sigh and glanced around to check that his mother had gone. 'Naomi,' he said weakly, failing to inject much enthusiasm into his voice.

She approached with her soft, tentative steps and lifted her face. He hesitated for a bare second before accepting that he had to kiss her cheek. Even her scent made nausea well up in his throat, along with the familiar side-order of guilt. It wasn't her fault he had too many hang-ups for a meaningful relationship.

'Is it okay that I'm here? I still had the ticket, so I thought...'

'It's fine,' he lied, hoping she'd read his body language and disappear quickly into the audience. On top of his background-level nerves and responsibility for the high emotional state of his students, Naomi being here was a kick to his stomach he could have done without.

Not her fault.

'Are you all right?' She reached a hand up to brush his hair back and run her fingertips over his forehead.

He tried to stop himself from flinching, but he must not have succeeded. Her gaze dropped and she pursed her lips in the closest thing to a frown Naomi ever wore. She was sweetness and light, gentle and soft – born to be every kid's favourite Reception teacher. And after six years of encouraging intimacy and dreams, he'd left her overnight. He still wasn't sure what explanation he should give her – what explanation he could give her.

'I need to prepare the kids.'

The stage door opened and Edie tumbled in with her violin case. He wasn't surprised to see her arrive late, but the thunderous expression on her face alarmed him.

Edie had always been an enthusiastic and sensitive learner, but something had changed at the end of the previous year and he'd grown used to picking up on her vulnerable moods. Her playing had become obsessive as she came to her music lessons increasingly exposed. He'd eventually heard the news of her parents' ongoing divorce through the staff grapevine. Edie never said anything, but he knew what was pouring out of her as she played. How many times had he done the same thing as a boy?

He'd done his best to create a safe space for her in their music lessons and he'd let her be, giving her no inkling that he was watching, ready to catch her. But he suspected Edie was tougher than she thought. Her mother, on the other hand...

'Louise', as she'd insisted he now think of her, came through the door, staring helplessly after her daughter. She always looked as though she were hurtling through life straddling a hydrogen bomb.

He'd purposefully taken no notice of her over the years he'd taught Edie. He paid attention to the children, not the parents. Then Louise had turned up outside his music room with a tear-stained face and a rumpled outfit and he was grimly concerned that that was the end of their professional distance.

But Edie was his concern tonight, not least because she was performing two solo pieces and was a member of both the violin ensemble and the choir. He didn't pause to dwell on Louise's long dark hair that rarely looked neat but always luxurious, or the way her baggy jumper looked careless and... friendly.

He searched around for a smile as he greeted Edie. 'You okay?' He kept his tone light.

But when she opened her mouth to reply, only a hiccough emerged and he glanced back up at Louise. She smiled tightly, her gaze an apology. She glanced at Naomi and failed to conceal a hint of curiosity. The back of his neck heated as he imagined her forming opinions about his ex.

'Her father's not coming,' Louise mumbled, and Edie hiccoughed again, before running for the green room.

Nick jostled Louise when they both went after her. She sprang back and swept her hair out of her face in a move that made it impossible for him to focus on anything else and he stammered an apology.

'I'll see you later, Nick?'

He turned back to Naomi, wondering how long he'd been staring at Louise. He winced at Naomi's kind gaze. 'I have to go,' he said, dismissing her far too rudely.

He followed Louise into the green room, to the chatter and restlessness and the smell of fear. He took a deep breath so it wouldn't choke him.

Edie stood stiffly, clutching her violin case. As usual, her hair was neat and her uniform immaculate, down to her ruffled socks. He approached to hear the end of Louise's halting attempt to comfort her. 'I'm sure he'll come to the next one.'

'He doesn't care,' Edie replied, her voice so thin it was almost broken. 'Why should I bother?'

Her emotion touched him, as it always did. It was the best and worst part of being a music teacher. He taught a raw and emotional method of communication. He couldn't stick to crotchets and legato. He had to deal with kids facing the staccato times in life, tied notes and syncopation, and occasionally the times when a sudden sforzando shook everything up.

But this wasn't a rehearsal. This was the culmination of Edie's hard work and passion and he wouldn't let anything or anybody take it from her.

He stooped to catch her downcast gaze and smiled faintly when her eyes begged him for answers he didn't have. 'Let's start warm-up, Edie,' he said gently. 'You haven't practised the Allegro for nothing.'

He could see she recognised the point he was trying to make as gently as he could. He knew she was performing one of her favourite pieces. He knew how it felt to let fingers fly over the sharp strings and conquer the cascading semi-quavers – control the music, when nothing else in life made sense.

He gripped her shoulder for the briefest moment. 'Him not being here is not a reflection on you or the hard work you've put in. He's let you down, but I know that, if you want to, you can get out there and make Handel proud.'

She smiled. 'He's been dead for, like, 300 years.'

Nick chuckled. 'Not quite 300. As long as you don't make him turn in his grave, I think you'll be okay.'

With a nod, and gripping her violin case tightly, she made her way to the row of empty cases. He straightened and found Louise staring after Edie, a grimace on her face.

'She'll be fine,' he assured her. 'It's probably best not to make a big deal of it. Nerves are natural.'

Her eyes darted back to him, clouded with emotion. 'I know. The music is the solution for her, not the problem.' She bit her lip as she studied him. His neck heated again. He didn't need the encouragement to look at her lips. What was wrong with him? Keeping emotional distance had never been a problem before. 'Thank you,' she muttered.

He dismissed her thanks with a wave of his hand – anything to stop her looking at him.

She smiled. 'Good luck and all that.' He froze and his expression must have been obviously stricken, because her smile vanished. 'What?'

He gave his head a little shake and forced a smile. 'Nothing.'

'Oh, shit!' she said, raising her hands. She talked more with her hands than his Italian grandmothers. 'I'm not supposed to say anything about luck, right?'

'It's a stupid superstition.' That had unfortunately been drilled into him when he was an impressionable child. 'Shit works though,' he added.

'What?'

'You can say merde for good luck. That's French for—'

'I know.' Her smile was back, but smaller and with an unsettling gleam of mischief that made him think of high heels and dressing in drag. 'It's one of the only French words I know. I wish you lots of merde, then.'

He should hurry her along and get back to work, but there was some value in being distracted from his own nerves – at least he could tell himself that. 'The expression you need is "in bocca al lupo".'

'That's all Greek to me.' She shrugged.

He grinned. 'Actually, it's Italian.'

'For shit?'

He laughed. The sound of stricken instruments being beaten with screeching bows rose behind him, but he grinned at her for a moment longer. 'No, it translates as something like "into the mouth of the wolf". It means good luck, especially for opera singers, but it works for orchestras, too.'

'You're throwing yourselves to the pack of baying wolves out there?'

The description was more appropriate than she realised. 'Paying wolves, as the PTA will be happy to see.'

She took a sudden step back and looked him up and down in

mock surprise. 'Why Mr Romano, I had no idea that you have a sense of humour!'

He knew she was joking, but he still felt the heat spread intolerably from his neck to his cheeks. A particularly loud screech from a violin made him jump. He raised his eyebrows ruefully. 'I teach them. A sense of humour is a requirement of the job.'

'Are you talking about our angelic children?'

'The ones I'm about to throw to the wolves, yes.'

'Well, in Berocca de lupus or whatever it was. I'll go join the wolves.'

'Crepi,' he replied out of habit. When she raised her eyebrows in question, he translated, 'May it die.'

'You musicians are crazy.'

3

Lou found her seat, feeling strangely light. She'd been fuming silently at Phil until Edie surely couldn't miss the steam coming out of her ears, but she wasn't even thinking about Phil any more. Even when she had to choose which of the three seats on the tickets to claim, the sinking feeling of betrayed disappointment didn't return.

Instead, her smile felt as though it were attached to a bunch of helium balloons and every time she blinked, she saw dimples and a charming blush. She'd had no idea thirty-six-year-old mothers went through a reverse teenage phase when faced with gorgeous, younger teachers. Life was full of surprises. It was possibly wrong, but she figured she deserved some kind of kick-back for all of the divorce crap she'd faced recently.

Nothing would ever happen for real. Tina and Zoe were wrong about that. Romantic – and intimate – interactions with any man were off limits until she'd emotionally processed the divorce – whenever that happened. And the pretty, young woman Mr Romano had been heatedly talking to when she arrived proved Lou was enjoying a one-sided crush that would never be reciprocated and certainly not acted upon. Did that give her the right to ogle his backside during the performance?

His first name was 'Nick'. It was a bit pedestrian, but it suited him in a way. Add in the 'Romano' and his ability to spout Italian at her and the overall package was quite a thrilling diversion for a Friday evening.

The audience of parents, grandparents and siblings was restless in the cramped seating. It was a sight better than squeezing everyone into the gym at school, but it came at a cost, in money and effort, to make use of the posh theatre at the private secondary school nearby. At least the theatre was full and she imagined the PTA would be happy with the funds raised.

Next year, everything would be different for Edie in secondary school. Her smile faded slightly, so she refused to dwell on the decisions she and Edie had made about next year and whether she would ever know if they were the right ones.

At least she was forming her plan for the summer and tonight she wasn't the one who mattered – Edie was.

The lights dimmed and the audience settled. A soft clang drew Lou's attention to the older woman next to her, who was opening a small tin of sweets. She caught Lou's eye and smiled, offering her the tin.

'Thanks,' Lou murmured and dug out a small, round sweet. She couldn't read the writing on the tin in the dim light, so she popped the sweet in her mouth without any further thought – and immediately gagged.

What was that? The woman smiled and nodded at her and Lou smiled back through a grimace, wondering if her tongue was being permanently damaged. There was a lemony undertone, but it wasn't a citrus sweet like anything she'd tasted before. The lemon was more bitter than sweet and a sharp, herbal flavour overwhelmed the familiar notes.

She sucked on it for as long as she could manage, but then gave in and crunched the rest of the sweet so at least it was gone. The woman glanced at her again and Lou rushed to paste her smile back in place.

The lights on stage came up and the head teacher walked out, thanking everyone for coming and waxing lyrical about the hard work and achievements of the children. When she introduced Mr Romano, he strode on to the stage with a tight smile.

Lou gave herself a moment to enjoy his broad shoulders and lean frame, looking especially good in a black suit. But she noticed the woman next to her, in her peripheral vision, and jumped when she realised the woman was still smiling at her. Lou smiled back and sank into her seat. Caught ogling the teacher by the grandma with the disgusting sweets. At least the low point of the night would be reached early.

The choir began to file on stage, each child awkward and different in their own way. Edie beamed from the back row. She always skipped happily out of rehearsal on choir day and had been full of enthusiasm for the short programme that night. Lou was glad that choir singing was a mandatory part of the music camp in the summer. Edie loved the violin, but choir made her blossom.

The children jostled each other and wriggled until Mr Romano raised his hands and settled them with a short gesture. He counted in the accompanist and then brought the choir to life with a sharp flourish. Lou kept her eyes trained on Edie and didn't let them drift to Mr Romano, but as the song drew to a climax, he snagged Lou's attention. He built crescendos with his arms and diminished the dynamic with his shoulders. He leaned down to his students, transfixing them with the intensity of his focus.

The next piece was a pop song with a sweet melody and a

subtle groove in the rhythm. As Mr Romano moved his shoulders and coaxed a gentle sound from the students, the sudden smiles on the faces of the children lifted the performance immediately. When he turned to cue a solo line from another year six girl, Lou saw he was mouthing the words.

Lou glanced self-consciously around her, but no one else seemed to be blushing – not even the smiling grandma, who looked as if she'd appreciate a good-looking man to go with her tangy sweets. Was Lou the only one who noticed that gorgeous... conducting?

She cleared her thoughts and settled back to watch Edie, her eyes bright, singing her heart out. If someone had told her eleven years ago that she could feel like this when she looked at her daughter, she wouldn't have believed them. Edie was sensitive, loving and funny – all of which shone through when she performed the music she loved. It made Lou's heart clog up with grateful wonder.

The children grew in confidence as the song progressed and Mr Romano held them back, pointing to his hand when they were getting ahead of the beat and using his fingers to encourage a light tone. Then all of a sudden, he ramped them up again, moving his arms as though he were controlling the sound with a superpower in his palms.

The choir hit the final note and held it; every pair of eyes trained on Mr Romano. With a decisive wave of his hand, he indicated the cut-off. He gave his fist a sharp shake, leaning towards to the students to share the victory. His hair was mussed and he was breathing heavily.

Lou could see why Edie loved her music lessons. Mr Romano made it come alive. It made her wish she were musical, but she'd long ago accepted that her joy in music was much greater than her ability.

The audience cheered and applauded as only proud parents could and suddenly Mr Romano was himself again, standing awkwardly to the side and blushing while he gestured to the students and gave his own applause above his head.

Edie filed off stage with the rest of the choir, her head high and proud, but Mr Romano remained standing to the side, his hands clasped in front of him and his feet planted wide.

The head teacher added her own applause as she stood by the microphone, waiting for the clapping to die down. 'Our choir is absolutely marvellous and a joy to listen to,' she said, to another spontaneous round of applause. 'Next we will welcome a series of students who will perform works they have been perfecting in their individual music lessons. We are so pleased to be able to offer violin and piano lessons at school and to hear our students perform this evening, whether they have been learning for six months or six years. The first student to take the stage is our year six music enthusiast, Edie Saunders.'

Lou grabbed for her handbag and started rummaging for her phone. Of course Edie would be first. She fumbled and dropped her phone as Edie strode on to the stage to polite applause. The thought of sending Phil the video made her hands shake, but she had to do it. Edie wanted him to see it and she needed to passive-aggressively chide him for disappointing their daughter.

Mr Romano helped Edie to settle her music into the stand, caught her eye with a smile and then sat at the piano. Lou tapped on her phone screen furiously, but stopped when the grandma next to her placed a firm hand on her arm. Lou looked up.

Grandma beckoned for Lou to give her the phone. 'I'll record. You watch.'

Lou stared at her, waiting for the catch. But the woman's caring smile and the glint of camaraderie in her eyes were impossible to resist. Lou swiped open the camera app and handed over her phone. 'Thank you,' she whispered. She was gripped by emotion as she turned to watch her daughter.

As the first high note reverberated around the theatre, she melted. She'd heard this piece at least a thousand times. She knew what speed Edie aimed to draw her bow along the string to create the exact quality of sound Lou was hearing now. The notes were more than sound. They were Edie's passion and achievement. Phil wasn't there to share it, but the tears pricking Lou's eyes weren't for him. They were for the incredible gift of being able to sit in the audience and just listen.

She didn't hear any mistakes. She didn't notice Mr Romano's piano accompaniment, let alone compare it to the scratchy recording Edie had used for practice. She wasn't on 'mum' mode, where she helped Edie follow Mr Romano's instructions for her practice. She simply felt. It stopped time for the duration of the piece and Lou felt so close to Edie, despite the rows of other people between them.

At the last few bars, Lou composed herself enough to appreciate Edie's mastery of the two trills and the gentle rallentando as the piece drew to a close. Her daughter was gifted. But, more than that, her daughter was inspired. And Lou was inspired by her.

The audience applauded and Lou dabbed at her eye before turning to the woman next to her. But she found herself looking into her own phone camera. She managed a weak smile before the woman mercifully stopped recording.

Lou clutched her phone to her chest when the woman gave it back. In spontaneous joy, she gripped the woman and one-arm-hugged her over the armrest between them, murmuring 'thank you' at least three times. The answering grip was firm and unreserved.

'It was my pleasure,' she said with an indulgent smile.

'No,' Lou insisted, still clutching her phone. 'You don't understand what that meant to me. To listen to her...'

The woman patted her arm as Lou shuffled back in her seat. 'I understand, pet.' Lou's smile grew at the sweet endearment that sounded odd in London, from this stranger with the bizarre sweets and knowing smile. 'I do,' she assured Lou. She pointed to Edie. 'That is your daughter.' Her finger swerved to the right to point at Mr Romano. 'And that is my son.'

Lou's smile faded as she processed that twist. She couldn't think of anything to say as she studied the older woman with the same curling hair as her son, the same dimples, but fairer colouring.

And then she remembered she'd been unrepentantly checking out Mr Romano during the choir performance. If the woman hadn't noticed then, she would definitely see something amiss now as Lou blushed hot to the tips of her ears.

'Ohhh,' she said to cover her choke.

'Twenty years ago, I was you,' the woman said thoughtfully. 'Except I was in Milan and my hair never looked as nice as yours.' She patted her curling grey bob.

Lou chuckled, mostly at the embarrassing situation, rather than the compliment to her hair. She might be the queen of disregard for fashion, but her long wavy hair was her indulgence. 'Th-thanks,' she stammered. 'You must be very proud,' she said, hoping that statement was safe.

'Oh, yes. He's such a committed teacher – and son. He might be thirty-two, but he's still the son of my heart.' She gave a sigh that was full of drama and brought a puzzled smile to Lou's face. 'And he looks great in a suit.'

Busted... Lou stared at her hands, not daring to meet her eye.

* * *

Nick was impressed with how the kids coped. Mistakes were made, but he'd prepared them for that and there were a lot of advantages to performing in front of an adoring, parental audience. It was a soft practice-landing for the round of exams he had to put them through in a month.

He still struggled to keep the grimace off his face when the head teacher announced the violin ensemble to end the concert. But he made sure the kids wouldn't notice anything as he ushered them on stage from the wings.

Edie sat in her position at the front and arranged her music. Most of the kids were craning their necks and searching the crowd, but not Edie. Nick tried to remember from previous years or parent evenings what her father even looked like, but drew a blank. She and her mum must have drawn a short straw, but Edie would transform it into magic with her music.

He wondered about Louise again, but bounced his thoughts back out of there. Even if she was mysteriously charming when vulnerable, she was one of those tall, gorgeous women who could swing her luxurious hair and never look twice at him.

After the last student had passed him and trotted on to the stage, he picked up his own violin, pretending his hand wasn't shaking. Focussing on the apprehensive faces of his students, he reminded himself to loosen his grip on the neck of the violin and forced himself on stage. The heat from the lights and applause of the audience threatened to bring everything back. He had to keep his focus on the kids.

The second violins could be distinguished by the more developed glaze of terror on their eyeballs as the moment approached to start the first piece. He hunkered down in front of them.

'Kids,' he began with half a smile, 'we successfully confused all of your parents at the beginning of term with the toilet-roll request. I reckon they think something sinister has been going on since we've been bringing cuddly toys to every practice. Tonight, let's show them. You know what to do.'

Some of the kids immediately responded to his firm nod, but many of them, as expected, just stared at him. His smile grew. 'You do know what to do, right?' The same nods, the same terrified stares. 'Oscar? Care to remind everyone?'

'Keep the bow straight.'

'Exactly. Imagine you're playing a toilet roll and not a violin. And?'

'Pretend you're playing for your soft toy and not...' His eyes darted into the audience.

Nick stuck his thumb over his shoulder. 'And not that bunch of pudgy pandas.' The children tittered and the first layer of terror dissipated. 'I've never seen so many pandas in one place. I thought they were endangered.' He stood. 'That's it. I'll see you all on the other side.'

He straightened and lifted his bow – the signal for the children to settle their violins under their sweaty chins. With a bar to set the tempo, he nodded to the first violins and they launched into the opening line.

When he lifted his own instrument, his concentration narrowed like tunnel vision. His chest tightened. His racing heartbeat interfered with the moderato. He was conducting with the rest of his body as best he could.

It wasn't nerves – not in the way the kids experienced it, where nonsense about pandas and the warm approbation of parents was enough to cut through the anxiety. For Nick, it was hardcore adrenaline combined with memories of humiliation, made worse by the school theatre setting.

With a nod to the second violins, he led them through the first line of their part. It was a simple line – the only difficulty was keeping time against the first violins. But as soon as his bow vibrated the string, one part of him shut down and another came to life. He fought against the desire to let it all out, to be the young virtuoso again. But he had too many traumatic memories of theatres and halls like this one.

He couldn't stop the pull of the music, calling for him to dive into oblivion, but he could ignore it – for the kids. He felt the relief from every child after they completed the difficult section. Their elation was familiar, but he couldn't allow it to come, yet. The piece wasn't finished.

He leaned towards them, stridently continuing with his bow. A squeak made the children wince, but Nick showed nothing on his face except the demand that they continue playing no matter what, until they reached the final notes of the piece.

Only after lifting his own bow – the signal for the children to follow suit – did he allow himself to join in their relief. It was almost as good as the feeling of mastering a jaw-dropping virtuoso piece.

He allowed them half a minute of glorious applause, sweeping relief and glowing pride before he handed off his violin and reeled them back in for the last piece. It was an easier song from the previous school year and a popular tune the audience would recognise. The only challenge was keeping the children from racing off with the tempo.

There was a smile on every face – on stage and in the audience – for the final moments of the concert. He gestured to the ensemble to stand for applause and shook Edie's hand with a grin – like the real orchestra leader she could be one day.

The head teacher shook his hand and he ushered the kids off stage, pausing for a deep breath outside the green room. It was done. He was annoyed at the scale of his relief. A school concert shouldn't be a big deal. He had to play from time to time. But he could imagine the looks if any of his students found out how much he hated it.

The green room was disorganised cacophony again and he clapped his hands together and held them high.

'Great job, kids. I'm proud of every one of you. Have a think about what you enjoyed most and tell me after the holidays. But most importantly, tell your parents I said you deserve a treat tonight for all your hard work!'

He waved off the children as they were collected by their parents. He shook hands and nodded and smiled and ignored his aching shoulders and thumping heart. His mother arrived and he clenched his teeth, although he was smiling.

He kissed her cheek and murmured equivocal responses to her encouraging words. Louise slipped into the room and grabbed Edie for an effusive hug that looked exceedingly pleasant. His mother slapped him on the arm and forced him to give her his proper attention.

'You can be so English, Nico. Take a compliment with grace.'

'Thank you, Mamma. But you have to admit I'm good at taking your Italian reprimands with grace.' He smiled.

Nick was surprised when Louise and Edie approached, not to speak to him, but to his mother.

'Thank you again, Greta,' Louise said warmly. *Greta?* What was his mother up to?

She tutted and waved her hand. 'It was nothing. But do introduce me to your lovely daughter.'

Louise lifted her eyes to his as though realising she hadn't greeted him. There was a pink tinge to her cheeks and a brightness to her expression that drew his gaze.

'Uh, this is Edie.' Lou wrapped an arm around her daughter's shoulders. 'This is Greta, Mr Romano's mother,' she said with a quirky shrug that acknowledged the awkwardness of the situation and carelessly tossed it away.

'Hello,' Edie said politely.

'Your playing was wonderful. You brought us all joy.'

'Greta and I sat together during the performance,' Louise explained, her eyes swerving back to him when he made some kind of relieved choking sound. Had he truly thought that his mother would set him up with Louise? It was his own fault for thinking such a ridiculous thing.

'Did you enjoy the performance?' his mother asked Edie, following up with more questions that made him wonder if she was thinking back to his early concerts, before he'd broken down.

'Your mum videoed Edie's performance for me so I could watch,' Louise commented. She was looking at him – warmly. It made him uncomfortable and oddly wistful. The adrenaline that had waned in his blood bubbled away again. 'It was so kind. I was in tears...' Her comment trailed off.

By the time he realised he'd been selfishly consumed in his own thoughts, he couldn't think of anything to say.

'I mean with her father not here...' She glanced away, blinking. 'God, you're going to think I cry all the time now.'

'Do you?'

She grimaced and he realised he'd said the wrong thing. 'I mean, of course not,' he said.

She chuckled weakly, giving him that look again. 'You were pretty good, too,' she said and his heart rate ratcheted up again. 'I didn't realise... you conducted and played with so much... passion.' The last word emerged as a kind of regretful choke.

He froze, the familiar flood of embarrassment stalling any response. His jaw clenched. She meant he looked like a freak when the music overcame him. He was well aware of the problem, although he thought he'd kept himself in check that evening.

'I'm sorry. I shouldn't have said anything,' she continued on a rush. 'I mean, I've been to every one of Edie's concerts over the past six years. I know exactly how you look when you conduct and absolutely nothing was different tonight.'

Nick studied her, baffled. She was twirling a strand of dark hair around her finger and her lips twisted with a range of emotions, so fast that he couldn't tell what sort. 'Are you sure you're okay?'

'Yes?' she squeaked. He had an unexpectedly strong urge to pluck the poor strand of hair from her fingers so she would stop mistreating it.

'I can understand it's not great, but I had no doubt Edie would do fine without... her father here,' he finished carefully.

She dropped the strand of hair and he breathed out again. She glanced at Edie and Greta, still deep in conversation, and dropped her voice low. 'Thanks. She wants him to come to the concert in Milan after the camp, but I doubt he will.' She winced. 'He's reminding me that the music is "my" thing with Edie and not his.'

'Ah, Edie tells me she is your student who has a place on the camp?' his mother interrupted. He nodded and Greta smiled and clapped her hands together. 'And Lou is going, as well?'

He nodded and glanced back at Louise. Yes, he was going to spend several weeks in close quarters with this woman. The summer camp was looking... interesting.

'Do you still need help planning the activity programme?' she asked.

'Yes, I haven't had time to look into it, yet. Perhaps you could stay for half an hour after school one day so we can go over the basics and then we can email from there.' He would be able to handle half an hour with her without doing something stupid like touching her hair, right?

'Nonsense!' his mother interjected. 'I wanted an excuse to make strudel. Can you come on Thursday? Perhaps Edie can help bake the strudel while you two... talk about your plans.'

Nick didn't dare look at Louise. He kept his eyes trained on his mother, hoping he was discouraging her subtly, but effectively.

'You live together?'

That snapped his blush into gear and the heat spread right up his neck. 'Temporarily,' he said. He risked a look at her. She was smiling at him, a warm, wry grin that washed over him like a hug.

'Nick gave up his flat for his ex-girlfriend when they split up,' his mother explained as though she were discussing the weather.

'I didn't mean to... pry, sorry.' He dismissed Lou's apology with a small shake of his head. 'Are you sure about Thursday?'

Greta confirmed with enthusiasm, but Louise was still looking at him. He smiled faintly. 'You'll enjoy the strudel. Give me your number and I'll text you the address.'

'I thought strudel was a German thing,' she said as she entered her number into his phone.

Greta opened her mouth to speak, but Nick cut her off before she could wax lyrical. 'Mum can explain it all when you come, but she's from Trentino, which isn't too far from Austria, and they're big fans of a strudel.'

'Is that why they got you to organise the camp? Because you're from the area?' she said. 'I've never been... anywhere really, so I don't know how many ideas I'll have, but I can do a Google search.'

'I'll appreciate the help.'

Her answering smile was a touch too bright and made him wonder what was going on inside her head.

'We'll see you Thursday, then.'

Greta could only wait the few seconds it took him to collect his briefcase and violin. 'Such a lovely girl.'

He had to assume she meant Edie. 'I'm not sure inviting them for strudel was the best idea. I have some professional distance to maintain until the end of the year – and the camp.'

She took his arm as they made their way out of the theatre, waving to the groundskeeper, who was locking up. 'I know professional distance is your speciality, but the camp is over three weeks, isn't it? That's a long time to be always professional. Better to break the ice now.'

'Okay. I'm glad it had nothing to do with... some nefarious plan to...'

'Settle you down? Why would I think of that?'

Her tone was cloyingly innocent. 'Why indeed?' he said, his tone discouraging a reply.

Of course, his mother didn't take the hint. She leaned up to say in a low whisper, 'Only because the woman was definitely staring at your... posteriore.'

He tripped on the doorstep. 'Thanks for that, Mamma,' he muttered.

4

'Is this... weird?' Edie asked as they stepped up to the front door of the little 1930s terrace.

'Definitely,' Lou grumbled.

'But why? It's not like Mr Romano spends the holidays in the music room.'

She gave Edie a dry look. 'We could have invited him to our house. He could have seen your vast collection of pink glittery unicorn books.'

Edie pursed her lips. 'Those books are still cool, you know.'

'Trust me, they won't be for long.'

'But I wouldn't mind if we'd invited Mr Romano to our house.'

Lou winced at the thought. The conversation was only sharpening the awkwardness of turning up on the teacher's doorstep during the holidays. She had to continue to think of him as 'Mr Romano', the hot teacher, rather than someone with a first name and a life. It was difficult when the front garden contained a chained-up bicycle that was carefully maintained and definitely not Greta's. Was that why he was so fit?

Lou lifted the knocker to redirect her thoughts. The door

opened immediately. Greta was wearing an apron decorated with petunias, but had obviously put her baking on hold to hover behind the door waiting for them.

She raised her arms in greeting and kissed them both on the cheek. 'Come in, come in. Nico?' She tut-tutted. 'He moves home and forgets all his manners.'

Edie straightened and Lou grinned an 'I told you this was awkward' at her. She ushered Edie inside and followed her into the cramped hall. 'Something smells amazing,' Lou said.

Greta waved her hand dismissively. 'I haven't even started. We still have to knead the pastry and cut the apples. I'm lucky to have an assistant. *Nico!*' Edie and Lou jumped. 'I worked out where I know you from, young lady.' Greta wagged a finger and Lou was stunned to see she meant *her* and not Edie. 'I have seen you read the news with that lovely voice. Very soothing. I like your news.'

Lou was torn between a laugh and a blush. It wasn't *her* news in any way, but a soothing voice was at least better than being complimented for her bland smile. Being pretty and forgettable was about the extent of her CV.

Mr Romano appeared from a doorway along the hall. 'No need to yell, Mum. I was just setting up the laptop.'

He approached in greeting, his smile tight with politeness, although it did nothing to stop the dimples. He was wearing a blue polo shirt that emphasised his broad shoulders. His hands were shoved into the pockets of dark jeans and he wore socks and neat Birkenstock slippers. If this was Mr Romano's attempt at casual, then Lou needed to invent a concept several steps below to describe her dressing habits. Perhaps this was how thirty-two-year-olds dressed these days – thirty-two-year-olds with continental European heritage, she corrected with a glance at the Birkenstocks.

Her hair was a flowing mess as usual and her hooded

cardigan hung carelessly off one shoulder. She imagined she'd draw disapproving looks in Milan, especially in the company of Mr 'Nico' Snappy Dresser Romano – and a bunch of kids she had to carefully insert into each mental picture so she remembered she was not going to be sitting on romantic squares with the teacher. Phil would have a field day if he could read her thoughts, not to mention what Zoe and Tina would do with that information.

Mr Romano disappeared back into the sitting room and Greta shooed her in after him. 'Coffee, pet?'

'A tea would be lovely. I go a bit... loopy when I drink coffee in the afternoon.'

Greta patted her arm and beckoned to Edie to follow her into the kitchen at the end of the hall. 'I'll bring the tea. You two get started.'

She turned back to find Mr Romano watching her, although he looked quickly away, busying himself with the laptop on the coffee table. When she sat beside him, he jumped.

She pointed at the screen. 'I need to be able to see it, too, right?'

He visibly shook himself. 'Yes.'

'I don't usually bite.' He straightened and she smacked herself for not resisting the weird urge to ruffle him up. 'Sorry. I don't know what's wrong with me,' she said, staring at the blank computer screen.

'You haven't even had a coffee.'

She chuckled. 'Trust me, you don't want to see that.'

He didn't reply for a long moment and she glanced up to find him studying her. 'Loopy Lou,' he murmured with a hint of a smile.

'That's me,' she said brightly, but there was a sigh waiting to escape when he turned away. That was her. Loopy Lou. No talent, just a good time.

'Should I call you "Lou" like Mum does, or would you prefer Louise?'

His teacher voice was back, so Lou pulled herself together. 'Lou is fine.' She tried to resist. She really tried. 'Does that mean I can call you Nico?'

He shot her a dark look that sent a juvenile pitter-patter through her torso.

'Sorry.' She dropped her gaze and mumbled, 'Mr Romano.'

He snorted. 'You'd better call me Nick.'

Greta arrived and placed a mug of tea in Lou's hands. 'Nick' was having black coffee. Lou glanced at him again as he absently acknowledged his mother and studied something on the computer screen. She got the impression he was avoiding Greta's gaze. He reached for the hardcore coffee and lifted it to his mouth.

Lou leaned in to see what he was looking at on the computer. But the sofa sagged in the middle and she lost her balance and fell into his shoulder. It would have been fine, except he smelled incredible – a kind of citrusy, cosy hug of a scent. And during the key seconds while she was inching her nose towards his collar, he was sloshing coffee in his lap.

She jerked back, settled her mug on to the coffee table and jumped up. 'Oh, God, I'm sorry. The s-sofa s-sags. I'll go get—'

She ran to the hall. 'Greta? Do you have a cloth? I've spilled Nick's coffee.' Greta appeared with a cloth, sweeping into the room and taking charge of the clean-up until Nick waved her away, took the cloth and cleaned up his own jeans, kneeling to scrub the sofa afterwards.

'Sorry,' Lou repeated.

'Don't worry about it.' Greta smiled as she took the cloth and left the room.

Nick was watching her again. 'You didn't spill my coffee. I did,' he pointed out.

She dismissed the statement with a wave of her hand. 'Shall we sit over here?' She gestured to a single armchair with a stool next to it. She didn't trust herself next to him any more. He moved the laptop in front of the armchair and tried to usher her into it, but she shook her head. 'You can drive.'

She perched on the stool next to him, but it wasn't much of an improvement. She had to lean over him to see the screen. Her brain was decidedly foggy. With some difficulty, she dragged her thoughts away from him for long enough to process the odd image she saw on the screen.

'We're going to make them do that?' The picture showed a woman in a bikini holding a paddle and standing jauntily on an oversized surfboard on the water.

'My cousin said it's all the rage at the moment on the lakes.'

Lou tilted her head and studied the picture. The woman looked as if she was having fun, but Lou couldn't see why.

'In my experience with these camps, there can be a real range of ability and... motivation among the kids. I wouldn't try anything like windsurfing because they might not be able to do it.'

'I don't think I could do that,' Lou said, gesturing to the screen. 'What if they can't swim?'

'They can wear life vests. Can you and Edie swim?'

'Of course,' she said defensively. 'But I get what you mean about "motivation". Aren't they going to want to spend all day on their phones or something? I know nothing about teenagers.' She grimaced. 'I hope you've got other helpers. I'm not very adventurous. I've never been to Italy. I don't know a word of Italian. I'm going to struggle to motivate myself, let alone move a bunch of stubborn kids. And I don't even know what that activity is called!'

'It's called stand-up paddleboarding, or SUP boarding, and I've never done it either, so no shame.' She glanced up at him to find a smile on his face. 'There will be other teachers from around the country and a handful of other parents coming, so it's not all on you. But I have the feeling you're going to be just what the kids need.'

She scowled at him. 'Don't use your teacher kindness on me. I see through you.'

He chuckled. 'Do you really think it's a bad idea? I've been struggling to come up with anything that would suit everyone.'

The little furrow between his eyes activated her sympathy and she studied the image on screen again, forcing herself to see it from a teenager's point of view and not her own. 'It's probably okay. I mean, someone's going to hate everything.'

'That's a good way of looking at it. I'll make a note of it. There's a good spot for it right near where we're staying, so we wouldn't need a whole day.'

'I assume we want to do a day on a boat on the lake? I thought we should do that early on so the kids get a feel for the place.' And she would, too.

'Definitely. We'll have to book well in advance for a group our size, so we should look into options.'

'Where are we staying again? Can you pull up the map?' It was overwhelming to see the lake and all the towns and monuments she couldn't even pronounce, let alone guide a group of children through, but Lou was excited. Screw her former insistence on all-inclusive holidays with no risk, no stress – and no challenge. She wanted to get out there and mispronounce everything, choose the dish she couldn't translate on the restaurant menu and try everything until she found something she was good at. Now she didn't have Phil watching, it felt possible.

Wasn't that the oddest side-effect of the divorce? She felt less powerful when it came to their joint decisions, but she wasn't afraid of being on her own – the opposite. She'd show him that failing at things didn't have to be part of who she was.

Nick indicated a spot on the eastern side of the lake. 'We're staying up in the hills behind Malcesine.' Lou repeated the pronunciation in her head several times, but feared she still wouldn't be able to say it properly. 'Mahl-*che*-see-neh,' Nick repeated slowly with a hint of a smile.

'Was I that obvious?'

'You've really never been to Italy before?'

She shook her head. 'I think I'm going to love it.' She laughed at the dreamy sound of her own voice. 'In a very serious, responsible adult kind of way, of course.'

'Don't worry, you'll have plenty of time to look around. Even I get a few days off when the guest conductor arrives in the third week. Do you have any plans?'

She had a whole document in her Notes app. 'Oh, nothing much, just yet. I thought I'd take a few workshops.'

'What sort of workshops? That sounds like a great idea. I know the sport side is important for these musical kids, but they might enjoy a workshop more.'

She stared at her hands in her lap. 'Nothing that would interest the kids, I don't think,' she muttered.

He watched her for a long moment. 'What?'

He only used that one word and then waited with an intensity that agitated her, but all her sheepishness couldn't hold it in. 'I want to find something I'm good at – talented at,' she explained on a rush. 'I suck at most things, to be honest. I'm not musical; I can't tell the difference between any leafy herbs and I hate cooking; I'm terrible at sport. I can't remember words in other languages. I will try, but it's not going to be my talent. I want to find something that's really my thing, you know? I haven't booked anything yet, but I've found a couple of local workshops around the lake. There's perfume-making in Sirmione and leatherwork in Riva. I'm looking at a couple of different photography courses and ceramics and I'd like to find a jewellery-making course or perhaps mosaics. I don't think there's much use in doing a cooking course because I know I don't like cooking, but I considered a cheesemaking workshop, or perhaps chocolate? Actually, maybe the kids would like to try chocolate-making. I could check if the place I found will take a large group of teenagers.' She eventually petered out when he didn't respond. Oops. Too much information.

'You want to find a talent?' he repeated.

She looked up, annoyed. 'That's what I said – at some length.' She'd expected him to look steam-rolled by her barrage of chatter, but he was rubbing his chin in a gesture that was more 'mad professor' than 'sexy younger teacher' and she was soon smiling again. 'I don't expect you to understand. You and Edie, you're special. You have the "music" thing. It's in your blood somehow.'

He leaned back in the armchair and sighed, a deep, long breath that held a secret he probably couldn't verbalise. He rubbed the fingertips of his left hand with the thumb. Lou knew he would have fat calluses, like Edie's. She looked up into his face so she didn't start to wonder what the calluses would feel like. His gaze was sharper than she'd seen it, with some of the restless energy of the concert.

'Talent doesn't solve your problems,' he said, his voice quiet.

Lou stilled instinctively at his tone. What problems did Nick have that he needed to solve? Could she sneak close enough to solve them for him without him raising a protest? The first step was the most difficult. She had to sit very quietly and very still, as if she weren't even there. Then, he might tell her. She wove her fingers together and tensed them to keep them still. When she had the urge to tap a foot, she smothered it.

Finally, her agonised waiting paid off and he started to speak. 'I wouldn't wish—'

Greta bustled in and Nick sat up straight, his hand returning to the keyboard.

'Strudel is in the oven. How's it going in here? Do you need any inspiration? More tea?' she asked. Nick handed over his cup with an inarticulate mumble.

'I'll have more tea with the strudel, thanks. I bet Edie enjoyed the baking. I never bake with her. I mean, I never bake.' Lou felt Nick's gaze on her. When she turned to him, his eyes were doubtful.

Greta left the room again and he shook his head. 'I don't believe you lack talent. It's something else.'

As much as his words warmed her, he obviously had no idea. She had three-and-a-half weeks in the Italian sunshine to sort herself out. She'd better make the most of it.

5

'Sunshine!' Lou raised her arms and did a wiggly dance as soon as they emerged through the doors of the airport on a warm Thursday in early August.

'Mum, you dork!' Edie groaned, glancing at her peers.

Lou wanted to smooth Edie's hair behind her ears in a soothing caress, but now was clearly not the time. 'I know every airport looks like Stansted, but we are in Verona and I am determined to love it.' After the year of the divorce and the teetering state of her career, she deserved that.

Phil wasn't coming to the competition. While that was both a blessing and a curse, her producer's flippant comment that she wanted a meeting with Lou after the holidays was definitely a curse – one she couldn't reasonably blame on Phil.

But she had a few weeks to leave life behind, to experience something different with Edie – and without Phil. She hadn't expected to feel so giddy.

'You're determined to love a taxi rank?' Edie asked.

'It's not a taxi rank, it's a—' she squinted at the sign '—solo arpeggio taxi. Sounds like just what we need!'

Nick stepped up beside her, a deep furrow between his brows and one hand holding a cart stacked with instruments. 'Solo parcheggio taxi,' he corrected without looking at her. 'Taxi parking only. I don't think they're requiring taxis to play arpeggios.' Edie giggled and Nick shared her smile. Lou pursed her lips, disgruntled.

He'd barely said hello to them so far. He'd been running around between parents and children, taking careful possession of valuable instruments, and was either supremely busy and stressed or doing a good job of avoiding her.

Ever since that afternoon at his mother's house where she'd lusted after him and gained a glimpse of whatever was hiding beneath his teacher façade, he'd carefully maintained his distance. She'd won a dimpled grin from him once, when Edie passed her grade six exam with distinction. Lou had nearly swooned.

She wasn't expecting he'd return her interest in him. She didn't even know what her interest in him meant, given the foundations of her existence had been broken up by the courts mere months ago. But she had hoped they would build some sort of friendship in preparation for the trip, enabling her to get over her juvenile crush on him.

As it was, she struggled to tear her eyes away from his scrunched brow. He glanced up from looking at his phone and she quickly erased any visible traces of attraction. His puzzled look was an improvement on the concerned furrows, but she imagined 'pretending I'm not lusting after you' was an odd look.

'Is everything okay?' she asked.

He nodded. 'But there's still time for that to change.'

'Why, Mr Romano!' she exclaimed, earning her a pinched look. 'I didn't think you were a "glass half empty" kind of guy.'

'Since you're in a "glass overflowing" sort of mood, I don't think that will be a problem. Are you going to insist on calling me "Mr Romano" for the whole trip?'

She crossed her arms over her chest and gave him a brilliant smile. He appeared to flinch away from her, so she toned it down. 'It depends on whether you're going to behave like a stuffy old teacher for the whole trip – when you're not treating me like comic relief.'

He sighed. 'I'm sorry. I enjoyed the laugh, but I should have realised it was at your expense. The responsibility is weighing heavily today. Not that that's an excuse.'

He clutched the luggage cart and Lou remembered the chaotic conversations at the check-in desk about the transportation of the instruments. 'It's okay. I didn't mind. I was just teasing.' He glanced back at her with a doubtful smile. 'Mr Romano,' she added with exaggerated courtesy.

A minibus drove up and his shoulders sagged with relief. 'Here,' he said and gestured to the luggage cart, which she took without question. He greeted the driver with a hug and some rapid words in Italian.

Lou couldn't help but stare. The sudden change in intonation transformed his voice. She suddenly realised how much he'd assimilated in London – or was he assimilating here?

When he came back to her with murmured thanks and grasped the handle of the cart, his thumb brushed hers and she dropped her hand in a hurry. Why couldn't she behave like a normal human being with him?

'Can you count the kids on to the bus? I'll take care of the instruments.'

She nodded and took a deep breath. She ushered Edie into the minibus, ready to count the twenty-one kids, one teacher and one more parent who had taken the same flight from London.

The other students, one more teacher and one parent were expected on later flights.

'Seat belts, everyone!' she called out. 'Take a seat next to someone. Find your new best friend.'

She'd counted twenty kids and looked up to find the pimply double-bass player wrestling his instrument into the trailer with Nick's help.

'I've just got this full-size one, Mr Romano. Maybe I should have brought the smaller one,' he said.

'Don't worry, Harry. You'll be glad to have this one for the competition!' he said with a heave. 'This case is solid,' he grunted.

With the instrument safely stowed, he waved the boy into the minibus and settled his hands on his hips, breathing out.

'I thought it better to stay out of that, although my upper-body strength might have helped,' Lou said, flexing an arm in a move intended to look like Schwarzenegger, but she knew looked more like a person in a T-Rex suit.

'Why do you have upper-body strength?'

'Edie was pretty clingy as a toddler. After she grew out of being carried, I had to keep up the weights otherwise I'd get teacher arm.' Great way to remind him she was the divorced mother of an eleven-year-old.

'Teacher arm?' he asked.

'You know, flabby bits here.' She turned back to find a crooked smile on his face. She wobbled between a laugh and a blush. She stood her ground as he approached the door of the minibus. If he was determined to tease her, surely she had reciprocal rights. It wasn't flirting. She grasped his forearm with one hand and reached for his upper arm with her other. 'Teacher arm,' she repeated, deadpan, while she pinched him.

He didn't flinch. He probably hadn't felt it. She ducked to stare at his arm. The muscle was rock hard. The look on his face told her he knew it. His lips twitched. 'Do you mean triceps?' She scrunched her nose at him. 'Don't underestimate a violin teacher.' His smile widened.

'Point taken, Mr Ro—' she hesitated for effect '—rock hard triceps.' She couldn't afford to linger to enjoy his grin. She needed her knees to remain solid to climb up into the minibus.

When she stepped in, there were two seats left, right behind the driver. Edie was one seat behind, talking to the pimply double-bass player.

'Ciao.' She smiled to the driver and took her seat by the window, turning to check on Edie.

Nick sat next to her and pointed out of the windscreen. 'Eyes forward.'

'What?'

He leaned close to speak quietly. 'I know she's the youngest in the orchestra, but this is going to be the best few weeks of her life. She needs you here, but in the background.'

Lou turned to him sharply. 'What makes you so sure she's going to love it?'

'I've been on music camp before. She's about to discover she's not as weird as Harriet Baker says she is.'

Lou gasped. 'Harriet who? What does she say?'

Nick gripped her elbow and turned her firmly back towards the driver. 'Shh.'

'Ow!' she said and pulled her arm back. Those fingers were lethal.

'Sorry,' he muttered. 'But don't freak out.'

'Don't tell me not to freak out if my daughter's being bullied and I didn't know anything about it,' she said on a hissing whisper.

'She's not being bullied. Trust me. I know the difference and I'm keeping an eye on it. You know what school kids are like when someone follows their own path instead of the crowd. You should be proud of her.'

Lou deflated slowly, her brow furrowing. Her fingers wound through a strand of her hair before she noticed what she was doing. She didn't remember hurtful comments in school, but she feared that was because she'd been Harriet Baker in this equation, not Edie Saunders.

'I am proud of her – immensely. Are you speaking from your own experience?'

He froze up, no doubt revealing more than he realised.

He turned away. 'My experience doesn't compare.'

'Why not? I bet you were a musical genius.'

The look of warning he sent her was confirmation of her suspicion that there was something behind this. 'Musical genius is a leading term. I just meant my schooling was different. I went to music school in Milan and when we moved to the UK, I could barely speak English. You see, it's not the same.'

The minibus slowed for the toll gates at the entrance to a motorway and Nick hurriedly checked his pockets for his wallet. The driver waved him back and they passed through an automated gate. He said something with a laugh and Nick smiled in response.

'Did he just call you "Nico"? I'm probably imagining things.'

'He's my uncle.'

'Seriously?'

'That's why we're here instead of closer to Milan. My mother grew up near the lake. The manager of the centre is an old friend of hers. She's moved back here, now – my mum, I mean.'

'Really? Greta's not in London any more? Did you get kicked out?'

His cheeks went pink. 'I moved out in plenty of time,' he said weakly.

One of the other teachers – an older woman from a school in Surrey – asked him a question, so Lou gave Edie a quick smile and then stared out of the window as their surroundings gradually turned from industrial grey to tentative green. At the first glimpse of the clay roof tiles of an Italian farmhouse, her giddy excitement returned. Every hoarding was exciting because it was in Italian and the unfamiliar brand names all sounded so fashionable.

Phil would laugh at her tolerantly and spout off what he knew about everything he saw. He always knew stuff. He'd always read more than she had. Everyone knew more and had read more than she had. If she made an observation, his response would be something dismissive. She was a sidekick – good for showing the strengths of the main character, but incapable of driving the plot.

A mountain rose in the distance and her thoughts of Phil drained away. The countryside opened out into fields of grapevines, neat vegetable crops and paddocks of horses, while that mountain loomed, distant with promise.

When they took an exit off the motorway, a rocky outcrop with a green skirt of forest rose next to a town baking in the sun. Palm trees were scattered among tall pines and spreading oaks and she couldn't decide if it felt like Scotland or southern Spain – or both.

'Don't peak too soon,' Nick said. 'Wait until you see the lake.'

She affected a shrug. 'I've seen lakes before.' But she couldn't suppress a grin. 'Did you come here on holiday as a kid?'

He nodded. 'I spent a lot of time around the lake with my cousins. But we lived in Milan, so I never got to be a sports nut like them. They're real mountain people, my extended family.'

'Maybe you'll be really good at stand-up paddleboarding. World champion!'

'Maybe you will be. You're the one looking for a talent.'

His tone held a note of scepticism, but she couldn't detect any judgement. Perhaps her judgement sensor had overloaded after so many years married to Phil. It was about time. 'I think you'll forgive me for saying I don't think either of us is going to be talented at stand-up paddleboarding.' She gave him a playful nudge.

But his answering smile was pained. 'They're going to hate it, aren't they?'

'Character building,' she countered.

'For us? Or them?'

She grinned. 'Definitely for us.'

He studied her with his wary intensity for a long moment, before succumbing to a smile that made her want to pack him up and put him in her pocket. And just like that, her desire to look out of the window and soak up the adventure disappeared in a puff of lust. This was not helping.

'Have you got your seat belt on?' he asked.

She raised her chin. 'Of course. And I told all the kids to do the same.'

'Good.' He looked out of the windscreen with a smile. 'Because this road is about to get interesting.'

The trees had thinned and the hills were grassy. Lou peered ahead, but she couldn't see what he meant. The road seemed to disappear into the hill. As they approached, she saw the arrows indicating a hairpin curve and the minibus lumbered around the bend. The road narrowed and the bus rocked through more curves as they rose through the hills.

They slowed even more as they began the descent. Trees blocked the view, but the blue sky and steep hill on either side of the road gave hints of what was to come. A cyclist pedalled furiously in the opposite lane and Nick gave a pent-up sigh. He was watching the cyclist, his eyes bright.

'That looks like so much fun,' she said with a grimace.

'Sarcasm aside, it really is. There's not much that compares to conquering a mountain on a bike.'

'When you said you weren't a sports nut, I didn't realise you meant you were a masochist instead.'

'All musicians are masochists, in one way or another,' he said flippantly. 'But anyone can cycle – and everyone does. It's a class-less sport around here. You don't have to have a fancy bike like that guy.'

'I can't.'

'Hmm?'

'I can't cycle. Not here, not anywhere. I cannot do it, Sam-I-am.'

'What?' He looked charmingly baffled. She'd seen that expression on his face a lot.

'You missed out on Dr Seuss during your childhood?'

'Ahh,' he said, very little the wiser. 'And you missed out on learning to ride a bicycle?'

'My parents were worried I'd fall on my face.' Because her face had been worth some money back then. It was still one of the only things that paid the bills.

'Was falling on your face something you did often?'

'Something like that,' she murmured.

'Do you want to learn?'

He was looking at her as though he believed she could. It was a sentiment she barely recognised. 'I'm thirty-seven,' she blurted out.

'And?'

His expression was perfectly serious. Damn him. 'My bones are brittle with age.'

He chuckled. 'You won't break any.'

'Are you offering to teach me?' She couldn't stop her voice from rising an octave or so.

'If you like.'

What would learning to cycle involve? Perhaps he would have to put his arms around her as she tried to balance. He might whisper instructions into her ear and wrap those hands gently around hers. She shivered and tried to shake the thought. More likely it would involve her bum sagging over the saddle and endless attempts to forget that he could see it.

She shook her head quickly. 'I don't think I would get the hang of it within the limits of your patience.' He opened his mouth to say something, but she waved a hand to stop him. 'I know, you have unusual reserves of patience, but I would be too much for you.'

He chuckled lightly. 'Possibly.'

In more ways than one... Why did she have the suspicion that they were on the same page with the double meaning? And why didn't he look put off? He now knew her age, her loser status, her lack of talent and her bad habit of running off at the mouth. Why was his expression still so warm? And why did she find him impossibly attractive? She would like to settle into an easy friendship, but instead she'd transformed into a ravenous cougar.

Her cheeks hot, she turned back to the window – and grabbed for the armrest of her seat as the minibus hurtled through another hairpin curve. Clay-rendered farmhouses surrounded by ordered groves of squat silver trees appeared with more regularity and when the minibus took the next curve, the view opened out suddenly to a stunning riviera of sun-drenched blue, green and terracotta.

'*That's* not a lake,' she breathed. The water glistened rippling gold in the afternoon sunlight. The mountains slid into the lake on two sides and, to the left, the shore was so distant that she could only see water, stretching to the hazy horizon. The dark blue of the middle graduated to turquoise at the shore. The pale blue sky hung suspended between the mountains; the clouds unable to touch the oasis of warmth beneath.

A town nestled below them, a cluster of baked terracotta roofs tumbling down to the ramparts of what used to be a castle and then to the edge of the lake. Masts swayed in the afternoon breeze – little yachts moored restfully in the tiny harbour.

'We're in Nice, right? Or some small town nearby,' she joked. 'And that's the Mediterranean?'

'Have you been to Nice?'

She shook her head. 'But I imagined it looked exactly like this.' She sighed. Nick said nothing, but when she turned to him, he was smiling at her. 'It looks nothing like this, does it?' she asked flatly.

'There are similarities.'

'Now you're just being nice.'

He shook his head. 'No, I understand why you'd think so. The yachts, the colour of the water – it's not too far off.' He was so cute, she didn't mind that he'd missed her joke.

'I think it was the palm trees that were most unexpected. Aren't we almost in the Alps?'

'Yes, the border with Austria used to run through here before the First World War. Switzerland is just over there a little bit. But *Lago di Garda* is a little piece of the Mediterranean that got lost. We even produce olive oil.'

'We? I thought you were the city boy from Milan?'

He cocked his head in acknowledgement, suddenly looking like the boy from Milan. 'My grandparents have an olive grove and a mill.'

'Really? That's so cool.'

He laughed. 'Yes, cooler than the city family from Milan. The farm is where my mum has moved back to.'

'Is it around here?'

'Yes, near the northern end of the lake.'

'I'm so jealous.' She sighed, looking out over the lake. 'I get to visit my parents at my old house in Royston.' She shuddered, thinking about that house, about her old room and what it looked like now – a shrine to things she'd needed to let go.

The view disappeared when they entered the town. Lou pressed her nose to the window, craning her neck to look along the narrow side streets and over the stone walls. They turned on to another main road and Nick pointed out the old town, which was now a pedestrian zone. Colourful shutters and stone balconies reminded her how far from London she'd come.

'Oh, look. Vino. I know what that shop sells. But what's Wein, then?'

'German.'

'What?'

'It's "wine" in German. They also sell Brot and Lebensmittel.'

'Vodka and vermouth?'

His expression lifted beyond his usual baffled charm and he burst into laughter. 'You crack me up, Lou. This camp is going to be interesting.'

She'd been thinking the same thing, but not because he was laughing at her bad jokes. 'I'm so pleased to be of service. But I do realise this is not a weeks-long hen do. What does it mean, then? Do you really speak German?'

He shrugged. 'Not really. It means "bread" and "groceries", and it's about my level of German. I know a few words from spending the summers here. I worked in a hotel when I was a student.'

'What, as a waiter?' He shook his head and the sheepish look gave him away immediately. 'Ah, you mean a posh hotel where you were in a string quartet playing Pachelbel's Canon on repeat for big money or something like that.'

'Something like that. Yes, I played in the hotel restaurant.'

'Pretty impressive.'

He rubbed the back of his neck in an odd gesture that she couldn't interpret. 'It paid the bills,' he muttered. 'Look, there's the beach.'

She turned eagerly back to the window. 'Oh my God, it's a real beach!'

'Well, yes.'

The clear blue-green water sparkled against the white pebble beach, still and inviting. Bright sun umbrellas shaded beachgoers. Palms and cypress trees lined the shore and the breathtaking mountain panorama completed a picture of an impossible place with the landscape of an entire continent.

'Please tell me we're going to get to come back here.'

'Don't worry. Malcesine is everything you want.'

He was right. As the minibus headed north along the lake, the mountains beside them grew steeper. The road was squeezed between water and rock, passing through towns that huddled on the shore, in the thrall of the stone massif taking shape above. The lake grew narrower, rendering the dramatic ridges and gullies on the other side in more detail.

Lou leaned over to see more of the mountains rising to their right, but her hand landed on Nick's thigh and she snatched it back before she had a chance to judge how seriously he took his cycling.

Soon after the sign announcing their entrance to Malcesine, the minibus took a sharp right on to a concrete road that rose steeply into the foothills. Shiny rhododendrons and pine branches poked above the stone walls on either side of the road and Lou noticed more of the squat, silvery trees. As the bus gained altitude and the hotels and holiday apartments thinned out, there were more and more of them in ordered plantations.

'Olive trees!' she realised suddenly. The low slopes were covered in them, contrasting with the dark cypress and pine on the wooded mountains. Above the treeline, the peaks rose – bare and grassy or imposing with pockmarked grey rock. The minibus trundled up around hairpin turns, giving Lou an alternating view of the lake below and the mountains above, until suddenly the trees opened out to reveal the town of Malcesine, romantic in every sense of the word.

Nick said something to his uncle and they pulled over at the edge of the road to enjoy the view. He stood and faced the kids in the bus. 'We're nearly there. But this—' he gestured out of the window with a smile '—is Malcesine.'

A tower of bright white stone, complete with crenellations and fit for a kidnapped princess, rose above the town, arrogantly facing the jagged rock of the mountains on the opposite shore. The warm colours of the town glowed in contrast to the still water. Streets clustered with orange clay roofs rambled up around the castle and down to the shore.

'The castle is a genuine eight hundred years old and has seen many battles. And this—' he gestured out of the opposite window and Lou ducked to see the view up the steep hill '—is Monte Baldo. The highest peak is nine hundred metres higher than Ben Nevis. It's a long way up.'

'What about the ice cream and the pizza?' asked one of the older students.

Nick grinned. 'I can promise pizza, pasta and gelato – not to mention risotto, polenta and rose cake. But I might make you climb that mountain to work it off.' There was a collective groan.

'You're not serious?' Lou asked under her breath. 'They'll mutiny.'

'Don't worry. This is the mountain with the cable car we discussed,' he said, refastening his seat belt.

'Oh,' Lou said and peered out at the towering ridge. 'Really? We can go up there?'

Nick chuckled. 'Going up there is the point.'

Lou stared the next time the minibus turned and gave her a view of the mountain. A few buildings were dotted on the high ridges.

When the minibus pulled to a stop at a gate, they were high above the town. The castle was exposed as a puny attempt to tame the wild landscape of rock and woods and the huge expanse of lake. They waited until an older woman appeared to unlock the gate so they could drive on. Trees formed a canopy over the bumpy driveway and they passed under a stone arch before coming to a halt on a gravel turnaround.

Lou jumped out eagerly and soaked in the view. The ground fell away in front of the drive – not too steeply, because a grove of olive trees had been planted. The lake glistened below.

'Isn't it beautiful?' Edie said and Lou wrapped her arm around her. 'I never imagined I would get to learn violin somewhere so beautiful.'

'Or that I would get to piggy-back on your success,' Lou said.

'Turn around!' Nick called out as he headed for the luggage trailer.

They turned and Lou's head dropped back as she gaped at the stunning stone chapel sitting meditatively at the base of a steep rocky incline. The white stone was rustic, the uneven bricks held together with pale mortar. A square bell-tower rose from the apex and an arched window that must be shining with light inside looked humble and dark from the outside.

A wall of the same rustic stone sheltered the cluster of buildings that made up the former convent. Palms peeked over the top and the fresh scent of pine and lemons and an alpine breeze hung in the air. As Lou took a deep breath, some hint of herbs reminded her of Greta and her strange sweets.

An ornate archway showed the way in. Lou wrestled the huge suitcase across the gravel while Edie pulled the smaller one and carried her violin.

'It's so quiet,' Edie said in a whisper as they approached the archway. As soon as she stopped hauling the suitcase, Lou appreciated what Edie meant. The silence settled on the convent as a presence.

Edie crossed under the archway and gasped in delight. 'It's magical, Mum!' Lou followed her through into an intimate square courtyard, lined with a vaulted cloister that was cool and silent, but containing an oasis of plants. A magnolia dominated the square, with oleander bushes and chrysanthemums flushing with colour beneath. A rock face rose directly behind, shadowed by twisted juniper trees and alive with moss, plants and flowers growing out of the cracks.

Lou craned her neck to look up, thinking about Nick and his mountains. What would it be like to just go up? She'd never wanted to do anything like that before. But if a group of crazy nuns had lived up here, anything was possible.

The campers, teachers and chaperones gathered in the courtyard, talking in hushed murmurs. Nick was the last through the archway, helping Harry with the double bass while carrying his own backpack and violin. He barely looked up, let alone appreciated their secluded surroundings.

He noticed her watching him. 'Everything okay?'

She grinned. 'This place is amazing.' He glanced around the cloister with a small smile. Mission 'cheer up the stressed teacher' accomplished. 'It's going to be a really special few weeks for us here,' she continued, but her throat closed as she played back her words in embarrassment. Who did he think she'd meant with the 'us'? 'For the kids, I mean,' she added.

'I suppose so,' he said, his voice even and kind, despite the weariness in his features. 'Don't forget about having a good time yourself. You have to find that talent.' His smile was so quick she didn't have time to work out if he was teasing her.

'Welcome, everyone!' called the slate-haired woman who had opened the gate. 'I'm so pleased to see you all, along with your lovely instruments!' she exclaimed. 'Welcome to the Eremo di Sant'Anna. My name is Cecilia and I can help you if you need something or want to ask some questions. Let me show you to the dormitory.'

6

Nick collapsed into the wicker chair and stretched out his legs. The last glow of orange lit the sky over the mountains. A cuckoo called nearby and he closed his eyes to listen, appreciating the odd acoustics of the rock overlooking the wide valley, as well as the slightly irregular cadence and muted quality of the birdcall.

It was going to be a special few weeks. He couldn't stop the smile. What was it about Lou that everything she said landed with the impact of an adrenaline injection? He'd been lost in the chaos of the day, the uncomfortable feeling of history and homecoming and the weight of responsibility for the young musicians. But she'd snapped him out of it for a few minutes with one amusingly ambiguous sentence.

Haunting the back of his mind was the competition – at the music school. In Milan. He sighed and opened his eyes. He was holding on to the 'glass half empty' attitude again. The kids' future would not look like his past.

With a creak from the back of his chair, the stem of a wine glass appeared in his field of vision, along with a thick curl of long brown hair. With a shot of anticipation and pleasure that he was too tired to suppress, he tipped his head up and smiled.

'Plying the teacher with alcohol?'

Lou leaned further over the chair so more of that luxurious hair flowed in his direction. Although slightly sheepish, her smile brightened her eyes and tipped up her lips.

'I thought you could do with a glass, after the day you've had.'

He swallowed a ball of something thick in his throat. She'd been watching him. 'I really could. Thanks.' He took the glass and watched her swish her hair back over her shoulder as she took the wicker chair next to his.

With even features, a flawless smile and impeccable posture, at first glance she was exactly as he'd expected for a beautiful woman who worked in front of a camera. But she was wearing an old hoodie, no make-up and had bare feet with multi-coloured toenails. There was little sign of her professional persona.

That lustrous hair suggested yet another side to her. It made him think of Circe, the mythical temptress who could turn men into animals. He'd rarely seen Lou with make-up on – except that day when she'd appeared in business clothes, high heels and smudged eye make-up and he'd wondered for the first time what was going on inside her head.

It would have been better if he'd never wondered. He suspected that inside Lou's mind was a weird and wonderful place that would make him smile and cringe and possibly never want to leave.

He watched her inspect her own glass, amused by the wild turn of his thoughts. It was preferable to ruminating on the competition and his return to the music school after sixteen years.

'Cheers.' He held out his glass.

She leaned over to clink her glass against his and took a sip. 'Mmm, Cecilia was right.'

'About what?'

'I asked if she had any local wine and she said this was what we needed. I don't know if I've ever tasted a sparkling red wine before.'

'Recioto della Valpolicella spumante,' he said, appreciating the familiar sweetness of the cold wine with the cherry notes that tasted of summer at the lake.

'I've heard of spumante.'

'It just means "sparkling" in Italian.'

'Oh.' The amused chagrin in her tone was recognisable. 'Either way, this is the perfect end to the day.' She took another sip and stared out at the mountains.

He was tempted to agree. 'Did Edie settle in okay?'

She nodded. 'She's sharing a room with Meg, one of the cellists. I think they'll get on okay.'

'And Helene?' he said, asking about Lou's roommate, another mother.

She peered at him over her wine glass as she took another sip. 'She's great. But she said you told her about me.'

He'd quickly realised Helene was a music enthusiast and a force of nature. She'd pummelled him with questions about the rehearsal schedule, routines and Maestro Eckert. In desperation, he'd changed the subject by coming up with something about Helene's lovely roommate, who came too easily to his mind. 'I just mentioned that you were friendly and keen to experience... everything.'

She grinned and he eased up again. 'Good. I like that.' She leaned her head back on the chair and stretched her long legs out in front of her. 'What was wrong with you, today?' she asked conversationally.

But her gentle tone couldn't soften the question. 'What are you talking about?'

'I understand it's stressful to transport a bunch of clueless kids and their valuable instruments, but you looked like you were leading us into battle against the barbarians, rather than taking us to a beautiful convent. I thought you would be excited about this trip.'

He frowned, wondering what to tell her. She would never understand if he tried to explain what had happened all those years ago. He couldn't explain why he simultaneously needed the music and was afraid of it. He hadn't realised it would be so hard to come back.

'It's a lot of pressure – the practical side and the... emotional side.' He winced and glanced up to gauge her response. She was watching him with a faint smile that allowed him to relax again and turn back to the sunset. 'I fear you'll see what I mean.'

'What are you afraid will go wrong? Whatever happens, we'll work it out. I broke my nose on a camp and, trust me, my mum thought it was the worst thing that could have happened, but it turned out fine.'

'I'm not sure I wanted to know that. What was it, tennis camp?'

She laughed. 'I was not allowed to play tennis.' She paused and an odd smile crossed her face. 'Don't hold it against me,' she began hesitantly, 'but I did a few modelling and... pageant things when I was younger.'

His mouth snapped shut and it took him a second to think of something to say. 'Beauty pageants?' he asked stupidly.

She gave him a dry look. 'I certainly didn't mean royal pageants. I know it's weird, but it's unfortunately true.'

'But did you learn, you know...?' He gestured vaguely to his face.

'Make-up? Why do you think I never wear the stuff any more?'

He smiled. 'You rebelled.'

She shrugged. 'We're all a reaction against our childhoods.'

'Perhaps,' he agreed half-heartedly.

'And I've seen this emotional side you speak of. Pageant girls can be more emotional than even you can imagine.'

'That's not quite what I meant,' he said, but he wasn't sure he wanted to go into it. The pressure of the music, the expectations, the judgement... He froze up just thinking about it.

'What did you mean, then?'

He sighed, thinking of the least he could say that would satisfy her. 'Playing music, well... you lose yourself a little. And finding your way back... sometimes you end up on a different path, or you don't come back at all.'

She watched him far too closely and he wondered what she saw. 'I kind of see what you mean,' she said gently. 'You put yourself under pressure to keep the kids' confidence up.'

'The camp has to be a safe place to work all this out.'

'Emotionally,' she completed for him with a nod. 'But that will also be fine. They have the best teacher.'

His laugh was brittle. 'You're just saying that to make me feel better.'

'Hear me out! I know you'll guide them through it. You'll be great. I mean, with your artistic temperament and all.'

'My what? I don't have an artistic temperament.' He forced the conviction into his tone even as it fled. God knew he did have an artistic temperament. That was the problem.

She nodded indulgently. 'Okay.'

He pursed his lips. 'But just forget about it. There are three teachers to look after that side of things. You and Helene and Tanya are just here to help – and have fun on your time off.'

'I can be responsible.'

'I never said you can't. You're just defensive.'

She spluttered a wordless response and he took a sip of his wine to cover his satisfied smile. 'You're one to talk, Mr "I don't have an artistic temperament".'

He smiled, the long day and his concerns about the camp and the competition dissolving with a fizz. 'I thought I was Mr Rock Hard Triceps?'

He could see her blush, more in the posture of her shoulders than on her features, as the light was fading. The silhouette of her fine, expressive face caught his attention. He could lean over and just – no, no and no.

'It's just my luck that you're Mr Photographic Memory,' she grumbled.

'I think you'll find that auditory memory is my strength, not visual.'

She leaned on the arm of her wicker chair, her nearness both a temptation and a curse. 'I think you'll find that arrogance is your strength, Mr Smug Bastard.'

He laughed. Before he could stop himself, he reached out for a strand of her hair. He pulled away again as soon as he realised what he was doing – and caught the uncertainty on her face. 'It comes with an artistic temperament, or so I understand.'

'I definitely don't have an artistic temperament,' she said with a crooked smile and leaned back into her chair.

'You're lucky,' he said, keeping his expression bland.

But the failing light must have made her sensitive to the catch in his voice he hadn't quite been able to hide. Either that or she was just sensitive to emotions – Circe with her animal power. 'Why? What's so hard about being a musical genius? What's lucky about being ordinary and talentless?'

'That's a bit harsh, isn't it?' he blurted out. She didn't reply. He couldn't see her clearly and wondered if he should turn a light on, but the darkness was disarming. He waited for her response, but she'd gone unusually quiet.

'They're not my words,' she eventually admitted. 'But that doesn't mean it's not true,' she continued more strongly. 'I've tried a lot of different things – music, dance, painting, sculpture, sport – and I've sucked at everything. But that doesn't mean I'm pushing Edie to compensate for my inadequacy. In fact, I don't even have Helene's talent for knowing stuff about music and good practice routines and all that.'

'Hey.' He grabbed her hand. He couldn't not. She quieted immediately. Her hand was warm and he should have let it go straight away – but he didn't. He ran a thumb over the back and tried to forget what his mother had said about her checking him out at the concert. It was a pleasant distraction, but a doomed one – especially when it was impossible not to realise she was talking about her ex-husband. 'He doesn't understand how important Edie's concerts are to her, so I doubt he knows anything about talent,' he said softly.

'But he's a TV producer. A lot of his work is with talented people. He knew I wasn't cut out to be a journalist, especially not after... But, hey, that's what I am good for: smiling and nodding and looking pleasant. I just didn't think that counted as a real talent. And he obviously thought so, too, since he said... You're hurting my hand.'

His fingers sprang open. 'Sorry.' He stared at her, no words coming. Where did he even start? 'He sounds like a smug bastard. And you know exactly what to do with those.'

She didn't react with the laugh he expected. Instead, she reached for the hand that had relinquished hers, clasped it for a moment, and then absently intertwined her fingers with his until their knuckles fitted together. He stared at their hands, unexpectedly moved by the image. 'You're nothing like him. I would never make that comparison.'

His emotions wobbly, he tried to turn away, but only succeeded in shifting his shoulders. His gaze remained trained on her. What was worse, she stared back. She was so beautiful – her hesitant breath, her warmth, her frank curiosity, her irrepressible humour. She was also suddenly close – and not just physically. She was crowding his spirit. He kind of liked it, but he couldn't stop the memories of the way Naomi had crowded him until he couldn't breathe. And Naomi was the kindest woman he'd ever met. The problem was him and his bloody artistic temperament, as Lou had called it.

Her other hand rose to his cheek and the air whooshed out of his lungs. On so many levels, nothing should happen, but something definitely happened inside him when the backs of her fingers touched down on his skin.

But the light blinked on suddenly and she jerked back. He steadied his wine glass, which he had forgotten he was still holding.

'Oh, sorry,' Helene said. Nick's face heated. He didn't dare look at Lou. 'Having the light on spoils the last of the view.' She went to turn it off again.

'It's probably better on, now,' Lou said, her voice even. Had he imagined that she'd just had her hand on his cheek? 'The light's faded completely. I was falling asleep!' She made a show of stretching and caught his eye. He swallowed his tongue at the mischief in her expression. Not his imagination.

'My vision is terrible in the dark,' Helene said. She raised her glass and Lou swiped hers from the table to match her. 'To a musical triumph,' Helene toasted with a smile.

'To no disasters,' Lou countered with a glance at Nick.

He lifted his own glass. 'To learning experiences – for everyone.'

'I like that one,' said Helene, pointing at Nick before taking a sip of her wine. 'Ooh, that's refreshing.' She sat back and looked between the two of them. He fought the rising blush. Surely, she couldn't see that they'd been a breath away from a kiss – or had he misread the situation entirely? A kiss? With Lou?

'We were just talking about Lou's plans,' he said, feeling her wary look and ignoring it. 'She's determined to spend the summer trying new skills to find her talent,' he began.

'What a fabulous idea!' Helene responded, not realising Nick hadn't finished. But what had he been going to say? 'I've been trying to work out how to tell her she doesn't need to find a talent to be worth something to someone'?

'Please tell me I can join in. I don't know what to do with myself while Jason is rehearsing. He hates me hovering, so can I tag along? You might be giving me just the nudge I needed! Aren't you brave!'

* * *

Lou shuffled back to her room from the communal bathroom, her mind blank of everything except the outline of Nick's features in the dark and how much she'd wanted to touch him. It was quite sad, really. She was finally letting go of her identity as Phil's wife and latching on to the first man who came into range. Urgh, it made her sound like a sniper peering through her scope. He was completely out of her league anyway – another stupid expression.

What would it be like to go on a date with Nick? Would it suddenly be awkward? She snapped herself out of it. It was *not* going to happen.

She clutched her bundle of clothes to her chest and listened only to the slap-slap of her slippers on the cool stone tiles. She'd been confused by the slippers provided in each of the rooms, but now she understood. The nuns must have lost toes up here in the winter. And they'd probably had to kiss each of the little icons in the niches along the hallway on their way to and from the toilet.

She heard voices at the end of the hall and immediately recognised Nick as the male voice. He was probably the only fully grown man in this convent. Both of the other teachers were female – the older Mrs Winkelmann and the dainty, young Miss Hwang –and all of the chaperones were mothers. As Lou arrived at the door of her room, she could clearly hear them speaking in Italian, so it was probably Cecilia. She was about to open the door and try to get to sleep, when Cecilia's voice rose in agitation. Nick soothed her, but there was resignation in his tone, too.

She peered around the corner and Nick immediately looked up and saw her. Busted, she padded over to them and tried not to notice that Nick was only wearing a T-shirt, printed with a faded treble clef, and what looked like a pair of boxer shorts. And, oh, boy, those were some gorgeous legs – he must really like cycling.

'Is everything okay?' she asked, tugging absently on a strip of lace before realising it was from her bra and shoving it under her other clothes.

'You know how we were talking about things going wrong?' he began.

'There will be no problem,' said Cecilia, squeezing his shoulder. 'In fact, the timing is quite good. You will love having your mother here.' His lips twitched and Lou suppressed a laugh. Nick's mother?

He turned to Lou. 'Cecilia's mother has to have an operation – quite urgent – and she'll need a few weeks of help during her recovery. My mother is able to cover for her, so there's no reason for Cecilia not to have the time off.'

Lou met his gaze carefully, her smile cleverly stuffed into a reproachful look, just as his matter-of-fact gaze held a definite eye-roll. 'I'd love to see Greta again.' She smiled sweetly.

'Ah, you have met Greta? She is my oldest, dearest friend!' Cecilia said. 'And when I suggested to her that she could come and manage the property for a few weeks, she was so excited to come and see Nico with his students.'

'You see, Cecilia has already mentioned this to her, so the problem is all solved.' His smile was wry.

'She will arrive in the morning – first thing.'

Lou spoke up. 'I'm sorry about your mother. I hope her operation is a complete success. You could leave now, if that would help. I'm sure we can cope with breakfast.'

'I'm pretty sure Mum will be here before breakfast,' Nick said.

Cecilia smiled. 'I think you are right.' She leaned up to kiss his cheek. 'Thank you, Nico. Your camp will be a wonderful success. Buonanotte, polpetto.'

She smiled to Lou and headed through the door to the manager's apartment. Lou watched her go to avoid meeting Nick's gaze, which the hairs on the back of her neck told her was trained right on her.

'You told me nothing would go wrong,' he said accusingly. But when she turned to him, he was smiling.

'One's mother coming doesn't count as something going wrong.'

'It is when one is in one's thirties and has spent months under the same roof as one's mother already this year!'

'At least if she's busy managing the place, she won't be eavesdropping on your rehearsals.'

He stood up straighter. 'Why would that be a problem?'

Lou watched him critically, suspicious of his studied blank look. Not that she would admit to having very sensitive journalistic instincts, but there was a story here. He was way too tense. 'I'm sure it's not,' she said with just enough doubt to make him narrow his eyes at her. 'You're the one who told me to back off from Edie. I'm just extrapolating.'

'I'm not sure I extrapolate well,' he grumbled.

'Diva,' she said, covering it with a cough.

He grinned suddenly and reached up to smooth her hair over her shoulder. She froze. Goosebumps prickled on her chest as her nerve endings stood to attention. Keep it cool, keep it cool.

'Beauty queen,' he accused, his smile gentle.

She wagged a finger at him. 'I told you about that to make you feel better, not so you could use it against me.'

He held up his hands. 'Only in self-defence! But it's interesting to know that about you. Your hair makes a little more sense, now.'

Her stomach dipped at the knowledge that he'd wondered about her hair, but also pinched her with the reality of her life. She was still the thirty-seven-year-old, talentless mother. And he didn't understand about her hair.

'I am vain about my hair, but not because of the pageants,' she said.

'I didn't mean to imply you were vain.'

She shook herself free of the memories of the lowest point in her life – a time she'd escaped and now celebrated by keeping her hair long and lustrous. 'I know,' she absolved him. 'Look,' she began, feeling as if she needed to broach the subject of the was-that-an-almost-kiss-or-am-I-delusional. 'About before...' The air thickened and she found herself staring at the treble clef sitting over his right pectoral muscle. Did that really say 'Royal College of Music'? Had he gone to the most prestigious music college in the country?

'You don't have to... We don't have to... It wasn't anything...'

She should have left him to muddle through the rest of the sentence. She sensed he wasn't about to press her against the doorframe and answer the question she hadn't asked in the way she truly wanted, so she went ahead with the awkward relationship reset. 'I know. We are on music camp. Tensions are high, et cetera, et cetera. No kissing.' She waved her hand dismissively.

He drew back to look at her. She felt a smile hidden somewhere in his expression, but she was struggling to find it under the blush. 'I didn't think... there would be any kissing... with you... us.' He made an abortive gesture and Lou had to order herself to stop looking at his hands. Those fingers were out-of-this-world attractive.

'Absolutely not,' she said with more force than she felt. 'Not if we were the last teacher and parent on the planet.'

He laughed, but it was stilted. 'It's clear,' he gave a tolerant smile. 'And don't worry about breakfast. I'll be up anyway. Save your energy for your chaperone duties tomorrow afternoon on the boat trip.'

She shook her head. 'No way. I offered to help with breakfast. I'm going to follow through. You sleep.'

'Maybe I can make the coffee, then.'

'Not if I get there first!'

'Goodnight, Lou,' he said with a smile that was finally close to the one she wanted – warm and amused.

'Buena naughty or whatever it was.'

He chuckled. 'Buonanotte, bella signora,' he said, the intonation floating pleasantly over her skin. 'E sogni d'oro – golden dreams,' he translated softly.

7

Lou oozed into the refectory the following morning at around seven. She had pulled a light robe over her pyjamas – because no one needed to get dressed to do breakfast – and scrunched her hair into a messy bun. It was summer holidays and too early even to do her hair properly. And she had no one to impress. No one at all.

The large stone hall was cool in the early light, but the windows on two sides revealed the promise of the morning. To the west was the olive grove, the golden lake and distant mountains, already gleaming in the sun. The north-facing windows looked into the quadrangle with the shiny magnolia and riotous flowers. The refectory itself had a vaulted brick ceiling, long trestle tables and niches full of woodwork, vases of flowers and arrangements of fruit.

Her fingers drifted over a candleholder formed out of a single piece of wood, sanded and polished smooth. She absently tested the ripeness of an apricot and her stomach rumbled. She looked up as she heard a gurgle and hiss from the kitchen, followed by the sudden, strong smell of coffee. The serving window was still closed, but the coffee smell wafted from the door, along with the sound of voices.

A sharp sentence in Italian made Lou smile. True to expectations, Greta had arrived already. She must have left home at the crack of dawn.

'It's not burned!' Nick replied defensively. 'I know how to make coffee. I can actually cook, too, if you'd ever let me near a stove!'

Greta said something in a wry tone.

'No,' he replied heatedly, 'Naomi didn't teach me to cook. I learned because I am a functional adult.'

Lou drifted closer to the kitchen as quietly as she could. It wasn't eavesdropping if she could only understand half of the conversation, right?

Greta said something more and Nick sighed. 'You're right. Thank you for coming. It's just...' Lou pricked up her ears. 'I don't want to talk about the competition, okay? At all. I have to do this my way.'

More Italian followed, in a conciliatory tone, but Lou's mind had conjured Frank Sinatra and she figured that was a sign that she should announce her presence.

'Good morning,' Lou said with a bright smile as she breezed into the kitchen.

'Ah!' Greta raised her hands and clasped Lou's shoulders as she leaned up to kiss her cheeks. 'Lou! So pleased to see you, pet. But didn't you sleep well?'

'Uh...' Lou glanced at Nick, although she was trying not to '... I slept fine.'

'But you look...' Greta trailed off.

'Lou always looks like that,' Nick explained, turning back to the aluminium coffee maker on the stove.

'Is that the way to talk to a lady?' Lou joked, sensing Greta was about to make a similar comment.

'I'm sure—' Greta began with a frown, but Lou cut her off.

'Don't worry. It's true. And Nick has seen me enough times on the school run to know I don't care.'

Greta looked put out, but turned back to the bench, where she was placing part-baked bread rolls on to trays to slip into the oven.

'Coffee?' Nick asked. Lou turned to find him holding out a large mug topped with a layer of milk froth. His expression was withdrawn and slightly apologetic. The accompanying kink of an eyebrow and wrinkle on his forehead were inexplicably sexy. Lou was in so much trouble.

'Mmm, thanks,' she said, taking the mug. 'The full barista service.'

He huffed a laugh and looked away. He handed his mother a milky coffee and took a sip of his own espresso before pouring the rest into an insulated pot, topping it up with hot water and closing the lid.

'What can I do to help?' she asked.

'Tell me about your journey,' Greta said.

'Seriously, I can help,' she insisted. She started opening cupboards. 'Is there cereal to put out or something?'

Nick gestured to two large glass dispensers on the bench, which she hadn't noticed. 'Done.'

'Milk?' He pointed to a jug. 'Butter?' Relaxing in a ceramic dish. 'Caviar?' He smiled witheringly at her.

'Didn't you say you wanted to set up the rehearsal space, Nico? I can do breakfast. You have a big day of practice anyway.' Greta shooed them both out of the kitchen. 'Take Lou with you to help.'

The air had already changed when they stepped out of the

refectory. The cool of the early morning in the hills was burning off, even before the direct sunlight had crept over the mountain. Warmth seemed to billow up off the lake and the olive groves. There was a tangy-sweet scent in the air that wasn't familiar.

'Caper bushes,' Nick said, pointing to a couple of trailing plants that appeared to be growing right out of the rock above the cloister. They were covered in white flowers. 'That's the smell. It will drive Mum crazy that they let them flower instead of harvesting the buds, but I can't imagine Cecilia getting up there on a ladder.'

'Does playing the violin give you mind-reading abilities?'

He flashed her a smile and shoved one hand in his pocket as they wandered along the cloister towards the chapel. She couldn't help but note his pressed chinos and fine-checked collared shirt. No wonder his mother thought she looked like a slob. 'It's conductors who have to be mind-readers,' he continued. 'But not necessary in this case. You had your nose up in the air like a puppy.'

'Do you mean caper like... capers? That's a flower?'

He nodded. 'My nonna pickles her own.'

She sniffed again. 'Perhaps I do have a good sense of smell,' she mused.

'Perhaps,' he responded noncommittally. 'Would that satisfy you that you have a talent?'

'It will help. I'm going on a perfume workshop tomorrow. I thought perhaps I'd be good at mixing scents and I could develop my knowledge of natural extracts and blending organic perfumes.' Not that mixing extracts would replace her income if that meeting with her executive producer went badly at the end of August. But she had to start somewhere.

His steps slowed as thoughts that were visible but not discernible moved across his face. 'Would you enjoy that?'

She shrugged and took a sip of her coffee. 'I'll find out.'

He pushed open the heavy wooden door of the chapel and ushered her through. 'Ladies first,' he muttered with a gleam in his eye.

Lou walked through and was struck by the quality of the light. The warm, pale stone concentrated the diffuse morning sun into a gentle welcome, like the opening pages of a book. Windows high up in one wall let in the direct morning sunlight, but the large west window was glowing. It was criss-crossed with diamond lead lighting and was lightly bevelled. Yellow panels with orange detailing complemented the warmth of the stone frame.

At the opposite end of the church stood a simple altar and, behind it, a sculpture of a woman and a child, stunningly carved in wood. The sculpture looked surreal in the nebulous light – more shadow than substance—and Lou stepped closer to stare at the serene, polished face of the mother. God knew she'd never looked like that with a baby on her knee.

'The light is amazing in here,' she murmured, moving her arm as though she could feel the particles. Nick didn't respond and when she turned to prompt him, she found him staring at her.

He cleared his throat and rubbed the back of his hand briefly on his forehead. 'It's the acoustics that strike me,' he commented.

'The what?' Lou called out in a loud, lilting voice that rang in the air of the small chapel.

He grinned. 'The a-cou-stics,' he sang in a simple – but perfect – arpeggio. It was her turn to stare. He had a gorgeous voice – smooth, modulated and resonating powerfully within the stone walls. When she didn't respond, he blushed and turned away, not quite quickly enough to hide the wince. There it was again. The contradiction in the man who lived the music for his students and refused it for himself. If she were a proper journalist, she'd get the story out of him.

He set down his coffee and opened a metallic travel crate, pulling out a folded music stand and handing it to her. She wordlessly followed his instructions, setting up the stands and hauling chairs into place until they'd formed the skeleton of a string orchestra.

'You overheard, then?' he said without looking at her, his hands busy with the conductor's music stand.

'Hmm?' She took a sip of her coffee.

'You're humming "My Way". I finally worked out why it's in both of our heads.'

She spluttered coffee. 'Sorry.' When he didn't volunteer anything else, she pushed. 'Did your mum force you to do competitions when you were younger? Is that the problem?'

'Don't jump to conclusions.'

She drew back suddenly at the short tone. 'Don't be such a bad-tempered prima donna.'

'I didn't invite you to eavesdrop and I certainly don't want to talk about it – which you may have worked out. You have your own goals to focus on.'

'Oh, very clever. You've worked out how to distract self-absorbed Lou from her feeble attempts to be kind!'

He straightened and looked her in the eye. His words had been rude, but she couldn't be hurt by them when he looked at her with such intensity. 'I didn't mean it like that. Don't ever think I don't like and respect you.' He paused and she used the moment to catch her breath. 'Even if I tell my mother you always look sloppy,' he muttered.

Being liked and respected by Nick Romano felt far better than it should have. She clutched her coffee cup as the warmth of his words raced through her. She took a step closer to him, fired up.

'And don't you go thinking this competition is all about you and this thing you don't want to talk about! This is a big deal for Edie and every other child in this orchestra. You work magic with the kids at school and they love you. I know life is hard sometimes, but you're starting rehearsals this morning, so please take your head out of your backside for their sakes!' Oh, shit, what had she just said? She braved a quick glance at his facial expression, braced for the worst. But, although his brow was furrowed, he was smiling. He took two heavy breaths.

'I needed to hear that,' he said, his voice trailing off. 'Lou,' he continued, one dimple peeking out, 'can I give you a hug?'

God, yes please! She composed herself carefully, placing her coffee on the windowsill. 'Sure.' She shrugged, but a twitch of his eyebrows made her wonder if she'd failed miserably at casualness. He took an awkward step in her direction and raised his arms. She resisted the urge to launch herself at him and took a matching step forward. They both guessed wrong and their arms collided. At least the murmured 'sorry' was in unison.

They finally found equilibrium, with one of her arms over his shoulder and the other around his back and his doing the opposite. And that's when she melted. It had been too long since someone had wrapped their arms around her. That would explain the cosy comfort infusing her muscles as her chest pressed against his and her hands clutched at him.

He gave her a squeeze, which nearly made her sigh with pleasure, but she realised it was the signal that she should let go. She pulled away and quickly reconfigured her expression.

'You're absolutely right.'

She laughed. 'That's music to my ears!'

'Thanks for the hug,' he murmured.

'Any time.' She couldn't help flashing him a smile and not caring if he interpreted it as flirting.

'I'm sorry I was rude. You didn't deserve that.'

Her smile dimmed. 'Thanks for the apology. You're allowed to have feelings. And... you know I like and respect you too, even when I'm telling you to get your head out of your backside – especially then.' That was good. That was Lou the powerful woman, who was absolutely right and useful and kind. And then she had to go and ruin it. 'It is a very nice backside.'

He blushed fetchingly and licked his lips, but his smile was worth it. 'Let's go get some breakfast,' he suggested, turning for the door. She gave herself an inward kick and followed, taking only the briefest moment – okay, a little longer than that – to appreciate that rear view.

* * *

Mixing perfume was *not* Lou's talent. Her first workshop of the trip had ended predictably in disaster.

It was a beautiful Saturday afternoon in Sirmione, on the southern shore of the lake, but Lou was disappointed and fed up. She eyed the relaxed patrons of the lakeside bar, thinking of Phil and wondering whether sitting in a café sipping Aperol Spritz might have been the more sensible idea.

'Do you think we have time for a drink before our ferry?' she asked Helene.

Helene hesitated, her gaze dropping to the wonky discoloured patch on Lou's jersey dress.

Lou sighed. 'I know. I stink. They probably wouldn't let me anywhere near a table and I'm not sure how well my taste buds work when all I can smell is camphor.'

'It's not as noticeable out in the fresh air,' Helene said.

The workshop had started well. Lou had been reasonably good at identifying natural extracts and categorising them as floral, woody or fougère, which she couldn't pronounce, but had recognised fairly well from the lingering memory of Phil's cologne. She'd also discovered she loved the pine-sweet freshness of the local juniper oil. Given the hint of gin in the scent, it wasn't surprising.

But she'd been distracted, thinking about the power of scent to bind memory and instead of extracting a small pipette of camphor oil as part of the middle note of her perfume, she'd managed to tip the bottle over. Any olfactory sensitivity she might have developed had not survived.

Had she truly expected to discover she had a gift for mixing fragrances? The chemical explanations of the different oils and how they react to the air had gone completely over her head. She'd simply enjoyed smelling the natural extracts and thinking of the flowers, fruit, leaves and wood that had produced the captivating scent – until her absent-mindedness had struck.

'Maybe we should have just spent the day exploring,' Lou grumbled as she gazed with longing at the panorama. They stood on the pebbly beach that snaked along the Sirmio Peninsula. Behind them rose the crenellated stone walls of the castle and, in front, the great expanse of the lake – green near the shore and within the battlements of the castle, but deep blue further out. The afternoon wind had picked up, sending the windsurfers surging on sudden gusts. The mountains near Malcesine and further north seemed a long way away from Sirmione, a cobbled town of narrow streets, the stone baking in the afternoon heat. 'Let's walk a little further.'

'We don't want to miss that ferry,' Helene reminded her.

'Don't worry. I don't want to repeat the bus trip from this morning.' In order to arrive in time for their workshop, they'd had to beg a lift from Greta into Malcesine and take the first bus.

'I wonder how the rehearsal went today,' Helene said for the hundredth time. 'Jason really enjoyed it yesterday, although it was only half a day of rehearsal, and he really can't wait until Maestro Eckert arrives.'

'Mr Romano is very good,' Lou defended Nick with more vehemence than was necessary. She cut herself off before she could say anything more that might clue Helene in to her inappropriate crush.

'Oh, yes. He's extremely talented – the only primary teacher in the country with high enough qualifications for this camp, I believe.' Lou thought of the Royal College of Music T-shirt. There was a lot about him she didn't know. 'Is Edie going to music school next year?'

Lou nodded. 'She's got a place at the Purcell School.'

'That's marvellous! I'm sure we'll see each other at orchestra performances for years to come! We were so relieved when Jason got into the Wells school. What second instrument does Edie play? Piano?'

Lou winced. 'Yes, but she hasn't done many exams.' She hesitated. 'My ex-husband thought it was too much for her.'

'Oh,' said Helene, but there was a wealth of horror in her tone. 'How many hours a day does she practise?'

'Two or three,' Lou answered vaguely.

'And what instrument do you play? All of this music makes me long to pick up my bow again, but I haven't played professionally since Jason was born. I played cello, but it's not a life that goes well with a family.'

'I don't play anything.'

'Sing?'

Lou shook her head. 'No ballet either – that's what my ex-husband's girlfriend does, so don't ask. I can't knit, I can't do complex sums in my head, I don't understand chemistry, I'm terrible at ball sports and I pull a muscle if I go running. That's me.'

'Oh,' said Helene again. 'What did you think of making perfume, then?'

'Your perfume was lovely – I think.' Lou gave her a lopsided grin and Helene took her arm and steered them back along the mediaeval lock to the other side of the peninsula, where the ferry collected its passengers. They strolled through the piazza, filled with relaxed tourists savouring enormous ice-cream sundaes.

'It was a wonderful diversion. I'm so glad I could come along. But if you want my perfume, you're welcome to it. I always wear "Aliage",' Helene said off-hand, as though Lou should have heard of the scent.

The funny-looking hydrofoil with its winged frame arrived, expelling its passengers, and Lou and Helene shuffled on. Lou pushed through the crowd of tourists and commuters to grab a seat near the front of the top deck. Life was too short for aisle seats when views were on offer.

As the hydrofoil picked up speed, she grinned out at the water, which felt far too large to be a lake. It was a huge body of fresh water with its own microclimate, surrounded by mountains that were the foothills of the Dolomites. The word 'lake' didn't cover it.

'This is a bit different from the boat we took yesterday!' Helene called out, holding the armrests in tight fists.

'I think the kids would have preferred the hydrofoil!' After the rehearsal in the morning, the whole group had taken a trip on a paddle boat up to the northern end of the lake. It had taken all afternoon to potter up and back and by the end, the kids had been looking more at their phones than at the scenery. But Lou had been delighted by everything they saw and disappointed she couldn't get out and explore every village.

Greta met them at Garda with her car – a snappy little Fiat, of course. 'What is that smell?' she exclaimed, but it didn't stop her from kissing both of Lou's cheeks.

'An... uh... incident at the perfume workshop,' Lou said. 'I'm going to stink out your car, sorry.'

Greta waved them in with a polite denial, but they had to make the trip with the windows open. When they pulled into the little car park at the convent, Nick and Edie were standing by the door to the quadrangle.

Lou went immediately to Edie. 'Is everything okay?'

She nodded brightly. 'I just wanted to see how it— Something smells terrible!' Lou winced.

'Is that an indication of the success of your trip?' Nick asked. She glanced at him, identifying the expected dry smile, but his eyes were kind. She also noticed he was dressed for cycling – a high-tech shirt and tight shorts. Lou mumbled a response to his question. 'Not your talent, then?' he asked.

'It required more fine motor skills and patience than I have – and too much chemistry. It was fun, though.'

'I didn't think... chemistry... was something you lacked,' Nick muttered.

Her mouth went dry. What was he implying? He was so hard to read and his expression so mild that she couldn't be sure her interpretation of his comment wasn't way off base.

'Care to explain that comment?' she asked, glancing meaningfully to his mother.

He coughed – probably to cover a splutter. 'I meant you're very good with people. Perhaps that's what makes you a good newsreader. The viewers feel like you're talking directly to them.'

Her skin prickled and, despite the urge to scoff, she couldn't think of a thing to say. Had he watched her then? She read the lunchtime news on weekdays, during school term. Had he looked her up on YouTube? She loved the possibility that he had – so much, that she forgave the chemistry comment.

She turned brightly to Edie. 'How was rehearsal?'

'Hard, but good,' she replied. 'I'm in the second violins.'

Lou studied her expression closely. Edie was used to being the best player in her school and this was her first experience of a lower rung of the pecking order. She certainly looked tired, but Edie had made an art form out of acting positive and Lou couldn't tell how discouraged she truly was.

She glanced at Nick to find him watching her just as closely. She straightened her shoulders. 'Are you expecting me to fly off the rails because she's not in the firsts?'

'Obviously I shouldn't have been.'

'I didn't realise Federico brought you his bike so you could lean it against the wall and chat, Nico,' Greta said as she approached with her car keys. 'Go for your bike ride, so you can get back in time for dinner – and let Lou wash off that smell!'

He clipped a helmet under his chin and grasped the handlebars of the bike. It looked old, but was built for speed, with those wonky handlebars and a lightweight frame.

'You really are a keen cyclist,' Lou commented, to give herself an excuse to linger until he set off.

He smiled faintly. 'I really am. You could learn, you know. It's a more useful skill than making perfume or candles or leather bags.'

She shuddered and waved him off. 'Each to his own. I'm going to have enough trouble with the paddleboarding on Tuesday.'

8

Nick's cousin Federico was firmly in Lou's bad books on Tuesday afternoon. She'd never met the man, but she couldn't forgive him for the indignity he had inflicted by suggesting to Nick that this activity was all the rage. The trendy instructors had insisted it was dead easy, but they'd failed to take into account that Louise Saunders was not made for stand-up paddleboarding.

Truly, she was wondering if her centre of gravity was somewhere different from a normal person's. No matter where she stood on the board, she wobbled. And once the wobbling reached critical momentum, that was it; it was only a question of whether she landed butt first or face first.

She tried to keep her feet planted on the board, but every time she glanced at them, one had shifted forward. And as soon as she looked down, the board seemed to grow a mind of its own, determined to throw her off.

Even Harry the skinny double-bass player – whose centre of gravity was definitely higher than a normal person's – had managed to stay up. Edie was making a decent effort – at both staying up and not laughing at Lou.

Helene had copped out and sat on the beach with five non-swimmers who had been too afraid to try, even with a life vest. The other thirty kids had seized paddles and headed out on the water – leaving Lou to helplessly pray to the gods of travel insurance. Tanya was fairly sturdy and paddled out a little further with the kids who caught on quickly. Miss Hwang – who had yet to let on what her first name was – glided comfortably in the middle, looking delicate and pretty in a swimsuit, and Lou stayed firmly in the shallows.

Nick was the last one to claim his rented board after completing the transaction with the SUP school. He assessed the situation with a wrinkle in his brow that reminded Lou of when she'd told him she'd broken her nose on a modelling camp. She was starting to realise what he was going through.

When his gaze reached her, she smiled sympathetically, only to feel a sudden wobble, sending her on to the front of the board with a splat. She grappled for the edges of the board, but slipped sideways, bringing the whole thing over on top of her.

She broke the surface of the water with a word that was not suitable for teenage ears. Clapping a hand over her mouth, she waited for the great maw of embarrassment to open beneath her, but instead the elastic of Nick's board shorts came into focus before her, along with a quick flash of skin that she shouldn't have so eagerly gawked at before his T-shirt billowed back into place.

'Do you need a hand?'

Her gaze jerked back up to his face. He'd taken off his glasses. Although she kind of missed the nerdy frames, he looked like a Gucci commercial. She blinked, trying to remember what he'd asked. Ah, did she need help? Probably, but not the sort of help he meant.

She shook her head and wobbled to her feet on the slippery stones. She flipped the board over and managed to capsize it on top of her once more before she succeeded in clambering up on to her knees.

'Actually, can you pass me the paddle?' She straightened her shoulders and swiped a strand of sodden hair off her face, although it set off another wobble and she had to throw her hands out for balance. Her T-shirt clung to her in soaked wrinkles.

'Any tips?' he asked and she looked up in surprise.

'You're asking me?'

He smiled – full dimple. Was that mix of amusement and kindness a teacher thing? Because she loved it. 'You look like your experience would be a helpful cautionary tale.'

'Good point.' She laughed. 'Let me just say it's not as easy as Miss Hwang makes it look!' She regretted mentioning the other teacher, when Nick turned to look at her in all her swimsuited, slim elegance. But his gaze didn't linger. 'And don't forget the leash.' Lou pointed to the Velcro tether on her ankle that ensured the board wouldn't drift away when she fell off.

'Right.' He fumbled for his own tether and hopped on one foot while he settled it in place. Then he squared his shoulders and took a deep breath. He glanced at her. 'This would be better without an audience.'

'Hey, Mr Romano! Look, I can do it!' called Harry.

'That's great!' he called back.

'This is music camp. The audience is unavoidable,' Lou pointed out. He winced. 'Just get on the board, Nick.'

With a grim laugh, he settled the paddle gingerly on the board and swung his knee up. He got up on all fours, but the back of the board sank into the water and he shuffled frantically forward, dropping the paddle. The board tipped sideways and he grabbed for the edges, floating slowly away.

He swore, clamping his mouth shut as though he could swallow the word.

'Let's throttle your cousin,' Lou said.

He laughed. 'Or pool our money for a hit man?' He looked at her urgently. 'What do I do now?'

Lou leaned gingerly forward and nudged his paddle with hers, sending it floating back towards him. 'Try to stand up!'

He settled the paddle on the board again and leaned on it with a grimace. The board shook as he jerked a knee up and settled one foot in the middle. The lake was oddly silent. Each and every student was watching him.

He got the other foot up and slowly rose to a standing position, the paddle waving madly in his hand. He swore again and the students nearby tittered. His gaze jerked up and he clenched his teeth.

'I can barely see a thing without my glasses.'

'That might be for the best right now.'

He managed one push with the paddle, then another. Harry cheered and the other students followed suit. Lou sat on her haunches to clap, but slipped backwards and plopped straight into the water. As she went down, she saw Nick wobble and then slide off. His head broke the water next to her and he swiped his hair out of his eyes.

Lou grinned and called out to the students: 'Was that a good stack? About an 8.7, I think.'

'9.1!'

'Only 7.9 for me!'

'I'd give you both a 9.5 for synchronised diving!'

'Why, thank you!' she replied, standing in the water to bow.

'Come on!' She grabbed Nick's arm and pulled him up next to her, pointedly ignoring the way his shirt stuck to his chest. She was blushing enough already.

His bow was much more graceful and, when he came up again, he was smiling. The students cheered and whistled. It was kind of fun, failing at this together. But she still wanted to kill Federico.

* * *

Nick prowled into the kitchen in search of a snack after the kids had been sent to their rooms for the night. Rummaging in the fridge for some olives or cheese, he jumped when the door of the cellar opened suddenly. But he wasn't surprised to see Lou step through with a bottle of wine in her hand. She raised an arm in greeting, but winced in pain and lowered it again. He knew how she felt.

'Did Mum give you the key to the wine cellar?'

'Yes, but don't look at me like I'm a boozy gin-mummy. Although a few more days like today and I might start to see the appeal.' She set the bottle down and locked the door behind her. 'Besides, it's creepy down there. One bottle is going to have to be enough – between three, if you're joining us.'

'Even between three it'll probably be enough to make these muscles feel worse tomorrow.'

She smiled and he grinned back helplessly. 'I hope mine can't possibly feel worse. Does that mean you don't want any?'

'I'd better take some for the team.'

Hyewon Hwang shuffled into the kitchen in a robe and fluffy slippers and made her way to the kettle. Lou stepped out of her path like a one-woman crowd parting. She watched Hyewon put the kettle on and fetch a mug. He wondered what Lou found interesting.

'We're going to sit and have a wine on the terrace, if you'd like to join us, Hyewon,' he said, wondering if that was what Lou had been angling for. His colleague was a brilliant cellist, but very reserved. Helene would probably like to break the ice, as well.

She turned, clutching her mug of tea. 'Thank you. I'll join you with my tea. I'll just go change into something warmer.' Only at that comment did Nick notice her legs were bare. She would not only feel the cool mountain air, but she'd also discover the range of biting insects that lived around the lake in summer.

When she left, he looked back to find Lou scowling. 'You were prepared to share our wine?'

He smiled, but there was an edge to her voice. 'Come on.' He grabbed three glasses and headed out to the terrace. He lit the citronella candle and shoved it under the coffee table before leaning back in the wicker chair and resting his head.

Lou and Helene chatted beside him. The convent was quiet, except for the soothing hum of cicadas. The air rising from the lake was damp and mild, tussling with the wild chill coming off the mountain above.

The camp was running smoothly. As long as they stayed by the lake, he'd be okay. It was stupid. He'd be fine in Milan as well, even if it didn't feel that way. After making a fool of himself on the lake but somehow turning the activity into a success, he could almost believe everything would go well. 'Somehow' was the wrong word, though. He knew exactly how it had turned into a success – or 'who' had turned it into one.

He glanced at Lou, her knees up under her chin as she sipped her wine. She was plastered to the back of the chair as though she'd never be able to move again, but she was still talking to Helene with that good-humoured chatter.

Hyewon arrived and he smiled at her when she hesitated to take the extra seat. He could imagine she was terribly shy. No one could play music with as much skill as she did without picking up some complexes along the way – and didn't he know it?

'It's so lovely out here, isn't it? Take a seat and drink your tea. What sort is it? Please call me Lou, by the way. I'm not really Mrs Saunders any more anyway.' Lou wrinkled her nose in a sorrowful sort of smile.

Hyewon sat with precision on the edge of the wicker chair. Nick cocked his head to look at her. What kind of crappy childhood had she had? A good step worse than his, he'd bet.

'You should call me Hyewon, then,' she said and took a sip of her tea, as though for strength. 'This is dandelion tea.'

'Sounds much more sensible than our grape tea. Cheers.' Lou raised her glass and took another sip before unfolding her legs with a sigh. 'And you did much better on the board than I did. You're probably not even suffering.'

'You don't use an English name?' Helene asked.

'I-I used to perform with my real name. It seemed unnecessary when I came to study in the UK.' She glanced at Nick and he mustered a sympathetic smile. Yep. A much more miserable childhood than his.

Helene launched happily into a discussion of vibrato technique and Hyewon seemed more comfortable talking shop, so Nick closed his eyes for a moment, enjoying the sweet, mild red wine on his tongue. He stretched his legs out, but bumped into Lou's feet. She retracted hers immediately and didn't look at him.

Hyewon didn't stay long and, when she stood to leave, Helene followed suit. 'I just want to go and talk to Jason before he falls asleep,' she said.

'You mean share the golden words from his teacher's lips,' Lou teased.

Helene gave a dismissive wave. 'I'll leave you to enjoy the golden words from your teacher's lips anyway.'

Nick snorted wine through his nose. It burned and set off a choking cough. He fumbled to set his glass on the coffee table. Lou thumped him on the back.

'Ow!' she said and pulled her hand back, waving it gently.

'That hurt *you*?'

'We need to make plans to kill your cousin,' she said, cradling her hand. 'I think I injured a tendon clutching that paddle for dear life.' She didn't say anything more, just tucked her feet back up underneath her. She sipped her wine and gazed across at the sky, just turning the royal blue of a summer night. She looked at ease, although his restlessness jumped a notch at being left alone with her. 'Did you know Miss Hwang before?' she asked, too casually.

'No. I met her once in London before we left because she was a bit nervous about her first camp, but that's all. Why?'

She ignored his question, causing a little tingle to run up the back of his neck. 'Is this your first camp?'

He shook his head. 'I went last time, too, although I wasn't organising. They usually struggle to find staff. Most teachers don't want to spend their holidays teaching – even if they're somewhere beautiful in Europe.'

'Why do *you* want to spend your holidays teaching?'

'I don't have other commitments,' he said dismissively.

'You used to have a girlfriend though, right?'

The tingle on the back of his neck turned hot. 'Yes,' was all he said in reply.

'What did she think of you leaving for several weeks on music camp with a whole lot of Miss Hwangs?'

'These camps aren't exactly conducive to illicit romance.'

Her laugh was bubbly and infectious. 'I suppose not.' She glanced at him and he felt the look much lower than he should have. This terrace had a strange effect on him – or she did. It was better to assume it was the quiet terrace. 'But when else are you going to see your colleagues in a swimsuit?'

He pressed his lips together to get his amusement under control. Hyewon might have been wearing a pretty swimsuit, but he couldn't have said what colour it was. All he could remember was the way Lou's shirt had stuck to her torso. The heat was back on his neck, thinking about how he'd tried to stop himself appreciating her long legs as she wobbled and flailed on the board.

'Are you jealous of Hyewon?' he asked tentatively.

Her blustery denial made him smile. 'Oh, psh, no, uh, of course not.' She grabbed a strand of her hair and ran it through her fingers. 'I mean, she's so pretty and capable and talented... Why would I be jealous?' Her voice trailed off. 'I can't even stay up on a frigging paddleboard,' she grumbled.

'We knew we weren't going to be world champions,' he said. 'And I think I owe you some thanks.'

She let go of the lock of hair and leaned forward with a smile. He was the jealous one. He was jealous of how easily she smiled, how she could shake everything off without recrimination or apology. 'I could take some gratitude. But what for?'

Her voice was low and, when she said gratitude, he couldn't be sure she hadn't meant it as a euphemism. He had to take a moment to stop thinking about kissing her.

'If you'd been a natural on the board, I would have looked like more of a loser.'

She chuckled. 'Happy to be of assistance. Perhaps that's my talent: looking like a loser.'

'Lou,' he said, more sharply than he'd intended. He grabbed

her hand before he could rein himself in. He held on tight, his grip forcing her eyes questioningly to his.

'Thank you,' he repeated, 'for showing me I don't have to take everything so seriously. I needed that today.' It was so still he could hear the gentle inhale and exhale through her lips. 'I'm g-glad...' He took another breath. He was staring at her. He should stop. 'I'm glad you came on the camp,' he finished, worried by the breathy sound of his voice.

Her hand came up and he froze. Her fingers slipped lightly into his hair and his eyes nearly lost focus at how good it felt. Strange that he could be so starved of affection when his mother insisted on so many hugs and kisses.

He leaned closer to her, slowly, but intentionally. Her sudden breath started up his tingles again. She leaned in, too, her face tipped up. *Crossing the line, crossing the line.* Somewhere in the back of his head, the alarm was sounding, but his pulse drowned it out.

'Mum!'

Lou crashed back into her chair so hard the wicker groaned. 'Shit,' she said under her breath, her hands smoothing her hair. Nick moved more slowly away, trying to keep the embarrassment and confusion at bay for as long as possible. The camp was the worst possible setting for an 'illicit romance', as he'd pointed out. But, for the first time, he was wondering if it would be fun. A bad idea, sure, but everything he did with Lou was fun.

By the time Edie appeared at the end of the cloister, Lou had fixed a mild, inquisitive expression to her face that he wasn't sure would convince her perceptive daughter. Luckily, Edie was preoccupied. She had a tissue partly obscuring her face.

'Sweetie?' Lou rushed over. 'Is it a nosebleed?' Edie nodded; her forehead creased with distress. 'Sit down.' She crouched in front of Edie, now settled in a wicker chair. 'I'll find you some more tissues. It'll stop in a minute. You know it always stops.'

Lou shuddered slightly and made to rise, but Nick finally spurred himself to action and stilled her with a hand on her shoulder. 'I'll get the tissues. You stay with her.' The look she gave him was an odd mix of gratitude and discomfort.

He returned with the tissues and a bin and noticed Lou's hands shaking as she opened the package and helped Edie swap her soiled tissue for a fresh one.

'Pop quiz, Edie,' he said, making both of them look up in surprise. 'What interval is this?' He hummed two notes.

'That's too easy,' she responded immediately. 'A third.'

'Okay, how about this?' He hummed two more notes from the same scale.

'A sixth,' she said.

He smiled. 'Good. Now change key.' He picked out two more notes.

'A fifth,' she said.

'Good. Can you tell me what time signature this is?' He hummed a snippet from the first movement of *Ein deutsches Requiem* by Brahms.

She considered for a moment. 'Four-four, surely. Why do you keep giving me easy questions?'

'All right. Listen carefully to this one.' He hummed the first line of Samuel Barber's *Adagio for Strings*, which was impossible to do without the crescendo and diminuendo, especially as the composer's own instructions were to play it expressively in a singing style.

Edie laughed and he grinned back. 'You're trying to trick me with that one, I think.'

'I didn't succeed?'

'Only because I've seen the sheet music on YouTube. What is it? Four-two?'

He nodded. 'With a five-two bar in the middle. I used to love that piece when I was your age, too.'

'You don't any more?'

He shrugged. 'I think you need to have stars in your eyes to pull off the Adagio. I can't handle the pathos any more.' Edie watched him in confusion and he smiled apologetically and glanced at Lou.

'Aren't you two the cutest little music nerds?' she said. He suspected she was simply filling the awkward silence, but he couldn't help feeling the prick of her words. Lou was fearless and fabulous and beautiful – too much for a repressed music nerd.

When she disappeared around the corridor to tuck Edie in, he lingered in uncertainty. After a few restless minutes, he gave up, took their glasses to the kitchen and shuffled back along the cold tiles in the direction of his room.

'Psst, Nick,' he heard as he passed her door. He turned, fighting the urge to smile. She had that effect on him, whether he liked it or not. She squeezed through a crack in the door and closed it behind her.

'Are you okay?' he asked.

She looked up in surprise. 'Yes.'

'You don't like blood?' he guessed.

She winced and nodded. 'Especially hers. Oh my God.' She shuddered and he watched her with interest as she tried to shake it off, but there was a shadow in her expression that he couldn't decipher. 'Thanks for helping.'

'No problem.'

She grabbed a strand of hair and hesitated. 'I'm sorry about before.'

'Before?'

She frowned and her disgruntled expression was so cute he had even more trouble keeping the smile off his face. He leaned against the doorframe and imagined telling her she looked cute. She would scoff that thirty-seven-year-old women weren't cute. And she probably wouldn't believe him when he insisted. And then he'd want to kiss her until she understood that she was attractive and funny and worth so much more than a guy who told her she was talentless.

'Nick, don't make me say it. I'm aware I can talk myself into dark corners. Throw me a bone, hey?'

That time he did smile. 'Sorry,' he said softly. He took a deep breath. 'Are you apologising for the fact that I almost kissed you? I think that was probably my line. I'm sorry I put you in that position.'

She ran out of words. It was rather satisfying. 'You...'

'Almost kissed you, yes. I didn't think I'd have to remind you.'

'You don't,' she squeaked.

She kept looking at him until his pulse was notching up again. Why was it so hard to leave? 'Are you sure?' Had he really just asked her that?

A long, laboured sigh escaped her lips and she sagged a little. 'Yes, I'm sure,' she said, her voice flat. '"The mum" is not supposed to be the heroine of the illicit romance on music camp, it would seem. Too many complications.'

He nodded, relieved and disappointed she'd given him the nudge he needed to draw away. 'Complications,' he repeated, 'yes.' He hesitated. 'But you know you're not just a two-dimensional character known as "the mum".'

A faint smile touched her lips and he felt closer to being able to leave her like that. 'Who am I, then, if not the uncoordinated, comic-relief mum?'

His answer spilled out before he could decide if it was a good idea or not. 'The hot mum.'

She snorted and slapped him on the arm. 'Get out of here, before your mother catches you flirting with the hot mum!'

He winced and scooted away backwards, smiling at her. 'Goodnight, Lou.'

'Goodnight, Nick.'

9

Lou felt like a hot mum as she strolled along the lakefront promenade at Bardolino on Thursday morning in her large sunglasses, a maxi dress and sandals. The lake was shallow and almost aqua as it lapped at the little port. Warm pink and orange houses with dark shutters and window boxes bursting with geraniums clustered on narrow streets. The landscape was surprisingly flat and Lou could believe she was by the sea, except for the wooded hill that rose to the north, hiding Malcesine from view, and the distant rock faces across the lake, hazy in the morning mist. The day was promising to be borderline uncomfortably hot and the water looked inviting.

Not as inviting as Nick's eyes in the moonlight, but that was a high bar.

After ducking down a slender side street for a cheaper breakfast cappuccino, Lou was wandering a few paces behind the purposeful Helene through the weekly market. She was off in her own world, recalling Nick saying he'd almost kissed her – or reliving the moment on the terrace where soft words and moonlight over the lake had conspired to make her think she could kiss him back.

She could still picture the way the light had glinted off his cheekbones. She couldn't believe she now knew how his springy curls felt between her fingers. She could still feel the way her heart had pounded as he'd approached – purposeful, certain.

But her character definitely wasn't the 'hot mum' and, whoever she was cast as for this part of her life, she didn't belong with the 'hot teacher', who could pick notes out of the air and sing them with the subtle power of an opera singer. He was clearly some kind of musical genius. She was dying to see him in action – more than just his restrained conducting.

'I have to get my husband a satchel.'

It took Lou a moment or two to tune back into the present. 'Your husband asked for a satchel?'

'Italy is the best place to buy nice leather satchels, you know.'

Lou supposed she had known, if she'd ever thought about it. 'What does he have to carry in a satchel?' She had gathered Helene's husband was some kind of engineering genius.

Helene looked at her without comprehension. 'He doesn't have to carry something. I mean, he can carry anything in a satchel. It's a convenient, fashionable staple item.'

'A satchel is a staple item?' She wondered if Phil had a satchel. She felt Nick would definitely have a satchel. She winced, realising she was thinking about two very different men, neither of whom should have been so much on her mind.

'A good one, yes. It has to be very expensive.' Helene patted her bag, which was draped securely across her body.

'I can't afford one, then,' Lou said.

Helene patted her on the arm. 'Maybe next time. You could get a bowl like this instead.' She drew Lou to a ceramics stall, stacked with chunky, hand-painted bowls and plates with alpine flower motifs, and salt-and-pepper shakers shaped like mushrooms.

'I might give it a miss.' She frowned, wondering how she'd get it home in one piece. 'Although I like the cheese bell.' It was shaped like a wheel of cheese. 'I like cheese.'

Helene smiled indulgently. 'So you've told me. Perhaps you'll be especially good at making it.'

'That's the idea,' Lou said, tossing her head and admiring a floral scarf.

Lou bought the scarf on a whim, but Helene's quest for a satchel went unfulfilled as they had to hurry to the meeting point for their cheesemaking workshop at a dairy in the hills behind Bardolino. So far so good. It was ten in the morning and she'd managed to keep her mind off Nick for a whole half-hour – in aggregate.

They joined their group and took a minibus into the country-side, arriving at the sprawling dairy which was covered in vines and looked out over vineyards and idyllic fields of grey cattle. Lou eagerly completed her outfit with an apron, gloves and a plastic bandanna over her hair and followed the trainer into the dairy kitchens. She would sacrifice a lot for cheese.

The cheesemaker explained everything simply until words like 'cultures' and 'casein' actually made sense. It all felt straight-forward and Lou hummed as she stirred her huge pot of milk sludge that would, through the magic of chemistry, biology, and time, become the crumbly hard cheese she loved.

But her mind predictably drifted as the minutes ticked by. What was she doing, flirting with someone – anyone – at this stage of her life? She'd thrown everything she had at Phil and their marriage. Perhaps she was too available? The only person she should be available to was Edie. Sure, her daughter had taken the changes in her stride – and seemed to be enjoying the camp despite Lou's romantic misadventures – but no kid was truly as well adjusted as Edie seemed. And if she'd seen her and Nick last night?

Lou shivered. What would Edie make of it? A little childish part of her wanted Edie to jump up and down in excitement at the prospect of her mum and her teacher getting it on. But that was terribly unrealistic and even Lou could see that.

'Signora Saunders? Signora? Louise?'

A nudge and an urgent hiss from Helene startled Lou out of her daydream. 'Lou!'

'Hmm?'

'Your thermometer!'

'Oh!' Lou took a startled look at her bubbling tub of curds and whey. Bubbling. Oh, dear. Not good. She swore. 'I'm so sorry.' She looked helplessly at the cheesemaker taking the workshop.

'Pull it off the heat,' the teacher said with a sigh.

Lou followed her instruction and peered into the sludge with a grimace. One less batch of Grana Padano to age in the cellar. She'd known herself well enough to steer clear of most cooking courses, but she'd thought cheesemaking would be a reasonable exception, as it wasn't really cooking. Except apparently you did cook the milk and starter cultures. And apparently, she still sucked at that.

She had more luck with the ricotta and mascarpone, which could not only be heated to a higher temperature, but also didn't require lengthy ripening, so she'd be able to take them back to the convent to revel in her success – lumpy and runny as they were. Toasting the end of the workshop with some punchy dry Amarone della Valpolicella and alpine cheese, under a trellis of vines overlooking a herd of peaceful cattle, Lou felt the day had been a success, even if artisan cheesemaking was not her talent.

'You know, in Japan, some people think European cheese is

the most disgusting thing in the world,' Helene said as she nabbed another morsel of the divine, crumbly Tombea.

'I didn't think you were from Japan,' said Lou.

'I'm not.' Lou felt stupid, but Helene sipped her wine and, in her typically unflappable manner, said no more about it. 'I was born in Hong Kong. My husband is Japanese.'

'Does he like cheese?'

'Only Cheddar. But he loves fish. I'm not allowed to come back until I've tried trout fresh from the lake.'

Lou tried not to grimace. 'I'm not big on fish.'

'Probably because you've only tried rubbery cod that's spent too long in the freezer.'

'Possibly,' she admitted, picking up a tiny square of toast elegantly topped with a whirl of bright yellow mousse. 'This is really good,' she said through her mouthful. 'Any idea what it is?'

Their workshop leader leaned over. 'Fish,' she said with a smile.

'What?'

'It's smoked trout and apple mousse.'

'Smoked what and what?'

'Trout and apple. With our local olive oil on the bread.'

'Oh, is the olive oil from the northern part of the lake?' Lou asked.

'No, our suppliers are around here.'

'Why are you asking about oil from the northern part of the lake?' asked Helene. 'Or did you mean the area around Malcesine?'

'Nick said his family own a mill in the north.'

'Ah,' Helene replied. What did she mean 'ah'? Was the ambiguity some kind of trap?

But Helene didn't take the topic any further and refrained

from winking or eyebrow waggling, so Lou assumed she hadn't noticed anything between her and Nick. *Huh*.

She realised Helene had asked her something and had to respond with a, 'Hmmm?' and hope she wasn't blushing.

'I know,' Helene said sympathetically. 'I'm wondering how the rehearsal went today, too. I'm not sure they're ready for the performance on Saturday.'

That didn't help to banish Lou's blush. She should be thinking about how Edie was doing today. She'd encouraged her to pursue music. Would Edie benefit from as much support as Helene gave her son? She wanted to ask Nick, but then realised her thoughts had returned right back to the place she should probably be avoiding.

'Jason told me they're struggling with the Jenkins. The second movement is so difficult to keep together.'

'They'll get there,' Lou said with a smile, remembering the Easter concert in London.

'But Maestro Eckert arrives in ten days!' It wasn't like Helene not to be exact. The maestro was arriving in eleven days, and Lou only knew that with such certainty because she'd pored over the dates with Nick.

'Why is everyone so scared of this maestro?'

Helene waved her hand dismissively. 'He's brilliant. That's all that matters.'

Lou swilled the last of her wine in the glass, staring at it. Helene was probably right. If you were brilliant, nothing else mattered. And if you weren't brilliant, well, you ended up blankly reading the lunchtime news and getting passed over for a brilliant dancer.

* * *

Rain battered the little convent and its indomitable cliff face the following morning as the kids ate their breakfast with sullen grimaces.

'Are we seriously going up a mountain today?' Edie leaned close to ask.

Lou took a sip of the cappuccino Nick had set in front of her five minutes before. She could get used to the authentic Italian breakfast. 'It's booked,' she said flatly.

'The weather is supposed to improve this afternoon,' Nick said weakly from a few seats along.

'This is nothing. It will be gone again in an hour,' Greta said with a smile, replenishing the basket of rolls on the table.

'I don't have a raincoat,' Edie's roommate, Meg, piped up.

'You can borrow mine,' Lou said. 'Did you leave it at home?'

She shook her head slowly. 'I don't have one.'

'Oh, sweetie. Sorry I asked.'

'It's okay. I mean, I don't usually need one. My driver takes me exactly where I need to go,' she said kindly.

Lou blinked. She caught a smile on Nick's face, but reached wordlessly for another roll. 'Wait!' She jerked her hand back at the sound of Greta's voice from behind her. She turned to see her approaching with a pretty glass bowl full of fresh summer berries and – yes! – Lou's own mascarpone.

'Now it's chilled overnight, you can taste it!' Greta set it before her with a flourish.

Edie and Meg leaned closer with interest. 'We might need a few spoons.' Lou grinned. 'But I'd better taste it first in case I spilled some of the vinegar from the ricotta into this mixture.' That gave her a bit more space. She dipped the spoon into creamy cheese, careful to avoid the plump blueberries and rasp-berries that would probably save the dish even if the mascarpone was rubbish. Perhaps that was why Greta had served it this way? There was only one way to find out.

Edie was looking at her with wide-eyed urgency, as though the success of Lou's mascarpone was as important as staying in time during the second movement of the Jenkins piece. It both touched Lou and pricked her conscience. Just how sad did her daughter think she was?

She glanced at Nick, to find his expression almost identical to Edie's, which touched her in a different way. 'Kids,' she groaned. 'It's cheese, not a live-action Disney adaptation.' She shoved the spoon in her mouth. It was creamy and rich. Not too sweet. It was mascarpone. 'It's pretty good,' she said with a shrug.

Greta handed out extra spoons and the girls dug in with a chorus of 'Mmmmm'. 'Can you make this when we get home, Mum?'

'Why not?'

'Can I try?' Nick asked with a smile.

'Sure.' She pushed the bowl in his direction and he took a spoonful. Lou caught herself staring at his lips and shook herself out of it, only to find her gaze on his hands. It was even dangerous to look at his hair, which was curling a lot in the humidity.

'Tastes like real mascarpone,' he said. 'Congratulations. You've found your talent.'

She sat back with a huff. 'This is not my talent.'

He sighed, as though her answer wasn't unexpected. 'Why not? It tastes good. You can make it at home.'

'It tastes good because the bowl is full of the freshest summer berries from the hillsides of Lombardy and Veneto.'

'And Lou's mascarpone,' he insisted.

'I burned the Grana Padano,' she said, lifting her chin.

His lips twitched and he crossed his arms over his chest. 'I bet they'll discover it's a wonderful new cheese variety.'

'I'm pretty sure I killed the cultures and they poured it down the drain.'

'Who's killing culture? You're not still talking about that terrible cinematic setting of the Vaughan Williams *Sea Symphonies*?' Helene said as she walked past on her way to sit with her son.

'I saw that,' Meg spoke up. 'My father cussed like a sailor and demanded his donation back.'

Lou pressed her lips together so she wouldn't laugh. 'We're just talking about the cheese controversy,' Lou explained. 'But the mascarpone is all right. It's probably yours.'

'No, no, no,' Greta said from behind the serving window. 'I took note. It's definitely yours.'

After breakfast, Lou took the opportunity of a rainy morning to read on the terrace and wander the cloisters. The heavy clouds streaking across the lake and the occasional burst of sunlight added drama to the already powerful landscape. The rain released the lavender and pine scents and the little quadrangle by the chapel was full of a sweet floral note she assumed was the oleander. It was better than any perfume she could have made.

The chapel was insulated for sound, so the hum of strings was muted in the cloister. Only the frequent pauses hinted at the trouble the orchestra was still having with the Jenkins. The door of the chapel opened as Lou was leaning over to sniff the oleander during a pause in the rain. Helene slipped out on tiptoe.

'What are you doing?' Lou hissed. 'Eavesdropping on rehearsal?'

'Just for a minute,' she admitted.

But Lou craned her neck to peer through the crack in the door, which Helene had left ajar. Edie was sitting, back straight, face eager, among the second violins. Nick was leaning heavily on his music stand and settling a solemn look on each section of the orchestra in turn. With his wild curls and the baton clutched in his hand, he looked the part of the mad conductor.

'I want to issue you all with a challenge,' he said quietly. He put down the baton and rubbed his forehead with the back of his hand. 'Close your folders.' Lou could have heard a penny drop in the little chapel. Although what she did hear was the startled plink of a string from a restless viola player. 'I don't expect you to know this piece by heart. But I want you to see that this movement is about more than what's on that sheet music. I don't care if you make mistakes – this time. Watch me and listen to your colleagues.' He raised his hands and the orchestra scrambled to take up their instruments.

He held his hands still for a long moment and Lou found her breath had stalled. Into the silence of the little chapel, while the pipes dripped with fresh rainwater and summer heat was starting to rise, he sang the first, pulsing bars of each of the lower string parts in a haunting tenor voice. Even the simple, repeated notes in tight rhythm sounded magical when he sang them, conducting himself with small hand movements and looking at each part as he sang their line.

The kids sat holding their instruments, staring. And then he sang the soaring, melancholy line of the violin solo – in the correct key, in falsetto. The orchestra gasped and Lou shivered. She'd never heard anything like it. There was something forbidden about hearing a man singing in the upper register, but it was so beautiful, she wouldn't accept the social norm that claimed his singing wasn't masculine.

All of a sudden, he straightened and raised his arms, counting the instruments in with a tight, 'Two, three, four!'

'He *is* some kind of musical genius,' Lou murmured as the orchestra came to life.

'I didn't realise he'd trained in voice. I wonder if that was his second study at music school,' Helene said in a loud whisper. 'I'd only heard of him as a violinist.'

'You'd heard of him?' Lou peered back through the door as the interplay of minor chords and dissonance made the air vibrate with... pathos, not that she'd ever reached for that word before. She peered intently at him, remembering what he'd said. Sweeping the orchestra through the dramatic harmonies, he didn't look like a stranger to emotion.

'Oh, I didn't remember the name at first, but I looked him up and remembered he gave a critically acclaimed performance of Bruch's No.1 when he was only fourteen – in Milan. But he never became a professional.'

Lou pressed her lips together as she watched. This was the man who tried to tell her that her talent could be making mascarpone, when he'd been a virtuoso violinist at fourteen. Gosh, no wonder Edie was so good. Why hadn't Lou thought to do a Google search on him? Hmm, possibly because looking up the primary school teacher on the Internet was an invasion of privacy.

But, goodness, if she'd thought Phil was bad for her self-confidence, anything... romance-y... with Nick would be disastrous. She could see it now: the child prodigy and the master of mascarpone. Not to mention he was five years younger!

He turned towards the violins and Lou shrank back from the crack in the door self-consciously. She grabbed Helene's arm and steered them back along the cloister, too quickly to appreciate the oleander that time. 'We should leave them to it. If we have to get these kids up a mountain this afternoon, I want a bit more rest first!' Helene looked longingly over her shoulder as Lou shepherded her away from the rehearsal.

* * *

The weather burned off so they were sweating in their rain jackets by the time they'd passed through the turnstiles at the valley station of the Funivia, which Lou immediately translated as 'fun street'.

It wasn't a bad description. The jaunty cable car whipped them up the steep slope so fast that her ears popped and she had the handrail in a death grip – and Edie's hand in another. At the midstation, they got out to photograph the panorama, the craggy castle at Malcesine looking puny in comparison to the grand mountains and turquoise expanse of lake.

And she couldn't believe that the view just kept getting better as they rode the larger, rotating cable car to the top. Every few metres of altitude revealed more mountain peaks in the distance. The journey was silent as the kids pressed their noses to the glass or held up their mobiles to capture the moment. A muted jangle reached Lou's ears occasionally – a rustic sort of sound like a wind chime, but more down-to-earth.

She leaned back and tugged on Nick's sleeve. 'What's the noise?' He looked questioningly at her and cocked his head to listen. 'That,' she said when it sounded again.

He grinned. 'Keep listening for the other clue.'

A few seconds later, she heard it again, followed by an unmistakable lowing. She gasped with delight. 'Cow bells! Oh, it's gorgeous. Sweetie, alpine cow bells! Like in *The Sound of Music*.'

'That was in Austria, Mum.' Edie laughed.

At the top of the cable car, the wind whipped Lou's hair into her face, but the sun was hot and sharp on the rocky meadows. The silence and the crystalline fresh air were pure summer – but summer as Lou had never experienced it before. There was no cloying, moist heat up here, just crisp, baking sunshine.

To one side, crazy paragliders threw themselves down the slope and off over the edge; to the other side, the terrain was dominated by a rocky outcrop and a small herd of goats, blending in with the stone. A caramel-coloured cow sauntered on the hill below, her bell clanging gently as she walked.

Nick waved them in the direction of the rocky outcrop and they trekked up to it.

'I feel like a real adventurer,' Lou whispered to Edie.

She chuckled. 'Mum, I'm eleven. You don't need to say that stuff to motivate me to walk any more.'

'Don't you find it exciting?'

She shrugged. 'I suppose.'

But Lou was not enough of an adventurer to look on with cheerful ambivalence as Nick scrambled up the rocks to the top of the outcrop. 'What are you doing?' she cried.

'No one else coming up?' He looked at the kids. Most looked back at him with the same horror Lou felt, but one or two followed his lead, squealing when they joined him at the top. 'Come on up here, Lou!' he called out. 'The view's amazing!'

'We're not insured for this!' she yelled back.

'You can't insure life!'

Her lips thinned. 'Yes, you can, you idiot!'

'Is it really dangerous?' Edie asked in a small voice.

Lou hesitated. 'I have no idea. I assume not very. You trust Mr Romano, don't you?' Edie nodded earnestly.

'Nothing would get me up there,' Helene said as she approached. 'Even if I was insured up to my armpits.'

'It's his head I'm worried about,' Lou muttered.

'His fingers,' Helene said with a gasp.

His backside, Lou added silently as he turned around to appreciate the view. He might be a musical genius with an artistic temperament, but that was a very nice behind.

He helped the kids down before anyone had a heart attack

and waved his arm to herd the group towards a gravel path heading off along the ridge. He set a quick pace.

'I'll stay towards the back,' Helene volunteered and Mrs Winkelmann went with her. Lou dragged Edie towards the front of the group – because of the mountain view and definitely not any other view.

'We've already come up nearly 1,800 metres with the cable car, but this isn't the top. Those,' called out Nick, pointing ahead, 'are the peaks of Monte Baldo.'

Lou couldn't help but pause as she soaked in the path winding and bobbling into the distance, towards a series of imposing crags.

'Pozzette, Longino and Valdritta, the highest, at 2,218 metres above sea level.' He counted them off.

Lou stared as she listened to his Italian intonation and stared at the great peaks.

'If anyone fancies,' he began again, his voice returning to his slightly posh Dulwich variety, 'we can hike there in about four hours, but you need decent shoes.'

'I'd need a lot more than decent shoes,' Lou said, her eyes still on the mountains.

'You don't think you could get up there?'

She looked back at him, startled by the sudden question. 'No way.'

'You might find it's like mascarpone: easier than you think.'

'Oh, shut up about the mascarpone.'

The wind picked up as they continued along the ridge, valleys dropping away to either side. When they arrived at the top of the chairlift on the other side of the Monte Baldo range, Lou was disappointed the walk had only been half an hour. How odd.

Four hours... No, she would hate it by the end.

She took one more look across at the peaks as the kids shuffled towards the turnstiles. What would it feel like to stand up there?

'You feel it, don't you?'

She jumped to hear Nick's voice at her ear. The words prickled over her skin. She felt a lot of things. But she knew he was talking about the desire to go up there – to the peak, where there would be nothing but rock and air.

'I have no idea why,' she said. He opened his mouth to say something, but she raised her hand, not stopping it in time and accidentally smooshing her fingers against his lips. She pulled her hand back quickly. Her voice shook more than she liked when she delivered her quip: 'If you were going to say "because it's there", you can forget it.'

He smiled. 'There's something about the mountains. We give them personal pronouns and personalities and want to conquer them like enemies, but they watch over our villages like benign gods.'

'That's poetic,' she said, not sure if she was teasing him.

'You could get to the top if you wanted – as long as you're not afraid of heights. Might be a better day than a craft workshop.' He smiled faintly and made his way to the turnstiles.

She shook her head once more at the distant peaks. If she discovered she could climb a mountain... she'd have to start wondering what other limitations she'd been placing on herself all this time.

10

Thank you, Herr Mozart. Nick stood before the crowd, baton clutched in both hands, and grinned. It always amazed him how much easier it was to take the approbation when he could stand to the side after his bow and show off his orchestra.

His orchestra... He rarely questioned his decision to teach at primary school, but when his gifted teenagers had nailed *Eine kleine Nachtmusik* for the captivated crowd, he almost wished he could experience this sort of exhilaration more often. But he knew that when the competition ended, he would have forgotten this thrill while drowning in pressure and anxiety – pressure and anxiety he would have felt even if they weren't performing at the Conservatorio. As much as he was wary of handing them over to Maestro Eckert, he was glad he wasn't conducting them himself at his old school.

'Grazie! Grazie mille per l'ascolto, signore e signori.' He raised his hands to clap the orchestra himself and, when the applause finally died down, he indicated they could file off the stage. Their exit was a mess of bumps and clangs that made him wince. He'd have to work on that. But they filed back to the bus and packed their instruments away without incident. Even the weather had held off for their outdoor performance by the Malcesine street market, although it was looking ominous now.

He gathered them on the path by the bus. He was about to speak, when a rumble of thunder interrupted him, filling the heavy air. The Lake Garda storm was a trifle early, but it looked typically dramatic.

He clapped his hands together to get their attention. 'I'll be quick!' he began. 'Choir pieces: lovely, but I didn't see enough eyes. I want dynamics. I want smooth phrasing. You'll get more of that from me than from the sheet music. Jenkins: you did it. Be proud of yourselves. Mozart: you knocked it out of the water. That is what we need to keep up. When you freeze up on stage in Milan, think of Malcesine, think of this stage and this audience today. That was your moment.'

Looking earnestly across the group of kids, his gaze landed on Lou, smiling with that brightness that made him stand straighter and wonder who had made her so lovely. Distracted, he forced his gaze back to the kids, running both hands absently through his hair. 'And now, you all deserve a trip to the pizzeria for lunch.'

The afternoon in Malcesine didn't turn out as expected; the storm hit as soon as they filed into the charming pizzeria. But the kids were in high spirits after their pizza and gelato and were more than satisfied with the afternoon's alternative entertainment: the convent's antiquated karaoke system.

'What, did the nuns used to use this?' Lou joked as she kneeled on the floor of the chapel, looking all over the unit for input options. The kids had more success when they took over. Someone produced a cable that could connect their tablet to the unit and the convent's Wi-Fi – which had thankfully been updated since the nuns left – did the rest. Nick watched them absently while he went through his score, marking things from the performance that day.

He recognised the squeak of Lou's old sneakers and the cadence of her steps before the brush of her knees against his forced him to look up and settle his glasses more firmly on his nose. She leaned on the arms of his chair. She had a frown on her face, but all Nick could process was how near she was, leaning over him with her hair tickling his forearms.

'Don't you ever get a break?' she asked in a scolding tone.

'Not until tomorrow,' he replied as evenly as he could. 'What workshop is it tomorrow? Nautical knots? Macramé?'

She laughed and he found himself staring at her mouth. It was awkward the way he couldn't keep his eyes off her – so unlike himself. He was a socks-on-in-bed kind of guy usually. 'No workshop tomorrow. I was going to check out a market with Edie, but she wants to go to the violin museum with Meg, Alison and Tanya and I don't fit in the car.'

'Are you okay with that?'

'It's fine, but bless you for asking!' She frowned. 'That sounded like my mother.'

He patted her hand. 'Don't worry about it, pet.'

She rewarded him with the laugh again. 'Why does your Italian mother call people "pet"? It's very sweet.'

'She uses cucciolo a lot in Italian. She must have asked someone what the equivalent was in English and it stuck.'

'Did she ask someone from Sunderland?'

'Maybe that's it.'

Edie appeared at Lou's side and tugged on her arm. 'Can you help me find a song?'

'What are you going to sing?' he asked.

'"Pressure" by Muse,' she said with a smile that was mostly brave but a tiny bit uncertain. Nick's eyebrows shot up.

'Great idea!' Lou said with a snap of her fingers. 'Get one of the other kids to sing the oo-oo bits.'

'You could,' Edie suggested, 'like we do in the car!'

But Lou dismissed the suggestion immediately. 'No way am I singing in front of your musical friends.'

* * *

Nick fitted in a quick escape into the olive grove with his violin in the early evening to burn off steam, but soon discovered he had been absent at a key moment of the day. He sat down at dinner and Lou plonked into the chair opposite him, giving him a long look.

'What?' he asked immediately.

She indicated Helene and Tanya at the other end of the table. 'They've got it all worked out. We're doing karaoke tonight.'

He froze at just the thought of getting up in front of an audience – even a small audience – and singing. Oh, God, could he get out of it?

While he was hesitating, Lou's mind was working – he could see it. The skin on the back of his neck prickled. 'I'm sure there's no expectation that you'll join in,' she said.

He squinted at her. 'No expectation?'

She waved her hands in some kind of shrug. 'Maybe a little bit of expectation.'

A smile pulled at his lips, which, adding to his pounding heart at the thought of performing, made him light-headed. 'A little bit?'

She scowled, but then shared his smile. 'Okay, Helene is desperate to hear you sing something. I tried to tell her you might not be keen.'

'How did you know I might not be keen?' he blurted out before he could reconsider.

She gave him a long look. 'You don't... share your musical gifts.'

He eyed her. 'You make it sound antisocial. It's not a choice I've made.'

Her look softened. 'Do you get stage fright or something?'

He looked away, studying the basket of bread with too much interest. 'A bit,' he vastly understated. He kept his eyes carefully averted. He was afraid of how much she saw, afraid of what she'd think if she knew the extent of his problems. More than that, he was terrified of what she'd think if she heard him sing. The boys at his school in England had made sure he'd never sing in public without their taunts of 'castrato' haunting him.

'Seriously, you don't have to sing.'

He sighed. 'I can play the accompaniment,' he said, hoping that would change the subject.

She drew back. 'You can play pop songs on the piano?'

'I can plonk out anything on the piano, if you give me a few minutes and a key.'

'Of course you can,' she grumbled.

She dragged a bottle of wine into the chapel an hour later when the kids were ensconced in their rooms and Adelaide Winkelmann was on duty reading a book in the corridor in case any curious feet should creep towards the chapel.

Nick turned from where he'd been fiddling on the piano to see Lou pouring four glasses of wine. 'Miss Hwang doesn't drink, does she?' Lou asked.

'Is she joining us?'

Lou looked up sharply and he couldn't stop the little buzz from thinking she was still jealous. 'She loves karaoke, apparently.' She handed him a glass and held hers out to clink. Helene,

Tanya and Hyewon drifted into the chapel and accepted their glasses.

'What are you going to sing?' he asked, smiling when Lou scrunched up her nose in thought. He pulled out his phone, typed a search, settled it on the polished wood music stand of the upright piano and played a couple of chords, squinting at the screen.

He must have done a reasonable fudge of 'Wannabe' because her gaze lifted and she chuckled. 'I would be a lousy Spice Girl,' she said.

'I didn't think they had one called "Lousy", but I couldn't be sure. I spent my teenage years buried in Brahms and Vivaldi.'

'Whereas I was listening to the Spice Girls and you probably weren't even a teenager in the nineties. I know which one of us is a proper musician.'

He shook his head. 'I'm a music teacher.'

She eyed him. 'You're a musician with a lot of hang-ups.' It was uncomfortably true. 'But no Spice Girls. I might be able to do Leonard Cohen's "Hallelujah" or something by Green Day.' She couldn't know that her eyes had a glow that he recognised. She was looking forward to trying it. He was learning that nothing kept Lou down – not even herself.

'Great choices, although I don't know if I could play Green Day very well.'

'What are you going to sing?' Helene asked.

'I'd rather just play.'

'Please! Sing me a classical piece. Was voice your second study at music school? Oh, or was piano?'

It wasn't pleasant to realise they knew so much about him. But the four faces were kind, interested. These were teachers and parents – his safe space. He didn't need to make a big deal about it. 'Voice at school, but piano at university,' he explained. He'd managed better when he'd discovered the freedom of keeping his back to the audience. 'Let's get started,' he said. End of topic. If only it were that simple in his own thoughts.

Helene, Hyewon and Tanya were unstoppable. Tanya belted out seventies pop with laughing tunelessness. Helene and Hyewon knew some of the same K-Pop, which they had to look up on the tablet, because Nick had never heard of them. They'd been going for nearly an hour before a gap of silence slipped into the chapel.

He nudged Lou with his shoulder. 'Your turn.'

She gave him a reproachful look, but drained her wine glass and retrieved the microphone. She flicked her hair over her shoulder and that was it – he was gone. Her tentative smile was warm and engaging. She fiddled with the microphone cord, looping it around her wrist and unravelling it again. She stepped from foot to foot in a little nervous dance. 'It's not the Spice Girls,' she began, smiling at him with the full force of her charm, 'but it's from around the same time. Helene, can you look up "Good Riddance" by Green Day?'

She took the tablet when Helene had found a karaoke track and nodded tensely as the rhythmic guitar chords started up. Nick knew the song, but, yeah, he'd been in primary school when it came out. And by the time he'd attended a normal secondary school that wasn't named after Giuseppe Verdi, he'd never had a chance at fitting in with the kids who liked this sort of music. She must have been every boy's crush in school – deservedly, he had to admit.

When she started to sing in that halting marcato unique to karaoke singing, her voice was a little tinny and scratchy. She used far too little diaphragm and not enough resonance. But the whimsy of her voice, reflected in her little grin, captured the mood of the song perfectly. A sarcastic smile showed on her lips a time or two, only deepening the skill of her interpretation.

He wondered if she was thinking of her ex-husband and it gave him a stomach cramp. It was a break-up song. Of course she was thinking of him – who else? It struck him that Naomi would never have sung a song about him – at any stage of their relationship. It was one of the things that had attracted him to her in the first place – she was as separate from his music as possible. But wasn't it also the reason he'd given up in the end?

His relationship criteria were a catch-22. His mother wasn't getting a daughter-in-law any time soon, that was for certain. There was too much of the repressed artist in him.

He winced. He was not an artist. He couldn't handle the life of an artist.

Lou's voice echoed through him as she sang, dredging up emotion he'd tried to bury. She claimed she wasn't musical – she certainly wasn't trained. And yet, her instincts and feelings were spot on. Music fed off instincts and feelings.

Her smile unfolded with the verses, as she sang the repetitive words about having the time of your life. By the time she reached the end, she'd lost the thoughtful whimsy and embraced her position on stage, holding the microphone high, before breaking into laughter when the song ended. Tanya, Helene and Hyewon applauded enthusiastically.

'Let me guess,' Nick said when the applause tapered off. 'Not your talent, but lots of fun?'

She stopped up short and looked at him. 'Are you implying something?' He hesitated, unprepared for the direct approach. He should have learned to expect the direct approach from Lou. 'Spit it out, Nick: my search for a talent is a load of crap. What good is making mascarpone if I'm terrible at everything important?'

'That's one thing you're very good at: putting words into other people's mouths.'

'That's a cop-out, if I ever heard one.' The others glanced between them warily. Did he want this to come to a head? With an audience? No.

He sucked in a deep breath and crossed his arms over his chest. 'Your first accusation is pretty close. Your search for a talent is a nice diversion and an interesting idea, but you're not going to find a talent that way. I'm not even sure you understand what a crock the word "talent" is.' He paused, but something he'd said had knocked the wind out of her and she didn't have anything to say. He looked her in the eye and continued. 'I'm not sure you really want a talent, anyway. Too much pressure.'

She laughed. But it wasn't a manic laugh of denial. It was bleak. '"With great power comes great responsibility."' She quoted darkly. 'Is that what you talented people say behind closed doors? Or are you too snobby for Spiderman?'

'I thought it was Winston Churchill,' Tanya murmured.

'Lou,' he said in a low voice.

But she didn't let him finish – not that he'd known what to say. Knowing what to say was her strength. 'Nick,' she said with a sigh, 'go play "Hallelujah" for me.'

He jumped up to the piano without hesitating. He watched her while she flipped through the tablet for the lyrics. Her expression was tight. As he stared at her, he had the distinct impression that, if it had been her on the stage at the Conservatorio that day sixteen years ago, she would have given it everything she had. It was he who had an issue with pressure.

It was a beautiful song, the melody and the words combining to reach the deepest emotions. But he could feel that she'd lost her groove. He hated it. But she continued singing, simply and mechanically, like knitting rather than artistic expression. But what was she looking for, with her talent search? Was she looking for a comforting hobby like knitting, or was she fumbling towards an experiment in artistic expression? Did she even know?

She smiled and curtsied neatly when the song finished and the other three applauded. She handed the tablet back to Helene, who immediately cued up more K-Pop. Nick hesitated for barely a second before following Lou back to her seat. He sat next to her, bumping her shoulder with his. It was the only thing he could do. She didn't move away, so he stilled, his shoulder against hers, and enjoyed the odd surge of... something. He didn't dare look at her, but the way she was threading and unthreading her hands in her lap indicated she was as distracted as he was by their conversation.

After Tanya managed a poor rendition of 'I'm a Believer' in an awkward key, there was a dangerous pause. He felt Lou turn her head and warily met her gaze. Her lips were pursed in lingering disgruntlement. She lifted her eyebrows in challenge. The gap in conversation lingered long enough for Helene to notice their silent communication.

'Nick! Please sing us something!'

Lou held her hand out for the tablet and he wondered whether she was going to spare him after all, but the glint in her eye worried him. Slowly and purposefully, she cued up a song, then stood to retrieve the microphone. When he'd heard enough of the introduction to recognise 'My Way', he understood what she was up to.

He closed his eyes for a second of hesitation, but when he opened them again and saw her approaching, a serious look on her face, he was compelled to do it. If she wanted to make him pay for rudely digging around for her true motivations, then that was fair enough. And if she was curious about his relationship with music, then it was her own fault.

He stood, straightened his trousers and reached for the microphone she held out. As he brushed past her, he muttered, 'You're taking responsibility for this.' He felt her pause, but didn't look back for her reaction.

He tried to keep it low-key. At least he thought he did. But he was standing on stage and there was some sort of audience in front of him and the physical memory of years of training made his voice soar in the tiny chapel. It was low in his register, but that was for the best. The worst of it was he knew he was singing Sinatra with the diction and resonance of an aria from an opera. His mind raced to separate the phrases in an expressive manner, to punctuate the music with appropriate dynamics. He couldn't help that he sounded like Pavarotti – actually, he sounded more like Giuseppe Giacomini, but anyone who'd heard him sing after he'd left music school had probably never heard of Giacomini and the boys at school in London had certainly preferred the previous comparison.

As the music came to an end and he carefully matched the final words to the pre-recorded ritardando, he knew what was coming. He took deep breaths to return his breathing to normal, and the details of the chapel and his small audience came back into focus, four pairs of wide eyes trained on him in shock.

When they didn't applaud, he set the microphone down with a sigh, took a theatrical bow and left the chapel with a tight, 'Goodnight.'

He caught Lou's mumble of 'artistic temperament' as he strode past, but he didn't want to stay for the conversation to follow. When he closed the door of his room behind him and leaned against it, hands shoved in his pockets, he was berating himself for being oversensitive and cursing the camp that had brought everything back. And he was wondering obsessively whether Lou would search him out – and whether he wanted her to.

'Just go,' Tanya said with a smile, after Lou's third attempt to join in with the conversation in her distracted state. 'Go and talk to Mr Romano. For all our sakes', you probably should.'

'Why not you or Helene?'

Tanya gave a significant cough, which heated Lou's face. But Helene said earnestly, 'You know him much better than we do. What was the matter, anyway? And what on earth is he doing hiding away at a primary school in South London? He's a fabulous tenor.'

'A regular Don Carlos,' Tanya said with a snicker.

Lou knew she needed to go. She'd put him in that situation, despite her instincts telling her one of his wild hang-ups would rear its head. Even though he'd come at her with accusations that felt suspiciously like the truth, he hadn't deserved that.

She dragged her feet, wondering what to say to him, wondering how he could be so gentle and encouraging with his students – and her – while punishing himself. She hated the idea that something as intrinsic to him as music could also make him uncomfortable.

When she drew up at his door, she wasn't sure how many minutes had passed since he'd stormed out. She forced herself to knock, still without a clue about what to say.

There was a rustling sound and then footsteps, then he wrenched the door open. His shirt was only half buttoned. Although he was a lot more covered than if he hadn't bothered to quickly rebutton it, the glimpses of skin with the finest dusting of chest hair seemed much more illicit, caught through his gaping shirt. She licked her lips and blushed bright red. When she raised her eyes apologetically, his gaze was dark.

'I'm sorry,' she blurted out. 'I knew you didn't want to do that and it was petty of me to make you, just because you were trying to help.'

'I could have refused.'

'I don't want to pry or anything. I mean, your business is your business. But I suspected... Wait? What did you say?'

'I could have refused,' he repeated gruffly.

'Huh,' was all she said at first. 'You said it was my responsibility.'

'I was being immature – and don't take that as an excuse to remind yourself that you're older than I am.'

She paused again. 'You're not angry with me?'

He hesitated. Her heart rate sped up. The silence wrapped thickly around her – around both of them. She stared at him – at the thoughts flickering across his expression, at the hint of a dimple that showed in his pensive look, at his wild, curling hair that reflected his agitation. It was so easy to imagine kissing him.

Then he sighed and the tension burst in a much less interesting way. 'No, I'm not angry with you. I probably shouldn't have said anything about your talent search. I've got no right to judge.'

'It's okay,' she insisted. 'In some ways it's just nice that you care.' She snapped her mouth shut. 'I mean, detached, professional sort of care. Not... anything else. I don't think... I mean, I'm not so conceited that I... Please save me, here.'

'I'm trying to think of something to say. It's certainly clear to me that you're not at all conceited.'

Lou grinned. She couldn't help it. 'You had plenty to say about me tonight.'

'And I was wrong, Lou – at least, I was wrong to make you question your enthusiasm.'

'But not about the talent search?'

'Exactly what is it about being talented that you want?'

She pressed her lips together. 'I don't know. That's the problem. I don't even understand talented people.' She eyed him. 'Including you.'

He snorted. 'I'm not "talented people".'

'You were a child prodigy,' she accused gently.

His gaze was reluctant. 'And I chose a different path. I'm not the best person to give you advice on finding your talents.' He said the word with disdain.

'You're the perfect person,' she said. 'I can take it. What do you really think?'

His expression was unreadable, but made her hot with emotion. 'You are more than talented.'

She was shocked into silence for a long moment, but when she thought back on his words with her brain instead of her heart, she immediately scoffed. 'I'm clearly not.'

'What you think of as talent is just sacrifice, hard work, motivation, time and help – with a good dose of obsession. If you want that, then get a therapist and throw away the rest of your life. What you have is much rarer: a natural openness, fearlessness, originality.'

Her retort melted. All of her insides melted. But there was a forlorn glint in his eye that reminded her of what she'd done to him that evening. He was far too generous to be trusted.

'It's really...' she considered her words carefully '... kind of you to say that, Nick.'

He smiled suddenly and ran a hand quickly through his hair. It was a smile with a deep, challenging twist. 'How did I know you were going to say that?'

She frowned. 'Well, I knew you were going to run off stage like a diva without waiting to hear how blown away we were by your performance!'

The hand that had been in his hair swiped across his forehead. She'd seen the gesture innumerable times now, but it made so little sense that night as she stared at him. Why the back of his hand? 'Yeah, because "Sinatra: The Opera" is exactly what the world needs right now.'

'So, you trained. What's so bad about that?' she challenged recklessly. 'And what was so bad about being a virtuoso violinist by fourteen?'

He completely shut down then and Lou winced before he'd even given the flippant answer she knew was coming. 'It's not something I can easily explain to someone who hasn't lived it,' he said.

'Like talentless Lou.' She grinned sharply.

'That's not what I meant.'

She shook her head. 'You can't have it both ways, Nick. You can't encourage me – and Edie, for God's sake – and have a different scale for yourself.'

'That's exactly what I have to do, if I want to continue to work in music.'

The question hung between them. Why didn't he play in public any more? Lou doubted he would tell her. He was still embarrassed. Feelings of inadequacy were something she was familiar with. She was desperate enough to study his hands, wondering if he'd been injured, but she'd seen him play with the violin ensemble in London – although she now realised how nervous he'd been.

'If I ask, will you tell me?'

'No.'

'We're allowed to discuss me, but not you?' He nodded. 'Fine,' she said, bracing her hand on his doorframe and leaning close. He drifted slightly backwards, giving her the confidence to move further into his personal space. When his citrus scent started to distract her, she stopped.

'You rocked Sinatra.'

He blushed. He was blinking behind his glasses so hard she could barely see his dark lashes. His jaw worked and the dimples appeared for less than a second. She suspected he didn't even know what he was feeling. 'I did not "rock" Sinatra. I sang it properly in front of an unappreciative crowd.'

'Helene appreciated it. Miss Hwang probably did, too.' She tried – oh, she tried – to keep her jealousy of the petite, talented Miss Hwang from her voice, but the way Nick cocked his head and studied her indicated she'd failed.

'And you? I can't imagine you like opera. Muse and Green Day and "rocking" bands, but not tenors who sing in Italian.'

She rather liked this tenor. It was inconvenient how much. 'I don't know much about opera,' she admitted. He looked as though he was going to say 'I told you so', so she held up a hand. She remembered accidentally pressing her fingers to his lips the day before and halted just in time. His eyes told her he remembered and, God, it was hard to resist. 'But I could listen to you singing Sinatra all day.' All night. She hoped the truth wasn't shining in her eyes. She was shocked by her own imagination. She was a thirty-seven-year-old mother and marriage ex-con. She was enjoying being free to not have sex. She didn't even look at pictures of hot guys any more – except of Henry Cavill, but she was human.

Why had his singing voice made her think of kisses on skin and a tight embrace?

'If we've...' He took a deep breath, but it didn't seem to be enough, because his chest was still rising and falling out of rhythm. 'Have we finished the apologies?' She didn't answer and he didn't wait long for her to respond. 'Because if we don't say goodnight, I might do something else I'd have to apologise for.'

His voice croaked upward at the end and she teetered in indecision. She didn't want to say goodnight. It was irresponsible and careless and her daughter was down the hall, along with all of his other students. But if he meant he would kiss her... Was that what he meant? It seemed so implausible, as she stared at the stormy expression on his handsome face, that his fervour was directed at her. Surely, she was reading this wrong.

There was only one way to find out. She struggled. But reason prevailed. She sucked in a breath through her nose and leaned close to kiss him softly on the cheek. It was both vastly insufficient and heady with potential.

'Goodnight,' she whispered. She must have imagined his shudder as she pulled away.

* * *

Lou slept through breakfast on Sunday morning. She'd sleepily farewelled Edie at stupid o'clock as she'd set off on the long drive to the violin museum with Tanya and Mrs Winkelmann, and then gone back to sleep.

Thinking that Phil probably thought she was doing this every morning of her 'holiday' ruined some of the enjoyment of the long sleep. But she'd needed the extra few hours after tossing and turning in a doze after she'd gone to bed close to midnight. Nick was bad for her hormones. She'd felt them zinging in her blood long after she'd said goodnight to him with the kiss on his cheek she was still replaying in high definition, simply for the enjoyment of remembering.

'Good morning, Lou!'

She almost jumped at the greeting from Greta as she shuffled into the refectory in search of coffee. Why was Greta so chipper in the morning? Because she'd been up for four hours already.

'Morning,' she replied, her voice alarmingly gravelly.

'Too much karaoke last night?' she asked with a smile.

'I only sang two songs. The others, though...'

'Did they get Nick to sing in the end?'

Lou studied Greta as subtly as she could. Her excessively casual tone and calling him Nick instead of Nico set off her sympathy. She could sense motherly concern. It gave her an uncomfortable flash of insight into her own future, with Edie at music school.

'We made him sing "My Way",' she said as evenly as she could. 'He was quite embarrassed afterwards, but I think he'll get over it.'

Greta met her gaze. Lou smiled faintly, her heart bleeding a trickle. Greta clutched her arm for a moment. If they'd known each other longer, it probably would have been a hug. 'Coffee,' she said firmly. 'Let me make you one.'

'I can do it – thanks.'

She shook her head. 'You let Nico make you a coffee every morning. Today, you'll let me.'

Lou nodded obediently. Had Nick really been making her a coffee every morning? She was mortified to think she hadn't taken note. When she thought back, she realised he'd set a foamy cappuccino in front of her, without fail, every morning of the camp so far and she'd only thanked him that first time. Something in her chest did a double flip and a couple of cartwheels.

The unsettled feeling only got worse when she watched Greta painstakingly making the cappuccino without a machine. They brewed coffee using a metal pot on the stove – a bigger one than Lou had ever seen – and then watered it down American-style in thermos pots to put out with the buffet.

But Lou's cappuccinos had been different. She vaguely remembered that first early morning, when she'd seen Nick steaming milk on the stove, but somehow hadn't remembered him using the French press to foam it. He'd done this for her every morning?

'Nick doesn't drink cappuccinos, does he?'

Greta shook her head. 'He doesn't have his Italian breakfast any more. I'm not sure how he copes with that double espresso on an empty stomach. But he's a good boy and makes one for me – and you. Would you like something to eat?'

'You really don't have to.'

'Yes, she would.'

Lou and Greta turned to see Nick walking into the kitchen, holding a crash helmet, fingerless gloves on his hands. His hair was a mess and he must have been wearing contacts because there was no sign of his glasses. He was sweaty and his legs were muddy and he looked utterly gorgeous. Lou couldn't help it. She soaked in the lean, muscular planes of his chest, revealed by the tight cycling vest.

It must be a warm morning out there. It was certainly hot in the kitchen. Her peripheral vision was telling her he was wearing bike shorts and she was trying hard to keep her eyes up. Until it reminded her, she could still picture Phil's... She nearly gagged.

'I have some croissant pastry. Take a seat and I'll bake you two some croissants.' Greta handed Lou her coffee and tried to usher them out of the kitchen.

Lou's brain switched back on sluggishly. 'Let me help, Greta. It's not your job to wait on me.' She glanced back up at Nick. 'And why are you speaking for me?'

He looked a shade sheepish. 'It's beautiful out there. You need to get outside.'

'Thanks, "Mum". I suppose I'll go for a walk later.'

'Go drink your coffee on the terrace, both of you,' Greta suggested. 'I'll bring you a croissant. I'll make more coffee.'

'I stink, Mum. I have to go have a shower.'

'As long as you don't preen for half an hour, you can shower while I bake the croissants,' she said with a pointed look. He gave her a disgruntled glance, but turned to go. 'Not too scruffy, either, Nico!' she called after him. 'Not if you're going to have coffee with a lady!'

Lou choked on her drink and set it down while she coughed. Greta walloped her on the back and she glanced up to share a look with Nick.

* * *

'Do you think your mum set us up on a date?' Lou couldn't help asking when they were settled in the wicker chairs, croissants, butter, rustic peach jam and fresh berries on a tray between them.

Nick was lounging in his chair, his legs stretched out in front. His hair was still damp, the curls springy, and the fresh smell of soap under his citrus cologne intoxicating. But there was something so satisfying about his relaxed pose – in stark contrast to the tight tension in Mr Romano the conductor. He glanced at her from where his head was resting on the back of the chair.

'If she did, she robbed me of the chance to make any effort myself,' he muttered.

'You don't think it's awkward?' she pushed.

His look was longer this time and she had no choice but to hold his gaze as warmth and speculation crossed his face. 'We're a bit past awkward, aren't we, Lou?'

Everything in her chest coiled up tight. Was he talking about friendship? 'I do a good line in awkward,' she mumbled.

His dimples appeared. 'That's okay. I like your awkward.'

She grabbed for a croissant and a plate and spooned a dollop of runny jam on to the edge. 'Where did you go on your bike?'

He grinned and took a sip of coffee. 'I finally got up there today – that route we drove on the first day.'

'You're insane.'

'You don't know what you're missing.'

'How long did it even take?'

'About three and a half hours.'

'Shi-i-i-i-i-it.'

'That's probably what my calves are going to be saying tomorrow, but we've got to knuckle down with rehearsal this week before the maestro gets here, so I wouldn't have had a chance to do it until my days off.'

She nodded. 'I've got three workshops this week because there are so many rehearsals planned.' They looked out over the silver olive trees, to the sparkling lake. The air was still light, but already hot with the promise of a scorching day and an afternoon heavy with humidity. 'You seem a bit too sporty for a music nerd,' she commented, hoping the easy silence would soften him to her nosiness.

'I'm not sporty and I certainly never was, in school.' He glanced at her. 'I was the skinny, weird kid who could sing like a girl. I only got into cycling when I came here to work in the summer. I don't think of it as exercise. I think of it as an outlet.'

'An outlet,' she repeated slowly. That sounded good. Perhaps she needed an outlet. It might stop her from using inappropriate humour as an outlet.

'Give it a go,' he blurted out.

'Cycling? Seriously, I'm pretty sure there's a reason why you're supposed to learn as a kid. Besides, what bike would I use?'

He squinted and looked her up and down in a way that made her tingle. 'You can use mine – well, Federico's. I can adjust the seat. We're about the same height, so it should be fine.'

'We are not the same height,' she insisted.

'What, do you think you're taller than me?'

She drew back. Of course she wasn't taller than Nick. But did he think of her as a tall woman? 'Are we seriously nearly the same height?'

He hesitated, studying her expression. 'I'm quite short and you're...' His gaze drifted to her legs again.

'Do not say "statuesque",' she said flatly.

He laughed, but quickly swallowed it. 'I wasn't going to. You have long legs.' Nick trying to keep a straight face was adorable. 'We're a similar height, unless you're in heels... or I am.'

She burst out laughing and he joined her. 'Fine. Since there's no harm in sucking at one more thing, I will get on this bike and give it a go.'

12

Lou regretted it as soon as she saw the bike. Where was she supposed to put her hands on the fancy handlebars? At least it appeared to have proper pedals, rather than those clippy ones that looked like guaranteed broken bones. She forced herself closer and stared at the bike, her stomach churning.

'You won't learn how to ride a bike in a day,' was the first thing he said.

Her gaze snapped to his, accusingly. 'Why didn't you tell me that before?'

'I'm telling you now.' He acknowledged her narrowed gaze with a nod. 'I know it's not nice to hear. It takes time to learn the balance – possibly longer for an adult who's never been on a bike before.'

'What's the point, then?'

He grasped her arm and turned her back. 'I want to show you that you could learn, if you wanted to.'

Her breath left her lungs in a whoosh. His expression was so earnest, so gorgeous. She was wobbly on her feet and she hadn't even got on the bicycle yet. 'Okay,' she said softly. 'I'll try.' *For you.*

His small smile started off all the sparks in her chest over again. 'You don't have to push yourself. I can hold on to the bike the whole time. And if you get scared, just tell me.'

She nodded. She was already scared – of how easy it would be to rely on those warm words and soft eyes. But he thought she was fearless.

Even getting on the thing was a challenge. He showed her where to put her hands and apologised that she'd have to swing her leg over the seat because it was a men's bike. But she got the impression that he enjoyed skimming his gaze over her bare legs, which helped. He'd lowered the seat so she could still touch the ground.

His hands held the handlebars firmly and their fingers overlapped as the bike wobbled. When she was steady, with her feet on the ground, he let go to arrange the pedals. He talked smoothly about keeping the wheels moving to maintain balance and about how starting off was very difficult at first, but got easier with time. But he stumbled on his words when he crouched down to fiddle with the pedals, nudging her calves with gentle fingers.

His lecture tapered off entirely when he stood and she turned to him in question. He was staring at her behind. She hadn't thought he was the type to ogle, but the evidence made her feel quite pleasant.

'Uh...' He attempted a sentence. 'I'm really sorry about this,' he stammered. She was going to say something poised and reassuring – and not at all embarrassed – when his hand came up and gripped the seat, the knuckle of his thumb poking her right in the rear. 'It doesn't have a luggage frame. I have to hold on here to keep you steady.'

'Steady' was a word that wouldn't apply to her for a long time if she kept up such close proximity to Nick. She kept her eyes averted.

'Are you right-footed?'

'No idea.'

'You probably are. We'll try with your right foot. Put it up on the pedal—'

The attempt to lift one foot up on to the pedal was all it took for the bike to tilt sharply to the right. Nick grabbed for her, his arms closing around her waist. The bike bumped her knee and threatened to pull them both over. He hauled her back with a grunt of effort. Her legs flailed. One hand grabbed for his neck. He took a couple of stumbling steps before both of her feet finally found solid ground and the bike clattered over.

She sighed with relief and her forehead fell to his chest. She was so embarrassed. She was doubly embarrassed by how good his arms felt, still tight around her. She must be starved of hugs.

'Um,' he said, his voice breathy. 'This is nice,' he murmured, as though his brain was only semi-functional. She could sympathise.

One of her arms was trapped against him and, really, they shouldn't be standing on the driveway hugging, so she was disappointed, but not surprised, when he let her go and stepped slowly back. Lou turned back to the bike with an accusing frown. She was going to get back on that thing, because now it was personal. She pulled it back upright and glanced at Nick.

He held the handlebars steady and their fingers repeated their little dance as she swung her leg over the seat. 'Those shorts are really distracting,' he muttered.

Lou would have snorted with laughter if she weren't so floored. This time, when his hand brushed her butt, she was feeling a whole lot besides embarrassment. And she wasn't sure how she was supposed to ride a bike when her heart was pounding.

'Right foot up on the pedal,' he repeated, but this time his voice was a murmur.

She managed to get her foot up this time, but her brain was mush. Perhaps it helped that she wasn't overthinking everything.

'You have to press with your right foot and quickly get your left foot up on the pedal. But keep the handlebars straight or you're going over again. Don't look at your feet. Look up at where you're going.'

Maybe cycling was like life: looking down at your feet made you wobble about everything.

The first couple of times she tried, her left foot didn't make it on to the pedal and he had to catch her. It worked once and she squealed as the bike lurched forward, dragging Nick with it. She put her feet down again immediately.

'Why did you stop?' he asked in chagrin.

'I didn't know what to do next!'

'You just pedal. I've got you. You have to do it before you can understand how to do it.' That definitely sounded like life.

She managed to pedal a few feet, Nick holding her firmly upright, but the sight of the steep slope to the road made her put her feet down in panic. He showed her the brakes, stepping up close behind her and closing his hands over hers on the handlebars to demonstrate. She wondered whether she could claim she hadn't understood the first time, because feeling his chest against her back again was pretty high on her list of priorities.

She had to admit she made progress – *she* made progress with *cycling*. Like most of her workshops, she'd had fun, but she hadn't been a natural. Nick's words from the night before were ringing in her ears when she thought about her quest for a talent. Sacrifice, hard work, time and help. She could see how she'd master cycling if she had those things. What if he was right? What if the only things that differentiated her from Winny the ballet dancer were her choices? What did that say about the choices she'd made so far?

Cycling was far too much like life. The instant her confidence wavered, so did the bike. Nick grabbed her as the bike made a dash for the bushes. She clutched him and he stumbled back, tripping on the grass. His hand accidentally pulled her T-shirt high up her back and, as he adjusted his grip, his palm landed flat on her skin, right where the clasp of her bra was.

She stared at Nick, her arms around his neck. One of his hands was up her shirt and the other one had tightened low on her hip. Her mind was suddenly clear of everything except their breathing and the expression on his face. It was glorious.

Then it got better. With an inarticulate mumble, he pressed his lips to hers. It wasn't the kiss of the mild-mannered teacher she'd known for six years. He lifted one hand to her face to tilt her head up and deepened the kiss and – oh, God – Nick Romano was kissing her with tongue. She didn't care who she was any more, as long as he didn't stop.

Hidden passions... Boy, had Tina been spot on. The kiss was crazy and intense. Her fingers tangled in his hair and his hand under her shirt roamed with far too much fire. He made a little needy sound and pulled her harder against him, his mouth moving urgently against hers.

She moaned – she actually moaned – and pulled his hand until it was planted on her backside. His fingers tightened and she had to break the kiss to gasp.

He hesitated, their lips still less than an inch apart. Lou panicked more than she had when the bike had grown a mind of its own. He wouldn't stop there? After clearing her mind of everything except the desire to run this to its conclusion, he would stop?

His eyes fluttered shut again and she could have melted with relief when his mouth touched hers again. But this kiss was different. It was long and slow. His arms stayed around her, but they held her tight, rather than exploring her body. His tongue pushed into her mouth, but gently.

How long they stood there under an olive tree, making out, she didn't know. But she learned a lot about the contours of his bristly jaw and the texture of his hair. When they pulled back at the same moment to stare at each other, she suspected he was looking at a new Lou, and maybe she was looking at a new Nick.

She clutched his shoulders, knowing they should start behaving like adults again, but not wanting to let him go.

'My mind is officially blown,' he murmured.

'My socks are officially knocked off.'

He grinned. She wanted to laugh. She wanted to dance. She wanted to exorcise that stupid spectre of Phil and everything he'd worn down in her over the twelve years they were together.

But even conjuring his name in her thoughts brought her down a notch. The sudden arrival of a little Fiat in the driveway squashed the last of the buoyant mood. Nick pulled her instinctively close at first, but then shoved her away again so hard she nearly fell.

'Oh, God, I'm sorry,' he murmured, running his hands along her arms.

'It's okay,' she breathed, because it was, when he had his palms on her skin like that.

'That's my mum's car,' he explained.

It was her turn to wrench away. Exactly how close had they been when Greta had turned into the driveway? Could she have seen anything? She had a sudden flash of how she'd feel if it were Edie who'd arrived back, and horror rose in her throat.

Greta pulled into a parking space and got out with a wave. 'How's it going?' she asked cheerfully.

'Great!' Lou said with false brightness.

'Uh, okay, I guess.'

Greta strode over with a big bag of market purchases. Nick scrambled to take it from her, but she shooed him away. 'Don't let me disturb you. I can take this in myself.' She smiled warmly at Lou. 'Good on you for trying, pet. It took me a good few years to get Nick on a bike. But he was so short as a child, and his balance was terrible.'

Lou thought back to the paddleboarding trip, but resisted the urge to tease him. He must be mortified enough. Besides, no matter how short and skinny he'd been as a kid, he kissed like a man now, and that was what counted.

'Are you going to get back on?' Greta asked, glancing at the bike, which had tumbled into a bush a few feet away.

Lou glanced at Nick and found him looking back at her. If they continued her lesson, they'd probably just end up under that olive tree with their tongues down each other's throats again. Sounded good to her.

'I think we were finished?' he said, and her disappointment was disproportionate, but unfortunately real. Damn him for being sensible.

'Yes, we were finished,' she confirmed.

'I wasn't quite sure if you were... finished... when I drove up,' Greta said lightly.

Lou nearly swallowed her tongue. Nick went red.

'I'll p-put the bike away,' he stammered and rushed off. Lou watched his retreat with a scowl.

She sighed and lifted her shoulders. 'I'll help you with your groceries, Greta. No objections!' She grasped the bag and slung it over her shoulder. She trailed Greta through the door and along the cloister.

'So,' Greta asked conversationally as their shoes scuffled on the cool stone. Lou cursed Nick for leaving her alone with his mother. 'Wedding bells or just sex?'

'Oh, God,' Lou groaned. 'What have I done?'

'Ah,' said Greta, patting her haltingly on the arm. 'Regrets.' She gave Lou an odd look.

Lou's shoulders sagged. Greta was wrong. She didn't regret a thing. But that didn't make it any easier to see where she could go from here.

* * *

The only thing worse than having his mother drive up while he was in a post-kiss clinch with a woman was having to teach the woman's daughter the next day. Edie was no problem – she never was – but Nick's thoughts kept returning to Lou. Mother and daughter both scrunched up their foreheads in concentration and there was something of Lou in Edie's smile. It was sweet.

He picked up his pencil and marked her music. 'You need to tighten up the phrasing here and use less articulation. This is extreme legato, as smooth as you can get it.' She nodded and lifted her bow again. 'And lift, just gently, on that note.' Her forehead furrowed again as she finished the phrase. 'Keep practising that part. You're nearly there.'

'Mr Romano.' He looked up and pasted on a detached smile. 'I find it really hard to play this part with the first violins. I get it every time in practice, but something stuffs it up when we play together.'

He grabbed his violin and rifled through his stack of music

until he found the part for the firsts. He could probably play it from memory, but he needed to concentrate on his student as well. 'Slowly first.' He nodded the tempo and they played the line together. As she'd said, she faltered at one point where one of Jenkins' unexpected contemporary harmonies sneaked into the otherwise traditional piece. 'You have excellent ears,' he said and she smiled in embarrassed pleasure, which also reminded him of Lou. 'You're expecting the usual baroque intervals. But it's supposed to sound like this. Once again, even more slowly.' They played again and she struggled through it, but at the cost of the dynamics and phrasing. After a few more times, she could reliably complete the line.

She released a huge breath and rested her violin on her lap. 'It's really hard.'

'That's the beauty of it.'

She looked up at him thoughtfully. 'My fingers disagree.' He grinned. Lou's sense of humour. 'Can we play the Tessarini duet?'

He glanced at the clock. They had five minutes left and they should probably use the time for the Jenkins, but he knew the feeling she wanted. She was tired and creatively depleted from the rehearsal that morning and she just wanted to enjoy a song she could play in her sleep. He couldn't say no.

With a quick nod, he lifted his violin and she rushed to do the same. They both played from memory. They'd played it so many times, it wasn't even recall memory, it was muscle memory. He'd quickly noticed she loved this piece and he suspected she'd disappeared into it at first instead of coming to terms with the divorce. He wondered what she felt when she played it now.

She giggled when they finished on an identical flourish. 'I missed playing that. It's not as good on my own, even though I've learned both parts, now.'

'Have you? I should have guessed. We can swap next time.'

'Mr Romano?' she asked as she fetched her violin case.

His stomach clenched in caution, as something in her tone reminded him of the tense discussion he'd had with his mother the night before, about getting involved with a woman whose head was messed up from a divorce. Greta had experience he couldn't dismiss and it was certainly true that he flinched when he imagined Lou still hung up on her ex-husband. But he also knew that his mother couldn't protect him from everything, even though she insisted on trying. He didn't *want* her to protect him.

'What is it, Edie?'

'I heard you went to the Conservatorio in Milan.'

His gaze snapped up. 'Yes.'

'What was it like?'

Alarms were screeching inside his head, but she deserved an answer that came from somewhere other than his panic response. 'Hard,' he said at first. 'So much rehearsal that you either learn to hate your instrument or you learn to live it.'

Her brow furrowed. 'Which one did you learn?'

He laughed. 'Both.' He sat again and gestured for her to do the same. 'Are you worried about Purcell?'

She scrunched up her nose. 'I wasn't.'

'But?'

'But... I don't want Mum to be so worried about me.'

Nick sighed and leaned back in his chair. 'Mothers are always worried about us.'

'Greta was worried about you?'

He snorted. 'Worried is an understatement. Your mum doesn't compare.'

'I might have to do a term of boarding school if she can't find a flat in time.'

'That might be hard.'

She shook her head. 'It's fine. I live between two houses

anyway. I've learned to get on with things myself. But what will Mum do if I'm away at school through the week?'

'I'm sure she'll cope, Edie. She's the parent.'

'I've been told that before,' she said indignantly. 'But it doesn't change the way things are. I was an accident, you know. She gave up everything for me.'

'I don't think that's how parents think of their children after they're born,' he said carefully. He was firmly in 'none of his business' territory, and yet he was curious and Edie obviously needed to talk.

'I know, and Mum is the best. Actually, I'm happy for her that she and Dad split up – now. I'm so happy she's getting out and trying all these things here in Italy. But she's put a lot of stuff on the line for me – and for Purcell. What if I do badly?'

'Then it wasn't for you and you change schools. Your mum will understand.'

She winced. 'But Dad won't. He'll blame her.'

The sinking feeling in Nick's stomach was nauseating. He told himself sternly that Edie's situation was different from what he'd experienced, but the feeling lingered.

'Edie?' They looked up to find Lou standing in the doorway, a frown on her face. 'Sweetie, if you're worried about something, you need to tell me.' She glanced at him. He met her disapproving gaze with a little frown, but inclined his head and closed his violin case. It couldn't be clearer. They'd shared one illadvised kiss. But it changed nothing. He was still just Edie's teacher and she expected him to maintain professional distance from her daughter. He was annoyed that it stung.

'I have to go anyway.' He glanced at Edie.

'Thanks, Mr Romano.'

He risked a glance at Lou. It was clear she had words for him – words she wouldn't say in front of Edie.

13

She knocked on his door before dinner. He glanced from her dark expression to the empty corridor behind her. 'You'd better come in.'

'I'm not going to ravish you.'

His eyes zeroed in on her mouth and he wasn't so sure he could say the same. Even fired up and brittle with emotion, she was too much for his senses. 'That wasn't what I was worried about. Come in and you can criticise me with more volume.'

Her shoulders drooped. 'How do you do that?' she said and followed him inside. He closed the door, leaving it open a crack out of some screwed sense of propriety.

'Do what?'

'Everything people throw at you; you just take it.'

He swallowed. 'What else am I supposed to do?'

'Defend yourself?'

'I will, when you're ready to listen.'

She crossed her arms over her chest. 'I'm one of your students now? Emotionally immature?'

'No,' he said softly. 'You're human.'

She shoved his shoulder and it was still better than her not touching him. 'And you're superhuman?'

'You know I'm not. I just know when to be detached.'

'Like when you kiss someone and then avoid them? That detached?' She nudged him again and this time he grabbed her hand, but she pulled it back immediately.

'Which issue are we addressing first? The kiss?'

'Didn't you get the email with the agenda?' she asked, her hand on her hip.

He tried very hard not to smile. He'd missed the cutting humour. Had it only been a day and a half? 'Sorry, I missed it. I've been avoiding you.'

Her reproachful look didn't land well because she knew he was joking and he knew she knew. 'But seriously, that conversation with Edie didn't sound like you being detached. It sounded like you getting personally involved.'

And she clearly didn't want him personally involved. 'She wanted advice. I tried to stay out of your business because I know she's fine.' He said the last sentence with his head ducked to catch her eye.

'How much has she told you, about the divorce?'

'Not much,' he reassured her. 'I know the timescale because her practice patterns obviously changed. And I know she used her music to cope. But that was the first time she's told me anything so personal.'

'Is she scared of going to Purcell?' she asked all of a sudden, her voice small.

'I thought you didn't want me getting involved?'

'I don't know what I want. Give me a break.'

He smiled. 'She would tell you if she didn't want to go to Purcell.'

'Do you think she should go?'

'I think you should trust your instincts.'

She scowled at him. 'I'm allowed to ask for a professional opinion.'

He hesitated. The opinion he wanted to give her was to get her ex out of her mind, but he could imagine how that would go down. And it certainly wasn't professional.

'She's certainly good enough – she got in, so that's not in question. She's self-aware. She works hard. She's got more emotional resources than I had at her age, but that's not saying much.' He trailed off, but it wasn't enough to prevent the curious light in Lou's eyes. 'She's worried about you,' he deflected, feeling a little guilty.

'Isn't everyone?' she grumbled. 'Unhinged Louise hasn't got her shit together,' she parroted.

Nick grimaced. He grasped her shoulders and, when she still didn't look up at him, he brushed his thumbs along her jaw. 'No one has their shit together.'

She blinked. 'That's a new one. I just can't decide if it's a platitude.'

'Trust me, it's the truth,' he said grimly.

'Are you implying that the impeccably dressed and very talented Mr Romano does not have his shit together?' she asked quietly.

'That's exactly what I'm saying.'

'And are you going to back that up with evidence or do you think I'm a gullible nitwit?'

The twinkle in her eye told him she'd trapped him on purpose. Something felt tingly and warm inside him. It wasn't how he'd expected he'd feel to be forced to divulge things about himself he rarely told anyone. 'You do realise this is a personal conversation, Mrs... oops. Sorry.'

She smiled faintly. 'Mrs Oops-Sorry realises this is a personal conversation and is suitably chastised. Now spit it out, Mr Artistic Temperament, or I will think you're patronising me.'

He ploughed ahead before he could overthink. 'I dated a woman because she understood nothing about music, and then I broke up with her again six years later for the same reason,' he admitted flatly.

She cocked her head. 'Immature.' She nodded. 'And both of them extremely poor reasons. Zero marks for self-awareness.'

His lips twitched. 'Playing a difficult piece on the violin gives me a huge amount of satisfaction – borderline egotistical pride.' He paused. His heart was suddenly racing. Why...? How had he managed to bring this up? 'But I'm too scared to play in front of an audience.'

She picked up on his wobbly mood and struggled for words. Was she going to ask? Of course she would. Then he could shock her with just how little shit he had together and how wrong she had been to think he was worth her attention.

'That's...' She took a deep breath and studied him until it made him uncomfortable. 'That's very sad,' she said evenly. 'But if it's right for you, then screw whoever made you feel bad about it.'

He sucked in a breath as an unexpectedly sharp emotion twisted inside him. He took a step towards her. 'Most disturbingly, my professional detachment is lying in pieces and I don't know how I broke it.' He reached up and tucked her hair over her shoulder.

'Who needs professional detachment?' she asked, her voice soft.

'We do,' he said. 'You do. I understand this is not an easy time for you. Kissing you wasn't the best thing I could have done.'

She sighed and sagged against the wall. 'Between the two of us, there's a lot of crap still sloshing around.'

He winced. 'That's... a revolting way of putting it.'

'I'm sorry I was angry with you. You didn't deserve it. I appreciate everything you've done for Edie and I can't quite imagine next year when you won't be her teacher any more. I hoped we'd be... friends still. It must be... music camp or something.'

'Or something,' he mumbled.

'How can you see all this so clearly?' she continued. 'I was angry and rude, but you knew it was my fault and not yours.'

'It wasn't your fault. And I don't see things clearly. I just know how murky our motivations can be.'

'Including our motivations for kissing each other?'

He studied her with a grim smile. 'Do we really want to examine our motivations?'

She smiled back, a little reticent, but warm. He wished things were different, but what 'different' would look like he didn't dare imagine. 'You don't want to admit to...' she leaned close and opened her mouth '... animal lust.'

He snorted. 'It's not really my style.'

She challenged him with a look. 'I was there. You almost consumed my face.' She kept watching him as his neck and cheeks heated. 'You're blushing.'

'I didn't intend to consume your face.'

'Well, that's what happened.'

He swallowed. 'Do I need to apologise?'

'I'm screwing with you, Nick. I haven't enjoyed a make-out session like that for twenty years. I mean, we probably shouldn't do it again, but... wow. If nothing else, a girl likes to know she's still got it.'

He blushed more deeply. Had he really kissed her so madly? He winced inwardly to realise it was just as bad in his memory as in hers – or good, depending on your definition.

'I've been trying not to think about it,' he grumbled.

'Your mother doesn't like me any more,' she said with a disgruntled frown. 'She wasn't actually trying to set us up on the terrace, I'm assuming. Or did she have me in mind for a daughter-in-law, until I gave her the impression I regretted kissing you?'

'You told her you regretted kissing me?'

'No, but that's the impression she got.'

He hesitated. 'Did you regret it?'

'You first,' she said drily. 'I'm not going to go out on a limb when you're the one who ran off and left me to deal with the witness.'

He chuckled. They were all wrong together – an absolute mess. And yet... 'I would do it again right now if there weren't a whole music camp outside that door.'

'Maybe we can just hug. That's a friendly thing to do, right?' she asked hopefully.

Aiming for reproachful, he failed miserably and ended up giving her an odd lopsided smile. It was just a hug, but his chest tightened and breathing became more difficult. 'Are you sure we should risk it?'

She went for an innocent look, but her cheeky smile derailed the attempt. 'Or I could kiss your cheek, if a hug doesn't do it for you?'

He shook his head. 'That was hot, when you did that,' he said, his voice embarrassingly rough.

'It was not,' she insisted.

'Don't make me prove it to you.' She grinned and he slammed his mouth shut. 'You're driving me crazy, Lou.'

Her smile dropped to rueful. 'I know, Nick. But I really need a hug.'

He wrapped his arms around her. She tucked her head into his neck. They'd worked out how to do it since that awkward clash of arms in the chapel.

There was no way he could step back, now. He was involved. The only question was how much she wanted him to be involved and how far he was prepared to trust her.

* * *

The days that week held a certain routine – a magical routine that involved daily glimpses of the lake and its lush palms and twisted pines and arriving home to the peace of the olive grove and the secluded convent.

Nick placed a cappuccino in front of her every morning and each time it was harder to keep her voice steady as she thanked him. She tried to keep her eyes off him but, judging by the number of times he caught her and gave her a little self-conscious smile, she wasn't doing a good job. Greta's worried looks suggested the same.

Lou and Helene's photography course took place in constant rain, but Lou figured there wasn't much lost because she struggled enough with composition without expecting to learn the intricacies of light. The main lesson she took away from the course was that you couldn't capture the lake in a photo. A photo could be amazing – there were enough craggy castles and dramatic rock faces to light up any old camera – but it couldn't do the lake justice. She was happier just gazing at the view than she was behind a camera, seeing objects as subjects rather than something real.

Helene had managed an amazing shot of a magnificent crested bird landing on the water with rock faces at the edge of focus in the background. Lou had only shown her photos to Edie and they'd enjoyed a good laugh at the out-takes and snuggled together and chatted afterwards.

Lou considered the glass-bead workshop a raging success,

because she'd held a blowtorch and not set anything on fire that wasn't supposed to be set on fire. Her beads were wonky, to put it mildly, but it didn't matter so much. She'd made a simple necklace with a large pulled pendant and four small beads separated by knots. She hoped Edie would like it. But Lou had hated the stress of working with hot molten glass and would be happy never to do it again.

She was glad Edie's eyes lit up when she saw the necklace and marvelled that Lou had made it herself – not for her own sake, but because Edie was looking tired. She would have been angry with Nick for creating such a punishing schedule, except that he looked tired, too. Mrs Winkelmann was going loudly to bed every night right after dinner at eight-thirty, announcing that this was always the toughest part of the camp. Miss Hwang looked ready to blow away on the breeze.

Helene made a very fine satchel at their leatherwork workshop on the Friday, but proclaimed it wouldn't do for her husband, as he needed a very expensive one. Lou thought it had been expensive enough, considering the price of the course. She had managed a small shoulder bag after accidentally shearing off a corner of her piece while she'd been distracted by the thought that she was working with the skin of a cow like the peaceful ones whose milk gave her cheese.

Saturday was a day off from rehearsal, for sightseeing. Months ago, when she'd planned the day with Nick, she'd been happy with the early departure to see the sanctuary of Madonna della Corona in the morning sunlight, but she hadn't foreseen how sluggish the group would be.

She sneaked into the kitchen early with a reusable coffee cup she'd picked up the day before, determined to make Nick a coffee for the minibus, since he usually looked as if he wanted to inject his morning coffee sludge rather than just drinking it, and they had to take their breakfast rolls with them. She explained her purpose as breezily as possible to Greta and did her best to ignore the look in her eye.

She was unreasonably disappointed when she discovered he was driving a second minibus to save the cost of hiring a larger coach for the whole group for the day. They separated the kids into the two buses and he talked at length to his uncle. Lou had plenty of time to notice his tired pallor and the button that he'd forgotten to close on his usually crisp shirt. But she didn't have long, after his uncle strode back to the larger minibus, to press the coffee cup into his hand, and certainly not long enough to enjoy his surprised smile and murmured thanks.

What should have been a majestic approach on foot to the stunning pilgrim church of Madonna della Corona became a grumbling shuffle of teenagers. Lou wondered if that was the collective noun for teenagers: a shuffle. But they summoned enough energy to take selfies when the basilica came into view, high up on a cliff, perched precariously under an overhang, its rose window and spire a part of the breathtaking landscape.

In the morning sunlight, it looked like something out of a fantasy. The interior was similarly unexpected, built into the rock and extending out from it. But the poor kids were so tired from the trudge up that Nick phoned his uncle to collect them from a nearer point for the way back, heading down early himself to collect the other bus.

The guided tour through the gardens of the Isola del Garda, with its lemon trees, olives, pears and summer flowers, was beautiful, but exhausting in the muggy heat. When they returned to Malcesine for the tour of the castle, Nick took pity on them and dropped some of the kids at the beach if they preferred, while Lou and Mrs Winkelmann supervised the group castle tour.

Edie stayed close throughout the day, which Lou enjoyed, but she noticed the change in her usually outgoing and energetic daughter.

'Everyone seems very tired,' Lou commented as they roamed the battlements of the castle, staring across at the lake or over the winding terracotta streets.

'It's the nature of it, I'm afraid,' Mrs Winkelmann said with a bob of her head. 'A bit of pressure at this stage and we'll pull together in time for the competition.'

Lou watched Edie's face carefully, noting the twitch of her brow. 'Perhaps everyone needs a full day off tomorrow, instead of just the afternoon,' Lou mused aloud.

Mrs Winkelmann waved her hand dismissively. 'Tomorrow's rehearsal will be the most valuable. You have to push through it.'

Lou couldn't help remembering Nick's comment that all musicians were masochists. 'But surely the kids will need some extra energy for Monday.' She was learning that saying the maestro's name wasn't a good idea.

'The kids have plenty of energy,' Mrs Winkelmann replied, incongruously. Lou frowned at her. 'It's Mr Romano who is lacking energy.'

'What?'

'The orchestra takes its cues from him, especially after more than two weeks of intense rehearsal. The kids are behaving like this because he's stressed, but it will be to their benefit in the long run. The maestro won't tolerate mistakes, so he has to put the pressure on now.'

Lou's stomach churned. She ushered Edie to the crenellated wall and changed the subject, pointing out the birds of prey swooping down from the mountain slopes and enjoying the swirling air above the lake.

'Are you worried about Maestro Eckert?' Lou asked Edie in a low voice.

Edie wrapped her arms around herself and her face contorted with a variety of emotions. 'I don't know,' she said eventually. 'I don't mind being challenged to play a piece perfectly. And if he's mean, then at least I know we don't deserve it.'

Lou swallowed. 'He'd better not be mean.'

Edie eyed her. 'Conductors can be mean, Mum. It's going to be worse at Purcell.'

She clenched her jaw. 'You're kids.'

Edie turned to her, her brow furrowed, but her eyes clear. 'We're some of the best musicians in the UK, as well as kids. It's an important experience. And, like I said, if he's mean, we'll know it's him, not us.'

Lou drew back and studied her daughter. In only eleven years, Edie had managed to surpass her mother in self-confidence. Given the poor start in life Lou had given her, she was flummoxed that she'd turned out so well. 'How can you possibly have so much confidence?' Perhaps confidence decreased with age. At least that would give Lou an excuse.

'Because Mr Romano isn't mean. Even when we make the same mistake over and over again, even when we're not trying hard enough or when we forget what he's just said, he understands.'

'It's not good to be too lenient.' Lou hadn't realised Mrs Winkelmann was still nearby. Lou clenched her teeth, wanting to defend Nick, to defend Edie, but what could she say, the untalented parent?

Edie wrinkled her nose. 'Mr Romano is not lenient.'

Mrs Winkelmann gave an affirming little nod. 'For such a young man, he does seem to be a remarkable conductor. I only hope it's enough for the competition.'

'You're going to do marvellously in the competition. No matter what place you come, you're going to make the whole country proud,' Lou insisted stubbornly. But Edie and Mrs Winkelmann exchanged an indulgent look.

'Thanks, Mum.' Edie smiled.

14

The convent was eerily quiet. There was no bustle coming from the kitchen, no slap of slippers on the flagstones, no beeping phones or grumbling teenagers. Just the heavy shadow of the maestro – a man who hadn't even turned up yet.

Lou had to get out. If she'd understood better, she would have booked a workshop for that day, instead of assuming she'd be busy helping. As it was, she could barely concentrate on her book and all she wanted to do was give Nick a hug. She made do with a walk.

She pulled on her trainers and tiptoed past the chapel, trying not to listen for the squeak of frustrated violin bows or Nick's clipped tones. She slipped through the door in the wall and stopped, struck afresh by the view, which, after two and a half weeks, should have been normal. She wasn't sure she'd ever think of the lake as anything other than magical.

Not sure which direction to take, she peered at the dirt paths heading invitingly off into nowhere, but didn't quite have the courage to just take one of them. A rustle from behind her made her look up from the maps app on her phone to see Greta emerging through the door, swishing in her outdoor gear.

'Oh, hello, Lou.'

'Hi,' she responded warily. 'Are you off somewhere?' It looked as though Greta regretted her question just as much as she did.

She eventually nodded. 'I'm going to collect mushrooms.'

'From the market?' Lou asked. Or from a dealer on a street corner somewhere? She tried not to smile at the image of Greta making a clandestine rendezvous for magic mushrooms.

Greta gave her a tolerant look. 'No, from the forest! Where do you think mushrooms come from?'

Lou had to admit – only to herself – that she'd never thought about where mushrooms came from, beyond Sainsbury's.

'Can I come?' The question even surprised Lou.

'If you like.'

It wasn't the most enthusiastic invitation, but Lou was suddenly burning to collect a wild mushroom. They hopped into Greta's Fiat and, half an hour later, pulled into a gravel parking space near the entrance to a dark pine forest. Lou breathed in deeply as they got out of the car. The air was heavy with moisture and earth.

Greta propped her backpack on her knee by the start of the forest trail and organised the contents. Lou watched with curiosity, but she recognised that Greta hadn't got over her funk yet, so Lou kept her distance.

'Hold this,' Greta said and handed her a reed basket.

'Are we going to visit Grandma?' Lou clamped her lips together at Greta's unimpressed look. She was supposed to be giving up the ill-targeted jokes.

Greta pulled out a knife and Lou took an involuntary step back. Greta looked up with a tolerant smile. 'It's not for bears – or wolves.'

'I didn't think so,' Lou insisted, pretending she wasn't worried by the sight of Greta wielding a knife.

Greta chuckled and headed for the trail. Once they'd gone a few hundred metres in, she swerved off the trail and bent down with a definite 'Hmmmm', gently poking in the leaf litter with a stick. Lou approached, but Greta held up a hand to stop her.

'Watch your step.'

Looking down, Lou noticed the scattered brown caps of enormous mushrooms. 'Wow!' Her mind travelled to the numerous Italian dishes she'd snickered at for the word 'funghi' and then wholeheartedly enjoyed – preferably with cream and garlic. 'They look tasty, even on the forest floor.'

'Boleto dorato. These ones are passable, but not the best. I think we'll leave them for now. I'm only allowed to collect two kilograms and I'm hoping for porcini, or some finferli.'

'Two kilograms? That sounds like a lot.'

'It won't be enough to cook everyone mushroom risotto.'

Lou smiled. 'If I get mushroom risotto, then I'm glad I came!'

Greta held up the knife. 'You might have to help.'

Lou held up the basket. 'I am helping!'

Greta gave her a little nod, which Lou took as a sign she was thawing. She followed Nick's mum further through the woods.

'There are some!' Lou pointed and Greta bent to look at them. Instead of big brown caps, these were delicate and white, almost lilac.

Greta shook her head. 'Also, not what we're looking for.'

'I'm assuming these aren't either,' Lou said, inspecting some flashy red ones with white spots. Even Lou got the impression those would be poisonous.

'Definitely not!'

'I had no idea there were so many mushrooms in the forest,' Lou said as she tramped after Greta, feeling the moisture seep into her trainers and eying Greta's hiking boots jealously. The sun broke through the canopy of pines and the taste of the air and touch of the sunshine made Lou smile.

Greta's eventual shout of, 'Aha!' was the first success of the morning. Greta took her knife and sliced through the bottom of a mushroom the size of her hand. It was brown on top with a curving, fat stalk. 'A porcino! I hope we find some more, but we might be too late. The rainy week means a lot of people will have been through here, looking. And it's early in the season. We don't get many mushrooms until the autumn.'

She brushed off her booty and handed it to Lou, to put the sticky thing into the basket. It didn't remain lonely for long. Greta soon pulled up a few more porcini and found a cluster of the yellowish ones she called finferli that made Lou's mouth water.

'What are they in English?'

'I've no idea. I never went foraging in London. I'll look it up later.'

The basket was about half full before Greta asked if Lou wanted to wield the knife. She showed her how to cut the mushroom at the base and it required a surprisingly strong, steady hand. Happy with two as her own booty, Lou handed the knife back and enjoyed trailing after Greta in the dappled sunshine.

'You've been very quiet,' Greta commented as she harvested another cluster of finferli.

'I thought you didn't want me to talk.'

'Why not?'

'Oh, I don't know, because you've been giving me the evil eye all week?'

'I don't have an evil eye,' Greta insisted.

'There are always times in our life for self-discovery,' Lou muttered.

Greta stopped and straightened. When she turned back to

Lou, she had a stern expression on her face, but it didn't stop the twinkle in her eye. 'Like the day you catch your adult son in a compromising position?'

Lou clamped her lips together. 'It wasn't that compromising. What does that mean anyway? Compromise what? His character? I'm ordinary and talentless, but I'm not that bad!'

Greta drew back and studied her. She shook her head slightly and turned to continue their ramble through the woods. 'Come on,' she said.

Lou followed, no longer thinking about mushrooms. 'I don't want to talk about Nick, you know,' she said.

'Okay,' Greta replied, her eyes combing the undergrowth once more.

'I mean, he's wonderful and you got it completely wrong when you thought I regretted kissing him.' Only the tiniest pause indicated Greta had heard, but Lou was requiring less and less encouragement as she tramped after her. 'But I know how much he beat himself up about his girlfriend – Naomi, was that her name? It would be so much worse with me. I suppose it's camp, and everything's a bit intense and it was a great kiss – oh my God, was it a great kiss. But I'm five years older than him, and I have a kid and sometimes I think of my ex-husband at the worst times.

'Even if I was some great talent at something, or understood something about this pressure, this obsession, I'm still a bit... broken, you know? I haven't really been... right for a long time and I just sort of find the little things that keep me going and for a while I'll do okay. But even Edie worries about me and she's only eleven. Nick doesn't want this kind of shit and I don't know if I can shove it away for long enough to have some kind of crazy fling – not that anything is possible in the convent full of teenagers and my daughter and his... you...'

The sudden lump in her throat finally achieved what presence of mind should have much earlier. Lou stopped talking in order to swallow the mortification. 'Do you think you can forget the inappropriate parts of that?' she asked, her voice oddly high-pitched.

When she looked up, Greta was facing her with a matter-of-fact expression, a huge mushroom in one hand and the knife in the other.

'Can you hold out the basket?' she asked and Lou shook herself into action. When the mushroom was stowed, they continued on.

'Are you angry with me?' Lou asked, figuring she no longer had anything to lose.

'No, pet,' Greta replied immediately. 'But I know better than to think anything I have to say will make a difference.'

'It might make me feel a bit less embarrassed,' Lou said.

When Greta laughed, Lou joined her with relief. 'You deal very well with embarrassment.'

She opened her mouth to disagree, but closed it again, thinking. 'I suppose that's true if your measure is Nick.'

Greta laughed again. 'He is very sensitive, but of course I don't have to tell you that. Has he told you about his schooling?'

'Not much. Sometimes I think I'm shaking the information out of him against his will.' She grimaced. It pinched to think how little he'd told her. She was always too busy bantering away her inadequacies. 'Is the competition being held at his old school?'

Greta nodded slowly. 'I probably shouldn't say too much. Mothers never have a reliable memory about their children's most difficult moments.'

Lou jerked her head up to stare. She thought back to the Easter concert. What had it been like for Greta to parent a prodigious musician? When had she and Nick's father divorced?

Greta patted the hand that was clutching the handle of the basket. 'You'll find your way,' she said gently.

'I have a terrible sense of direction.'

'It's because you're still in the valley. Climb the mountain and you'll find your path.' She set off again before Lou could decide if that was just a really catchy platitude or some deep truth she could aspire to grasp. The valley analogy struck a chord. The years after Edie was born felt like a dangerous ravine and she still wasn't sure how she'd crawled back out of it. And Phil? He was a wide valley between two mountains where the sun never penetrated. She'd been lost in that valley for a long time, staring up at mountains that had always looked impossible to climb.

She couldn't help but remember Nick telling her she could make it to the top if she wanted to. But he was part of this magical place where the ocean got lost in the mountains and delicious dinners grew spontaneously out of the forest floor.

When the basket was full, Greta led Lou back to the car. It was a mystery to Lou how she knew the right way among the narrow, criss-crossing paths. Lou's feet were sore and she had no idea how far they'd walked.

It was past lunchtime, but Greta assured her the cook had saved food for them. Lou wondered if Edie had worried, but she was probably happily chatting to Meg and enjoying the adrenaline of the last rehearsal before the arrival of the maestro.

Lou's stomach rumbled loudly as Greta's little Fiat turned up the driveway to the convent. 'It's the mushrooms. They're making me hungry,' she joked.

'You'll have to wait until tonight for those,' Greta warned her. She held out her little tin of sweets. Lou reached for one without thinking, but hesitated when the tangy scent reminded her of the last time she'd tried one. 'It's a different flavour this time,' Greta prompted, shaking the tin.

'Oh, in that case...' Lou grabbed one and popped it into her mouth – and grimaced. 'There are two varieties of foul sweets in Italy? What flavour is this one supposed to be?'

'Propoli. Er, it's kind of like beeswax.'

Lou gagged, squeezing her eyes shut as she crunched the hard sweet.

When they pulled into a spot, there was an unfamiliar car parked by the olive grove. Lou inspected it curiously, but the hire car company sticker didn't answer her questions. Had the maestro arrived a day early? Helene would be beside herself! Nick, too, on the opposite end of the scale.

But when they entered the cloister, Lou realised her mistake. She froze, basket of enormous mushrooms on her arm, and stared at Edie's pinched expression. A shower of dread flowed through her body. Her nose itched. Her mouth was dry. Her heart pounded and her thoughts scrambled. This was not good.

Her gaze flitted to Nick, standing to the side, speaking to the new arrivals. He noticed her glance and cocked his head slightly, concerned.

'I'm sure we'll work something out,' he said stiltedly.

No... Lou didn't want to work anything out. She wanted to pack them into the hired SUV and send them back down the mountain. She wanted to scream like the wronged woman she was, insisting they weren't welcome to intrude on her little mountain retreat unannounced. It was arrogant and rude to turn up suddenly and they had no right to make Nick – and Greta – work around their sudden arrival. What did they expect? Did he want to stay?

Lou shivered in distaste, realising belatedly what a haven the convent had become, with Edie and Nick and Helene and even Greta when she'd still been sporting her evil eye. How dare he take this from her?

She struggled to force her feet forward. Greta was looking at her curiously. It must have been obvious from her expression who the new arrivals were, because Greta stepped forward and introduced herself as the stand-in manager of the convent and asked what exactly could she do for them.

Lou zoned out of the awkward introductions.

'I'm terribly sorry it's last minute, but our plans changed and, as soon as we were able, I wanted to come and see Edie.'

He always sounded so reasonable. Even Greta was smiling graciously, despite the inconvenience. He pretended to be a doting father and suddenly any amount of rudeness was forgiven. Well, it didn't work on Lou. Snapped out of her dread by his appalling charm, she bustled forward.

'Ah, there you are, Lou,' he said in that smooth, easy-listening voice. She drew herself up for the accustomed cheek-kiss that was equally unpleasant for both of them.

Her lips contorted into a fake smile. 'Hello, Phil.'

15

'Psst!'

Nick jumped at the whisper right in his ear and whirled, dropping several bedsheets in the process.

'Fuck, I'm sorry,' Lou groaned when she saw what had happened. They both ducked to retrieve the sheets and nearly bumped heads. The only other time he'd heard that word on her lips, she'd been wobbling for her life on a paddleboard. He wondered if it was an indication of her mental state.

'Give me the sheets,' she said briskly, flinging her hair back from her face.

'I can do it,' he said evenly.

'There's no way I'm going to let you make their beds, you masochistic moron, so give me the sheets.'

The curse word had definitely been an indication of her mental state. 'You're going to make their beds? Who's the masochist now?'

'I've made his bloody bed enough times in my bloody life!' she hissed.

'Exactly, so let me do it.'

'No way! I brought them here. Let me fix it!' She grabbed for the sheets, but he refused to release them. When she tugged harder, he stepped forward to maintain balance and found himself much closer to her. It gave him an idea – one he probably shouldn't have had. He dropped the sheets, grabbed her upper arms and steered her into the big linen cupboard, pulling the door to behind him and flicking on the light.

Once she recovered from her surprise, she started to splutter some kind of protest, but it fizzled quickly. Nick stilled, feeling helpless and frustrated as he watched the emotions flicker across her face. She didn't want him involved, but he couldn't stand by and watch her put herself down. Ever since the handsome and unnecessarily charming Phil Saunders had shown up, the soul had somehow been sucked out of the convent.

'It's not your fault!' he said, struggling to keep his tone even.

'He's my ex-husband!'

Nick threw up a hand. 'Exactly! He probably divorced you because he didn't want to be responsible to you any more – the smarmy prick – but somehow you're still responsible for him? It's classic Lou! Absolutely classic!'

Her jaw clenched and his stomach sank with the suspicion that he'd made her feel worse. How else was he supposed to get through to her? As they stood in the linen cupboard staring at each other, sucking in agitated breaths, one other way came to mind. He swallowed.

'That was unnecessary,' she said through gritted teeth.

'If it wasn't necessary, I wouldn't have bloody well said it! None of us are judging you based on his behaviour! Only you! You're your own harshest critic and I hate it!'

She narrowed her eyes and folded her arms across her chest. 'You don't have to hang around.'

'I want to hang around.' He paused for emphasis. 'I want to

hang around you!' His heart pounded with the thrill of blurting out the truth. He got on a bit of a roll. 'I want to walk along the lake holding your hand and listening to you talk. I want to take you out to dinner and feed you olives and give you a goodnight kiss that will keep you awake for hours thinking about me!'

Why was he saying all this out loud? He was the last man she'd want to fall at her feet in awkward devotion. He'd gone way too far, but seeing Phil had set something off inside him. She'd been married to the guy – for a long time. She would have looked gorgeous on his arm as he charmed and networked his way around London being the big man he obviously thought he was. At one stage, she must have been in love with him, the confident, superior jerk.

He winced at his own thoughts. Just because her ex-husband reminded him of the boys from school who'd made his life hell, didn't mean he could take it out on Lou.

'I don't like olives,' she muttered, staring at him.

Her words brought the tension inside him crashing down and he burst out laughing – wry, hopeless laughter. He grasped her shoulders and pulled her to him, feeling everything else drain away as her arms came around him and her head tucked into his neck – she didn't fit under his chin.

'Let me make the damn bed, Lou,' he whispered, pressing a kiss to her forehead. 'He's got no rights to you any more and you have no responsibility to him – especially if he understands so little about you that he thinks you're ordinary!'

'But you're busy and stressed and you don't deserve my—'

'"Your" what? He's not "your" anything, right?'

She pulled back to stare at him in dismay. He shook his head slowly and sighed. He smoothed her hair back, smiling bleakly at the realisation that he finally had his hands in her luxurious hair, as he'd always wanted.

He just wished she would stop reducing herself to being that idiot's ex-wife.

'Oh, Nick,' she sighed, her forehead falling to his chest.

'I'm sorry to be overbearing,' he said softly. 'I do understand this must be hard for you.'

Her fist tightened in his shirt, sending pleasant shots of emotion along his spine. 'Don't apologise,' she whispered.

'I won't if you won't.'

He felt her chuckle under his hands splayed on her back. She relaxed slowly into him and his eyes drifted closed. He hadn't been in any state for further emotional shocks. He was about to deliver his poor orchestra into the hands of a professional conductor. Without firm instructions from the maestro, he'd second-guessed himself all week, worried his interpretation would differ and that the kids would end up in the firing line, then hearing his old maestro telling him a musician needed to be able to take anything the conductor threw at them.

And then Phil had shown up, laying bare the odd connection he'd felt to Lou from that moment early in the year when he'd finally looked up and seen her for herself. He'd been leaning on her without realising it, without having the right to. She shouldn't have to prop up him or dodgy Phil.

But here she was again, seeping into his bloodstream with her soft hair and warm scent, melting into his arms with some power he hadn't realised existed. And he let it all go – the fear, the tension, the lonely pressure. She snuggled closer with a sigh and he swayed on his feet, with tiredness and contentment.

He made the mistake of leaning back – or was his mistake forgetting it was a door behind him and not a wall? Either way, one moment they were locked in a profound embrace and the next they were flying through the door of the linen cupboard and plummeting towards the cold pavers of the hallway.

He threw one hand around her waist and flailed with the other to break their fall. He landed heavily on his backside. She came down on top of him and, if it hadn't been for the stabbing pain in his posterior, he might have quite enjoyed the feeling of her sprawled on top of him, her knees on either side of his hips and her hair filling his vision.

'What the...?'

She scrambled off him and hauled herself to her feet. He just sat there and blinked for a moment while she swept her hair out of her face and smoothed her clothes – and her expression. When he glanced up to see Mr Smug Bastard and his dainty girl-friend, he had the mad urge to drag Lou back and kiss her sense-less, but that was a minefield of motivations he didn't care to examine, so he just retrieved the dropped sheets and stood.

'We were getting you some sheets,' Lou said, her voice breezy and empty.

'Just what we were coming in search of,' Phil said in that patronising tone that he dressed up as friendliness. 'Although I didn't expect them to... fall out of the cupboard.'

Nick hated that she blushed, but he hadn't expected any other reaction. She didn't want him to be involved. He didn't want to feel involved.

'Let me take them, darling.' The girlfriend – Ginny? Penny? He couldn't remember – took the sheets while Nick was still wondering who she was calling darling. 'We can sort the beds. I feel so terrible about intruding without notice.'

'Yes, uh, sorry for the trouble.'

Nick noticed Phil wasn't looking at Lou when he said it. He wanted the apology for her, not himself. He managed some sort of smile. 'Well, goodnight. You know where I am if you need anything.'

Phil took one more look at Lou; something sharp in his gaze made Nick shuffle closer. But Phil glanced curiously between them and Lou sidled away again awkwardly.

'Goodnight, then,' Phil said, a hundred hints in his voice – or in Nick's imagination.

Nick glanced at Lou, but she didn't look at him as she drifted slowly in the direction of her room. But when Phil and his girlfriend disappeared around the corner, she turned back suddenly. The cheeky smile on her face was the Lou he'd missed. He shouldn't have been so happy to see her smile, but everything inside him lifted.

She approached with swift steps and stopped in front of him. 'I don't like olives,' she repeated steadily. After the slightest hesitation, she continued, her voice breathy. 'But the rest of it sounds pretty good to me.'

She stood looking at him for a long moment while he grasped her meaning and his blood began to flow with heat. He licked his lips, struggling for a reply.

'Ask me some time?' she asked in a small voice, one corner of her mouth kicked up in an enchanting smile.

He cleared his throat. 'Definitely,' he said.

* * *

Why hadn't she kissed him? Of all the thoughts to be running through her head the day after Phil's arrival, she was inordinately pleased that that one was dominant. A cuddle with Nick in the linen cupboard had been exactly what she'd needed to restore that thing that Phil scared off whenever she saw him – her self-respect. But the cuddle would have been much better if she'd planted a kiss on Nick before they'd fallen through the door.

'Are you all right, Mum?' Edie asked and Lou realised she must have been smiling into her coffee again – her lovely frothy cappuccino, which was going down a treat while Phil and Winny were sipping the stuff out of the pot.

'I'm great, sweetheart. Are you all ready for this morning?' She gave Edie a squeeze.

'What's happening this morning?' Phil asked.

'The maestro arrives!' She couldn't help adding sarcastic emphasis to the word 'maestro', but she wasn't worried anyone else would pick up on it.

'I can't believe today's the day!' Helene bustled by, returning to sit with Lou and her odd family when she'd fetched a bowl of cereal.

'Is he staying here?'

'Here?' Helene looked horrified. 'No, he's at a hotel somewhere nearby and will travel here for rehearsal each day.'

Lou gave Phil a look, hoping he'd get the hint that he could do the same, but his gaze hardened and her mood slipped again. What did that look mean? Why had they arrived out of the blue? She'd thought they were on the Canary Islands, or was it Madeira, or the Faroe Islands? Some island she'd had no interest in and didn't want to have any interest in – except that Phil had that weird look in his eye.

'I don't know why he'd want to stay somewhere else. It's beautiful here,' he said with one of his signature smiles. Helene smiled back, but Lou went cold in her stomach. 'What are your plans for the morning, Lou?'

She felt like a deer in the headlights. 'I might take a walk.'

'You don't have any more workshops, Mum?' Edie asked and Lou looked at her roll to hide the blush. Why did Phil's presence suddenly make her embarrassed about her quest?

She shook her head. 'I thought I might be needed more

during this stage of the camp, given the amount of rehearsal you guys are going to be doing.'

'Now we're here, too, Phil was very keen to spend time with Edie. You could take some time for yourself,' Winny suggested. Lou, Phil and Edie all froze at that statement, but she didn't seem to notice. 'You could even take a night to go off exploring.'

She felt the ripple through Edie and it was thankfully enough to snap her out of her self-pity. 'I've seen lots of the lake already. It's so beautiful around here.'

'I feel like we have some catching up to do,' Phil said, that odd look on his face again. 'Would you like to come for a drive with us this morning, Lou?'

She grabbed her coffee for something to do with her mouth other than gaping. No, she would not like to go for a drive with Phil the superior bastard and his girlfriend.

'You go. I'd rather stay local.' Lou pushed up from the table as soon as her coffee was finished, wrapping her roll in a serviette. 'You guys have fun this morning!' she said as she made her escape. She wanted to find where Nick was hiding. But to her displeasure, Phil stood and followed her into the corridor. She turned to face him with her arms across her chest and a less-than-subtle foot-tap.

'Do you have a minute?'

She pursed her lips. Could she pretend she didn't without sounding like the unreasonable one? 'What's on your mind?' she asked, deciding that pretending to be interested would expedite the conversation.

'I just think...'

Lou raised her eyebrows, prompting him and trying not to marvel at the sight of him struggling for words. Her curiosity was unwillingly piqued.

'I think we should talk. There could be some... improvement in our communication... for Edie's sake, of course.'

'Of course,' she sighed. She knew he was always happy to use Edie to get his way.

'But now is obviously not the right time.' It wasn't? When would be a better time for a horrible conversation she didn't want to have? 'Let's go for coffee this afternoon – without Winny.'

The suggestion sat heavily in her stomach like excess acid, but her rational brain insisted this was an adult thing she had to do – for Edie's sake. Managing Phil was unfortunately part of her job description as 'ex-wife'. 'I'm not sure Winny will like that idea.'

'Oh, she'll understand,' he countered immediately.

She will, will she? Lou prised her jaw apart before she cracked a tooth. It was so obvious to Winny that his ex was a loser, she wouldn't worry about a tête-à-tête? 'Fine. We can go to a café in Malcesine.'

'Great. Thanks, Lou.'

Once again, she came out of the exchange feeling like the unreasonable one, the childish one. He kissed her cheek and headed back into the refectory, leaving Lou deflated and in no state to cheer Nick up, as she'd wanted to.

When she looked up, it was to find the subject of her search already in view. Nick stood at the end of the corridor, his arms full of folders, watching her warily. She winced.

'Can I help you with those?' she asked, gesturing to the folders.

'Sure.' He shrugged. She approached and took a couple, not looking at him. 'I'm taking them through to the chapel.'

They walked silently through the cloister, sunlight bursting into the courtyard in an affront to their separate miseries. She dumped the folders next to his and finally looked up. He looked as though he'd barely slept. And yet the concern in his eyes warmed her – and reminded her to get her head out of her own backside, as she'd challenged him to do weeks ago.

He was very close. She could see the little reflection of herself in his glasses. She could feel the warmth of him – or was that just her memory of the night before?

'You know,' she began quietly, enjoying the unruly curl that fell over his forehead when he cocked his head to listen, 'this unresolved sexual tension thing between us is so much better than anything else in my life right now.'

He chuckled and gently extracted the strand of hair she hadn't realised she was worrying, smoothing his fingers through the hair around her face. 'Unresolved, huh?' His lips landed on her forehead and her spine turned to jelly. She clutched his biceps – or were they triceps? – for balance.

'I don't know how we're supposed to... resolve... anything with a bunch of kids around,' she said in mock seriousness.

He groaned something that sounded like her name and finally pulled her close, his lips searching. She opened her mouth in anticipation.

'He's here! He's here!'

Thank God Helene had shrieked instead of rushing into the chapel like a normal person. They both cursed, Nick's choice of word slightly fouler than Lou's. She broke into giggles and pulled away. He gave her a look that suggested he didn't find it quite so funny.

The door to the chapel finally banged open.

'Quick! He's getting out of the car!' Helene waved them forward.

Nick squeezed her hand and she stared at their linked fingers. She hadn't held hands with a man for... quite a long time. It had probably been one of the first signs that Phil had lost interest in her – not that she'd realised it at the time.

Nick tugged, trying to draw her out to greet the maestro. Frowning, annoyed she was thinking of Phil again and wanting more time alone with Nick, she resisted until he dropped her hand.

16

How quickly could she get this over with?

She gave Phil a perfunctory smile as she plonked herself into the seat opposite him. He'd muttered something about giving her the seat with the better view of the lake and she was still trying to interpret his motives.

The afternoon sun was at the 'burning' stage and she was roasting under the light scarf from the Bardolino market, but didn't dare pull it off because she didn't want her shoulders to turn crispy. She'd pulled on her maxi dress, trying to recapture the 'hot mum' feeling but Phil seemed to suck away some part of her, like a personality vampire.

She was also, for the first time, genuinely distracted by the progress of the rehearsal up at the convent. The maestro was the sort of man who would never deign to speak to a lowly parent, but, judging from Nick's crumbling expressions, he was a hard man. Smiling, teasing, fervent Nick had been absent since the moment that morning when she'd come so close to getting a stolen kiss.

But before she could head back up the hill and ask Edie, and hopefully Nick, how the first day had gone, she had to deal with whatever Phil wanted from her.

'So, what needs to improve with my communication? Did you send me an agenda for this meeting? The slides in advance would have been helpful – and the interview questions. You know I'm no good off the cuff.'

'This isn't a confrontation.'

His soft statement still felt like a slap. Was she being oversensitive? Or was that what he would think? Oh, God, he hadn't said a thing and she was already realising the truth of Nick's accusation the night before.

Phil was still in her life – in her head – even though he shouldn't have been.

He continued speaking, something about keeping channels open and maintaining the relationship, since they still shared so much. But Lou was barely listening.

She was horrified. Twelve years of second-guessing herself to avoid his backhanded censure and anticipating his irritation; twelve years of knowing he'd only married her because he'd accidentally knocked her up, and she'd developed a little Phil, like a bizarre kind of abscess, who'd taken over her thinking and given her no hope of rebuilding something of a life without him.

But she still needed to manage his disapproval in situations like this, to keep the peace and make it easier to work together – to keep the bloody communication channels open.

'I just need you to let me in a bit more. I miss the way we used to talk about Edie. I miss Edie. I miss... you,' he finally said, and Lou sat up straight so quickly her trendy metal chair wobbled on the cobblestones.

What the hell did that mean? And what gave him the right to bandy about vague phrases like that after more than a year of awkward coolness? The smarmy prick.

Remembering Nick's description of Phil from the night before turned her tingles into a full-blown rush of indignation. He needed her to let him in? He wanted even more from her when everything she'd given him, every sacrifice she'd made, had never been enough? She couldn't do it. She wouldn't. If he wanted something, he was going to have to get it himself. And if he didn't, it would be his own fault.

She was tempted to cross her arms over her chest, but she didn't want to be on the defensive any more. Instead, she leaned on the table and steepled her fingers and made her opening gambit. 'If you miss Edie, why do you consistently miss her concerts?'

He hesitated. One point to Louise. 'Well... I... It's always been your thing with her.'

She laughed. 'What's your thing with her, then?' Point two to the hot mum.

'Well, she's always so busy with the music.'

'Which I push her into to compensate for my own glaring lack of talent.'

'I wouldn't quite put it that way.' He frowned and sat back in his chair. His even tone sent her scrambling to defend herself, to placate him and prove herself. But she stopped. She stilled and quietly refused to back down.

'You did,' she said with a smile. 'You did put it that way.'

'But the amount she practises, she doesn't have time for anything else!'

'Have you asked her if she wants to do anything else?'

His silence was point three. She hadn't realised scoring points against her ex-husband could be so satisfying.

'Have you offered to spend time with her? Have you asked her what she'd like to do with you?'

'No, but she's a kid. Don't put the responsibility back on her.'

Lou sat back in her chair. 'I'm not putting it on her. I'm putting the responsibility on you. I guarantee you, if you ask her, she will say she wants you to come to her concerts most of all – at least make a gesture of understanding her passion.'

His disgruntled frown felt like another point. 'I'm here now.'

Lou nodded slowly. 'She'll appreciate it at the competition. And you might get an idea of how much satisfaction she gets from her music.'

His shoulders jerked slightly and he took a sip of his coffee with a titter of relief. Was that what she used to look like to him? But she wasn't going to let him off so easily.

'Why are you here?'

His gaze jerked up. Lou tried not to show it in her expression, but her acerbic defiance was hardening into anger. She would like to have been wrong. Actually, no, she was okay with being angry.

'Do I need a reason?'

Her lips thinned at his tone – so light and reasonable, but veiling a threat she would once have heeded without hesitation. 'It depends on whether you have a reason or not. What happened to the Canary Islands?'

'Actually, it was Mykonos.'

'Obviously, I didn't remember and I don't particularly care. Why the change of plans?'

He studied her, as though calculating how much he could get away with. But she was on to him. He sighed suddenly and glanced away. 'I just wasn't sure, you know.'

'I don't know, and I won't know until you tell me what you're talking about.'

'How are we supposed to know we've made the right choices?'

'We don't. But we've made them. All we can do is make more choices.'

He was silent for a long moment, watching her so intently that she would have blushed if it were anyone other than Phil. When was the last time he'd studied her with his full attention?

'I just kept thinking about everything I've given up...' His eyes crinkled in an odd way that Lou found strangely pathetic. His hand snaked across the table towards her and she looked on in horror as his fingers found her knuckles and brushed affectionately over the skin. She pulled her hand back.

'I do that, too, thinking about everything I gave up,' she said. His smile told her he thought he'd won a point. 'Everything I gave up during the years we were married, I mean.'

'What?'

She took a deep breath. 'Do you have any idea how selfish it is to come here and hint vaguely that you regret allowing our marriage to fail, while your girlfriend is off somewhere wondering when you're going to get back, and your ex-wife has worked her butt off to smooth the transition for our daughter?'

'I'm not saying we should get back together.'

She thought he must be able to see the steam coming out of her ears. 'Of course you're not, thank God! You're not mature enough to face the full consequences of any of your decisions or own up to making mistakes!'

'Lou...'

'Yes?'

'Where has all this come from?'

'Does it matter?'

'I suppose I'd hoped for... the old you when we had this conversation.'

Lou nodded. 'I'm pleased to disappoint you.'

'But you should know,' he began and her stomach coiled right up tight again. She should have known Phil wouldn't let her have even that meagre victory. 'A new start doesn't solve anything. I'm pleased you're not clinging to the grief for our marriage and you must know I worried so much about... you... getting...'

'Depressed?' She said the word because it didn't have the same 'gasp-groan' connotations for her as it did for him. She was the one who'd lived it.

'Exactly,' he replied. 'But I don't want to see you get hurt because you're throwing yourself into this trip to ignore the grief.'

She wanted to laugh in his face – or at least smile coldly. But the statement was a bucket of ice-cold water on her spine. Was that what she was doing with her doomed talent search? Was it what she was doing with Nick? She was stricken at the thought. Was she some kind of depressed emotional parasite who was nothing without a male host? She certainly felt that was all she'd been for the twelve years of her marriage.

But she *wasn't* with Nick. And she was under no illusion that anything between them would work for the long-term. And she didn't even really believe the nice things he said about her. The only thing she'd started to believe was that she might not be responsible for Phil's rudeness. And she was bloody well sticking to that.

'Moving on quickly hasn't worked out so well for you?' she asked, managing a flippant tone, even though she could feel her expression was stony.

He hesitated and his lips squashed together in a bloodless grimace. 'I wouldn't compare your workshops with my relationship,' he said smoothly. The smarmy prick.

She sat back, refusing to bite. She might not have her shit together, but she knew she wasn't playing his games any more. 'Are you and Winny having problems?'

His spluttered 'no' provided much more of an answer than he would verbalise. The pinch of sympathy for Winny was new and totally unprompted, and Lou was rather proud of herself. Phil wasn't good at relationships. When she'd been twenty-five (and pregnant), she'd assumed he hadn't settled down by thirty-two because he was so career-driven. She wasn't prepared to defend forty-four-year-old Phil. He was a lousy partner. It hadn't been all her fault. The truth brought a glimmer of relief to light the way ahead.

She didn't want to spend another minute in his presence. It wasn't her job to hear him out now, even though he'd opened his mouth to say something.

'I'm done, Phil,' she muttered, bending to fetch some money out of her handbag.

'What?'

She placed money for the coffee on the table and stood. 'There is no problem with our communication that you can't fix – you. Edie will happily do something with you if *you* ask her – she's generous like that, unlike me. But music is her passion – something I don't even understand, let alone encourage. If you seriously want to feel like family, then you're welcome to – without me. Stay at camp, experience it with her, listen to her and re-establish your relationship, but don't bring me into it. In fact, I'm going to do as Winny suggested and go off on my own for a few days so you can enjoy sole responsibility for our daughter. That's the conversation that you said you wanted – tick.' She continued before he could come up with something to take the wind out of her sails. 'As to the conversation you really wanted, you've got some nerve falling back on me because you're finally discovering a relationship is hard work. I'm glad Winny has more backbone than I ever did. Good luck trying to grow into a functional adult.'

She whirled around to make a dramatic exit, complete with triumph, but her handbag snagged on the chair and she had to turn back to free it. Of course, she couldn't resist a quick glance at his reaction. Seeing Phil lost for words was a reward she'd never thought she'd earn, and the glint of respect caught her by surprise.

* * *

She was robbed of her dramatic exit twice, the second time by the realisation that Phil had driven them down in the hired SUV and she'd just stranded herself in Malcesine. It wasn't the worst place to be stranded with her ruminations.

She brooded along the narrow streets lined with colourful rendered houses, their window boxes full of petunias, and terraces sheltered by vines. She cogitated fiercely through the squares that jumped out suddenly from the tiny lanes. She mulled everything over as she ducked into the salumeria and spent enough on cheese to ensure that she'd never be able to afford a decent satchel.

She bought herself a cheeky pallina of stracciatella gelato and stood under the chestnut tree in the square trying to talk herself into graceful acceptance of the fact that she was going to have to walk all the way up the hill in her sandals while Phil had the air-conditioned hire car. Who was the functional adult now?

The rehearsal would be over by now. She much preferred her thoughts to be up the hill with Edie and Nick. If only her body were up there, too. With a sigh, she pulled out her phone and plotted a route up the hill.

When her maps app suggested a narrow walking trail, the undertaking became less onerous and almost exciting. She left the baking labyrinth of Malcesine behind and headed uphill, following the road at first. She stopped to admire a little shrine, painted brightly with a religious scene, which made the asphalt turning area with big bins into a charming spot to stop and check her map.

She turned on to a road that quickly petered out into a dirt track and the forest closed around her before she could appreciate that it was the blank section of the map on her phone. Her eyes searched reflexively for mushrooms, but she had no hope of identifying the ones she saw and no knife, so she turned her face up and enjoyed the smell of pine and the play of light between the spindly trunks.

She emerged out of the forest again into a field of wild grass that was so pale it was like stepping through a portal to another world. Lou was shocked to see she was nearly back. A wall in the distance marked the boundary of the olive grove by the convent. She was surprised to realise she'd left her pent-up anger somewhere in the forest among the majestic trees and the fresh scent of peace.

She clambered up through the grass, cutting through the field in the direction of the little gate with the stone arch. She'd left the heavy heat and heavy heart of the town behind.

In her blissful clear-headedness, she didn't notice the figure, three or four trees ahead, until the sudden sound of a violin soared over the olive trees and out to the lake. She stopped suddenly. Her skin tingled and she shivered, despite the warmth from the sun and the lake at her back.

He was turned away from her, with only the top of his profile visible above his violin. His hair was curling wildly, shaking with each stroke of the bow. His body lurched with the music, energy rippling through him from the fine tension in his bow arm to the fingers of his left hand, moving furiously over the strings.

He was spectacular. His eyes were closed, his face pinched with concentration. And he serenaded the olive trees with the passion of the virtuoso violinist he could have been.

His performance was both riveting and unbearably intimate. A large part of her wanted to run and leave him alone but watching him brought a flicker of understanding about his obsession.

She didn't recognise the piece he played – a wild melody of lilting quavers and sudden intervals that sounded alive in its own right. Watching the music pour out of him, she guessed he was improvising or had written the piece himself, and she felt humbled by the enormity of his talent.

But he didn't use his talent to excuse his faults or bring others down. He'd given up the chance of personal glory to teach a bunch of kids how to enjoy music. And he thought she was the talented one.

She leaned back against a tree, the gnarled ridges of the trunk anchoring her thoughts in this grove, in this moment, and closed her eyes. Phil's comments didn't matter any more. It didn't matter that she couldn't create beauty from some great talent. She could listen. She could feel.

The music stopped suddenly and she jerked her head up, opening her eyes. She wasn't surprised to meet his gaze. She blushed fiercely, utterly confused about what she should be feeling. What she did feel was privileged, touched and a little bit healed.

He was breathing hard, his chest rising and falling. He raised a hand, swiping the back of it along his forehead, the bow in his hand finally explaining the gesture she'd seen so many times. She didn't know how he was going to react.

She wanted to kiss him... so very badly.

17

Nick waited for the wave of embarrassment to engulf him. Performing in front of an audience always turned him back into the stuttering only-child whose parents argued about him and whose so-called friends were either jealous or derisive.

Lou should fall into the latter category. She was a charming, stunning woman, who didn't share his musical obsession. But she was looking at him with such softness in her eyes that the slight tang of awkwardness was barely discernible. He didn't feel judged. He felt seen. He felt wanted.

He blinked to clear the drips of sweat out of his eyes. God, what had she seen? It had been a particularly wearing day, leading to a particularly energetic release with his violin. He was such a weirdo. And now she knew.

But he couldn't work out if he minded or not. In all the years he'd been with Naomi, she'd never seen him play like that. He'd been horrified just imagining it. But something light, almost the feeling of laughter, was bubbling in his chest in response to Lou's gaze – to her presence. He supposed he didn't mind. The realisation was pleasant – more than pleasant.

He switched his bow to the other hand, dangling both the violin and the bow in one hand while he ran the other along the back of his head, the tension slowly draining out of him.

'You might have to say something so I don't feel embarrassed,' he called out.

She smiled, one of her blinding grins that shot through him with sudden warmth. He grinned back. 'I'm sorry I listened,' she said softly. 'I know you don't like to have an audience.'

His grin faltered, not because his mood dropped, but because it soared. How did she see so much? She listened to him – to what he said and what he couldn't say. He'd never had the guts to tell her the full story, but she grasped enough, she understood on an emotional level. It was exhilarating.

He swallowed. 'I seem to be surprisingly okay about you hearing.'

She released a deep breath and he realised she'd been wary of his reaction. 'I'm glad. Because I couldn't seem to regret listening. It was like... I don't know. It was intimate, like... sex?'

He spluttered and blushed. 'It was not like sex.' But he was laughing too hard to convince her the comparison didn't fly.

'I don't know, it was kind of hot.'

His blush spread and deepened, making him blink again. The warm afternoon wasn't helping. He couldn't help thinking back to that morning's almost-kiss, to the effect she had on him.

'It was not hot,' he insisted.

She gave him a lopsided smile. 'I'm the woman here and I, uh, beg to differ.'

He snorted through a half-laugh, half-gasp and rubbed a hand over his face. 'You're certainly helping me to feel less embarrassed about the music.'

Her smile was cheeky as she slowly stepped closer. He soaked her up with his eyes. She stopped next to him, her shoulder brushing his, and they looked out at the view of the lake through the silver leaves of the olive trees.

'Do you want to tell me about it?'

He gave her a sidelong grin. 'You're good at that.'

'What? I'm interested. If you don't want to tell me, I'll respect that, but watching you play was kind of like a missing piece I needed to see. But I still don't understand why it's a big deal for you to play in public.'

He sucked on his lips as he thought about her simple question. He grabbed her hand and she shimmied her fingers in between his, giving him the shot of confidence he'd needed.

'It started at music school,' he began quietly. 'I always had stage fright; that's par for the course. Even Chopin famously had stage fright. But then... my parents started arguing about it.' As he could have predicted, she winced. He shook his head. 'This isn't Edie's story. It's mine.' She squeezed his hand and rested her cheek briefly on his shoulder. With Lou by his side and the sunshine on his face, among the heightened colours of the lake, the trees, the wildflowers and the shadow of the mountain, the moment was right.

'I had started thinking about quitting music school, especially after a new maestro took over my orchestra. My teacher had his own way of pushing me through the fear that probably didn't help, but, Stockholm syndrome or whatever, I would never have attributed any blame to him. Mum wanted to take me out of school straight away, but Dad decided I had to push through it or all my hard work would be wasted.'

'Oh, my God, they were both wrong.'

He glanced at her with a smile. 'You worked that out straight away.'

'I have some... perspective,' she said, wrinkling her nose.

'I suppose you do,' he murmured. 'Anyway, their marriage was obviously failing. I got a bit trapped in a feedback loop of not coping and then I screwed up, massively, on stage during a concert.' He shivered at the memory and her hand clamped around his forearm. 'And then I just didn't know what I wanted any more. I couldn't continue at music school, because I wasn't prepared to perform again. I kind of... shut down. I think Mum panicked and decided I had to leave Milan. We stayed here at the lake with my grandparents for a few months, but she decided we needed a completely new start – how much of that was to do with my dad, I don't know. Anyway, she got a job and we moved to London.'

'And she didn't send you back to music school.'

He shook his head, wondering if he could get away with not spilling the next part. God, why did he have such a stupid sob story?

'Much worse than your history as a beauty queen,' he said.

She laughed bleakly. 'I don't know about that, but don't distract me. I still don't understand why you're embarrassed when you do perform, since you obviously rediscovered your love of music.'

'I don't perform,' he insisted. She sent him a dubious look. 'I don't count karaoke.'

'What about the school concert?'

He sighed, knowing his blush gave him away. 'It's stupid.'

'I'm pretty sure it's not as stupid as my answers to the general knowledge questions at the pageants. Out with it. Were you booed off stage during the school musical? I did the school musical, by the way. I sucked, but I managed to make everyone clap for me anyway.'

He smiled faintly at her. 'I can imagine that. But I had the opposite problem.'

'What, you were so good that everyone hated you?'

He squeezed one eye shut as he considered her wording. He'd never thought of it like that. 'I suppose that's right. I was small and skinny and new and I didn't speak English. But I'd started playing violin again – obsessively, by myself, and I managed to talk myself back into orchestra performances, just no solos. I walked into the position of first violin and ruffled a few feathers. Plus, it was a boys' school with way too much testosterone and I was an easy target.'

Her nostrils flared. 'You were bullied,' she finished, unnecessarily.

He shrugged. 'Yeah,' he said uneasily, his hand limp in hers. But she hung on.

'Don't dismiss it! I can't believe everything you went through, and you're still full of encouragement for the kids – all the kids. That's more strength than I've ever seen in one person.'

He stared at his violin, hanging from his hand. He could get used to this: violin in one hand, Lou's hand in the other, her warm words ringing in his ears and burrowing into his chest. 'It's my little way of getting back at them,' he said softly.

She gave him one of her brilliant smiles and that was enough reward for pulling through and moving past the poisoned words of his former classmates. 'That's why you became a teacher,' she said gently.

He nodded and looked away when her gaze became too warm. 'That and the fact that I rarely have to explain my name in a school setting. The boys at school had endless fun at the expense of my name.' He smiled through her quizzical look. 'What did you think Nick was short for?'

She drew back and looked him up and down. 'You're going to tell me your name isn't actually Nicholas? Although, now that I say it, it does sound kind of wrong.'

'In what way exactly?' He cocked his head.

'I don't know. I'm now thinking it's not Italian. But you know how little I know about Italy. Am I right?' He nodded. 'So, what's the Italian version of Nicholas, then?'

'You know it as a female name,' he explained.

Her brows rose. 'Ah. I see.'

He smiled ruefully. 'You see.'

'Like Andrea Boccelli. Nicola Romano.'

He nodded. 'That's me.'

'Oh, God, you poor thing.'

'That's why I don't mind Mr Ro-Rock Hard Triceps.'

She pinched him, but he figured he deserved it. They both fell silent, but the warm hum between them hung pleasantly and he had no intention of releasing her hand. He was quite enjoying the absence of judgement – and the fear of judgement. 'I'm glad you found a way to devote your life to music anyway,' she said softly. 'Your playing just then... it touched me.'

His throat grew thick. He retrieved the memory of her standing under the silver olive tree, her eyes closed, her hair moving lightly in the breeze, living the music he was creating for her. It was a singular experience, a memory he suspected he would keep for special occasions. 'I hate the pressure, but I love the music,' he murmured.

'That's fair enough.'

He chuckled and nudged her with his shoulder. 'Try telling that to Maestro Eckert.'

She looked up at him in sudden alarm. 'The competition! You're going back to your old school.'

He nodded evenly. 'It's getting harder to pretend it isn't coming. I'm feeding them to the wolves for real this time.'

'But you've prepared them so well! The concert on Saturday – it was fantastic! And the way you coach them through their mistakes while still building their confidence! It's amazing, Nick.'

She had a remarkable record of saying the right thing. But in the minefield of his hopes and fears, she was never going to get a perfect score. His stomach sank. This, too, was only a brief, peaceful interlude. The reality that had sent him off into the olive grove to sweat out his frustration returned with menace.

'You wouldn't be saying that if you'd seen the rehearsal today,' he grumbled.

'Edie said yesterday that if the maestro was mean, she'd at least have the confidence to keep going – because of you.'

He grimaced. Edie's hope and trust in him were misplaced. How had he ever thought he could guide them through this? 'She might have something different to say this evening.'

'I'll ask her,' Lou said stubbornly, obviously unwilling to believe him. 'What was so bad about the rehearsal?'

'Where do I start?' he spluttered, dropping her hand. 'Let's see: they picked up on none of the changes in dynamics in the Mozart. The tempo was so off they stopped and started through the entire rehearsal. Of course, they got lost in the second move-ment of the Jenkins. Meg came to see me in tears at lunchtime saying they wanted to go on strike, and I think that's the end of any chance at mutual respect between the maestro and the orchestra.'

Lou's furrowed brow was cute and kissable, even in the midst of his misery. 'Did he try to earn their respect?' she asked. He smiled faintly, but she shook her head to cut off his reply. 'You can't excuse behaviour just because someone has convinced everyone they're brilliant and powerful. Isn't the job of a conductor to listen to the musicians and bring out their talent?'

He sighed. 'Yes, but—'

'No buts! You're the brilliant conductor here, not him! You made a bunch of primary-school kids wielding violins into some kind of ensemble! If Maestro-bloody-Eckert needs a super-duper orchestra to showcase his talents, but can't get these amazing kids to stay in time, then he can shove his credentials. You should conduct them.' He paled at that suggestion. 'You're worth twenty Maestro Eckerts – a hundred!'

He loved the flash in her eyes, but he couldn't change the situation with spunk. 'This is the way things are. They're preparing for high-pressure careers on stage. I knew this, I knew the maestro by reputation, and I didn't prepare them. I should have been harsh and made them cut off their grumbling and everything else except the music. But I haven't had the heart to do it. I keep thinking about the competition and just being too... kind to them.'

Her look was warm and doubtful. But his responsibilities wouldn't go away – at least not until tomorrow when he could take a day off and try not to think about it.

'The kids will be okay,' she insisted.

He sighed. 'Some of them will,' he agreed haltingly, glancing apologetically at Lou.

'Meaning, you think Edie won't cope,' she accused, her expression hardening.

He nodded, taking her disapproval as his due. 'She's my student. Of course she won't cope.' He turned to trudge back up the hill and end this soft reprieve he didn't deserve.

She stepped in front of him, blocking his path. He looked up into her face, an inch or two higher than his, standing on the hill like this.

One of her hands landed on his shoulder, firm and warm. Her other hand brushed his cheek intolerably. 'Nick,' she said forcefully, challenging him not to look away – as though he had a choice. 'You've given Edie something much more important than training on how to play the violin.' His heart pricked up against the orders of his brain. He strained unconsciously closer. 'You've given her a love for it, which she will have for the rest of her life, maestro or no maestro. Phil always said I pushed her. I mean, I sat with her and listened every time she practised at the beginning – through all those awful notes before she got the hang of tuning. But I didn't push her. She practises because she loves it, because you gave her the passion for it. Phil was wrong about that.'

He stared at her, feeling the warmth of her palm rising and falling with his deep breaths. His fears, his passions, clashed with the frustration and longing he felt for her – to see herself, to accept herself.

'Phil was wrong about a lot of things,' he murmured.

'He is,' she agreed with a little smile that sent his thoughts right back to the unresolved sexual tension. 'He would be so surprised to hear I have a massive crush on you.'

'A crush, huh?' He smiled ruefully. Oh, well, he could live with that, as long as she didn't take her hands away. 'I have a thing for the hot mum, too.'

'I was wondering...'

He loved her playful tone. 'Yes?'

'I really liked the... when you consumed my face.'

He snorted, snaking his arms around her waist. 'That's not the hottest way to express that, you know.' He stared up into her eyes, enjoying having her close, feeling like the only two people in the world.

'Does it put you off?'

He grinned. 'No.'

'Good,' she whispered and dipped her head. He breathed in and leaned up to her. One hand tangled in her hair. Was escaping reality with her for a moment truly going to be so easy?

Her phone rang.

'For fuck's sake,' she muttered. Staring up to the sky with a grimace, she pulled away and rummaged in her bag. 'It's Edie,' she explained. 'She's probably wondering where I am.'

He inclined his head and gestured up the hill. 'Let's walk, then.' She nodded apologetically and took the call.

* * *

'Are you sure this is okay?' Lou asked Edie for at least the fiftieth time as she waited for Greta to take her to Malcesine that afternoon. 'You're not just agreeing because you're worried about me?'

'No, Mum. It's fine. And I'll call you if I need anything. It's not like we've been inseparable during the camp, is it?'

She studied Edie's face; the sharpening features a reminder that her little girl was stepping out into the world. 'Your dad wants to spend time with you.'

Edie's only reaction was a nod and Lou breathed out slowly in relief. She mustn't have noticed Lou's tension regarding Phil. 'I think it's good for you to... not be here.' Or perhaps she had.

'What exactly does that mean?'

Edie gave her a peeved look that Lou was pretty sure she was going to come to know well in future. 'Don't take it the wrong way! I'm not trying to get rid of you!'

'I wasn't thinking that,' she said, but part of her had been.

'But that's exactly it. As soon as Dad shows up, you're suddenly... sad,' Edie said, a stricken look on her face. Lou drew back, wondering why everyone else seemed to cut to the heart of her issues. First Nick, now Edie. Was it so obvious she wasn't through to the other side of the divorce yet? 'This camp has been great. I've loved all the activities and getting to rehearse with these older kids has been really good preparation for Purcell. And I've been happy to see you doing stuff, too, and helping Mr Romano.'

Lou tried very hard not to blush at the mention of Nick. Edie was keen to deal with the divorce with a maturity that shouldn't have been expected of an eleven-year-old, but Lou never wanted to imagine her with enough maturity to deal with the attraction between her and Nick.

'I just know that if you and Dad are both here, it won't quite be the same. I'm happy for you to go – as long as you're back to hang out on Thursday.'

'I wouldn't miss it. And if my hotel is crappy I might be back tomorrow!' She pulled Edie in for a fierce hug. 'Any idea what you want to do on Thursday? It sounds like everyone's going to mutiny against the proposed high ropes course. I don't know what we were thinking.'

Edie shrugged. 'I don't know yet. But I want to hang out with you before we head to Milan.'

'Definitely. Are you sure everything's okay with the maestro? Nick seemed a bit... upset.'

Edie smiled faintly. 'He's just protective of us. I think it's a good combination – at least, I hope so. The maestro is really tough, but we'll do better tomorrow. We might do better when "Nick" isn't watching from the corner.' She said his name with a cheeky smile that brought heat to Lou's cheeks again. She hoped Edie was only amused that her teacher had a first name and not at the idea of Lou having a raging crush on him. 'Have fun at your hotel!' she said and dived back in for another hug as Greta appeared, holding her car keys.

'Ready to go? Let me put your bag in the car.'

Helene appeared through the door in the wall, waving. 'I won't know what to do with myself, all alone in our room!'

Lou smiled. 'I'll be back for one last night on Thursday. We can have a slumber party.' She gave Helene a quick hug. 'Don't worry too much about the rehearsals.'

'Oh, I won't. Maestro Eckert is sure to turn them around. You know the amazing work he did with the Prague Philharmonic.'

Lou didn't know, but she nodded anyway. She squeezed Edie's hand once more and headed for Greta's car. Movement in her peripheral vision made her turn back to see Nick rushing through the door and coming to a sudden stop like the Road Runner.

'You *are* going!' he blurted out. Edie and Helene turned to him curiously and he blushed, making Lou blush, which stretched the tension between them to unbearable. She should have explained her decision to him before arriving back at the convent full of teenagers – and mothers and ex-husbands.

'You both have a couple of days off,' Greta pointed out.

Lou looked back at Nick. He looked at her. She was both tongue-tied and unable to say anything in front of their audience. He had her phone number. She widened her eyes at him, hoping he'd pick up the stupid hint that now would be a good time to go on a date, if he ever intended to ask her.

A real date. Could she do it? A man who wasn't Phil? Was it fair that the first attribute she thought of was that he wasn't Phil? Not that she would have thought it, if Phil hadn't shown up to burst her lakeside bubble.

Either way, he probably wouldn't pick up that her weird look was a hint. She wasn't going to take the initiative and call him. She would probably have to content herself with a nice bath.

18

Lou awoke the next morning to the sound of her phone ringing. She fumbled for it, blinking in surprise to see it was nine o'clock. She rarely slept so late. It wasn't as though she'd been up late the night before. Her tiny hotel room didn't even have a bathtub and she'd only had Italian terrestrial TV channels. She'd finished her book, then ummed and ahhed about joining Netflix, until she'd worked out that the Wi-Fi was too slow anyway and gone to sleep.

The hotel was tucked into the warren of streets in the centre of Malcesine and there was a tempting gelateria in the street below, but it wasn't exactly a luxury retreat. She was just thankful it had been available, because anything was preferable to sitting across the breakfast table from Phil.

And pining for Nick.

She winced. She was doing far too much pining. She was even embarrassing herself.

After coming to terms with her lie-in, she then realised that it was Nick calling and sat bolt upright.

'Hello? Is everything okay?' she asked.

'Yeah.' There was a pause. 'Hi, nothing's wrong.'

'Oh, good.' She blushed and was terrified it would show in her voice. 'Sorry. Hi! What's up?'

'I was wondering... Do you want to come outside?'

She blinked. 'Outside?' Was that code for some kind of date or was it her wishful thinking?

'Yeah, outside your hotel. I'm here.'

Her heart pinged into her throat and back in an excited bounce. 'Here, here?'

He chuckled and the sound curled up in her stomach. 'Yes, here, in Via Bottura.' She just managed to cut off the excited squeal. She had Nick to herself. Finally! 'Are you okay?' he asked. Perhaps she hadn't quite succeeded in quashing the squeal.

'Yeah,' she said, trying to get her voice under control. 'Just let me get dressed.'

'Oh, God, I'm sorry. Were you asleep?'

'It's okay. I never sleep this late normally – the mum thing, you know.' She slammed her mouth shut. She was going on a date. No more mentions of 'mum things'.

'Okay.'

'Sorry, I'll be five minutes – maybe ten. But don't go anywhere!'

'I won't.' She could hear the smile in his voice and her own grin stretched off her face. 'You might want to wear trousers.'

She bounded down the stairs of the hotel ten – okay, fifteen – minutes later, hoping she'd cobbled together a date look, but in too much of a hurry to see him to take any more time. She flipped her hair over her shoulder, straightened and opened the main door with a big smile.

Her smile only got bigger when she saw him. His arms were crossed over his chest, his hair was curling with that unruly wave she never wanted him to tame and he was wearing one of his 'Nick ensembles' of a patterned, collared shirt and a nice pair of trousers. She didn't care if that made him more fashionable than she was. She got to look at him.

He was leaning against a pastel-blue Vespa, a helmet dangling from his hand and another hanging on the handlebar. She stopped just outside the door, soaking in the perfection of the image. A day on Lake Garda. On a Vespa. With a gorgeous man, who made her laugh and think and feel. She took a second to appreciate it.

He gestured haltingly to the Vespa. 'It's my cousin's. I went and picked it up this morning, in case you wanted to... go for a ride.'

'Cousin Federico?' she asked. His brow furrowed slightly, but he nodded. Lou grinned. 'Then he's absolved. This is awesome, Nick. I can't wait.'

He laughed and she skipped down the steps. He came close and she lifted her face up. Was this it? Would she finally get another kiss? He brushed her hair back and settled the helmet on her head, his touch gentle as he secured it under her chin.

But he didn't kiss her. Perhaps this wasn't a date. Perhaps this was some sort of pity-prize for being pushed off music camp. To be honest, it didn't matter what it was. Not only would she get the best tour of the lake on the back of a Vespa, but she could wrap her arms around him and snuggle in while she did.

He sat on the front of the leather cushion and patted the back. Lou grinned. She settled on the seat and scooted right up behind him. She slid her hands around his chest and breathed in. Her mind filled with the feel of the fine cotton of his shirt and the warmth of his skin beneath. He smelled good – nothing like Phil, she realised with satisfaction. And even if this wasn't a date, it was the best date she'd ever had.

'Hold on,' he said with a smile as he fastened his own helmet and grasped the handlebars. The Vespa took off with a little cough and Lou whooped as they putted through the narrow streets and out to the main road.

Clinging to him wasn't only for pleasure as they picked up speed on the Strada Regionale. The wind whipped her hair. They zipped along the road with the lake twinkling peacefully alongside and the mountains looming dramatically as they headed north.

They passed the scene of their paddleboarding triumph and she squeezed him in a hug she hoped he felt. He pressed her hand to his chest in response.

They whipped past sparkling green coves of sun-drenched stones and clear water. She laughed and hung on as the Vespa tipped around the bends. Windsurfers and little sailboats dotted the lake and the green-and-grey ridges of rock on the other side blinked gently in the morning sunlight.

Up ahead, a rock face tumbled over the road, but they zoomed through a series of tunnels, the air suddenly cool. When they burst back out into the sunlight, Nick pulled the scooter on to a wide shoulder and parked, turning off the ignition. The view was gorgeous – lake and mountains and the town of Riva del Garda, bordered by a dramatic diagonal ridge of rock. It was a gorgeous, sunny day, and the distant alpine peaks were also visible.

'Breakfast stop,' Nick said with a smile. 'Off you hop.' He popped open the seat and retrieved two wrapped packages. She peered inside to see a bottle of orange juice as well. He checked one of the packages and handed it to her. 'I think that's your cheese, by the way.'

She unwrapped one end and grinned, finding a fresh panini loaded with the cheese she'd bought the day before, and stuffed with salad. Nick hopped up on to the stone wall and Lou followed suit, keeping her shoulder against his.

She wrinkled her nose. 'That smells fishy.'

'Mmmhmm,' he replied, obviously enjoying his bite. 'Sardines.'

'Urgh,' she said, making him chuckle. No kissing for the moment, then, she thought petulantly. She fetched the orange juice and looked in the corners for cups, but didn't find any.

'Ah,' said Nick with a frown. 'I knew something about this wasn't going to go smoothly.'

Lou smiled and shrugged, pulling the cap off the juice and taking a swig, before handing it to him to do the same. 'I would have gone crazy by now if I worried about germs all the time. Lazy mum thing.' She inwardly slapped herself. She wasn't supposed to be mentioning the mum thing.

'Right,' Nick said when he hopped off the wall, brushing crumbs off his trousers. 'Are you ready for the highlight of the ride'

'It gets better? This has been so amazing already.'

'I hope you're not sick of me yet.' He smiled wryly.

She hopped off the wall and gave him a reproachful look. 'If you say stuff like that, then I'll worry, too. It's hard enough to accept that you want to spend your day off with me.'

'Days off,' he murmured.

A little thrill zipped through her, cosy feelings at the words he'd said and... hotter ones at the thought of what he might be implying. But, no, she couldn't be certain that he meant days and nights. She wasn't ready anyway, but would she ever be? Could she afford to waste this opportunity? It might be wonderful. It might ruin everything. But what did they have to ruin?

Sometimes it felt as if they had a lot.

They continued north, popping through the tunnel under Riva's strange diagonal mountain and along the waterfront. The town was already baking in the summer sun. Swimmers filled the coves and the heat was almost enough for Lou to wish she were up at a higher altitude, like a crazy hiker. The mountain rising up to the west, with a little white tower looking down on the town, looked inviting.

They scooted past the mediaeval fortress, and pulled up so Lou could get off and snap some pictures of the clock tower and the brightly coloured buildings on the main square, right on the lake. Lou stared up past the white tower at the jagged ridge above.

'You know you want to go up there,' Nick said with a smile.

'Is there a cable car?' He shook his head and she grimaced. 'Then it's not likely.'

'It's just walking,' he insisted. 'You might have to work up to a via ferrata – that's a steep hike, where you need climbing equipment.' She shuddered. 'But you could do any hike you wanted. Look, that one there is Cima Valdritta.' He pointed back across the lake. 'The highest of the Monte Baldo peaks. You could get up there if you wanted to. I could take you tomorrow.'

'No way,' she said, not sure if she was saying no, she couldn't, or no, she wouldn't. Part of her really wanted to go up there, but she'd never been hiking in her life. She enjoyed a nice ramble in the countryside like any other British person, but these were mountains. They didn't have those in London. 'Have you been up there before?'

'Once, years ago. The last part is a bit of a scramble, but the rest is a fairly easy hike.'

She sighed. '"Valdritta" is a very evocative name, but I don't think there's any way little old Lou is going to make it up there tomorrow.' She glanced at him glumly, wondering if that meant he'd do his own thing tomorrow. But he was smiling at her.

'Maybe next time? How about a warm-up hike somewhere else tomorrow?'

With a warm-up together in her hotel room tonight? If that

was what he meant, she was all in. Gosh, what was wrong with her? Perhaps if he just got on with it and kissed her, she'd stop wondering if they were going to end up tangled in bed. It had been such a long time since she'd thought so much about... tangling.

He grabbed her hand and she had to force her mind back to what he'd just said so she didn't blurt out anything about sex. 'How about a warm-up "walk" tomorrow, then?' he asked more gently.

She grinned. She was grinning like a fool today and she didn't care. 'Yes. I can wholeheartedly agree to a walk.'

'A long one?' he asked hopefully.

She wasn't sure if he was hopeful of the exercise or more time together. She decided there was no harm in believing the latter. 'A long one,' she agreed.

'Good,' he said, his gaze lingering on her face for long enough that the heat rushed to her cheeks. Was he going to kiss her now? Or now? How about now? 'Come on. Let's head to the next stop on your tour.'

She tried not to look disappointed. 'I didn't realise this was an organised tour.'

He shrugged. 'Just a few places I thought you'd like.' He grabbed her hand as they walked back to the Vespa. She clung to his hand, slipping her fingers in between his. She'd probably enjoy Siberia if she got to hold his hand.

The next stop wasn't far; a car park at the bottom of some terraced gardens. A pink-and-cream villa accented with palms was set among the thick pine and cypress trees – an oasis against the mountain backdrop.

'Parco Grotta Cascata Varone,' Lou read.

'What do you think it means?' Nick asked.

She gave him a shove and hopped off the Vespa. 'I know a trap when I see one. Of course, it's a grotty old park with cases of Peroni.'

He burst into laughter and tugged her back to plant a kiss on her cheek. It was about two inches too far to the left of where she wanted a kiss, but she still blushed. And then he blushed. They were hopeless.

'Come on,' he said, taking her hand and tugging her up to the villa.

It was not a grotty old park at all. It was a wonderland of ravines and waterfalls among walls of mountain rock. The only complaint Lou had was that she was too busy gaping at the cascades and skyscrapers of rock to talk to Nick. And she was too scared of falling to let go of the handrails of the metal walkways bolted into the rock faces, which meant they couldn't even hold hands.

As they wandered back to the Vespa, Nick looked at his watch.

'You probably had other things you wanted to do on your day off – like bike riding.'

He looked at her with an odd expression.

'It's been really lovely,' she rushed on. 'I would never have found this stuff on my own and, now I know it's here, I wouldn't have missed it. It's so kind of you to bring me.'

He hesitated again and her uncertainty grew. Should she offer to go back to Malcesine so he could have his freedom again? She obviously shouldn't have hoped this would turn into a real date. She wouldn't have minded a few days ago. She'd had an amazing morning exploring her new favourite place in the whole world. So what, if she couldn't kiss Nick while she was doing it? He'd explained he wasn't in any shape for a serious relationship anyway. It was probably sensible not to kiss if it wasn't going to go anywhere and, God knew, she shouldn't be having any kind of relationship, serious or not.

He brushed his hand over his forehead and the action made her smile faintly. Sometimes it felt as if she knew him so well. 'Is that supposed to be a hint that I should take you back to Malcesine?' he asked. After another pause and a lick of his lips, he continued, 'Or have I not been clear enough?'

The warmth in his eyes behind his glasses, the uncertainty in his smile, gently subdued her self-doubt. Maybe she would get that kiss some time this century. 'I think,' she began stiltedly, 'I'm not... confident enough to pick up on hints right now.'

'Right,' he said with a deep breath and a little nod.

And now... kiss me! Go!

He didn't. She obviously wasn't the only one who couldn't pick up on hints. But he was building up to something. 'I was hoping you'd want to come with me for lunch with my grandparents.'

Whoa. That was a bit beyond a date. Being on music camp with his mother was awkward enough.

Something of her feelings must have shown on her face, because he quickly reassured her. 'I know you don't like olives, but I thought you might like to see the farm and the press. And my nonna makes her own ravioli.'

She grasped his arm. 'Oh, my gosh, take me there, right now.'

He chuckled. 'I didn't mean... I mean... to be honest, Nonna will probably ask when we're getting married, but the ravioli is worth the embarrassment – trust me.'

'I might even consider marrying you for your nonna.'

His laugh was almost a splutter. 'It's good to know what my assets are.'

'You've got a lot of assets,' she replied, trying to keep a straight face.

* * *

It was a beautiful afternoon up at the farmhouse that reminded Nick of childhood holidays, as well as those dramatic few months following his parents' separation. He'd never appreciated how lucky he was to have the place in his family, until he'd seen Lou's enchantment with the old stone house, tucked up in the hills with a view into a lush valley and a glimpse of the lake.

He set the table for lunch, slowly and with a smile. His nonno was in his element, using his charmingly bad English, which was peppered with German, to take Lou through an olive-oil tasting.

'It is very... sharp,' he said with a flourish.

Lou stared blankly at him. 'Spicy, Nonno. Spicy. Not sharp,' Nick called out.

If it weren't for the constant urge to kiss her, he would have felt remarkably content. But every time he accidentally blurted out his half-formed ideas about where their relationship could go, she got a weird look on her face.

It had felt good to finally explain to her about school, music and his confusion about life, but he also had to accept that now she knew that he lost his head when he played the violin, he'd been the runty music nerd at school – and a floundering sort of cop-out at life.

She was hung up on Phil and worried about Edie and he wasn't tough enough for adulting. But he wasn't mature enough to follow his sensible thoughts and keep everything on a friends-only level. No, he had to touch her and dream and remember what it felt like to have his fingers in her hair.

He'd booked a restaurant for that evening and the reminder was slapping him in the back of the head regularly. It was a romantic restaurant tucked up on the hill behind Malcesine. A table for two. He couldn't take her there and claim it was part of the friendly service. He either had to cancel the booking or ask her out – properly, with intentions.

He had no idea what those intentions were. He was too preoccupied with the thought of kissing her. Perhaps it was all just a bizarre outlet for the pressure he was under. That didn't sound fair to her. But his outburst in the linen cupboard two nights ago was so out of character that he must be cracking.

Nonna gave him a knowing look as she brought plates out to the terrace and he quickly rearranged his expression. She was as robust as ever, in her bright apron, but he could see the slow changes that had brought his mother back home.

His uncle appeared and he noticed his nonno ushering Lou back to the table from the makeshift tasting station he'd set up for her.

'I had no idea olive oil was supposed to be spicy.'

Nick smiled. Her inexhaustible curiosity was a joy. 'But on the roof of the mouth, not the tongue,' he explained.

'Yeah, your nonno showed me how to do the weird click thing on the palate. I hope I didn't spit on him. Oh, hello.' She greeted his uncle with a smile and accepted the cheek kisses. Nick watched distractedly until he realised he was staring so much his whole family must suspect something.

Although his nonna apologised that it was just a simple lunch, it wasn't, of course. Watching Lou suppress a moan at the mushroom ravioli was like accidentally catching a glimpse of someone in the shower. If they'd been alone, he probably wouldn't have been fit company. It didn't bode well for his fast-diminishing plans for the evening.

After finishing the secondi of pike with garlic and capers, which she obviously enjoyed more than she'd expected, she smiled brightly at Nonna. 'Thank you so much. I won't need to eat all week.'

Nick scrunched up his napkin and tried not to take the

comment personally. She didn't know he'd planned to take her to dinner that night. He hadn't bloody well asked her.

His uncle insisted on giving her a tour of the groves and the olive press after lunch and she was either very polite or genuinely interested in the ten varieties of olives and their different characteristics. Since she was Lou, he suspected it was probably the latter. Was there anything she wasn't interested in?

'You must come back and stay in the autumn, and help with the harvest. Nico often comes during his... half-term, you call it?'

Nick was enough of a Lou expert to recognise the slight blush. 'Thank you for the invitation. It's a beautiful place, here.' The wistful note in her voice should have been a pleasant sound, but it made him realise she didn't think she would ever come back.

Lou let out a huge sigh as they strolled back to the Vespa. He silently took the bottle of olive oil and jar of almond-stuffed olives his nonno had given her and stowed them under the seat. She'd obviously been too polite to decline the olives. He propped up the jar next to the plastic bag containing the hiking boots his nonna had lent him for Lou to wear. He only had to convince her to use them.

'Where was cousin Federico, then?' she asked lightly. 'I'm going to start thinking he doesn't exist.'

'He works at a hotel in Riva. If you're so interested, I could take you there,' he said, annoyed at himself for the edge to his voice and hoping she didn't notice. Was he jealous of his own cousin? A man she'd never met?

'Nick,' she said, her voice steely. His gaze jerked up to hers. 'I'm not interested in your cousin.' Her lips pursed in a combative frown that was far too engaging. 'Do you think I'm hung up on every guy except you?'

Whoa. His heart rate sped up. He was heading right back to linen-cupboard territory. What was wrong with him when she was around? But she had a point. 'No,' he began, swallowing in hesitation. He squeezed his eyes shut. 'But I've spent the whole day kicking myself for not asking you out and I'm a bit of a wreck. I'm sorry. You deserve better.'

When he opened his eyes again, she was suddenly a whole lot closer and her eyes were trained on him. 'Let me be clear: are you trying to ask me out? On a real date?'

He laughed hopelessly. 'I'm even worse at this than I thought,' he muttered.

'Yes or no,' she prompted. Her lips twitched.

'Yes,' he said immediately. 'I booked a restaurant and everything. And now you're stuffed.'

She nodded thoughtfully. 'And you haven't asked me yet, because you're still deciding?'

'No,' he said. 'Because I'm a wimp.'

'I know I'm very scary.'

'You have no idea,' he mumbled.

Her sceptical look gave her a little double chin and he wanted to drag her into the nearest linen cupboard. 'I promise, despite the stupid joke I made about your nonna, I'm not out to marry you. I'm safe for a date.'

He nodded. 'A date.' Why did it feel like so much more than that? Was it because he was supposed to be the teacher on this camp? They had less than a week left and then Edie wasn't his student any more. It hardly seemed to be a line to worry about crossing. And yet, a date felt like the wrong route to be taking if they were planning to say goodbye forever. 'I haven't had one of those in a long time.'

'Huh. When I last went on a first date, you were a teenager.'

He propped his hands on his hips. 'My last first date was with a twenty-two-year-old.' He winced.

She tutted, but was clearly suppressing a smile. 'Sounds like you were the cradle snatcher that time. My last first date was an M&S sandwich on a park bench – that I had to fetch myself!'

'You fetched a park bench?'

She poked him and her smile broke out. 'No, I didn't fetch a park bench.'

'But you did marry the guy,' he grumbled. He couldn't seem to help his dark tone when he thought of Phil.

'I might have had to fetch my own sandwich, but at least he asked me out properly.'

Nick grinned as inspiration struck. 'Challenge accepted,' he said and hopped on to the Vespa. She questioned him with a look, but got on behind him, her hands closing around him.

Ten minutes later, he turned on to a bumpy road through olive groves. 'Close your eyes!' he called back over the sound of the engine. When he pulled on to the side of the road, he got off the scooter and helped Lou do the same, tugging off her helmet. He turned her blindly towards the view, wanting to pull her against him but contenting himself with standing close.

'I have a question for you, and then you can open your eyes,' he murmured. His hand brushed hers and before he realised what he'd done, he'd threaded his fingers through hers. 'Will you come for a romantic dinner with me?'

After the day they'd spent, after the weeks of dancing around each other at the convent, the tension felt so much bigger than it should have.

Her answer wasn't in doubt, but the outcome of the evening felt suddenly like a turning point.

'Yes, Nick. I'd love to,' she said, her voice unsteady.

He breathed out slowly, catching a strand of her hair on a gust. He waited until the ball of emotion in his throat cleared – or until she made a joke and broke the tension. He needed her to make a joke. The view, the intimacy, the contentment – it was too good.

She turned suddenly and opened her eyes. 'But I demand payment,' she said.

A smile pulled at his lips. He could rely on Lou to lighten the mood. 'Of course.'

'A kiss.'

'Now? Sure.' Did he sound too eager?

'Hmm,' she said in slow indecision. 'I really want that kiss.'

'I know what you mean.'

'But I have the feeling there's an amazing view behind me.'

'Also true.'

'Bugger it.' She leaned forward slowly and pressed her lips to his. His heart pounded. He needed something to hold him on the earth and he found her hair, her cheek. She was a reason to stay right where he was and be happy – to be who he was and be happy.

The dramatic view of the castle set atop a huge rock formation and the town of Arco below didn't seem so spectacular any more.

19

'I have to come back here one day,' Lou said dreamily as she finished her wine and gazed out over the rooftops of Malcesine and out to the lake.

'The camp isn't exactly conducive to tourism,' Nick replied carefully, reminding himself that just because he interpreted her comment to mean they'd never see each other again after Milan, didn't mean she'd been thinking about it.

'And I wasted my time on the workshops.'

'You think it was a waste of time?'

'You do.'

He studied her. 'I didn't mean they were a waste of time. I meant you don't need to have a natural talent for something to be who you are. You don't have to put yourself under pressure to be good at things.'

'Well, I've been watching a group of very talented people put themselves under pressure to create something beautiful. I want to be part of that – part of something.'

He wanted to insist that she was part of that, but he suspected she would see through the platitude. Providing moral support wasn't the same as playing second violin. 'I understand that. You want a creative outlet and a sense of community.'

She laughed. 'I've been so stupid.'

'No, you haven't, Lou,' he insisted immediately, his hand hovering over hers. 'You're just expressing something most of us are too afraid to express.'

'I think Phil's going through something similar,' she said suddenly. He tried not to wince at the change of subject. 'I wondered even... whether he's having some kind of mid-life crisis. I was so convinced the divorce was because of me. He never really wanted me anyway, no matter how hard I tried. But... maybe that was his fault. And maybe I lost a bit of myself trying to be what he wanted.'

He allowed his hand to drop on to hers. He had no idea what to say. He'd never committed to Naomi the way she had to Phil. The only thing he'd committed to was his violin.

'Oh, God, I'm sorry. I don't want to spend the evening talking about Phil – or mum stuff, or my stupid quest for a talent. I'm a terrible date.'

'I'd rather talk about this than books or movies,' he commented lightly.

She sighed. 'You were the one who told me I was still hung up on the smarmy prick.'

He winced. 'And I still asked you out, so don't apologise.'

She was looking at him with a glint in her eye that made him want to blush. He wanted to know what she was thinking... but, on the other hand, perhaps that was dangerous territory.

'Let's go get gelato and walk along the lake,' she said with a smile.

He waved the waiter over to pay for the meal and when he glanced back at Lou, she had that glint in her eye again.

'What?' he asked. It was better than assuming and blushing.

Spots of colour on her cheeks didn't help his assumptions. 'You speaking Italian. It's...'

'My mother tongue?' he prompted, trying to shove his hammering heart back down from his throat.

She scrunched up her nose. 'I was going to say "hot".'

He coughed. 'Gelato,' he said, clearing his throat and grabbing her hand. He'd been reflexively grabbing her hand all day. Why did it feel unbearably sensual to do so now? His thumb brushed hopelessly over the back of her hand and she shivered lightly. What the hell were they doing?

Peach gelato and the evening breeze off the lake helped cool his thoughts as they walked along the Lungolago. They bumped into each other lightly every few steps. He couldn't seem to tear himself far enough away.

'I assume the coconut is good?' he asked, his voice alarmingly rough.

She raised an eyebrow at him. 'Am I making too much noise?'

'Uh...' He rubbed the back of his head. 'Depends on why you're making the noise.' His comment trailed off.

'Because I'm enjoying my ice cream.'

'In that case, carry on. I'll try to ignore you.'

'And because I like the funny sigh you keep making.'

He choked on a laugh. 'Are we going hiking tomorrow?' he asked, needing to change the subject. 'I checked your shoes at the farm and you have the same size as my nonna, so I've got shoes for you.'

'Your nonna has hiking boots?'

'Everyone has hiking boots.'

'Except talentless Lou.'

'Stop it, or I will steal a lick from your ice cream.'

She burst into laughter. 'Was that your teacher voice?'

'I hope my teacher voice is a bit more serious than that!'

'You've scared me into saying I'll come hiking with you.'

'Good... I think. I'll look for a route.'

'Not the summit,' she insisted.

'You'd love the summit.'

'I would lose my lunch on the summit.'

'I'll pick you up after breakfast, anyway. We can head off before it gets too hot.'

She nodded, but didn't say anything further. He risked a glance at her, but, in the dim light of the lamps along the footpath, he had no idea what she was thinking.

She was oddly quiet for the walk back to her hotel, where he'd parked the Vespa. The weather had turned during their moonlit walk, clouds gathering ominously. He'd thought the date had been a success, but now she'd gone quiet, he wanted his chatty, easy-going Lou back. Had the date been a stupid idea? She paused at the bottom of the steps up to the front door of the B&B.

'So, about nine again?' he asked.

'Sounds good.'

He frowned. He felt muddled. 'You're very quiet,' he commented.

'Shouldn't it be a relief that I'm thinking before I speak for once?' She took half a step closer and his breathing went crazy.

'It depends on what you're going to say,' he squeaked. 'To be honest, I think I prefer you off the cuff.'

She smiled wryly. 'I don't think I own any cuffs.'

Then her smile vanished and her gaze flew to his in alarm that matched the inappropriate heat of his response.

'I didn't mean handcuffs. Honestly! I didn't mean that!'

'Of course not,' he quickly agreed.

'I just really want to invite you in for a drink, but I don't know if I have... anything in my... minibar... that you'd be interested in.'

The breath whooshed right out of him. 'I'm pretty easy. I'll drink anything,' he said, hoping he didn't sound too eager.

Her smile was giddy and he took a step closer because he couldn't stay back. 'And here I was thinking I was using minibar as a euphemism,' she murmured.

He stared at her as understanding slowly crowded out disbelief. He tried to take regular breaths, but he still felt as though he was hyperventilating. She was warm and funny and, with her hair falling over her face in the breeze, sexy as hell.

He hesitated. Was he really going to do this? Him the weird, repressed musician with Lou the vivacious hot mum? 'You know, I'm not very good at euphemisms. Or sex.' Her smile dimmed and he couldn't take it. 'But actually, I really, really like your... minibar.'

She grinned and his blood fired up again. 'You'd better come in, then,' she said.

He couldn't have said what the room furnishings were like. He could barely remember his own name when he pounced on her as soon as she closed the door. They'd blown all restraint. The first kiss was like a burst pressure valve, with the force of weeks of tension, that had barely survived the public interactions that had been charged with attraction from the beginning of the camp.

Spurred on by her grasping fingers and clumsy teeth, he pressed her into the door and swept his tongue into her mouth. Kisses became messy moans and frantic hands, as though they were both afraid the other one would change their mind.

Although alarmed at the speed of their fumbling advances towards the sex they probably weren't ready for, he ran with it and soon they'd toppled on to the bed in a tangle. His glasses were dislodged, but he was too busy running his hands under her shirt to bother to find them. They rolled over a couple of times, wrestling with clothes.

She'd just shimmied out of her shirt and flung her hair back, making his heart stop, when an urgent reminder intruded.

'Shit,' he muttered, grabbing her hips to still her and flopping his head back on the pillow.

'What?' she asked, blinking.

'I don't suppose you have any condoms?'

She froze and blushed deep red. 'Shit,' she repeated with a grimace. 'A pair of amateurs we turned out to be.'

As his blood rushed in confusion, he couldn't help smiling at her. He sat up and wrapped his arms around her. 'It's my fault. I was thinking about this... I mean, I tried not to. I didn't want to be a... presumptive jerk, you know, but I could at least have...'

'I'm pretty sure I thought about this more than you did, Nick,' she said drily, snuggling into him. Tingles spread through his whole body and he was either deliriously happy or the weight of her on his thighs was interfering with his circulation. Either way, he wasn't going to move her until he had to. 'And the woman can just as easily buy the condoms, if she's going to open up the minibar.'

'Do you think if I went and got some,' he asked lightly, 'you might still be... keen... when I got back?'

She drew back, which disappointed him until he caught sight of her smile – warm, affectionate and a little bit naughty. 'I think I'd still be keen if you insisted we walk on hot coals and shards of glass beforehand.'

'Are the hot coals supposed to be a euphemism? Or the shards of glass?' He winced.

She burst out laughing.

* * *

Lou sat cross-legged on the bed and waited for the doubts to roll in like the clouds that had gathered during their moonlit walk. It would probably be easier if the box of condoms Nick was fetching never got opened. Sex might unleash a host of feelings she would prefer shut away.

She forced herself to picture Phil naked and remember how weird and perfunctory their sex life had become at the end. Although he was handsome and in decent shape, the image still made her shudder. How long had she ignored the fact that she hadn't wanted him sexually? The separation had brought relief in that regard. She'd been happy to have no expectations on her body.

Until now...

Not that Nick had expectations. Something burned in her chest when her thoughts returned to his sudden fervour, as though he couldn't believe his luck. She clutched her arms around herself and grinned like a fool. Nick thought he was the lucky one?

A sudden flash of lightning through the window startled her and she jumped up to peer out into the little alley. It was pouring with rain. And Nick was on a Vespa.

She threw her shirt back on, did up her trousers – how had they come undone? – and rushed along the hall to watch for him. Five minutes later, she saw the lights of the Vespa through the driving rain and threw open the door for him.

'Hey,' he said with a smile. It made everything easier that he was nervous, too.

'Come inside. I can't believe I let you go out in the storm!' She dragged him back into her room, fetching the extra towel from the bathroom and wrapping it around his neck.

'I wanted to,' he assured her, then seemed to choke on his own admission. She'd never imagined a man as cute as Nick could exist, let alone go out in the rain to fetch condoms for her. 'And it wasn't raining so hard when I left,' he added. He placed the box on the desk and ran the towel over his hair. 'How are those second thoughts going?' he asked, his voice low.

'You're the one who's had a cold shower,' she said carefully.

'A cold shower doesn't work... when it comes to you,' he murmured.

She melted, joining the puddle that was pooling on the floorboards at his feet. Her feelings were hot and consuming. The wisdom of her actions blurred and the intimacy, the recognition of each other, became more important.

'But, Lou...'

She didn't want to hear his reservations. She was sick of listening to her own. She stepped close and pressed a light kiss on to his lips. His eyes fluttered closed behind his glasses and he sighed, his lips searching for hers after she drew away. But she didn't return to his mouth – not yet. She got to work on the buttons of his sodden shirt. He watched her with a turbulent look.

'I had my second thoughts,' she murmured. 'And third, and fourth. I don't know if it's fair to you to be close like this when my life feels like a shambles.' He was about to contradict her, so she kissed him again. 'But I don't think anything is going to make me stop wanting to be with you tonight.'

'Tonight,' he whispered with a rough nod. 'And tomorrow.'

She reached the last button and tugged the shirt out of his trousers and off over his shoulders. His skin was cold and he shivered as she ran her palms over his chest and down his arms. She tore off her shirt again and wrapped her arms around him. He buried his face in her hair. Tonight and tomorrow. She hoped it would be enough; she hoped it wouldn't be too much.

The second attempt was much slower, with long kisses and

fervent touches. But Lou's perspective began to dip and lose focus in the onslaught of sensation. His hitched breaths and aching touches exposed the need she couldn't afford to acknowledge. She felt the intensity and desperation in him as they grasped for something neither of them thought possible. She held on tight and travelled with him, through passion to vulnerability and the ultimate intimacy of a simultaneous climax.

The storm must have passed, because, after they'd finished, all she could hear was his breathing and hers. The squeeze of her heart was almost unbearable as she held him close through his heaving breaths. He lifted his head and straightened his arms in an attempt to keep his weight off her, and gave her a glimpse of his blinking astonishment, but his forehead fell back to her chest in apparent exhaustion. She was a bit strung out herself.

He eventually flopped on his back next to her and she had to face how wrenching it was to let him go, even only a foot away.

'Not good at sex, huh?' she said when she'd recovered enough of her voice.

He managed a half-hearted laugh. 'It was your fault,' he responded, his voice gravelly.

'My fault you sold yourself short?'

His hand groped for her as he squeezed his eyes shut, then opened them. 'Your fault that was the best sex of my life,' he explained. Lou's blood surged again at his words. A deep place inside her stored them away.

But she reacted with a smug smile. 'At least now you know you like saggy boobs and a mum-tum.'

He propped himself up on one elbow, despite the effort it obviously took him, and stared at her face. His hair was curling and she had to pinch herself that she'd just made wild love with the gorgeous Nick Romano. 'It was you. It was the sounds you made,' he said, his voice high with disbelief. 'For an auditory person, Lou... I've never heard anything so hot!'

Warmth swept up her chest and something alarming pricked behind her eyes. Phil had always told her to be quiet – Edie, the neighbours, someone might hear. It was too much, too difficult to think Nick liked even that about her – not when everything she did still reminded her of Phil. Why couldn't she have met Nick in a couple of years, after she'd allowed the echoes of Phil's words to fade? And why was Nick so amazing that he'd surely get sick of the strung-out mum who was crippled with self-doubt?

But she burrowed into him when he flopped back on to the bed after disposing of the condom.

'Are you okay?' he asked, his fingers gently sweeping over her hair.

'Yes. You can go to sleep, Nick,' she whispered.

'Yeah, I think I'm about to pass out,' he murmured.

* * *

Nick arrived back at the hotel the following morning still in a ridiculously good mood. Oh, he knew this wasn't the start of anything real. Lou hadn't said anything, but he had felt it when she drew away the night before. But he'd been in too deep a post-sex stupor to do anything about it.

Then waking up with his face covered in her hair and arms full of her warm, naked body had set him up for a few days at least. When she'd rolled over and pulled him on top of her for round two, he'd suspected he'd be set for the rest of the year.

She must have been watching for him, because she opened the door of the B&B with a bright smile after he pulled up. He tugged her close for a long kiss, reaching up to tangle his fingers in her hair and realising she'd tied it up in a low bun under her hat. Had he ever seen her with her hair up?

'Did you manage to avoid Greta?'

'Of course not. But I did manage to avoid Edie until I'd show-ered and changed.' He caught her apologetic gaze. 'It's okay, Lou. I do know you have a daughter and I understand a bit about kids.'

Her expression wobbled for a moment and he wondered if bundling her back into the hotel room and having another go at what it turned out they were remarkably good at would make her feel better about herself. But he knew she'd love the hike he'd picked out.

'Edie was fine, by the way. She was eating breakfast with Meg. And there was no sign of Phil or what's-her-name.'

'Winny,' Lou informed him with a dry smile. 'Thanks for the update.'

He just nodded in response. 'How are the shoes?'

'Fine, I think. I still can't believe I'm borrowing your grand-mother's hiking boots.'

'You'll have to get your own next time.' Another wobble to her smile. It was a miracle they'd finally ended up in bed together, given how much still held them apart. He gathered her close again. 'Hey, don't worry about me. I know where this is at. It's not all your responsibility.'

'What did you tell your mum?'

'As little as possible,' he replied. 'I'm pretty sure she worked out where I was last night, but I'll talk to her about it privately later and she won't interfere. You do know she doesn't disapprove of you, right?'

She gave a little smile. 'We kind of bonded over the mushrooms.'

'You're lucky she let you go with her. She's competitive about mushroom foraging. Ready to go?'

'As ready as I'll ever be. But that seems to be my motto for the past few days.' Her voice trailed off at the end.

He parked the Vespa in a small town tucked in the mountains behind the lake and headed back out of town, pointing out the signs for the Sentiero della Pace.

'This is the Peace Trail. It's 500 kilometres long and some parts are 3000 metres or more above sea level.'

'I'm not going to ask why someone would need 500 kilometres of hiking trail.'

'You might get an idea today,' he suggested with a grin.

'And I might twist my ankle at the first turn.'

His grin widened. 'If we get stuck up on the mountain overnight, I'll happily share my body heat.'

She slapped him on the arm. 'You'd better carry me back down.'

'My cousin is in the soccorso alpino, so he can come and rescue you.'

'Maybe I should twist my ankle if it means I get to meet cousin Federico. He's some kind of mountain rescue guy?'

'And much more attractive than I am,' Nick said, aiming for flippant.

'What am I doing with you, then?'

He glanced at her, hoping she couldn't tell how much churning was going on inside him. She was clearly joking about Federico, but just the throwaway mention of being 'with' him made everything flip over again inside.

'You're conquering a mountain with me,' he said.

She paused and turned to him with a sceptical smile. 'Am I really?'

He took her hand. 'Of course. I said I could have taken you up to Valdritta, but I appreciate you need to mentally prepare for that one. So, welcome to your own personal mountain to conquer, 1600 metres above sea level, 360-degree panoramic views, a real croce di vetta.'

'That's the cross on the summit? Oh my God, I've seen them from a distance.'

'Exactly. This one's for you today. It's not an easy hike, but I'm looking forward to seeing you do it.'

She looked up the trail with a grin that struck him with the power of a Brahms concerto. How did she not recognise her incredible talent for tackling life head-on with a smile? He knew it hadn't been easy for her, but she didn't just accept life's lemons, she grabbed them off the tree and made silly faces with them. It made him want to dream. 'What's it called?' she asked, her voice hushed.

'Monte Biaena.'

'Monte Biaena,' she repeated with much better pronunciation than she would give herself credit for. 'Let's do this.'

20

'Holy crap,' she gasped, propping her fists on her knees to rest for a moment. 'This is a lot of uphill. And don't tell me it's a bloody mountain.' At least Nick had the decency to look sweaty and tired himself. He handed her a bottle of water and she guzzled the last of it.

'Do you need a pep talk?'

She chuckled. 'Nope. I just need new knees.'

'I think we have to wait about thirty-five years for those.'

'Forty years for you – young thing.'

'Just wait. At the top, I bet there'll be a bunch of seniors with their Nordic walking sticks.'

She straightened to waggle a finger at him. 'Because they've got new knees, damn them!'

He packed away the water bottle and took her hand with a laugh. 'Come on.'

She grimaced at their joined hands and then shook him loose. 'Too sweaty.'

Then, before she was ready, the forest abruptly stopped and a sun-drenched grassy plateau stretched out – and up – before them. Then there was the view. She paused and stared. Not far ahead, the meadow fell suddenly away and a rich green valley spread out before them, a river winding whimsically through it. The deep-green forested hills on either side rose, steep and disorderly, up to rocky caps. She was at once so high above civilisation and so far below the strange rocky otherworld above.

The air was different up here, almost crystalline. Despite the breeze, the plateau seemed still and immutable. She stopped and closed her eyes.

'Uh, Lou,' came Nick's voice from very close. 'I'm pleased you're enjoying this, but we're so close to the summit. The view is much better from up there.'

Her eyes flew open. 'What? The summit?'

'That is where we're aiming.'

'But... it was supposed to be harder.'

His smile was twitchy and lopsided, but had that giddy affection she was coming to love. 'It *was* hard. Ask your knees.'

After a thrilling stroll along the plateau, slowly coming to appreciate the sheer drop into the valley below, the cross came into view, sitting dramatically on a rise. Beyond the cross there was nothing but air.

'Is that safe?' she asked, her voice unsteady.

'I wouldn't recommend falling off.'

'Now is not the time to joke, Nick.'

'It's the perfect time to joke. You can do this. There's even a whopping great cross to hang on to when you get up there. You don't have to go too close to the edge.'

Staring at the cross, she knew there wasn't a choice. She was going up there. Her tired legs forgotten, she headed straight for the peak. She didn't care if Nick was chuckling warmly behind her. She was claiming that summit.

The last few feet of elevation were a little hairy as the grass hid the rocky terrain, but Nick's nonna's trusty shoes kept her feet steady and her single-mindedness did the rest. And then she was grabbing at the metal cross to haul herself up on to the little concrete platform above... thin air.

Before her, stretched the deep valley. To either side, she finally saw the extent of the steep cliff and jutting rock.

'Turn around,' she heard Nick call and she craned her neck to see him while clutching the cross with quivering arms. Then she caught sight of the lake. It was the northern corner, crowded by rock faces and greens and greys and blues. The huge hunk of rock blocking out part of her view of the lake must be Monte Baldo.

'And turn again.'

She could hear the smile in his voice and matched it. Hugging the cross so she didn't start to feel afraid, she swung around and caught sight of the other rocky mountain rising above the forest they'd hiked through. And beyond that... endless alpine peaks, still imposing, even in the distance.

She did another slow turn to appreciate the panorama. 'This is incredible. I can see... everything! Take a photo! Take a photo of me!' She patted her pocket for her phone, but didn't like the feeling of letting go of the cross while, three feet away, the land dropped suddenly away.

'I'll take it with mine. I'll make sure you get a decent version so you can frame it.'

'That sounds so stupid, but I just might.'

'It's not stupid. Just think of all those burly mountaineering types. Their flats are full of photos of themselves in precarious situations.'

She smiled and he snapped the first photo. 'I won't ever be a mountaineering type,' she said, wondering if she might have been, in another life.

'Maybe not, but you're up a mountain.'

Her smile stretched. 'I am. I'm up a bloody mountain.' He snapped another photo. She glanced at Nick, a few feet below. 'Can we take a selfie?'

'Sure.' He shrugged. His steps were much more secure as he joined her on the plinth. He wrapped one arm around her, anchoring it on the cross, and held the other one up to take the photo. 'Hmm, you had your eyes closed,' he muttered after checking the photo. 'Let's take another one.'

Instead of focussing on the warmth of his body next to hers, the familiar tickle of his aftershave, she forced her eyes open and looked at the image of the two of them. His handsome face was just as much of an attraction as the dramatic view. The picture she made, turned slightly to him, her smile contented and... believing... made her knees weaker than the prospect of the sheer drop behind her.

She wanted to frame that photo. She wanted to keep believing.

* * *

Lou came down from her mountaintop experience slowly. Physically descending the mountain was the first challenge, especially on the parts where the trail was so steep and rocky that she had to cling to the metal rope bolted to the rock face. But she shocked herself by loving it.

The first blow to her mood came when Nick explained that he had to be back at the convent that night. She convinced him to come into her room before driving up; it was worth it just for his sheepish smile as he did up his trousers before leaving. The lingering kiss he gave her at the door was good enough to melt her poor knees again, but she was grumpy that he had to say goodbye.

Greta's speculating look when she picked her up after a late breakfast on Thursday morning was the next part of Lou's crash back to earth and the expression on Edie's face when the Fiat pulled up outside the walls of the convent banished the last of her high spirits. Edie was waiting with Nick by the door and rushed at Lou as soon as she got out of the car.

'I missed you,' she whispered and something inside Lou shattered. This was the one thing in her life she couldn't mess up: her relationship with her daughter. She looked up, resisting the gathering tears, and caught sight of Nick, watching her carefully, his expression grave.

'I missed you, too, sweetheart,' she said, squeezing Edie again, as though it would help her get her head screwed on straight. 'Is everything okay?' Edie's shrug said more than any words could have. Lou clutched her shoulders. 'Is it the maestro? Rehearsal?' Edie shrugged again and Lou's alarm notched up.

'It's okay,' Edie murmured. Lou could have throttled Maestro Eckert. She looked up at Nick, demanding the answer of him, as she couldn't get anything out of Edie.

'He's added an extra rehearsal today because he thinks they're not ready. And... he could probably be a bit more encouraging.'

Nick's blank tone made Lou's shoulders droop. He didn't deserve to be stuck in the middle when he'd worked so hard to build the orchestra.

Edie sighed, clutching her elbows. Lou could still picture her half her current size with her cuddly crocodile held tight in her arms. It still shocked Lou how helpless and vulnerable Edie had been. 'It's just disappointing, because we'd been having such a good time.' Her lips thinned.

'We can't have a good time all the time,' Lou said gently.

'It's not just that.' Edie's voice lost its conviction. 'It's Dad,' she said apologetically, glancing between Lou and Nick.

Lou froze. Her arm came around Edie again. Everything in her chest that had started to come loose tightened up again, choking her. Her eyes strayed back to Nick, not sure what she was trying to get from him. Whatever it was, she shouldn't be looking to him for it.

'Uh, I'll...' he began, his voice trailing off. 'I'll talk to you later, then.' He swallowed. She smiled awkward thanks, her feelings a pathetic mix of embarrassment and regret.

After he'd left, Lou shepherded Edie to a bench in the cloister, facing the cool quadrangle with the magnolia. When Edie dropped her guard, her expression was pained.

'I don't know... if I'm supposed to tell you this stuff,' she mumbled.

'It's important that you can tell me anything, sweetheart.'

'But it's about Dad, not you. And I don't want to make it even more difficult between you two.'

Lou sighed. 'That's very considerate of you, but my feelings about your dad are not your responsibility.' She heard Nick's voice in her head, telling her that Phil's behaviour wasn't her responsibility. But it wasn't the same. Nick had no idea what she owed Edie – and, to a degree, Phil. 'If something's bothering you, I need to know so I can help you.'

She nodded, so accepting. 'I think they're arguing... a lot – Dad and Winny.'

'Oh, sweetheart, that's not something you need to worry about. Dad will work it out.'

'But they're arguing about me.'

Lou's anger balled immediately in her stomach. It took effort to keep her expression in check. 'What makes you say that?'

'I heard them.'

Lou swallowed and counted to three to make sure she didn't explode in front of Edie. 'You'd better tell me exactly what happened.'

'Last night I had another nosebleed.' Lou shuddered, but kept her mouth clamped shut. 'I had a tissue, so I stopped it at first, but then I needed another one, so I went to find Dad. But I could hear them behind the door before I even knocked. Winny said something about Dad rubbing you and me in her face because he obviously didn't care about my competition. She was actually pretty understanding yesterday after the terrible rehearsal. I mean, ballet sounds even worse than this, by the way.'

Lou nodded.

'Then Dad said he didn't have to care about my music to live up to his responsibilities,' Edie continued, her voice starting to quaver, and Lou winced. 'Then he said something about me needing him to balance out your wild ideas about me becoming a professional musician when it's just setting me up for disappointment.' She hiccoughed and grimaced, her lip trembling. 'And after the day we'd spent in rehearsal, trying so hard and failing and being told we couldn't do it over and over again...'

'You started to worry he was right?' Lou prompted.

Edie nodded and shoved the ball of her hand into her eye. 'Is he? I don't know why I'd go through this stuff with the maestro if I'm going to end up failing every audition.'

Lou frowned. Nick's words about hard work and obsession rose in her thoughts again, and his relationship with music. 'If you want it enough, you won't fail. I know how hard you work.'

'What if I don't want it enough? Or I'm just lazy?'

'You're not lazy. And if it turns out you don't want a professional career as a musician, then you could be a music teacher.'

Her head came up. 'Like Mr Romano.'

'Exactly.'

'I don't know if I'll ever be as good as Mr Romano,' Edie admitted faintly.

'I'm sure he would disagree, sweetheart. But I'm beginning to understand. He's a bit special. But I'm certain he enjoys it – and you would, too, if you decided not to pursue performance.'

Edie stared out at the blooming cloister. 'You're right. I think I just hated the rehearsal so much yesterday. I'd forgotten how it feels when I play my favourite pieces – like the Tessarini duet.'

'I'd love to hear you play that together,' Lou said. She'd heard both parts of the duet endlessly from Edie's room. 'But what does Dad know about your playing? He hasn't seen you perform in the past year. He's not saying it because of you.'

'Then why is he saying it?'

'Because of me, and Winny,' she said, trailing off. But the answer was unsatisfactory. 'And himself,' she added. 'He's saying it because he doesn't have all the answers, and that's scary sometimes. He's afraid he's losing touch with you.'

'And discouraging me is supposed to help with that?'

'He didn't realise you were listening.' Lou couldn't believe she was defending Phil, but Edie deserved the best from both her parents. 'It doesn't excuse him, but he might have thought harder about what he was saying if you'd been in the room. Besides, you're going to knock his socks off in the competition.'

Edie smiled weakly. 'I'm not so sure about that. Maestro Eckert seems to think we all suck.'

'That also says more about him than it does about you.'

'Yeah, well, competitions might be more about the judges than the participants.'

Lou gave her a squeeze. 'We'll see how it all goes, sweetheart. Either way, we'll be sharing an enormous dish of gelato at the airport on Monday to celebrate your first international competition. We'll hang on to the good bits, hey?'

Edie looked wistfully up at the rock face above the quadrangle. 'Do you think I'll have a teacher like Mr Romano at Purcell?'

Lou's heart squeezed uncomfortably. 'I'm not sure there are too many people like Mr Romano in the world,' she murmured.

'Are you over Dad? I mean, like, have you moved on and stuff?'

Lou couldn't stop the jerk of surprise. 'What? Where did that come from?'

'You're still pretty young, Mum. I mean, if Dad found Winny, why wouldn't you... get a boyfriend? If you were over him.'

Lou let out her breath on a slow huff. 'I don't know if I could... do that, sweetheart. Boyfriends are complicated. Getting over someone isn't just a "snap your fingers and you're done" sort of thing.'

Edie nodded sympathetically and leaned her head on Lou's shoulder. She enjoyed the affectionate ease, the glimmer of hope it gave her. All of the past eleven years – even the lows of the first three – had been worth the effort. 'I'm happy to have you to myself,' Edie said softly. 'I just thought... I thought maybe you and Mr Romano liked each other enough to get together. That would have been nice.'

Lou smiled faintly as her stomach did somersaults. It would have been nice. If only he weren't so talented and wonderful, she might have believed he'd settle for her. But if Phil had never settled for her, she'd never ask Nick to do that.

* * *

Lou cuddled up with Edie that night with her eyes open while her daughter went to sleep. Bedtime cuddles had become an ironic habit in the past year. How hard had it been for Lou in the beginning with baby Edie in the bed, the bleating newborn who wouldn't tolerate being separated from her mother for a second. Now Lou was the one who wanted the closeness, the reassurance of Edie's well-being.

Helene was up reading – and messaging Jason along the hall – but Edie drifted off peacefully in Lou's bed. After enjoying the last of the sleepy cuddles, Lou crept out of the bed and through the door with a whispered, 'I'll be back in a bit,' to Helene.

It was their last night in the convent. Lou wandered slowly along the hall, even though her destination was clear. She enjoyed the coolness of the tiles on the soles of her feet, the still and lonely air, the hushed peace of the place women had come to for centuries to leave the world behind. Lou had hoped to find herself here, or something similarly trite. It wasn't surprising that she hadn't found any answers. She didn't even know where to start with the questions. But something *had* changed.

Maybe it was just the sex. She suppressed a smile and made her way out to the terrace. But the terrace had only one occupant, and it wasn't the one she'd hoped to see.

'Are you still awake, Lou? Would you like a glass of wine?' Greta asked.

Lou wished she didn't feel so awkward, but the 'mother-of-the-man-you've-just-had-sex-with' thing was... uncomfortable. She decided it was best to face it head-on. 'Do you know if Nick is still up?'

'No, he's gone to bed. Big day tomorrow.'

'Of course,' Lou murmured. She hadn't meant to make Greta defend him. 'Yes, I'll have a small glass of wine, thank you.' She flopped into one of the wicker chairs, staring out at the scattered lights and the moonlight reflected off the lake.

'What did you think of the farm on Tuesday?' Greta asked, pouring the wine.

Lou's eyes flickered to her, but it could have been an innocent question. She hadn't actually slept with Nick at that point. 'It was lovely. I can't believe there are trees there that are older than both of your parents. I'm glad I got to see it.'

Greta nodded. 'And my mother's hiking boots? Did you use them?'

Lou felt the heat rising to her cheeks, but the dim light from the citronella candle was mercifully low enough to hide her embarrassment. 'Yes. Didn't Nick tell you? We went up a mountain.' She grinned, remembering. 'I made it to the top. I could barely believe it. Monte Biaena, it was called.'

'One of our local peaks, near the farm. That's not an easy climb for a beginner!'

'It's not?'

'Not at all. It's very steep.'

Lou tried to chuckle, but she was too thoughtful. Why had Nick chosen a difficult hike? Because he'd known she could do it. Her face warmed even more, heat rising from the ache in her chest.

'I'm sorry,' she said suddenly. Greta didn't say anything in response, but she leaned forward slowly to peer at Lou in the dim light. Her silence was a definite prompt to explain herself. 'I'm sorry if I hurt Nick,' she blurted out. She wasn't sure if she was speaking in the past, present or future.

'Why would you hurt Nick?' Greta asked carefully.

'I'm a mess, Greta,' Lou said with a shake of her head. 'And he doesn't deserve to get dragged in.'

'Isn't getting dragged in his decision?'

Lou frowned. Why wasn't Greta looking at her with disapproval? Lou wanted a scolding, not the glow of concern in her eyes. 'I wouldn't want him to sacrifice anything for me. I have my challenges and I'm not... worth...' she sighed and glanced up at the tiled awning '... him. I'm not worth him.'

Greta didn't respond for a long time. 'What challenges do you think you are the only one to have?'

Lou shivered and gathered her cardigan around herself. Greta didn't understand. Lou had had to share her challenges with Phil, especially at the beginning, and it had left her in the state she was in today. Something whispered that Nick was different, but she'd been helpless for too long after Edie was born and again when Phil left. She couldn't do it again.

'You remember I've been through a divorce, too,' Greta prompted.

Lou nodded, more out of politeness than anything else. 'I know. And I know you argued about Nick's musical career. I know you understand a lot of what I've been through.'

Greta inclined her head thoughtfully. 'I know what it's like to feel like you have no more space in your life.'

'I have space. All of the workshops? I did them because I have so much damn space.'

'And you enjoyed them, which is wonderful. But I don't mean time. I mean... space in your heart. You expend all of your energy for other people until you have nothing else.'

Lou snorted. 'I'm not that much of a martyr.'

'You wouldn't give up everything for Edie?'

'Of course I would. I'm her mother!'

'And to maintain a functional relationship with Phil?'

Lou nodded again. 'Those aren't choices.'

'But you can't serve Edie if you're miserable.'

'I'm not miserable!' she insisted.

'Fair enough,' continued Greta. 'But as Nick got older, I realised something.'

Lou nodded and sipped her wine, waiting for Greta to get it

over with. If she wanted to get her advice off her chest, that was fine.

'I realised that what he wanted was for me to be happy, too.'

Lou rested her head back against the wicker chair, remembering Nick doing the same, trying to picture his face in her mind because that was what she most wanted to see. 'That sounds like Nick. I know Edie wants me to be happy.' In fact, Edie wanted her to be happy with Nick, which was probably what Greta was hinting at. Why didn't anyone understand it just wouldn't happen? She didn't want to pull him down and have him resent her as Phil did.

'But will you let someone make you happy?'

'I don't need someone else to make me happy!' Lou snapped. 'Sorry, I'm just... tired... and there's a lot going on.'

'I can see that, pet. But just remember what I said: you deserve to be happy.'

Lou laughed, but with no humour. 'I'll remember.'

* * *

Lou was grinding her teeth at the remembered comment the following day in the car on the way to Milan. A three-hour drive with her ex-husband and his snippy girlfriend wasn't exactly what she would have chosen to make herself happy.

Edie had been right. There was some uncomfortable energy between the couple. But Lou didn't particularly care. She just wanted him to keep it to himself.

They drove through the outskirts of Milan, with its grand glass and stucco buildings and graffitied corners, and the magic of the weeks at the lake felt a long way away already. The frenetic pace was immediately noticeable. Well-dressed men and women weaved along the pavements with purpose, metro stations buzzed and the public squares were full of tourists. Lou wondered what background Nick would have given, if he'd been there. She wondered where his family had lived, whether it had been an apartment in one of the tall stone buildings with Juliet balconies and decorative pediments.

They met the group at the Conservatorio for a tour. Lou was distracted, looking out for Nick, but he didn't come. The other kids had been handed over to their parents and Miss Hwang was absent, too. He probably had work to do and he certainly didn't need the tour of his old school.

The group moved through the hallowed halls of the great music university and associated secondary school and Lou struggled to respond adequately to Edie's enthusiasm – much less to Helene's ecstatic excitement, although it did feel like a magical, cloistered realm where music reigned.

Only in the modern auditorium did Lou stop and take a good look, picturing a very young Nick on stage with his violin. Tomorrow, it would be Edie's turn. She hoped it would do both herself and Nick good to see Edie on stage, enjoying herself. At least Lou hoped she'd enjoy herself. She hoped Phil hadn't spoiled her pleasure in the music.

They checked into the university residence a few streets away, where students from five different countries were staying during the competition. Edie was assigned a bed in a twin room with Meg, but Lou was across the communal living area in a double room by herself, so she suspected Edie would come in with her. Helene was along the hall with the boys and Lou's room was far too empty all of a sudden. Like her life? Oh, God, what a stupid thought. Just because the holiday was over didn't mean that real life sucked. Greta thought she needed space in her life? All she had was space.

Will you let someone make you happy?

It was trite nonsense, but it was already haunting her. Focussing on her own happiness would be selfish, and she'd seen the damage done by being selfish when she'd struggled to adapt after Edie was born. She knew, after that brush with darkness, that happiness was a state of mind, not a set of circumstances. It wasn't something she should expect from another person.

But it was disconcerting how much happiness, in her imagination, looked remarkably like a set of circumstances in which she saw Nick every day.

Her reality at dinner was different: a jittery pre-teen, an ex who was full of bluster and his very absent girlfriend. It didn't help that the mushrooms in her risotto didn't compare to freshly picked porcini from a Trentino forest, the olive oil on the bread was flat and bland and the wine an easy chianti, which was neither as complex as the Amarone or as refreshing as the Recioto della Valpolicella.

Phil had picked the restaurant, as usual. Lou felt slightly claustrophobic returning to the routine from earlier family holidays, but it hadn't occurred to Phil that she might have some experience with the regional cuisine. She was a long way from the lake and she seemed to have left her confidence behind. Perhaps Phil understood the well-dressed, successful people of Milan better than she did.

Most ominously, he made no mention of Winny's absence. Lou wished he'd just blurt out that she'd left him and let her and Edie get on with dinner. Instead, he sat, alone and taking up too much space, trying to behave like his usual self.

Then, outside the residence, he pulled Lou aside before leaving for his own hotel. Unease rose in her chest.

'Can I talk to you?' he asked.

No. Whatever it is, please sort it out yourself. And please stop making everything about you, because your daughter is performing in the most prestigious competition of her life tomorrow and she needs your support.

'Okay,' she said instead. He glanced pointedly at Edie and Lou gritted her teeth. 'Edie, maybe you could go on up. I'll be there soon.' Lou frowned at Phil. She would give him three minutes.

'I can't help wondering,' he began, dropping his chin to give her his serious look, but she was struggling to take him seriously any more. 'I can't help wondering if there was something I could have done... differently... where it wouldn't feel as though we'd lost so much.'

She couldn't not respond to the grief in his voice. She knew it intimately. 'I'm sure there was, Phil,' she said more gently than she'd expected.

'Was? What about for the future?'

'It depends on what you want.' If he meant he was ready to listen to her and Edie, she would cut him some slack. If he meant anything about his relationship with her... No. He probably didn't mean that. But if he did... just no.

Her breath hitched to realise that her feelings about the marriage and divorce had changed. She no longer looked back and saw herself as Phil's other half. She had still been Lou, even at the lowest point. She had tried. She had built some kind of family, some kind of life. The divorce didn't suddenly make her invalid. The space that Phil had taken up in her life had finally shrunk.

'I think Winny might have left,' he muttered, 'permanently.'

Lou sighed and gave him a faint, sympathetic smile. 'I'm sorry.' He looked lost. She'd never thought she'd see the inimitable Phil Saunders, master of all he produced, looking lost. An inappropriate laugh rose up in her chest. He was just as screwed up as she was. 'Maybe you'll make up.'

His brow furrowed. 'How would you feel about that?'

'My feelings haven't mattered to you before. It's your life.'

'I'm sorry, Lou. You've obviously grown and changed, and I'm proud of you for doing that. I... I don't know what I want any more.'

'You might find that's been the case for longer than you think.'

21

Nick walked quickly to shake off the memories, which were starting to choke him. He'd avoided the Conservatorio this afternoon, but it would be waiting for him tomorrow, along with the maestro and the kids who had trusted him.

He'd just had dinner with his father. He'd accomplished the obligatory meal and awkward conversation. Neither of them had wanted to talk about the competition or the Conservatorio, so topics had been limited. Now, Nick only had to shake off the confusion and lingering guilt about his parents. He didn't think they'd seen each other at all in the past sixteen years. Compared to them, Lou and Phil were a model in amicable divorces.

Speaking of Lou and Phil, Nick turned the corner and stopped short to see them engrossed in conversation at the door of the residence hall. Lou wasn't angry. He could tell straight away. In fact, she had an odd smile on her face. His heart beat in his ears, although he didn't want to acknowledge his feelings – feelings he was beginning to suspect went deeper than he'd intended. He knew where Lou's priorities lay. Because of Edie,

Phil would always be among her priorities. She didn't need to be responsible for Nick's ragged feelings as well.

'I keep wondering what would have happened if... if Edie hadn't come along quite so soon,' Phil muttered, but the words reached Nick's ears.

'That's a lot of wondering – without much purpose,' Lou said, cocking her head. She stood tall, her hair moving slightly in the breeze, and he hoped Phil would realise one day just how spectacular she was.

'I wasn't always fair to you. I know you struggled—'

'And you were there to help when I was struggling, so that's not the point.'

'Still, I might owe you an apology.' *Might?* Nick gritted his teeth. 'Perhaps I expected too much of you.' The words turned Nick's stomach. What a jerk. He'd spent years not appreciating an incredible woman and, when he finally stepped back to examine his own behaviour, all he could come up with was that he should have settled for her and her flaws that only existed in his own mind?

For God's sake, Nick expected the world from Lou and had no doubt she would be everything he imagined – if she didn't feel so trapped. He breathed out slowly through his nose.

'I appreciate the apology,' Lou said, her voice soft.

'I'd like to start again. I'd like to do better this time.'

Nick froze. He shouldn't be listening to this conversation. It wasn't just a moral dilemma; his chest was starting to ache and he had to get away.

'Phil...' she said, loosening her crossed arms.

Nick couldn't have said if it was an invitation or not, but Phil took it as one. He wrapped his arms around her. The strength of Nick's distaste surprised him. Was it the thought of her cuddling with the man who had stripped her confidence? He screwed his eyes shut. It was more, but he couldn't afford to think about it. At least now he understood why he'd been happy to stay with Naomi all those years. It had been better than this. Great way to wake up to the fact that his passion would never go away – by falling in love with a woman who wouldn't let herself love him back.

When he opened his eyes again, Phil was leaning down and Nick choked, falling into a coughing fit. Lou and Phil jerked apart and Nick forced his legs into action. He strode past, sparing them only the briefest of glances.

'Sorry to interrupt.' He held up his hand. 'I'll see you in the morning.' He closed the door firmly behind him.

When there was a knock at his door twenty minutes later, he shouldn't have been surprised. But he'd been too eager to fall into a dark mood that was the unfortunate flipside of his creative zeal – or *artistic temperament*, as she'd called it.

He wrenched the door open and skewered her with a look that hid nothing. She drew back, but then frowned, unimpressed. 'Stop jumping to conclusions,' she said peevishly. 'Can I come in?'

His heart tripped at her implication, and in anticipation of her company – alone, in his room. He'd missed her. Two days of nothing more than glances and he'd missed her. Not good. 'Sure, make yourself at home,' he said.

'Sarcasm isn't really you,' she said with a frown as she swept in.

'Neither is jealousy,' he muttered.

She froze and her gaze rose slowly to his. 'Nick...' Her regretful apology was coming more quickly than he'd expected.

He held up a hand. 'Don't worry about it. I'm not really angry with you.'

'I'm not getting back together with Phil.'

'That wasn't what...' His brain reacted sluggishly. He sighed. 'I knew that... on some level.'

'You know me well enough for that.' Did he? A large part of him protested that he knew her better than she knew herself. Another part of him found her such a mystery that he had no hope of working her out.

'I suppose I do,' he said, rubbing his forehead.

She smiled ruefully. 'If you think I'd be capable of sleeping with you and then getting back together with Phil two days later, I hate to imagine your impression of me.'

'That's not... I'm sorry. It was more a reflection on me than on you. I know you have a lot... going on.' He arranged his features into a suitably understanding expression. He knew she had so much going on that she wouldn't consider turning their affair into something more.

'You do, too,' she said. 'You avoided the Conservatorio this afternoon.'

'I've been there before.' He shrugged.

She chuckled. 'I wasn't disputing that. Are you going to be okay, tomorrow?'

'I'd better be.' His lips twitched with the weird urge to smile. 'I don't have to get up on stage until the choir competition on Sunday,' he pointed out.

'Are any of your old teachers still here?'

'I haven't looked,' he said. 'I'll be fine. You've told me plenty of times you have your own responsibilities. You don't need to add me to them.'

She mashed her lips together, disgruntled. It was so cute, some of his bad mood stubbornly lifted. But he clung to it for protection.

'We had sex and now you're grumpy as heck. How is that not my responsibility?'

'How do you know they're related?'

'You're not denying it.' Damn, she had a point. 'I wouldn't have let it happen if I'd known you were going to blame me.'

His head snapped up. 'I'm not blaming you. I'll take my share of responsibility for amazing sex. You're the one who blames yourself for everything!'

'What's your problem? I've told you I'm not getting back together with Phil. Are you angry with me for making you realise you're allowed to feel stuff?'

'No,' he responded immediately, his face hot. She stared at him, strong and smart and so much more than just talented. 'I'm angry with you for not realising the same about yourself.'

She drew back, her nostrils flaring. He'd made a hit, but there was no satisfaction in it – for either of them. 'You don't know what you're talking about.'

He gave her a narrow look. 'I thought you said I know you well.'

She crumbled as he watched. Her shoulders sank, her lips trembled. He took a step closer in alarm, but she withdrew with a finality that scared him.

He nodded sharply. 'Okay, I get the message. Phil can hug you, but I can't,' he grumbled.

'He's Edie's father,' she said, her voice strained. 'And, for better or for worse, he knows some things about me that you don't.'

He hated this. He hated the idea that she was so stuck in what she thought she couldn't do. Whatever she was talking about, he didn't like being in the dark.

'I know some things about you that he doesn't,' he insisted. She studied him, her expression tumultuous. 'I know that you have endless curiosity. I know that you're too funny to worry about being embarrassed. I know that people warm to you immediately and feel safe with you. And you have a great capability for joy and love. Phil doesn't know any of that. If he did, he would never have let you go.'

She flinched and he wondered if he'd just made everything worse. She shook her head slowly. 'You don't understand.' Her denial was firm. She stilled, staring at the institutional carpet of the residence hall. 'When I had Edie,' she began, the words torn from her, 'I fell apart. It has a nice, clinical name: post-natal depression. I had post-natal depression. I was depressed. You get the idea. End of story. But for fuck's sake, that description doesn't begin to cover the way I failed her – the way I failed them!' He would have been happy to hear the strength back in her voice, but it was so brittle, he didn't trust it. And he was upset to discover that she had been right: he hadn't known this important thing about her.

'This one thing I had to do with my life, the greatest responsibility in the world, and I wanted to give her back. She cried all the time. I hated breastfeeding. I was terrified. She had constant nappy rash because I didn't change her. She didn't put on much weight and I can't really remember how much I tried. And Phil held it together. He got me help – professional help, because I was beyond anything else. He made me take the pills. He made sure Edie was okay. He pulled us through.'

And then he left you... But Nick finally understood why she couldn't see that betrayal for what it was. He understood why he couldn't tell her she could let it go. He felt trapped and torn... and most definitely in love.

'I haven't been the same since – or, more specifically, I was always prone to that. On the surface, everything is fine. I'm a bloody pageant girl on the outside. But underneath, I'm a mess.'

'Lou...' He was tongue-tied. What could he say? His reaction was beside the point. And blurting out 'I love you' would achieve nothing until she could believe him. Would she ever?

'Thanks for telling me,' he murmured. 'I can't imagine what you went through and I understand how that puts Phil in your life... forever.' He wanted a hug – for purely selfish reasons. Had his stupid jealousy ruined his chances? 'But I think you're doing a pretty good job of being who you are, and everyone loves you for it.'

She snorted. 'Yeah, because I lead the way in school-run slovenliness. That's not what I meant about being okay on the surface.'

'I know you didn't mean that. But you put people at ease; you make them smile. It's because you don't try to be someone you're not.'

'Like you do,' she said, so softly he wasn't sure if she'd meant him to hear.

'Exactly,' he agreed fiercely.

She shook her head. 'If people are comfortable around me, it's because I'm non-threatening, which is code for "I suck". Trust me, it's a thing.' He tried to interrupt, but she shook her head. 'Do you know I only have my job because of Phil pulling strings? I might lose it after the summer. I have a big meeting with my boss. I trained as a journalist, but I was never cut out for it and after Edie... I couldn't stomach anything hard-hitting. I do the froth and I read the news that no one watches.'

He wondered whether she was going to help the film crew coming tomorrow. He'd forgotten to ask her about it during their two days together and assumed it was none of his business anyway. The way Phil had expressed it on Monday, it was his project, but he could imagine Lou making a good contribution to the piece, if her TV personality was like her own – earnest, curious and charming.

'The people who do watch your bulletin like it. And the froth can be just as important as the hard-hitting stories. Do you think teaching kids to appreciate music is useless because it doesn't contribute to society?'

'Don't you dare! It contributes to their lives!'

'And your news bulletin contributes to the lives of lots of lonely people who are home during the day!'

She drew back and he hoped he'd at least scored that point. He couldn't heal her wounds relating to motherhood – he wasn't sure anyone could, even Lou herself – but, regarding her work, she might be more open to reasoning.

'I'm a regular public service broadcaster,' she drawled.

He raised his hands as if to say, 'I rest my case.' 'And funny!'

Her fists landed on her hips. 'Do you know why I'm so vain about my hair? And don't tell me I'm not vain. I know how much time and energy I spend making my hair this ridiculously shiny.'

He hesitated over the quick change of direction. 'It is pretty spectacular,' he murmured.

'Because all my hair fell out. I had crazy wisps for years after she was born, blotchy skin and weight that fluctuated depending on how I was managing. I wore a wig to my job interview. My hair is real now, but it's a stupid, lingering weakness. I'm only as good as the people who need me and what do they care about my hair?'

'They care that you respect yourself. And they know that you're even more amazing inside.'

She sucked in a startled breath. 'You're the most hypocritical man I've met! How can you hide yourself away, afraid of the opinions of others, and think I'm the amazing one?'

'Because you don't hide, no matter what life throws at you! You're right, I'm grumpy and a hypocrite. I wonder why you bothered to sleep with me.'

'Maybe I like grumpy and hypocritical. And you're handsome as heck, you know.'

His cheeks heated and he stared at her. What was he supposed to do in three days when he didn't have an excuse to see her any more? Could he quickly backtrack to the friends thing? He doubted it. He felt way too much when she was in the room with him. He took a deep breath. 'You like grumpy and hypocritical, but you don't believe I might like you?'

She rolled her eyes. 'What happened to the burden of your talent and escaping your rampant feelings?'

He sighed. He'd been an idiot to be so confused. His music had nothing to do with his ability to love and be loved. 'I think we both know I was talking shit.'

She smiled, but it was sharp with regret. 'Whereas my problems are even bigger than I admitted,' she said. She raised her hands haltingly, settling them high on his chest and stroking his shoulders, fondly, like a friend – or a child. 'If you're ready to be who you are, then I'll be happy for you. But you don't need me bringing you confusion and failure.'

He straightened and her hands fell to her sides. 'I understand I can't tell you what to feel, but I won't let you make assumptions about what I feel. I know this is not a forever thing and I won't make demands on you, but you have brought me a lot more than confusion and failure already.' He'd shocked her into silence, so he ran with it. 'Your hair is very beautiful, but you've got something a lot shinier, a lot healthier than your gorgeous hair. It's your gorgeous heart. That's the part I'm going to miss.'

Her eyes closed slowly. 'Thank you,' she murmured.

He shook his head. 'You can thank me by believing me.' Her wince was enough of an answer to how likely that was. He sighed. He needed a way out – he needed to give her a way out of this conversation, of the relationship, even though that stung. 'I'll probably be... pretty busy over the next couple of days,' he finished weakly.

She nodded. 'Let me know if I can help.'

'I will, but the organisers should have everything in hand. Maybe you could go and see the sights of Milan.'

She scowled. 'Maybe I could.'

He stared at her, trying to force himself to move, but he missed his chance. With a quick frown, she grabbed a fistful of his shirt and pulled herself up to kiss him. The tension in the air cracked immediately, breaking in the storm of a kiss that could be their last. He grabbed her and pulled her closer. If she thought he should embrace his feelings, then she would have to experience them, too. He opened his mouth and kissed her hard while she looped her arms around his neck and hung on. Her familiar scent reminded him of intimacy and contentment. He tore away before he started thinking about the skin under her clothes.

She released a long breath on a whistle. 'I didn't really mean for that to happen.'

'I know.'

She leaned up one more time and gave him a soft, sweet kiss that was just as devastating. 'Thank you for being wonderful – for being you,' she murmured. She glanced back up into his face. 'Goodnight.'

He didn't return her tentative smile. He crossed his arms over his suddenly aching chest. 'Good night,' he whispered, watching her gravely as she turned and left.

22

Lou and Edie found their rehearsal room with some difficulty in the rabbit warren of the Conservatorio the next morning. Edie was brimming with energy, which made Lou wary. Would she crash too soon? She might have worried less if Edie had admitted to feeling nervous, but she'd insisted she was fine.

The orchestra was setting up and Nick and the maestro were already there when they arrived – as well as a film crew. Lou stopped and stared. They wore lanyards from her TV station. She didn't know all of the crews, but she was certain she should have known of this one. They were standing to the side with Phil and Nick as the camerawoman unpacked her things.

'Lou!' Phil looked up with a smile. 'You know Chris and Tam from the station?'

'No, actually,' she muttered.

'You *are* here!' one of the women exclaimed and shook Lou's hand warmly. 'I got the impression from Phil that you wouldn't be here.'

'I could say the same about you,' Lou said through gritted teeth.

'You didn't know they were filming?' Nick asked.

'I thought you'd told her,' Phil said.

Nick gave Phil a grim look. 'Why would I have told her?' *Why indeed?* Did Phil know they'd spent the two days together?

'You knew?' Lou asked Nick, discomfort rising in her throat. What was going on?

He nodded. 'Phil took me through it on Monday. We had to organise permission forms and a schedule. He didn't tell you?'

She shook her head silently, feeling Nick's concerned gaze on her. But she was looking at Phil. He'd had ample opportunity to mention it. Her stomach clenched in resentment. He didn't want her involved.

'What are you filming?'

The two women from the film crew glanced at each other and Lou felt the heat rise to her cheeks. 'It's a spot for *How and Why*.' One of the women named a kids' documentary show. 'It's just a ten-minute slot.'

Lou glanced at Edie. She didn't seem surprised. Lou was the only one who'd missed the memo. 'That's great,' she bit out and turned back to Edie.

When she'd waved Edie off towards the orchestra, she turned to find Chris – or was it Tam? – standing awkwardly behind her. 'Feel free to say no. You must be busy, or we would have planned this from the beginning.' She paused and Lou must have given her a withering look because she stood up straighter and continued. 'I mean, I think it would be perfect. We've only got budget for voiceover, but... you're here and... your kid is playing. You'd be the perfect presenter for this spot. I don't know why Phil didn't think of it.'

Lou froze. She knew. She'd never been anyone's perfect anything. She'd been a disappointing pageant girl, a broken mother and an inadequate wife. 'You want me to present?'

'You probably have a lot to do. And it's not ideal with no notice! I wish we'd been able to plan it!'

Chris-or-Tam did a good job of not running her eyes over Lou's outfit, which featured an ancient T-shirt and a scruffy pair of cut-offs. She'd been too daunted by the fashionable Milanese to make any effort.

'What have you planned?'

'After grabbing a snippet from the rehearsal, we're going to take some shots around Milan and then come back for the first part of the competition this afternoon. We don't have the text written yet because we were going to add that later.'

Lou's mind worked. She could already picture the spot coming together, an introduction filmed in front of the stunning cathedral, shots of nervous kids, the intense concentration and challenge of the competition. It would be a great story to tell. She was halfway to writing it in her head.

'I'd love to present it,' she said before she could talk herself out of it. 'I'll just run back and get changed. I'll start scribbling a few words down and we can grab a few pieces to camera so we have a selection when we get back to the studio.'

'Great!' The woman looked genuinely chuffed that Lou was willing to do it. What alternate universe was this?

She didn't bother to inform Phil, and Nick had disappeared, so she dashed out of the room alone. Helene was in the corridor, hovering.

'Do you think they'll let me stay in the rehearsal?' she asked.

'Maybe later,' Lou said. She paused. 'But first, I need your help for half an hour. Do you have any make-up?'

Helene frowned at her. 'Yes. What's going on?'

'Come on. I'll explain on the way.'

* * *

'The competition takes place every four years, each time in a different city. This year's location is Milan or, as the Italians call it, Milano – a historic city where the composer Verdi found success, and the home of the famous La Scala theatre, which has been a top venue for classical music for centuries.' Lou walked slowly forward in the sunshine, keeping her eyes on the camera. 'We're here in the Piazza del Duo-shit!' She flapped her hands in frustration. She looked up to find Chris and Tam grinning at her. 'I can't pronounce it! Duow-mow. Doo-o-mo. For fuck's sake! Are you still filming?'

'No,' Tam said, her smile much too innocent and her quick finger on the button betraying her.

Lou laughed and pulled out her phone, listening to Google Translate saying the word a few more times. She wished Nick were there to demonstrate the pronunciation in a way that would give her an excuse to stare at his mouth. She wished Nick were there for any reason. It was a beautiful, sunny morning on the stunning central square in front of the cathedral, surrounded by grand buildings with arches and ornamental pediments and fine stone. She longed to be able to soak it in with her hand tucked in his. It wasn't a good sign for her bright, independent future as a single woman – the bright future she was going to make for herself, damn it! Phil could go stick his opinions and his hypocritical overtures of friendship, or whatever the hell he wanted.

She was enjoying herself. The mispronunciation wasn't the first mistake she'd made and it wouldn't be the last, but Chris and Tam were a fun team and, in the warm Italian sunshine, fresh from her weeks at the lake, the pressure was off. Lou wanted to share her enthusiasm for the camp, for the sights and smells of the city.

They'd rushed madly across Milan, grabbing a shot of the La Scala theatre, where the competition finalists would play tomorrow night; the inside of the elegant Galleria Vittorio Emanuele II; an alternative piece-to-camera outside the mediaeval castle and a quick trip past the picturesque Naviglio Grande canal.

Lou would come back, she decided, although what she would think about Nick's home town after she'd arrived back in England and accepted reality, she couldn't say. She already missed Lake Garda, the hot and cool air, the forests, mountains, terracotta villages – and the convent. But would she be able to go back? Would it all be a disappointment without Nick as her guide?

She was, thankfully, too busy to grapple with the reality that awaited her on Monday morning when they flew home to London. They arrived back at the Conservatorio in time to fudge another piece-to-camera in the cloistered courtyard and meet Edie when she emerged from rehearsal for lunch. She looked alarmingly worn out.

Lou's gaze rose automatically to search out Nick. When she found him, he gave her a helpless shrug and a grim smile. She wrapped her arm around Edie ready to listen, but Edie just sighed and laid her head on Lou's shoulder.

In the canteen, Lou grabbed food in a hurry and plonked down next to Nick, nabbing the seat quickly before another hovering parent could claim it. He looked up with a half-smile for Lou and something warmer for Edie, who sat, hunched and silent, next to Lou and took a lacklustre bite of her pasta.

'What's really going on?' He shrugged and opened his mouth, but Lou slapped his arm with the backs of her fingers before he could begin. 'And whatever it is, it's not your fault. That is the wrong answer.'

His smile grew, but Phil chose that moment to sit opposite them and Lou felt suddenly like a teenager sitting next to her crush, trying to hide her feelings while the rest of the class looked on with knowing sniggers. She eyed Phil. His expression was blank – too blank.

'It was a hard rehearsal. We knew it would be, but...'

'It's no fun,' Edie blurted out.

'The performance will be,' Nick assured her.

'Even though the maestro thinks we don't have a chance of being finalists?'

He paused. 'The maestro might be obsessed with the competition, but we don't have to be.'

'You don't think we'll make it either!'

Lou watched Edie, before shooting Nick an accusatory look, but it was half-hearted. She understood the lesson he had to help them through. And she knew how hard it was for him. Unable to stop herself, she squeezed his hand between their chairs.

'I don't know why they put the kids through this,' Phil grumbled. 'It's not as though they're learning much, under all this pressure.'

Lou bristled, wondering how she'd ever put up with him. She leaned close to Edie. 'You know I never won a pageant – ever.'

She glanced up with a reluctant smile. 'I know, Mum.'

'You've worked hard on this. You're playing in the best orchestra you've ever been part of. You've mastered the Jenkins. You all know how much you've achieved.'

She could feel Nick's eyes on her as she spoke. Why was she so warm whenever he was next to her? She'd expected the intimacy to fade the further they travelled from the lake. They'd return to being acquaintances back on British soil. But although they'd had no chance to speak privately, let alone do anything else privately, the awareness of him next to her had only grown.

He caught up to her in the corridor after lunch. 'Hey,' was all he said at first.

She stopped walking and leaned against the wall to take a good look at him. 'Hey,' she replied with a knowing smile.

'Your filming seems to be going well,' he said, inclining his head.

'Is there an "I told you so" hidden in there somewhere?'

'I might have been thinking of saying that, but now I wouldn't dream of it.'

'But you have to tell me if Edie needs me and I'm off somewhere with the crew.' His smile dimmed and Lou could have kicked herself. 'Forget that. I shouldn't have asked. Phil and I will manage.'

He studied her for a long time, the light banter gone. 'You'll manage,' he said finally, but she couldn't help wondering if he'd wanted to say something else.

'How are you doing?'

He was making a valiant effort to keep his emotions off his face, but she noticed the sudden rise and fall of his chest and interpreted his abortive hand gestures. She wondered if she was allowed to give him a hug.

'I'm in the background until tomorrow, so it's fine.'

Heavy footsteps sounded behind her and Nick's quick step back and indrawn breath worried Lou. She glanced behind her with a grimace to see Phil and the TV crew approaching. Lou felt, rather than saw, Phil's look.

'Oh, are you ready for the interview?'

Her head snapped up. 'You agreed to be interviewed?' Nick swallowed and shrugged. She sighed. 'You don't have to.'

He gave her a sceptical look. 'Don't I? At least now I get to be interviewed by you.'

She couldn't quite stifle her smile. 'I'll try to be gentle.'

He glanced at the TV crew. 'I'll go find a room where we can record.'

'Great, thanks,' said Chris. She turned to Lou with a smile after Nick had gone on ahead. 'So, you two are... friendly, then?'

Lou didn't dare look at Phil, but she could feel him there – in an entirely different way from how she felt Nick. 'We've been at camp for three weeks already and I've known him for years.' She nearly choked again to hear the last bit. What would Phil think?

'What happens at band camp stays at band camp?' Chris laughed.

'He's a little young for you, isn't he?'

Phil's mild words sent such a shot of ice over her skin. 'Nick might be twelve years younger than you Phil, but he's not a fresh-faced teenager,' she said with a tight smile. She made a neat turn on her sneakers and headed off in the direction Nick had taken.

She hadn't cooled down by the time Chris fell into step beside her. 'Nice one,' Chris said out of the side of her mouth. Lou looked up in surprise to see her pointed wink.

'He is too young for me,' she muttered.

'He doesn't seem to think so.'

'And too hot for me,' she added ruefully.

Chris chuckled. 'He is hot. You get a massive green light from me to get it on with him.'

'Th-thanks,' Lou stuttered.

'Unless you already have.' If Lou's blush hadn't given her away, her mortified stare certainly did. 'Ooh, I thought so! Wow, good going, you! Hot, young lover. You deserve it, sweetie. You absolutely deserve it.'

Lou laughed, but it was mixed with an odd bleakness at Chris' turn of phrase. Maybe she did deserve a hot, young lover. But she wanted love. Until she could get past the hefty mistakes she'd made, until she found what she was worth, she didn't have the space for love.

* * *

'Nick.'

He stopped talking. He wasn't sure what he was rambling on about anyway. The camera was burning his skin, making him feel prickly all over and out of breath. 'What?'

'Shhh. The camera's not rolling.'

'What?'

'It sucked too much. I gave them the signal to cut.'

He crossed his arms over his chest and gave her a sharp look. 'I went through that for nothing?'

'Do you think it was any less painful for us?'

'I'm sorry I'm not your ideal talent,' he said, giving her a pointed look. He wasn't her ideal boyfriend either – that much was clear. She didn't even want him to help look out for Edie. Whether she was just trapped in her own insecurities or truly didn't feel enough, the result was the same: no more Lou after tomorrow night.

'I know your talent lays in other areas,' she said with such a straight face he suspected she hadn't intended to make him think about his talent in the bedroom. She was so bad for him, making him feel things that weren't constructive, challenging views that had protected him since before that day when he'd lost it on stage in this very building. And yet, she made him feel incredibly good.

Not for the first time, he began to realise the way he'd viewed the world pre-Lou had been missing key components. His obsessive tendencies with music weren't incompatible with a relationship. His fears and hang-ups had nothing to do with love. But his previous relationships had also had nothing to do with love, because that was what this was.

'What do you want me to talk about, then?'

'Feelings,' she said. He almost choked. 'The viewers – who are also kids – want to know what it feels like to get out there. You're the best person for the job.'

'You're rubbing it in,' he accused.

'But you know it's true.'

'Okay,' he said and sat back. They were in an otherwise empty green room. The orchestra competition was due to start in just under an hour. He was in love with Lou. There were a lot of feelings. 'Everyone gets stage fright. Some people experience it more strongly than others and it's one of the most difficult parts of playing music.'

'What can you do to get through it?'

'Sometimes nothing. Sometimes you play terrified – terribly. Sometimes you find it fades once you get into the music, which is why it's good to know the beginning of each piece by heart. It's incredibly personal, walking on stage and interpreting a piece of music – especially when you know you're going to be judged on it. And that's why it really is true that anyone who simply walks on stage and makes it through their piece is a competition winner.'

'Even if they come last?'

'Learning to deal with disappointment is part of the challenge. Someone has to come last. But if you lose with grace and keep going, that's more powerful than winning every competition. You have to keep it all about the music. To get wrapped up in winning and losing is to trivialise the experience.'

'Do you think they're going to do well?'

'They're going to do incredibly. Whether we spend this evening elated or wallowing in disappointment, they've done well, they've learned and they've worked hard together.'

'That's lovely to say, but do you mean it?'

He looked up at her in surprise. 'Of course.'

'What about you? If they don't make it through, are you going to sit back and think how much passion you've shared with them?

How much joy and confidence you've brought them? Are you going to accept your success?'

God, she was good. 'I know what you're doing, Lou,' he said. He'd worked out that the camera was rolling, but it didn't matter any more. He pierced her with a look. 'I will if you will.' Did she have any idea that he meant not only accepting themselves, but accepting each other?

'It doesn't work like that.' She sighed. 'I can't make you believe in yourself.'

'And I can't make you stop believing Phil.' He stood swiftly with a quick apology to the camera crew. 'I need to get back to the orchestra for warm-up.'

23

The detachment of the camera was exactly what Lou needed. Her head was a mess. She'd hated seeing Edie discouraged before the competition, was frustrated with Nick, angry with Phil and... disappointed in herself. Nothing new, then.

If she'd been sitting next to Phil in the audience... She didn't finish the thought. Better that she was watching the performance with Tam through the viewfinder of the camera. Maestro Eckert strode on stage, full of self-importance, and Lou couldn't help comparing him unfavourably with Nick. She tried to tell herself it was just because his rear profile was nothing to look at, but she knew it was because she would never meet anyone as wonderful as Nick again. Why did he have to be so great? Give him a few flaws and she might be able to swallow her pride and ask him out in London. But she couldn't bear it if it went to hell after she'd fallen in love with him... properly.

And then there was Edie. As Tam zoomed in and panned across the orchestra, Lou watched for the glimpse of her daughter's dear, determined face. Her jaw was set and she looked as though she were in detention, rather than an orchestra performance. It reminded Lou of the 'talent' round of the awful pageants she'd lived for, for too many years – she'd never succeeded in anything except making herself feel like a failure.

But the orchestra wasn't a failure. They looked grim; from Meg, the charming cellist, to earnest, pimply Harry, but they were playing with sweat and defiance. Lou searched out Helene in the crowd, in time to see her shaking her head. Lou's shoulders slumped. What chance did they have?

Even Lou could tell their *Eine kleine Nachtmusik* didn't have the finesse of some of the other performances. And the Jenkins was difficult.

She clapped and cheered after they finished the Jenkins, not caring that the back row swivelled to give her disapproving looks. But it wasn't enough. They weren't finalists. That was the end for Nick and Edie's orchestra.

She grabbed Edie in a hug as soon as the audience dispersed, and felt her crumple. The tears were unexpected. Lou knew the camera was still rolling and probably trained on them because it was a good shot, so she smoothed Edie's hair and kept her face averted, tucking her firmly against her chest.

'I don't know what to do, Mum. It was so hard. What if Purcell is like that all the time?'

She floundered; her own head too mixed up to provide reassurance. 'We'll be okay, sweetheart. I can't promise everything will be fine, but we'll work it out when it comes. Just think, you might have a teacher like Nick.'

She settled immediately. 'I wish I could still have... Nick... as my teacher.'

'I know, sweetheart,' she murmured. 'We all wish we could keep Nick.'

* * *

On Sunday morning, Lou dashed out for takeaway breakfast from the pasticceria across the street. It probably wasn't healthy to eat peach tart and strudel for breakfast, but Lou wanted to make sure Edie had something in her stomach.

Thinking of performance nerves brought her thoughts back around to Nick and she bought an extra coffee in case she saw him. Just as she was about to pick up her paper bag from the counter, she heard her phone vibrate and grabbed it eagerly. But it was just Phil, announcing he was outside the residence.

She replied quickly and juggled her order back across the road until he could take the bag and one of the coffees from her. She stifled a scowl to see Nick's coffee pilfered so thoughtlessly. But her resentment wilted again when she remembered she hadn't seen much of Nick, nor was she likely to that day. If he was avoiding her, it was probably for the best.

They turned into the hall leading to their door, to the sound of violins – two of them. Lou slowed her steps, stopping completely before she arrived at the open door. It was a lively minuet; the two instruments overlapped and echoed, sweeping through harmonic interactions in the complementary melodies. The piece moved on to a minor key, bringing in hints of an expressive melody that gradually took prominence and brought back the joyful major key.

Lou knew the piece. She could probably have sung along with each part. But she'd never heard it like this. She'd never heard her daughter and the man who was so much more than her teacher playing a violin duet together. She didn't know anything about technique, but she could feel it. She sensed what Edie had inherited from him in six years of lessons. What had he said all those nights ago at the convent? It was pathos. Lou's emotions were engaged, tugged this way and that by the skill and passion of their playing.

No wonder he felt so exposed on stage. No wonder the clueless boys at school had ridiculed him. In the intimate vulnerability of his performance, he held a power they couldn't ever understand. She had the urge to protect him, to make sure no one forced him to play ever again, except when he was playing for himself. She blinked back tears, hoping Phil wasn't watching her.

Nick had taught Edie with the same delicate touch and she'd grown and blossomed in response. She'd embraced her passion and used it to get through the toughest time in her life. Was that what Lou had wanted from a talent, something to get her through?

Her mind whirled with thoughts of hard work and sacrifice, of finding space in her life to be happy. Oh, God, had Greta and Nick been right? Had her search for a talent been doomed from the start because she wasn't willing to open up to it, to create space for her own happiness? But how could she, when her failed marriage was such dead space in her heart?

She wanted to savour how she felt at that moment, responding to their music, their emotion. Listening to them playing together, she could almost believe it was possible.

What was she supposed to do? Nick wasn't Edie's teacher any more after today. He had no reason to see them ever again. She couldn't give him a reason until she was sure she could accept the ups and downs of her feelings for him. He deserved so much better.

What did she deserve? *Will you let someone make you happy?* How could she, when her life was full of doubts and mistakes? At least she didn't include Phil in that calculation any more. For that moment, listening to the music stirring her soul, she was happy – deeply, tearfully happy.

She swiped at her eyes as the song ended and she stepped

through the door with a bright smile. 'I've never heard both parts of that together! It's just beautiful, you two!'

They were sitting on the sofa in the shared living room, Meg and her mother watching while eating breakfast at the table. Edie flicked her hair back and stowed her violin, approaching for a hug.

'Oh, hi Dad,' she said, giving him a hug too.

Lou's eyes fell on Nick, who stiffened when Phil followed her in. She put the breakfast on the table and went to the kitchenette to fetch a glass of water. Nick followed her.

'Are you okay?'

She turned slowly, with no idea what emotions showed on her face. 'Thank you,' she murmured. Nick shook his head, dismissive, as usual. 'I can see she's doing better, now.'

'Thank Tessarini,' he quipped.

Lou frowned at him. 'Thank *you*.' Her eyes were hot again and she turned away in case more tears fell.

His hand on her shoulder stilled her. He drew close enough for her to hear his breath and long for something she couldn't have. 'What's wrong?'

She blinked madly and risked a glance at him as the silence stretched. 'I'm okay.'

'Is it Phil?'

'No,' she insisted immediately, glad it was true. But she couldn't exactly tell him she was messed up about him and not her ex.

'Edie's going to do fine.'

'I know.' He dropped his hand from her shoulder with half a shrug that told her she was acting strangely. 'What about you?'

His eyes narrowed. 'What about me?'

'You have to conduct this morning.'

'Thanks for reminding me,' he said drily.

She leaned closer and dropped her voice. 'If you get nervous, just remember I'm out there with a camera crew, appreciating your backside,' she murmured.

He ran a hand through his hair and blushed. His embarrassed smile was one of her favourites. She nudged his chest with her shoulder.

'Are you eating?'

Swear words filled Lou's head at the sound of Phil's voice from behind them. Nick squeezed her shoulders briefly. 'I should go. I'll see you at the choir competition.' She nodded, unwilling to say goodbye and still angry at Phil for interrupting.

He'd opened Lou's purchases and set them out on the table for Edie. 'Can I talk to you for a moment outside?' he asked.

She glanced at Edie, who was looking between them with uncertainty. 'Just for a moment. We have to get Edie to the green room soon.'

'Of course.' Phil smiled graciously – at least, it should have been gracious, but it felt smarmy and cloying.

Phil didn't wait long after closing the door behind them. 'Is that teacher the reason you don't want to talk about improving our relationship?'

She released a long breath and shook her head. 'Phil, please let's not do this today.'

'I'm worried about you.'

'I thought getting divorced absolved you from any concern for me! That's what you wanted, wasn't it?'

'Of course not,' he insisted, but he paused, running out of words. His mind was working, but at least he realised that almost anything he said at that moment would be offensive. 'I don't want you getting hurt,' he finally settled on with his familiar gruffness that was nothing more than arrogance.

'Just because you're discovering relationships aren't all plain sailing even when they don't involve me, doesn't mean I'm doing even worse!'

'You're in a relationship? With Mr Romano? It just doesn't add up, Lou. He's young and he doesn't have kids and he's...'

Lou laughed ruefully. 'Talented? That's what you were going to say, right?' She shook her head. 'I don't have to listen to this. I'd prefer it if you kept your observations for your own relationship and for our daughter's well-being. You signed away any rights to my love life months ago – and gave up any interest much earlier! Today is not about you!'

She flung the door open and returned to Edie. Their last day at music camp. She wanted Phil out of her head, even if he was right.

Today wasn't about her, either. It was about Edie – and Nick. She would enjoy the day for their sakes. She'd live in the moment, starting with enjoying a quiet, delicious breakfast with Edie.

She was glad she'd ordered so much cake.

* * *

Nick couldn't get Lou out of his head. Perhaps it was because he was hanging on to the last threads of their flirtatious banter. Perhaps it was because he was heading back to his grandparents' house that evening after the concert, never to see her again.

That sounded terribly dramatic. If only he had a way to keep seeing her until she worked out what she wanted.

He'd loved seeing the other side of her – the side that worked behind and in front of the camera. She clicked into place, expressing her tireless enthusiasm, curiosity and instinct for people and a story. Lou might think she wasn't talented enough to be in her industry, but he suspected her boss disagreed.

The thought brought him right back to Phil and he needed to rein himself in before his passions started to force their way through the cracks. He had a choir to conduct, music to escape into and a past to ignore. At least his preoccupation with saying goodbye to Lou had given him a new perspective. He wasn't looking forward to facing his old professore, but it didn't feel like the drama it had before.

His orchestra had come together into a decent choir. And Maestro Eckert hadn't interfered to mess with his methods – or his head. So, with a measure of pride and a dose of embarrassment at the thought that Lou was checking out his backside, he walked on stage to the muted applause of the small audience. If they were named finalists, they would perform that evening in the gala concert at the La Scala theatre. The orchestra performance had missed its target, but it wasn't over for the choir, yet.

He'd chosen to start with the Verdi chorus from *Nabucco*, because the kids loved it and had reacted with wide-eyed enthusiasm when he'd told them they might get to perform it in the theatre where the opera had debuted. The sweeping melody of the 'Chorus of the Hebrew Slaves' caught him up every time. The kids held the tension of the music and sang from their hearts and Nick knew that, even if Lou had spent the first few bars appreciating his backside, she would have forgotten all about it by the time they broke into glorious harmony at the line about the golden harp.

When they reached the end of the piece, fading to a compelling pianissimo with all the diaphragm tension he'd asked of them, he cut them off with a triumphant gesture and a grin. He knew he must have looked like an idiot up there, waving his hands around as though holding the voices in the air, but the kids had exceeded his expectations and the music had been magnificent.

If he'd thought the 'Chorus of the Hebrew Slaves' had gone well, the kids blew him away with their performance of the second piece, a renaissance setting of 'Ave Verum Corpus' by the English composer William Byrd. The quality of the sound they achieved was better than he'd ever heard from them, sharp and timeless. It was everything he'd tried to teach them – the highs and lows of living the music.

In the euphoria of learning that their performance had earned them a place in the final concert, he wondered if Lou had been right. He'd always felt like a failure in the music world and a misfit outside it. But could he find a place between both? Had he already found it?

Had he already found it with Lou and Edie? It was a dangerous thought that spiralled as he sent Edie on to the stage for her virtuoso performance after lunch. He caught Lou's eye, where she sat in the audience. He wished he could hold her hand through this – for his own sake as well as hers. Edie was so young, but Lou had done such a good job of listening to her, supporting her and loving her.

Edie's touch on the bow was always delicate and heartfelt. He could hear her nerves in the sound, but she leaned into it instead of freezing up. And she won her place on stage at La Scala that night. He was both awash with pride and terrified for her. It was surreal hiding backstage while his old teacher told her in his stilted English that she needed to develop some discipline with her technique, but her interpretation was wonderful.

Unfortunately, Edie coming to the attention of professore Aliberti meant he did, too.

'Nicola Romano!' he called out when Nick had been trying to make a quick exit after the virtuoso rounds.

He turned slowly. 'Professore.'

'Piacere di rivederti qui. I didn't realise you were teaching.'

'I'm flattered you remember me, prof.'

The look on his face took him back to his teenage years in a heartbeat. 'What a ridiculous comment. Of course I remember you. Do you play professionally? I never heard of you again.' That day sixteen years ago hung in the air, not to be forgotten, nor mentioned.

Nick straightened his shoulders. 'No, I don't play professionally.'

'Che peccato. A shame, a shame. But it's good to see you teaching.'

'Grazie.' Muttering something about getting ready for the concert, he escaped. It was an odd anticlimax, being back here, speaking to the prof. He'd always felt his life had ended that day, but it hadn't. It hadn't even been the end of his career in music. It had simply been a step on his path. He hoped to have as much peace about this... thing... with Lou, given time. It certainly felt like a step on his path too.

Nick walked past her, as she chatted charmingly into the camera outside the theatre, as he arrived with Hyewon for the concert that night. He paused to smile. How did Lou have no idea what effect her charm had on people?

When the camera stopped rolling, Lou turned to approach him, but he waved her away with some kind of excuse. He felt far too philosophical for banter with Lou, and he had to be able to say goodbye to her without something breaking.

After the adrenaline of the weekend, the tension of the packed weeks of music camp, he had all kinds of feelings about tonight. The worst was an odd foreboding, which wasn't rational. It was only a concert. It wouldn't be any worse than his cramped-up disaster on stage when he was younger, and he'd just discovered even that hadn't been the end of him. It was just a concert. He wasn't going to make a fool of himself.

He was going to make a fool of himself.

He hesitated, trembling, as sweat gathered under his shirt. His tie was choking him. His hands were slippery, making him terrified he was going to lose his hold on the delicate neck of the violin. He lifted the back of his bow hand to his forehead to swipe back his hair – and the perspiration that threatened to drip into his eyes.

The stage beckoned and, beyond that, a large audience of Milanese music enthusiasts and families of teenage musicians from across Europe. He'd played at La Scala before, seen the blur of the grand red-and-gold boxes lit with the elaborate chandelier that hung from the stuccoed ceiling. But that time, although he'd been similarly terrified, at least his name had been on the programme.

What the hell was he doing?

He glanced back at Edie's white face. Had Lou, by some miracle, made the sprint backstage already to work her magic on her terrified daughter? Nick had known it would end badly when Phil had accompanied her backstage. It was possible he hadn't intended harm, but harm was what he'd done.

'I'm so surprised and impressed, sweetheart. I mean, I thought this was just... you wanted to be a music nerd, you know, but to play in a theatre like this... it's really something. You must be so nervous about walking out there, but I can't believe you've made it so far...'

Nick had nearly retched on her behalf. 'Music nerd'? Phil truly was one of the boys who'd made his life hell in school. He was 'surprised'? She'd worked hard for years to get where she was and he 'couldn't believe it'? Nick had rushed to abort the conversation, but it had been too late. Edie had frozen up and demanded her mother, in a sudden panic. Nick had been only too happy to send Phil to fetch her while he attempted damage control.

'It's okay,' he'd grasped her shoulders and said. 'Just breathe for a moment. We're still here.'

'I can't go out there!' she'd choked, her tears beginning to flow. 'But if I don't go out there, then I'll disappoint you!'

'Don't think about me, Edie. I don't care if you go out there or not. I only care about how you feel about your playing.'

'So... I don't have to go out there?'

That was a difficult question. He couldn't help thinking about his younger self. His mother would have said no, he didn't have to, and flitted him out of the theatre in a protective embrace. He'd winced at the image. Maestro Eckert and his ilk, many of the faces from Nick's own education, would have pushed him out with the heel of a handmade leather shoe and told him to toughen up. But there had to be another way.

'If you don't go out there, you won't learn what you're capable of. I believe you can play that piece with such beauty that the audience will feel it in their blood.'

She wiped her nose with her sleeve. 'But I'm shaking. I can't even hold my violin!'

He nodded grimly. 'I never told you...' He took a deep breath. 'I feel like this every time I have to step on stage.' Her eyes widened. 'I was ashamed to feel that way, but even I'm not too old to learn it's okay. But I also stuffed up once – badly enough that I thought I wanted to quit music. I don't think it will happen to you, but it might. It's a brave thing to stand up there and believe you belong there, in front of all those people. But it's worth it for the music. It's worth it because every time you play, your heart and soul heal a little more. And, Edie, my heart and soul heal, too.'

She sobbed once and swallowed. 'Dad doesn't think... he doesn't think I should go to Purcell.'

'You do. Your mum does. I do.'

'I need Mum... I can't... What if she doesn't make it here in time? Maybe the next person should go on.'

The student before Edie in the programme had already returned backstage and the applause had died down.

He winced. 'You're the last one,' he said apologetically.

She shook her head vigorously. 'I can't! I'm not a prodigy like these others! I'm just an ordinary kid! I can't go out there!'

'Edie,' he said, his voice surprisingly even. 'I'm an ordinary teacher. I was called a prodigy once and some people might say I failed to reach my potential.' He paused as she frowned at him. 'I'm terrified at the thought, but even I can go out there.'

'What?'

He swallowed. This was crazy. His heart was already pounding and he hadn't taken a single step towards the stage. 'I'm going to go out there. Your mum will be here in a minute and I hope she can talk you into sharing your talent, your passion for the music. In the meantime, I'm going to go out there and make a short apology. If that's not enough time, I'm going to play something.'

'What are you going to play?' she asked. Half his mouth kicked up in a smile at how easily he'd distracted her. The half of him that wasn't trembling in terror soared with hope for his talented student.

'I have no idea.'

He'd grabbed the first violin he'd seen, quickly checked the tuning and stumbled to the black curtain. Now, he had to follow through. He took one more moment to sweat and fret before spilling on to the stage with an undignified lurch.

He stepped up to the microphone at the side of the stage. 'Uh, buonasera, signore e signori. Good evening. There has been a short delay with the last performer, Edie Saunders from the United Kingdom.' He glanced back, hoping she might appear, but she didn't. The accompanist looked up in confusion.

He couldn't hear anything except the rush of his blood and the erratic beat of his heart. That could have been because of the heavy silence in the enormous theatre, or it could have been because of the surge of chemicals in his brain trying to shut everything down.

Asking himself what he was doing was the wrong question. *Why* was he doing it? It was for Edie, to prove something to her, to prove something to himself, and because he would put himself through hell for her – and for her mother.

He grimaced. He was standing on stage like a fool, pouring with sweat, because he was in love. It was a poor time to have come to terms with his intense, emotional side. But hadn't Lou taught him there was no time like the present?

'While we give Edie Saunders a chance to get ready, I will play a short piece,' he said, his voice trailing off.

* * *

'What is he doing?' Lou hissed as soon as she arrived backstage. She glanced at Edie, but her daughter seemed to have forgotten her own crisis in her fascination at seeing her teacher standing in front of the crowd, alone, setting a violin on his shoulder. Edie peered through the black curtain and Lou drew up beside her, wrapping an arm around her waist and peering out above Edie's head.

Nick drew the bow across one string, shakily. Lou could see the odd energy in him, his defences caving in as he poured himself out for the music. That single note, drawn out with an ebb-and-flow of diminuendo and crescendo, trapped the audience. And then, as though he were pulling the music out like an endless scarf from a magician's hat, more notes flowed: furious quavers pooling into sudden longer notes and flying free again in a compelling melody. A simple line of climbing crotchets appeared below the dancing tune; Nick's bow and fingers suddenly creating an orchestra of sound. And as he played, his body arched with the music, pouring the notes and phrases into the audience and drawing back to float with the sudden harmonies that emerged.

'Do you know the piece?' Lou whispered to Edie. Her daughter shook her head silently. Oh. My. God. Nick was standing in front of a vast, international audience, playing something he'd written himself.

His bow was firm, but his body was trembling – except for his left hand, steady on the strings or wavering to produce stunning vibrato. The piece built to a climax where he leaned back so far Lou wondered if she was going to have to dash out and catch him. Then he plucked the strings in delicate rhythm before one last legato sweep to the final notes.

He tugged the violin from his neck and slumped. The audience erupted in sudden applause that appeared to wake him from a trance. He bowed once, tottering on his feet, and rushed off stage.

Lou did have to catch him. He landed heavily in her arms and she dragged him to a chair.

'Edie?' he said softly.

'I'm going,' the girl said with a wide-eyed nod. She swallowed once and strode out on to the stage.

Lou's chest rose and fell with enormous breaths as she held Nick to her chest and listened to Edie's first notes. She closed her eyes, pulling the moment into her heart so she could live it for years to come. Edie had done it. She was playing with her heart, in front of a vast audience. Nick made a wet patch through her shirt with the perspiration from his forehead as he leaned on her, but she didn't want to move. They stayed still and silent until Edie's last note.

'She did it,' Lou murmured as the audience broke into applause.

'She fumbled the andante, but recovered well.'

'Oh, shut up,' she whispered. Lou felt him smile against her.

'I might pass out and you won't have to worry about that any more.'

She tightened her arms reflexively around him. 'I can't believe you did that.'

'Neither can I.'

She wanted to ask him how he felt, but it was a trite question when he was still dragging in shaky breaths. He hadn't been kidding about the stage fright. 'Why did you do it?'

'Why do you think?' he asked with an odd laugh. 'For Edie. For you. For me and my years of stupidity. God, it was awful, but it's done now.'

She shivered at his words. For Edie... And he'd done it for her as well? What did that even mean?

'Can you take the violin before I drop it? It might need... disinfecting.' He grimaced and handed her the instrument, which was covered in sweat droplets. 'I don't even know who it belongs to.'

'Charming, Nick.' She chuckled and gave him another squeeze.

'You lovebirds had better finish your cuddle before she comes back.'

Lou gritted her teeth. She wanted to hold on to Nick just to spite Phil – actually, she wanted to hold on to Nick for a lot of reasons, only one of which was to spite Phil. But he was right – so she eased away slowly.

'Thanks for the hug,' Nick said softly.

She wanted to reply 'any time', but it reminded her that tomorrow would be the last time. What was she going to do without him?

But as people burst backstage to speak to him – in Italian and English, all in the same dumbfounded tone – she was more certain than ever that she would have to find a way to do without him. The world had rediscovered his talent. She was just loopy Lou who liked to smile and pretend she never felt the weight of her own failures.

She grabbed Edie in a fierce hug and drifted away from the commotion around Nick. She and Edie were done for the night. The choir had already performed and they would sit in the audience to watch the orchestras.

'You were amazing, sweetheart. You always are, but tonight, you not only nailed your piece, you went out there when you weren't feeling your best. That's a skill I wish I had.'

'Thanks,' Edie replied with a watery smile. 'I don't know what came over me. All of a sudden, I was terrified. But, Mum,' she said, her brow furrowed, 'I've never heard Mr Romano play like that before.'

'I don't think anyone has.'

'He doesn't play, because he's scared.' Lou nodded grimly. 'But why would he be so scared when he can play like that?'

'I hope you never need to understand, sweetheart. People are complex creatures.'

Lou rummaged until she found an empty violin case, then took out a pack of wet-wipes – she was a mum after all – and cleaned off the chin-rest and the finger-board of the violin as best she could before stowing it in its case. She took one more look at Nick, who was teetering on his feet, but surrounded by a well-meaning crowd. She took a deep breath and headed for the door.

'We can go now?'

Lou didn't turn to look at Phil, wishing she'd been able to forget he was there for a few more minutes. She simply nodded and felt him following, as though they were still a family unit. She would do a lot to minimise Edie's trauma about the divorce, but she didn't want him anywhere near her – not after she'd been through so much to get him out of her head.

As Edie took the first step out of the room, Lou looked back, finding Nick's eyes on her. She wanted to stay. But she wouldn't hold him back. She couldn't cope if she ever thought Nick held her in contempt. Next to him, she'd only ever be talentless Lou.

* * *

It was a very different Nick who bid the children and parents farewell in the foyer of the theatre, shaking hands and smiling warmly. He spent barely five minutes with the three of them, most of that with Edie. He shook Lou's hand, to her utter shock, and she stared at it, tingling with the awareness of something she didn't grasp yet, but which was going to hurt when realisation came.

Phil saw them to the door of the residence and said goodbye. Lou breathed out – finally. In their room, Lou broke open the snacks she'd bought the day before and spread them on the bed.

'Sleepover snacks!' Edie said with a grin. 'Mum, you're the best!'

'I thought you'd need some regenerative treats tonight.' She smiled at Edie's glee, but, seeing the sweets in their little tin, she remembered Greta at the concert in London.

'Are you okay?' Edie asked, nibbling on some odd cheese-flavoured crisps that had looked less weird in the corner shop.

'I should be asking you that!' Lou said too brightly. 'I can't believe you played in that theatre! In Milan!'

She wrinkled her nose in an unexpected grimace. 'That's what Dad said.'

'What? What did he say? What was it exactly that upset you?'

Edie sighed. 'Dad just made me feel like a fake. The other kids were all so talented. I know I only got to play tonight because the judges liked my interpretation. I wasn't technically as good as some of the kids who missed out. And Dad made me think about all that again at the wrong moment.'

Lou couldn't think of anything to say. Phil made Lou feel like a fake, too. He didn't realise he was doing it – he'd deluded himself into thinking he was the big man, using his influence magnanimously for others. Her biggest mistake was believing him.

Get Phil out of your head...

She was so used to questioning her judgement and doubting her abilities. She couldn't blame Phil for everything, but she needed to recognise that little voice he'd amplified in her and stamp it out. She didn't need a new talent. She needed to value the ones she already had – the ones Nick had tried to make her see.

Far from pushing Edie to make up for her own inadequacies, as Phil had accused her of, she'd used her daughter as an excuse to hold herself back. *Can you let someone make you happy?* She'd crowded out that possibility by filling up her spirit with all her mistakes and failings until there wasn't space for anything else. Not only was happiness what Edie would want for her, but believing she had to limit herself because of the mistakes she'd made with Edie, at the beginning, would lump her daughter with a burden of responsibility that she didn't deserve.

Lou had danced around her fear of falling back into depression after the divorce without facing it head-on. The fear was still with her, taking up space she was beginning to realise she wanted for other things. Unless she let something go, she couldn't let anything – or anyone – in.

She hadn't found a new talent, but she'd found reasons to live life to the full, reasons she wanted to hang on to. She'd found beauty in sights and scents, in making people laugh or think or ask questions. She'd found Helene's straightforward kindness, the kids' youthful confusion and Greta's no-nonsense hospitality. She'd climbed a bloody mountain. Those were the things she wanted to bring into the rest of her life. She wanted to fill her mind with the good things. She loved Edie. Hell, she loved Nick. That was worth something more than a talent.

She'd been so self-absorbed, searching for the way forward, that it had taken the time at the lake to make her see life was great as she was – if only she'd look up and let go.

And Nick... He wasn't her reason to move forward. She'd been worried about latching on to him to make up for her floundering life. She'd pushed him away, certain he didn't fit. But he'd been her friend, in the sweetest sense of the word. And now, with or without him, she wanted the space in her life for enjoyment, for friendships and happiness – not the constant questions and fear.

Then it struck her. She wanted to let him in. He was handsome and talented and cared about her daughter and was basically her dream guy. And if he wanted her, if she could believe he did, why couldn't she make the space for him?

Idiot!

He'd got up on stage for Edie – for her, he'd said. He'd said he was interested in her. If there was any chance she could believe him, why had she walked away from him tonight?

Double idiot!

'Mum? Don't be upset about Dad. I can usually filter out the stuff that... doesn't help. I just freaked out tonight.'

Lou stared at her daughter and squeezed her hand. 'I'm proud of you, sweetheart. Not just because of tonight. I'm so proud of your music, but I'm prouder of who you are. No matter what you decide to do with your talents, you're wise and sensitive and strong and I've learned so much watching you live your life.'

The tears shining in Edie's eyes started off Lou's own. Edie dived into her arms and they clung to each other.

'I love you, Mum,' Edie murmured.

'I love you too, sweetheart.'

'And I'm proud of you, too. I know you haven't always been happy, but you're always there for me – and everyone else. You're the best friend anyone could have.' Edie pulled back, her question creeping into her eyes before she dared to voice it. 'Are you sad about Mr Romano?'

Tears were still running down Lou's face and she added a grimace and a tentative smile to the mad mix of emotions, 'Yes,' she admitted.

'It's probably silly of me to have hoped...'

Lou tightened her arms around Edie. 'No, hope is what I needed, but I don't know if... it's too late?'

Edie patted her arm in a way that made Lou grin. 'How about you sleep on it? I know he likes you – a lot. Maybe you could ask him... you know.'

Lou stared at the ceiling, fighting a huge, hopeful grin. 'Ask him to be my boyfriend?'

Edie poked her. 'Mum, that's so primary school!'

'Would it be weird? If I ask your teacher to be my boyfriend?'

Edie gave Lou a withering look. 'He's not my teacher any more.'

'But it's embarrassing. I'm your mum. I want a boyfriend.' Lou winced.

'What was embarrassing was how you used to stare at him.'

'I did not!' she denied, knowing Edie was right.

'Seriously, Mum, I'm happy for you.'

'If he feels the same way,' she groaned. Her head fell into her hands.

25

'I can't believe you didn't find a satchel! But, you know, maybe your husband will want to come back with you to find one he likes. I would have failed to find one on purpose!'

'You're planning to come back?' Helene asked.

'Of course. This wasn't nearly enough time to explore.'

'I suppose that's true for Milan. But we saw the theatre and that was the most important thing.'

'You'll be back again, won't you? Soon?' Mrs Winkelmann asked, approaching with a clipboard. 'In the half term, wasn't it? For the olive harvest?'

Lou looked at her blankly. 'No, I haven't made any plans.' Although, now Mrs Winkelmann had said it, Lou was desperate to come back to the farm in October. But she had to find Nick first and then... oh, God, she didn't dare think of what came next.

'Oh, I'm sorry. I thought you and Mr Romano were... never mind.'

Lou turned awkwardly away before Mrs Winkelmann could see her blush, only to encounter Helene's wide-eyed stare. 'You and Mr Romano...? Oh my God. How did I not see this?'

'I have no idea, Helene.' Lou wrapped an arm around her friend's shoulders fondly. 'But it's nothing.' She grimaced.

'Yet,' Edie piped up and Lou shushed her with a look.

'That would explain why you're still here,' Mrs Winkelmann commented.

'What do you mean?'

'He left to go back to his family last night.'

Lou's breath left her suddenly. 'He left? Last night?'

Mrs Winkelmann finally looked up from her clipboard. 'That was the purpose of saying goodbye to you all after the concert.'

Lou's chest froze up. She'd had no idea it had truly meant goodbye. Was this the end of her hopes? Did his quiet exit mean he wouldn't hear her out even if...? Even if what? He wasn't there to hear her say anything.

With his perfect sense of bad timing, Phil arrived with his suitcase. He kissed Lou's cheek while she was too distracted to wonder if she should protest. 'Morning. Miss Hwang said I was okay to catch a lift to the airport with you all this morning.' He gave Lou a smile. 'I'm booked on your flight. I'll try to wangle seats together.'

Mrs Winkelmann gave him a disgruntled look that made Lou like her a little more, but wrote his name on her list. 'Right, you can put your luggage under the bus and keep your instruments with you, please,' she called out when the coach pulled up.

As Harry emerged, rolling his double bass with help from his mother, the memories began to prick and she panicked. She couldn't leave without talking to Nick. If she couldn't speak to him, she'd talk herself out of it once they arrived back in London.

Phil turned where he'd stopped on the second step up into the coach. 'Lou? Are you coming?'

She glanced at Edie. She hesitated, but her conviction didn't waver. And when her daughter smiled, she returned it with a growing sense of her ability to make things right.

'No,' she said lightly. 'I'm not coming.'

'What?' His tone flattened.

'I'm going back to the lake.'

'You're going back to your toy boy.'

'Think very carefully before you make our relationship like this, Phil,' she said softly. She drew Edie close. 'Is this okay? You're supposed to be with me until the end of the week, but I could try—'

'I'm coming with you.' Edie lifted up on to her toes in excitement, clutching her violin.

Lou turned to Phil, trying to tamp down her excitement at what was certain to be a mad caper. 'I'll have her back when we agreed. Have a good flight.' Lou turned away with her head high, feeling poised and ready for adventure – until she realised she'd forgotten their suitcases and had to race back as the driver was closing the luggage compartment.

They linked arms and set off, like the Gilmore Girls, except they were dragging suitcases across Milan, navigating the tram tracks and the endless grid of streets lined with historic and contemporary apartment buildings, offices, and cafés. As the adrenaline receded, Lou also realised she had no idea where they were going.

She stopped, looking for shade and finding it only under the eaves of a little news-stand plastered with magazine covers of elegant-looking men. She drew Edie into the shade, trying to ignore the scorching look a model was giving them from a poster. She knew Italians made nice suits, but she hadn't realised they also produced lovely Jockey shorts.

'We need a plan,' she said, sounding much more confident than she felt.

Edie eyed her. 'We need the Internet.'

'Good point.' Lou laughed and pulled out her phone. 'And I need to remember where that farm was!'

Edie's smile slipped. 'You don't have an address?' Lou grimly shook her head. 'Can you find it again on a map?'

'I bloody hope so,' she muttered.

'Mum, this is crazy. Maybe you should just call him.'

'I can't call him! At least not until we've become so lost, we turn up in Stars Hollow.' Edie appreciated the joke only enough for a half-hearted chuckle. 'But I know where we need to go first.' She flagged down a passing woman in pristine white capris and heels. 'Uh, scusi! Scusi, signora, I mean signorina, I mean, sorry, I have no idea how old you are. Dove la stazione? Il treno?'

The woman eyed their suitcases. 'Do you mean Central Station? It's a long way from here. You're going to want to get the tram,' she said, in an American accent.

They took the tram, after the woman had pointed them in the direction of a tram stop and told them to buy a ticket from the magazine seller. When the tram terminated at the Piazza del Duomo, Lou had an inkling that they'd got on the wrong one.

After pausing to pinch each other with the view of the ornate marble façade of the cathedral and the nineteenth-century grandeur of the Galleria Vittorio Emanuele II, they accosted another helpful passer-by, who pointed them towards the Metro. After puzzling out the network maps in their underground carriage, they made the successful transfer and arrived at Milano Centrale.

By the end of the day, Lou counted back the various means of transport they'd taken that day and reached eight. The tram and two metro trains were only the beginning.

Edie stared at the high ceilings of the station atrium and its art deco reliefs of roman soldiers and enormous posters of beautiful people advertising beautiful fashion items, while Lou pored over her maps app until she thought she'd found the right village.

'There's a train station here,' she said, swiping across to a town several miles east of the lake, 'and a bus that should stop here. Now we just need a ticket.'

After passing under an enormous sign reading 'BIGLIETTERIA' (Lou had a giggle: 'Those are very big letters!'), they took one look at the queue and returned to the ticket machines. They argued with the machine and ended up with a ticket that Lou hoped was for the right train. They had just enough time to grab a couple of panini piled with Parma ham and find the platform. They collapsed into their seats and, as the train pulled out of the grand station, Lou's doubts crowded in again.

Was she really racing across northern Italy to stand awkwardly in front of Nick and tell him she liked him and wanted to be his girlfriend? Or, even worse, that she was in love with him and she wanted to have his babies? Oh, God, she hadn't thought that far. Strike the babies. She already had one. And what did Nick think of that? Surely a young, handsome guy didn't want to have to wait around for the babysitter to go out on a date – or, worse, stop by Phil's to drop Edie off.

She scolded herself for the lapse. That was yesterday's Lou talking. She wasn't contemplating a Tinder date and he wasn't a random toy boy. He was Nick. And the only problem he'd ever had with Edie was when Lou had used her as an excuse.

Their train pulled into Verona with a few minutes' delay, so they held hands and dashed to the departures board to find their connection. They hauled their luggage on to the regional train heading for Bolzano, adrenaline pumping, just as the conductor blew her whistle.

'I can't believe we made it,' Lou puffed.

Her tension ticked up with the passing minutes. Edie managed to read a book, but Lou was barely paying attention to the changing scenery. When the train pulled up to the station called Mori, the pine and herbs in the air, the mountain cliffs extending in all directions and the sharp, clear sunlight made her come to her senses.

She stepped off the train with an odd smile, feeling as though she was exactly where she wanted to be – if she could just find the right bus stop.

A bus pulled up, labelled with route number '1' for 'Marco'. The driver, who she couldn't help but think of as Marco, was fond of shaking his head and speaking the weird mix of English and German peculiar to people from this region. He kept pointing and saying 'Mori'. Weren't they already in Mori?

When a passenger called out from the back, the driver said, 'Scusa, we go, jetzt,' and waved them off the steps.

Lou released a huge breath. They found a park bench – no shade, but at least it was somewhere to collapse in the afternoon heat – and Edie propped her head up with her elbows on her knees. 'What do we do now?'

'We pray to the god of Google,' Lou groaned and fetched her phone. Edie's stomach rumbled loudly. The Parma ham panini had been delicious, but they'd scoffed it before twelve because that was what happened when you sat on a train, and they hadn't had time to get anything else.

She thought about Nick's nonna's ravioli and her mouth watered. Perhaps she should just call him. But it was after 2.30 and they'd probably finished eating. And she wanted to prove herself with a dramatic entrance – either that, or she was just terrified.

'Okay,' she said, taking a deep breath. 'Apparently there's another bus stop back there somewhere. But if we get stuck, there's always a taxi.'

'Except you don't have an address,' Edie pointed out.

Lou grimaced. 'Details, details.' She tugged Edie up off the bench and marched for the bus stop.

They missed the bus.

'Why does it only run every two hours?' Edie asked, scrunching up her nose at the timetable.

'Because this isn't London,' grumbled Lou. She checked her phone. At this rate, it would be past five o'clock when they arrived in the town that she wasn't even sure was the right one. Swear words were bouncing around in her head.

A bus pulled up at the stop, this one the number '2'. 'I wonder if this one goes to "Giovanni",' Lou muttered, earning Edie's weird look. It helpfully went to 'Mori', which was at least a step closer than the desolate railway station and motorway bridge they'd spent the last half an hour at.

When they stepped off the bus, in the centre of the little town, Edie gasped. An imposing cliff rose directly above the town, a church nestled against it, high up among the trees and rock.

'There are people climbing!' Edie said.

Lou squinted at the crazy little silhouettes and wondered if one of them was Nick's cousin Federico.

'Right,' she said, feeling as if this were definitely a caper from an eighties comedy film and not sure whether she was the straight character or the silly one. 'First stop: pizza. Then: taxi or bus, depending on how long it takes us to eat the pizza.'

Edie raised one finger. 'Do I get a say?'

'Depending on what your say is.'

'First stop: pizza. Second stop: gelato.'

'Absolutely. Thank you for correcting my oversight.'

* * *

At twenty past five, they climbed wearily off the bus.

'Please tell me this looks right, Mum,' Edie said out of the corner of her mouth. All they could see were forested mountains and rocky crags, with a few terracotta-tiled roofs hinting at a steep village below.

'Hmm,' was all she allowed herself to say at first. When they rounded the corner and she saw the freestanding clock tower by the church, she released an enormous sigh of relief. 'I remember that church. This is the right village!'

Her elation lasted as long as it took for her to realise she wasn't exactly sure which direction to go from there. She remembered the farm lay on a road heading out of town, but which road? They dragged their suitcases along the bumpy track into the village. It was a pretty mix of wood-and-stone houses and walled terraces, carved directly into the hillside. Palms mingled with birch trees in the bizarre Garda mix, although Lou couldn't have said how close they were to the lake.

She took a chance on a road that could have been right, but, after a hot five minutes of puffing uphill, she decided it definitely wasn't. Edie made a choking sound and sat on her suitcase with a plonk.

'I'm sorry, sweetie,' Lou said.

'It's okay, Mum. It's been fun so far – an adventure.'

'But now we're tired and thirsty and in the middle of nowhere,' Lou completed for her. She hoped it wasn't a metaphor for her love life. 'I wonder if I can call a taxi from here?' She pulled out her phone, only to discover she didn't have data coverage. She groaned and plonked down next to Edie.

A rumble in the distance grew steadily louder, accompanied by a mechanical cough and the occasional crunch of tyres. A rusty blue tractor pulling a trailer full of branches bumbled around the corner. It stopped in front of them and the wizened driver opened the door. 'Salve, signore!' Lou had no hope of catching the rest.

Edie tapped her on the arm. 'Maybe he knows the farm,' she said urgently.

Lou hauled herself up and rummaged around for a smile. 'I'm sorry, I don't speak Italian.'

'Bene, bene. I help you?' He gestured to the road. 'Valle San Felice?' he said, naming the town they'd just left.

Lou shook her head. 'We're looking for an olive farm. Uh, oliva. Famiglia Zanoni.' She thought the word 'famiglia' might actually be Italian, because it made her think of gangsters.

'Zanoni?' he repeated. She nodded eagerly. 'Federico Zanoni?'

Lou chuckled. She hoped it was a name that ran in the family. Nick had introduced his grandparents simply as Nonna and Nonno. 'Yes, I think so!'

He waved a hand and nodded reassuringly. 'I know.' He hopped down from the tractor and gestured towards the door in welcome.

Lou shared a glance with Edie as he heaved their suitcases into his trailer and they climbed into the cab. They bumped and rumbled into the town, Lou and Edie perched on either side of their hero. When he pulled into a familiar driveway, Lou's stomach cramped and her blood rushed suddenly in her ears. What the hell was she going to say to him? She should have practised something. She'd had all day.

Finally, they had arrived. She'd chased him across the country and now she was standing on the sun-drenched terrace with its glimpse of the lake between the hills, the shuttered farmhouse quietly waiting to witness her blubbering declaration.

Greta emerged from the house and stared; her hands frozen around a tea towel. Their rescuer deposited their suitcases at their feet and greeted Greta with kisses, although she struggled to tear her eyes away from Lou and Edie. Lou blushed bright red.

Nick's nonna appeared, remembering her manners where Greta appeared to have forgotten hers. She kissed both of them in welcome and flung the door wide, chatting away in Italian as she gestured for them to come in. But Lou didn't move. She glanced at Greta, then at the house, as the tractor began its rumble back into the village.

Then a slow smile crossed Greta's features, tinged with wonder and bewilderment. She approached with swift steps and grasped Lou's forearms. 'Lou,' she said with a nod of her head. Lou's heart started pounding again at the warmth – approval – in her gaze.

She opened her mouth to say something but she couldn't find the right words. Greta understood she'd spent the whole day chasing him. She understood what it meant.

'He's not here.'

'What?'

Edie groaned. 'You're kidding! How many buses is it going to take this time?'

Lou stared at the sky and tried not to hyperventilate.

'Don't worry. He'll be back soon. He's just gone for a walk. I think...' She gave Lou an assessing look. 'He needed some time to himself.'

Lou's stomach dropped. 'Which way did he go? When did he leave?' she blurted out.

Nonna waved from the door. 'Come! Drink!'

Lou shook her head. 'Which way? Did he say?'

Greta gave her another little smile and said something to Nonna. Then she took Lou's arm. 'Get out your phone and I'll show you.' Lou scrambled to do as she asked. 'Here, this is the way. Follow the road to the next town and then take this turn. He was going to this lookout.'

Nonna appeared with a glass of water and Lou could have groaned in pleasure. 'Grazie,' she murmured and downed the water.

'Are you sure you wouldn't rather wait?'

'Definitely not,' Lou said, clearing her throat.

Greta smiled in amusement. 'At least leave the poor child with us while you trek on.'

Lou glanced at Edie, who was already being led away by Nonna. She shrugged and gave Lou a thumbs-up.

'Wait, let me get you the shoes!'

Lou took them with thanks and sat on the bench under the awning to put them on. 'It's nice to be back here,' she said softly, looking out at the terraced hill below and the peaks across the valley.

'That's what Nick said.' Greta rattled another little tin of sweets in Lou's direction. She eyed the tin with mistrust, but gritted her teeth and popped one in her mouth. It wasn't horrible. It had just the right amount of tang to blend seamlessly with the herbal note that she almost recognised.

'Lemon and sage,' Greta explained.

'I actually like it,' Lou said. 'Are your sweets some kind of test?'

She chuckled. 'No, pet. I just like watching your reaction.'

Lou glanced haltingly at Greta. 'Would you like to hear now that you were right or wait and see how this pans out first?'

Greta chuckled again and sat next to her on the bench, clasping her hands. 'I'm fairly sure how it will pan out.'

'I didn't expect it. I wasn't ready,' Lou said as she pulled the laces tight.

'But you're here now. And that's what matters.'

She took a deep breath and stood. 'That's right. I'm here now. And I know what matters to me.'

26

Nick wasn't hiking. He was barely walking. Instead, he was wandering, meandering – and stumbling, when his thoughts crowded him too closely. The dappled shade of the trees over the trail brought a soothing cool after a hot day. An occasional twist of the path and break in the trees heralded a stunning view into the valley to Torbole and then the lake. But views and forests and walking trails were better with Lou.

He wasn't entirely sure what had happened to him. He'd come on the camp, tense and resentful of being forced to bring kids here, to the scene of his failures. And then Lou had happened. From the first day she'd had an unpredictable effect on his feelings. She made him laugh when he'd thought he couldn't. She'd made him see new facets of every situation and appreciate things he'd never noticed.

On the second morning, watching her enjoy the light in the tiny, crumbling chapel, she'd moved him. He should have known that morning how much trouble he was in. But how could he have known, when he'd never felt anything like this before?

On the last night, he'd stood on stage in front of an audience of hundreds at the La Scala theatre. And all he'd been able to think about was Lou leaving with Phil afterwards. But what could he do about it?

He was lost. Thankfully, not geographically lost, but he couldn't decide what to do. Leaving Milan last night had been both terrible and an aching relief. Saying goodbye to her had put him under too much pressure and he'd shut down rather than do it properly. He might regret that for the rest of his life. Unless he did something about it.

But did he have the courage to ask her on a date back in the real world? To ask for a place in her complicated life? She was charismatic and engaging; it was impossible not to love her. He imagined everyone who saw her on screen fell a little bit in love with her. Once they saw the spot for the kids' show, where she'd revealed a little more of her personality, she would have even more fans.

And he wanted to be her biggest one. But he was... not charismatic or engaging. Or funny. It turned out he could get up on stage when Edie needed him to, so perhaps he wasn't as useless as he'd thought, but did he and Lou fit together?

It didn't matter that she wasn't a musician. She understood him anyway. It had been foolish to think his passion for music had any impact on his relationships. He simply hadn't trusted Naomi enough with his feelings – had been too afraid of ridicule.

But Lou had cared enough to discover who he was before he'd wanted to let her in. She'd accepted him before she understood how much it meant. She had far more trouble accepting herself.

His mind slipped back to the surreal moments after he'd stumbled off stage. He'd felt as though he were having a heart attack, but it was worth it to know he'd done something for her, to show her how much she was worth – to him. It had been the proudest moment of his life, and not because of the shocked faces of the professors who'd thronged him afterwards.

His priorities had changed. He couldn't afford to dwell on the fear any more. Yes, she was gorgeous and had been married to a man who triggered Nick's fears and weaknesses, but none of that mattered when they were together. He had to find a way to make her see it.

He was heading back down the hill now. The walk hadn't cleared his head, so he might as well head back to the farm, to his mother's concerned looks and Nonna's comfort food. In another few days it would stop reminding him of pulling up on the Vespa with Lou pressed into his back and watching her charm his family.

The path narrowed to a stony trail and he heard the footsteps of another late walker heading in the opposite direction. He pulled to the side to allow them to pass. But when the other person appeared, he thought he must be imagining things until she smiled.

He stared, flooded with sudden happiness. He'd missed her. It had been less than a day.

He glanced behind her and didn't see anyone else. He stood like an idiot, staring at her and wondering when his capacity to make decisions would return.

'Hey,' she said, her smile tipping into cheeky as she shoved her hands into the pockets of her light trousers. She was wearing Nonna's hiking boots.

'I'm so happy to see you,' he blurted out.

She laughed and so did he – in disbelief, hope and utter shock at how much seeing her again affected him. 'I'm happy to see you, too!' She smiled again and he wobbled. 'Do you need to sit down? Have I given you a heart attack?'

'I hope not,' he murmured. She had a good enough hold on his heart to make him wonder.

'I should have called you, but...' She stared out at the view, the crags and forest and smooth valley below. She didn't seem to see it any more than he did. She lifted her shoulders and grimaced.

'It's a nice surprise, Lou,' he said softly.

She released a pent-up breath. 'Oh, good. That's it. I wanted to surprise you. Well, I wanted to show you...' She paused and her cheeks turned pink. 'I don't know what I was thinking coming all this way without calling. You are...' She hesitated.

'I am?'

'...probably...'

'About a second away from kissing you unless you tell me that's not why you're here,' he completed for her on a rush.

'It's definitely why I'm here!' she squealed and reached for him.

They met in the middle. And it turned out he'd missed her even more than he'd realised. His brain checked out as her lips met his for a kiss that made up for every moment of miserable uncertainty he'd experienced since he'd left her hotel room on Wednesday night. There was nothing uncertain about the way she gripped his shirt and opened her mouth.

He wrapped his arms around her, feeling every detail of her body close to his, to communicate how much he felt when they touched – and kissed.

'You have no idea how much I needed that.'

Her hands came up, one cupping his cheek and the other stroking his hair. 'I have some idea,' she whispered.

He pressed another kiss on her lips and drew back to look at her. 'So, why didn't you fly back home today? If it was just for that kiss, then I kind of get it because... wow. But did you need something else?'

She stared at him for a long moment. 'You,' she said so quietly it was almost more breath than voice. 'I need you.'

Shock and warmth shot through him with crackling intensity. How amazing would it be to have Lou relying on him, to be her partner, her rock – now he knew he was capable of it?

'You don't need me, Lou. You can do anything you want. You're so full of life and spirit. You don't need me,' he said gently.

He watched shadows pass briefly across her expression and wondered if she was going to deny it. But, instead, she cupped his jaw. 'You're right. What I meant was, I want you,' she said.

He clutched her waist, where he hadn't been able to let her go. His heart pounded. Did she know what those words meant to him? Did she mean it the way he wanted her to mean it? His eyes stung and he hoped it was only sweat. She swiped her hand over her forehead and a quick smile flashed on her face.

'I have taken eight different forms of transport to get to you, starting at nine o'clock this morning, because I didn't know you'd left Milan last night!' Her voice shook. 'I'd do a lot more than that to keep you in my life – our lives. I thought I didn't have space for you in the mess of my life, but, bloody hell, if you want the mess, then I'll *make* space for you!'

He stared at her, this beautiful, remarkable woman, as elation tipped up his mouth into a goofy grin. 'Lou, I love you,' he whispered.

* * *

Lou let out some kind of squeak. It wasn't a sound she'd intended to make – she would have preferred a more elegant response – but her heart was so gloriously full of wonderful emotions and her vision was blurring.

He'd just said everything she'd ever hoped to hear.

The second sound to emerge from her mouth was a choking snort, which resulted in a coughing fit. She threw a hand out to steady herself on his shoulder. Then, because that wasn't enough, she dropped her forehead to his chest and sucked in huge breaths.

'Um, do you need a hug or the Heimlich manoeuvre?'

'Hug,' she scratched out. His arms came up and she pressed into him. He was a lovely height for her. Her chin nestled pleasantly just above his collarbone.

'I love you, too,' she murmured, unable to resist a quick kiss just below his jaw.

He jumped. 'This is crazy. Did you just say...?'

'I love you. Yes. I said it. I mean it. I probably don't deserve you, but screw it. I'm—'

He kissed her. Boy, the man could kiss. All those hidden passions were a huge turn-on. She whimpered. His hand roved further south and he broke off with a wince and a muttered apology on a tight breath.

'No need to apologise,' she replied, clearing her throat. 'It's quite good for my ego that you can't keep your hands off me.'

'I really can't,' he agreed. 'But that was a warning. If you ever suggest you don't deserve something, that's what I'm going to do to you.'

She grinned. 'Yes, Mr Romano.'

He blushed dark red and she giggled. 'I'm serious, Lou. You're the most wonderful, sensitive, compassionate, funny and *talented* woman I have ever met. And I will kiss you senseless if you ever say otherwise.'

She stared at him, his dark eyes piercing with fervour, his hair wild from her fingers. 'But—' He kissed her again – short and hard this time. She smiled when he drew back. 'You can't be right—'

His lips met hers again, but this time they were both laughing too hard to manage more than a sloppy, affectionate swipe. She hooked her arm around his neck and pressed one last kiss to his lips before drawing back to look at him with a smile.

'I have a very important question to ask you, which is going to come out like something one embarrassed kid would say to another, but I'm serious, okay?'

His puzzled smile was full-dimpled and she had to stop for a moment to kiss him again.

'Nick, I love you. That's not the kid bit,' she said at his questioning look. 'This is the kid bit.' She paused for dramatic effect, which was, perhaps, one of her talents. 'Will you be my boyfriend?'

He grinned and tightened his arms around her.

'I would love to be your boyfriend,' he murmured.

She crumbled again, a teary, laughing, elated heap of crazy emotions, clinging to him. She settled her forehead against his, breathing in the intimacy of the moment. He kissed her again – slowly, softly, deeply – and she decided to believe him. She was extremely talented at loving Nick – among many other things. More importantly, she had a daughter and a boyfriend who loved her for who she was.

* * *

They strolled back to the farm holding hands, bumping shoulders and stopping often to laugh and kiss and prolong the time alone. Images and feelings from the past few weeks – the past six months – coalesced pleasantly in her mind, settling into the new paradigm. Lou was happy. She was happy to make Nick happy – and Edie.

'Edie's back at the farm with your mum and nonna,' she told Nick.

He nodded slowly. 'I take it she knows why you both took – eight, was it? – different forms of transport to come after me?' He stopped to nuzzle her ear. 'I'm impressed, by the way.'

She grinned. 'My plan worked,' she said with a mock-maniacal laugh. 'And, yes, Edie knew exactly what we were doing and even sat through a few of my awkward moments of doubt.' He squeezed her hand and his smile slipped. 'Oh, don't worry. I was just being dramatic. I knew what I wanted by the time we left Milan – by the time I went to sleep last night. Getting on the wrong tram didn't stop me, waiting two hours for a bus didn't stop me – although, to be honest, it meant we got pizza and gelato.'

'And what does she think? Of us?' He grinned. 'Being boyfriend and girlfriend?'

Lou smiled ruefully and thought back. 'She mentioned it earlier – a long time before I was prepared to consider it.'

'Really? When?'

'After we... after I... Although she doesn't know that, of course,' she rushed on.

'Just take a deep breath, Lou. We'll work out how to do this. We don't have to have all the answers straight away. But I'm here for you – both of you.'

She rested her forehead on his shoulder for a few breaths. 'I know. You were there for us even before I decided to let you in.' She straightened and smiled at him. 'I can't believe you went out on stage for her.'

'I can't either,' he said with a huff. 'But I wanted to prove something to you. Edie makes being with you more desirable, not less. She means a lot to me. As you started to mean something to me, too, she became even dearer. I understand you're circumspect about sharing responsibility for her, but I want the whole package.'

She stopped and stared at him until he winced and blushed.

'Am I coming on too strong? Please don't back off.'

She laughed in disbelief. 'How can you keep getting more perfect?' He gave her a look. 'I mean, I know you can be grumpy and too worried about what other people think.' She paused.

'Now's the time for the "but",' he grumbled.

'But I'm so happy,' she said, her voice flying up at the end.

'Good,' he murmured, dropping a kiss to her hairline. 'That's exactly what I want to hear you say.'

She smiled. 'Do you want to hear me say how handsome you are and how long I had a massive crush on you?' He blushed. 'And how much I love that blush?'

'If you had a crush on me for so long, why did you put me through the past few weeks? The almost-kisses? I wasn't sure if I was in love or needed to see a therapist.'

'I'm sorry,' she said with a smile and a placating kiss. 'You were right,' she admitted. 'I had Phil in my head, crowding out what was truly important.'

'I could have dealt with you more gently. I know from watching my own parents that... maybe I was afraid you'd never come to terms with it. My mum has never... I was selfish, as well. I wanted you for a while, too, even though I had some stupid ideas about why it was a bad idea.'

'Ooh, tell me more.'

He chuckled. 'About how long I've wanted you? I think you know the day it started.'

She stopped and stared at him. She did know. It was when she'd started breaking out to be herself, when she'd looked a mess and felt just as bad, but she'd started on the road to her own future.

'The day I told you—'

'I'd look good in high heels – yes. I've barely been able to take my eyes off you since.' He paused. 'And then it got worse when we got to the convent and I started getting to know you properly. I fell completely in love with you somewhere between the paddle-boarding and the bike riding. And there was no turning back after seeing the look on your face at the summit of Monte Biaena.'

'And I didn't fully understand you until I heard you play the violin under the olive trees,' she added softly, watching him.

He nodded slowly. 'That took away my excuses. I clearly don't need to hide from you.'

She smiled and drew him down for one more kiss as they arrived at the driveway to the farm. 'You don't. Just don't make me come after you on a tractor ever again.'

'A tractor?' He smiled a whisper from her lips.

'I really wanted to get back to you.'

'I really want to kiss you before my mother sees us.'

'What are you waiting for?'

He tilted his head and her breath caught in anticipation.

'Nico! Dinner is on the table! You can save that for later!'

Lou groaned. 'Not again!'

EPILOGUE

'The wind up here is wild. I didn't expect that. But the view is... incredible. I think that's probably Switzerland over there. When a mountain looks like a little pile of dirt... that's perspective, you know. You can't believe it until you're actually up here. Touching this cross is so hard to describe. It's 2,200 metres above sea level and the lake is basically at sea level. That's more than a mile down there. And it's steep – too steep for any vehicle except a person on foot. And – oh my God, Edie, you made it up! Sweetheart, come up here to the cross! Turn off the camera, I'm blubbering!'

'It's great TV, Lou.' The camera operator laughed.

She gave him a dry look. 'At least people will get a genuine impression of what it's like to slog up a mountain.' She'd tied her hair back in a bun, but it hadn't survived well under her hat and a good portion of it was now whipping around her face. Her cheeks were blotchy from sweat and sun and wind.

But she was bursting with pride. She stood at the summit of Valdritta, the highest peak of the Monte Baldo range. The lunar landscape at the top of the crag was spectacular and otherworldly. It contributed to her sense of disbelief at the past year of her life.

Not only was she even more deeply in love with Nick, now they'd supported and enjoyed each other for a year, but she'd had her own humorous documentary series commissioned, entitled *Give Life a Go*. Her fears had all been in her head. The station was happy with her work and interested in offering her more opportunities. It turned out her audience enjoyed her sympathetic style.

Edie had settled in at Purcell and was relishing the challenge. She read lots of pink glittery unicorn books on her long train journey to school. Lou had looked for a flat in Watford, but Edie had been happy to commute from London in the hope that Nick would be around more. When Nick had stammered that he'd love to move in with them, they'd found a flat with a better tube connection for Edie and an easy cycle for Nick.

Edie still enjoyed playing duets with Nick more than anything she'd learned at school. It made Lou's heart burst every time she heard them. She loved it every time Nick played, knowing she was privileged to hear him because he loved her and he felt safe with her.

He'd had requests to play one or two concerts from connections who had been at La Scala that night, but he'd declined. Lou had just smiled and hugged him and told him that, if he was ever ready, she'd be there to catch him when he tumbled offstage. And if not, watching him play was a huge turn-on and she was happy to keep her reaction to his lyrical interpretation private.

She'd caught him writing music a few times and gently teased him until he'd admitted he'd considered going back to study composition, if he could study part-time around his work. Lou would never be prouder of him than when she attended the primary school concerts where he worked magic, passing on his passion in the most amazing way.

Watching him holding Edie's hand as she navigated the rocks and tried not to look down, Lou felt her heart tumble again – a sensation she was slowly getting used to. He was handsome and kind and real – and somehow, he was hers.

Lou held out one arm to Edie as she clung to the metal cross. Edie squealed as she let go of Nick's hand and grabbed for Lou's. They clung to each other, the summit cross between them.

'Smile!' called Nick, casually perched on the rocks, holding his phone up for a photo. 'I knew you could do it!'

'You knew I'd be a teary mess at the top, too!'

'I think you'll remember I told you to bring tissues!' He grinned.

'I thought that was because you were going to propose up here, you idiot!'

He froze and Lou slammed her mouth shut. She didn't understand why Nick found her loose mouth so endearing.

'I didn't think… I thought it was too soon.'

'Well, now I've gone and ruined it, I may as well keep digging.' She laughed, light-headed. It was probably the altitude making her crazy, but it didn't matter. She knew what she wanted. 'Nick Romano, will you marry me? Turn off the bloody camera!' she called to the cheeky cameraman. 'I love you.'

'Yes!' he called out, loudly over the wind. 'Yes, Lou. I'd love to get married. And I love how you asked.' Edie gasped and squealed in delight.

Lou shrugged, blinking wildly against the fresh tears. 'It was a spur-of-the-moment thing.'

'You have the best ideas. And I love you – always.'

The tears were falling in earnest, now. 'I've ruined the piece,' she blubbered to the cameraman. 'And I think I'm stuck.' She made the mistake of peering down towards the lake, at the steep incline and piles of loose rocks at the bottom.

'Don't worry, Mum,' said Edie, squeezing her hands. 'You can do it.'

Lou grinned at her daughter through the tears. 'I can, can't I?'

ACKNOWLEDGMENTS

I wrote this book during the first COVID lockdown in spring 2020, when the world was watching northern Italy. The news of the doctors and nurses and all the staff at the hospitals in Lombardy working so hard with no knowledge of the disease and few extra resources was definitely on my mind while writing. Because of their brave stories, Lake Garda became an even more magical place in this book, embodying hope for all of us, and I got tears in my eyes when the last COVID patient was released from hospital in Bergamo after the first wave. It's an amazing part of the world and I hope they don't have to experience anything like that again.

I need to thank my crew of beta readers, the two Lucys and R. B. Owen, for allowing me to experiment on them with their emotional reactions to the characters. My husband gets an extra-special mention this time, because he was always 100 per cent behind me when I wanted to write, despite everything else going on during the lockdown with home-schooling etc.

My editor, Sarah, and the marketing team at Boldwood Books have also been champions, helping me through these first two books where everything has been new for me.

I'll also add a few special mentions of people and groups who influenced this book: my lovely old choirs, Eltham Choral Society (we had so much fun singing the 'Chorus of the Hebrew Slaves', didn't we?), Blackheath Choir and even St Peters Chorale a very long time ago. And also, the National Childbirth Trust (NCT), which had a profound impact on my early parenting and my thoughts about that time of life. My thanks to Jessie Klug for her endless enthusiasm for Schwammerlsuchen, the Austrian version of mushroom hunting, that inspired a pivotal scene!

And, because a dedicated research trip this year wasn't possible because, you know, 2020, the Assessorato al Turismo in Malcesine, the Paolo Bonomelli Olive Farm and all the wonderful bloggers and individuals who leave reviews and information on the Internet for others – and the people who post amusing SUP board fails on YouTube!

MORE FROM LEONIE MACK

We hope you enjoyed reading *Italy Ever After*. If you did, please leave a review.

If you'd like to gift a copy, this book is also available as an ebook, digital audio download and audiobook CD.

Sign up to Leonie Mack's mailing list for news, competitions and updates on future books.

https://bit.ly/LeonieMackNewsletter

My Christmas Number One, another wonderful read from Leonie Mack is out now.

ABOUT THE AUTHOR

Leonie Mack is a bestselling romantic novelist. Having lived in London for many years her home is now in Germany with her husband and three children. Leonie loves train travel, medieval towns, hiking and happy endings!

Visit Leonie's website: https://leoniemack.com/

Follow Leonie on social media:

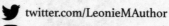 twitter.com/LeonieMAuthor

 instagram.com/leoniejmack

facebook.com/LeonieJMack

Boldwood

Boldwood Books is an award-winning fiction publishing company seeking out the best stories from around the world.

Find out more at www.boldwoodbooks.com

Join our reader community for brilliant books, competitions and offers!

Follow us
@BoldwoodBooks
@BookandTonic

Sign up to our weekly deals newsletter

https://bit.ly/BoldwoodBNewsletter